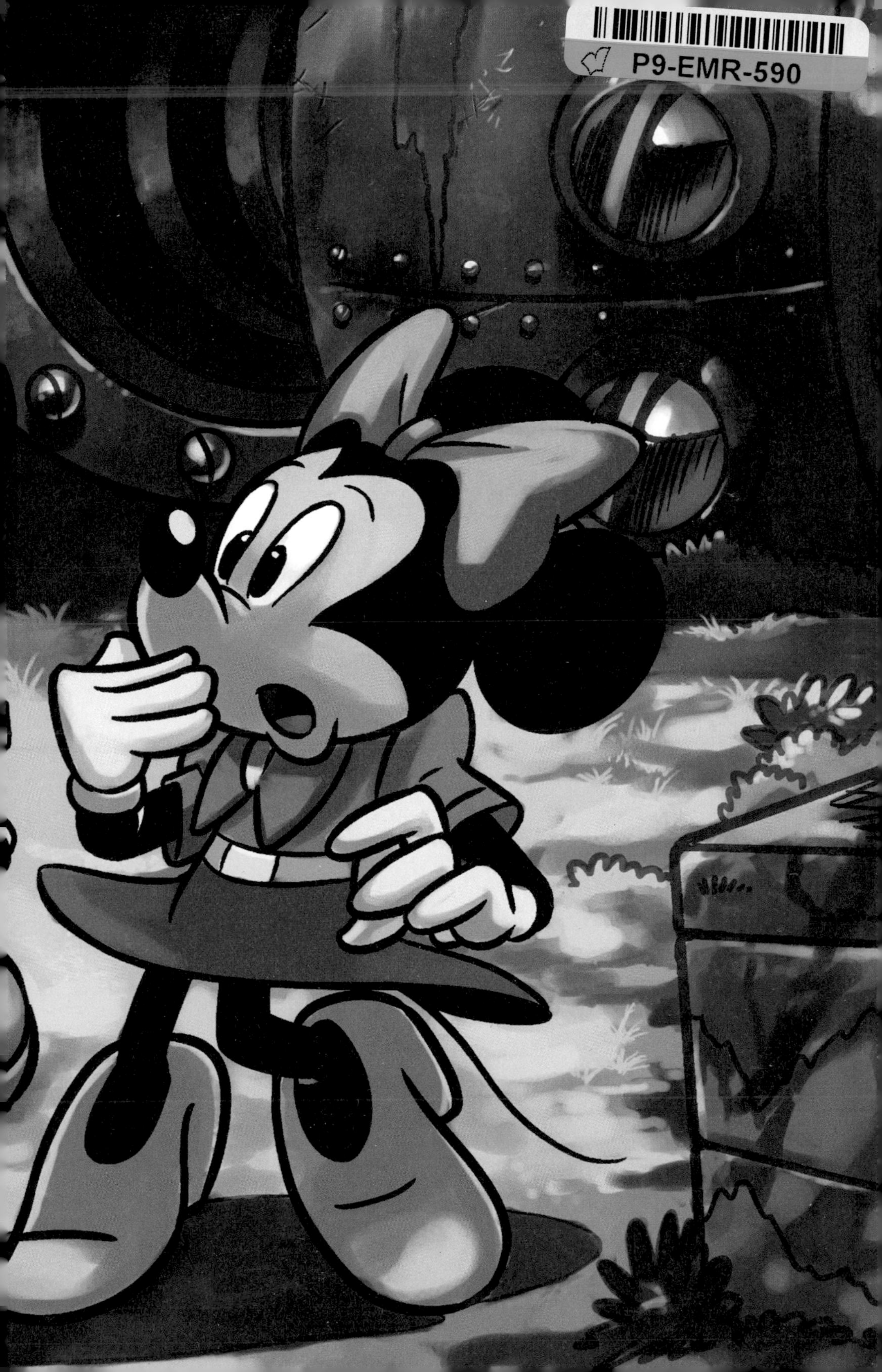

MICKEY MOUSE AND THE WORLD TO COME

BOOM Kids!

ROSS RICHIE
chief executive officer

MARK WAID
editor-in-chief

ADAM FORTIER
vice president,
new business

WES HARRIS
vice president,
publishing

LANCE KREITER
vice president,
licensing & merchandising

CHIP MOSHER
marketing director

MATT GAGNON
managing editor

FIRST EDITION: MAY 2010

10 9 8 7 6 5 4 3 2 1

FOR INFORMATION REGARDING THE CPSIA ON THIS PRINTED MATERIAL
CALL: 203-595-3636 AND PROVIDE REFERENCE # EAST – 66658

MICKEY MOUSE AND THE WORLD TO COME – published by BOOM Kids!, a division of Boom Entertainment, Inc. All contents © 2010 Walt Disney Company. BOOM Kids! and the BOOM Kids! logo are trademarks of Boom Entertainment, Inc., registered in various countries and categories. All rights reserved.

Office of publication: 6310 San Vicente Blvd Ste 404, Los Angeles, CA 90048-5457.

A catalog record for this book is available from OCLC and on our website www.boom-kids.com on the Librarians page.

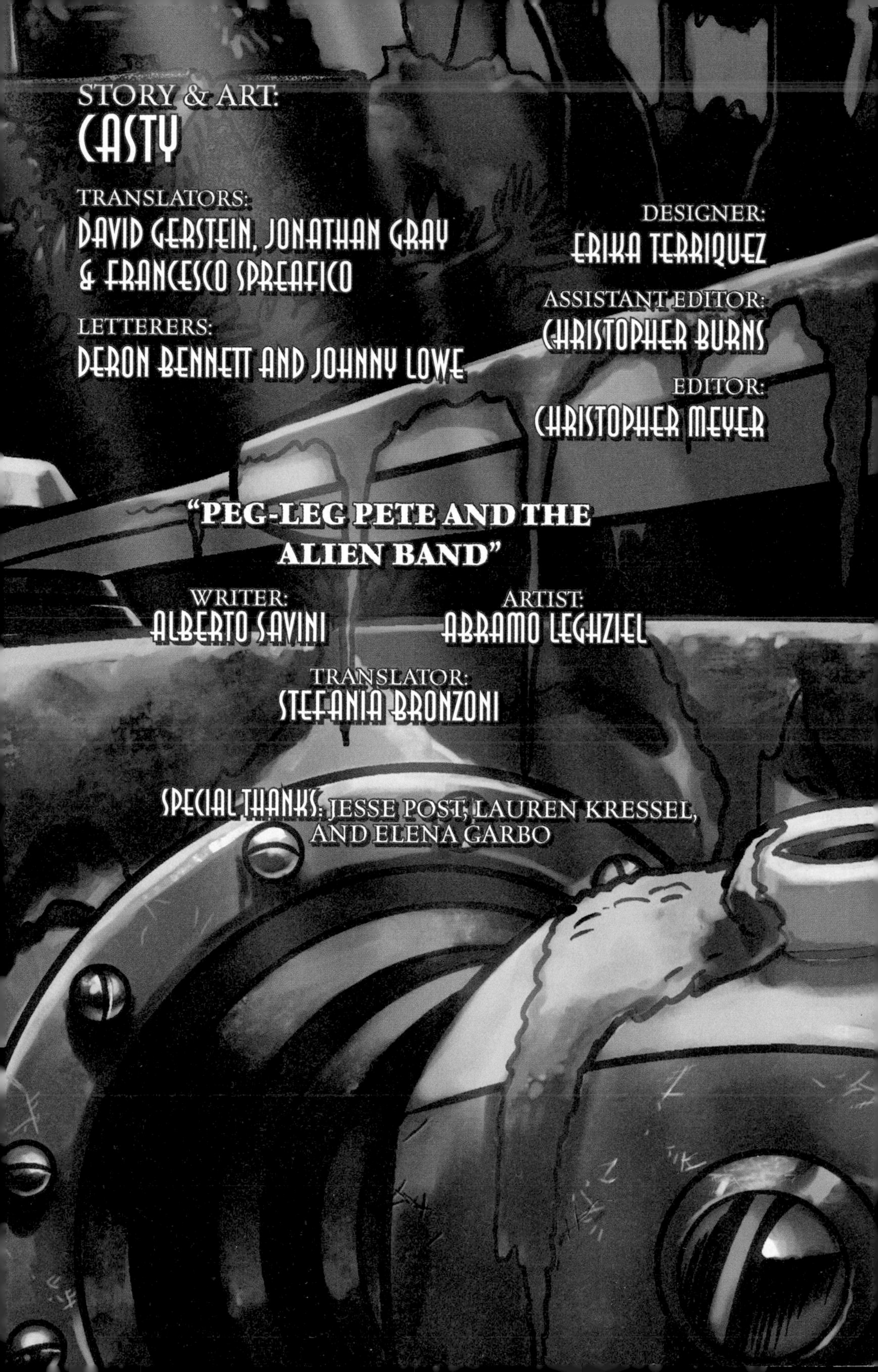

STORY & ART:
CASTY

TRANSLATORS:
DAVID GERSTEIN, JONATHAN GRAY & FRANCESCO SPREAFICO

LETTERERS:
DERON BENNETT AND JOHNNY LOWE

DESIGNER:
ERIKA TERRIQUEZ

ASSISTANT EDITOR:
CHRISTOPHER BURNS

EDITOR:
CHRISTOPHER MEYER

"PEG-LEG PETE AND THE ALIEN BAND"

WRITER:
ALBERTO SAVINI

ARTIST:
ABRAMO LEGHZIEL

TRANSLATOR:
STEFANIA BRONZONI

SPECIAL THANKS: JESSE POST, LAUREN KRESSEL, AND ELENA GARBO

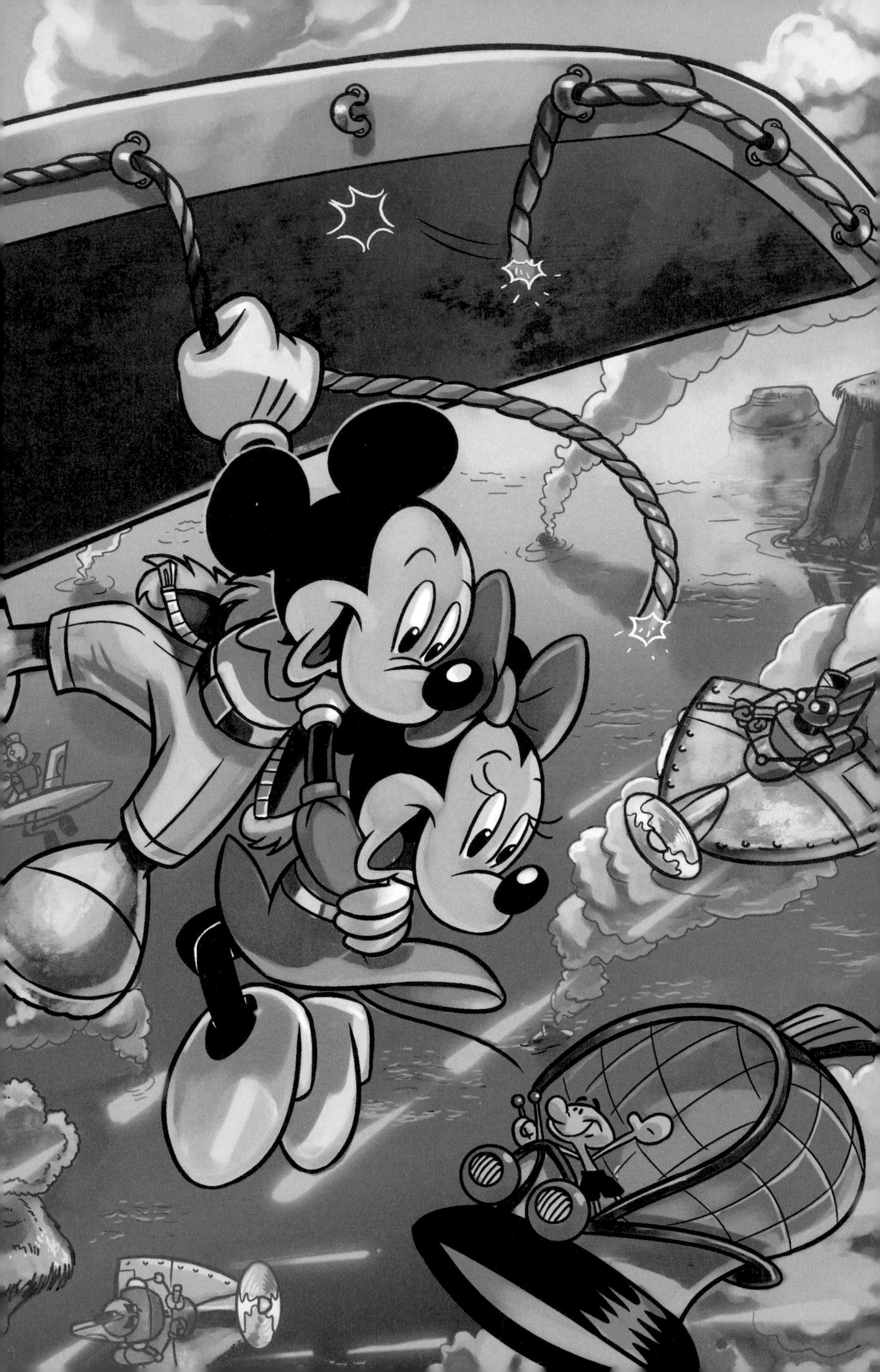

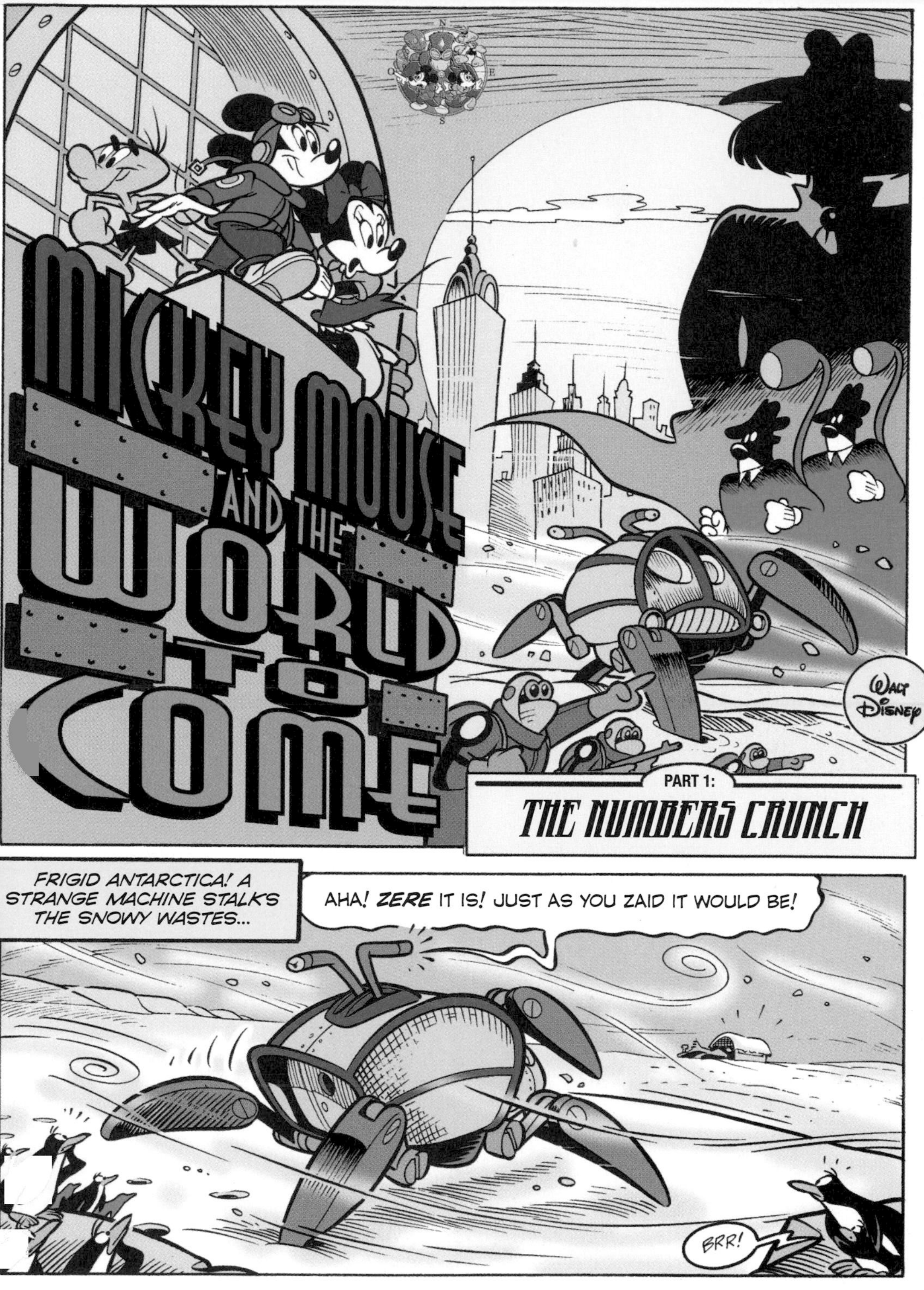
MICKEY MOUSE AND THE WORLD TO COME
WALT DISNEY
PART 1:
THE NUMBERS CRUNCH
FRIGID ANTARCTICA! A STRANGE MACHINE STALKS THE SNOWY WASTES...
AHA! ZERE IT IS! JUST AS YOU ZAID IT WOULD BE!
BRR!

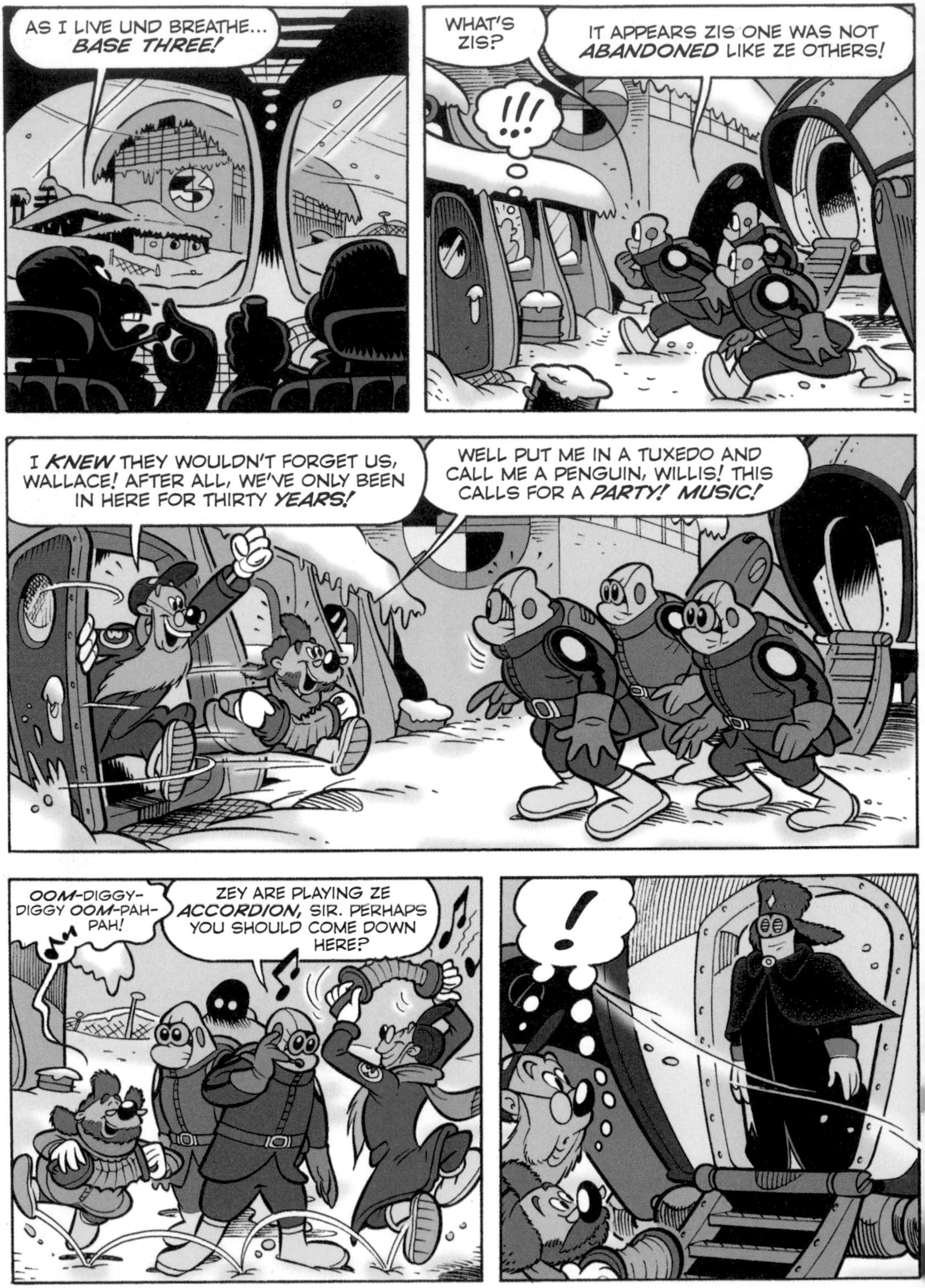

AS I LIVE UND BREATHE... BASE THREE!
WHAT'S ZIS?
IT APPEARS ZIS ONE WAS NOT ABANDONED LIKE ZE OTHERS!
!!!
I KNEW THEY WOULDN'T FORGET US, WALLACE! AFTER ALL, WE'VE ONLY BEEN IN HERE FOR THIRTY YEARS!
WELL PUT ME IN A TUXEDO AND CALL ME A PENGUIN, WILLIS! THIS CALLS FOR A PARTY! MUSIC!
OOM-DIGGY-DIGGY OOM-PAH-PAH!
ZEY ARE PLAYING ZE ACCORDION, SIR. PERHAPS YOU SHOULD COME DOWN HERE?
!

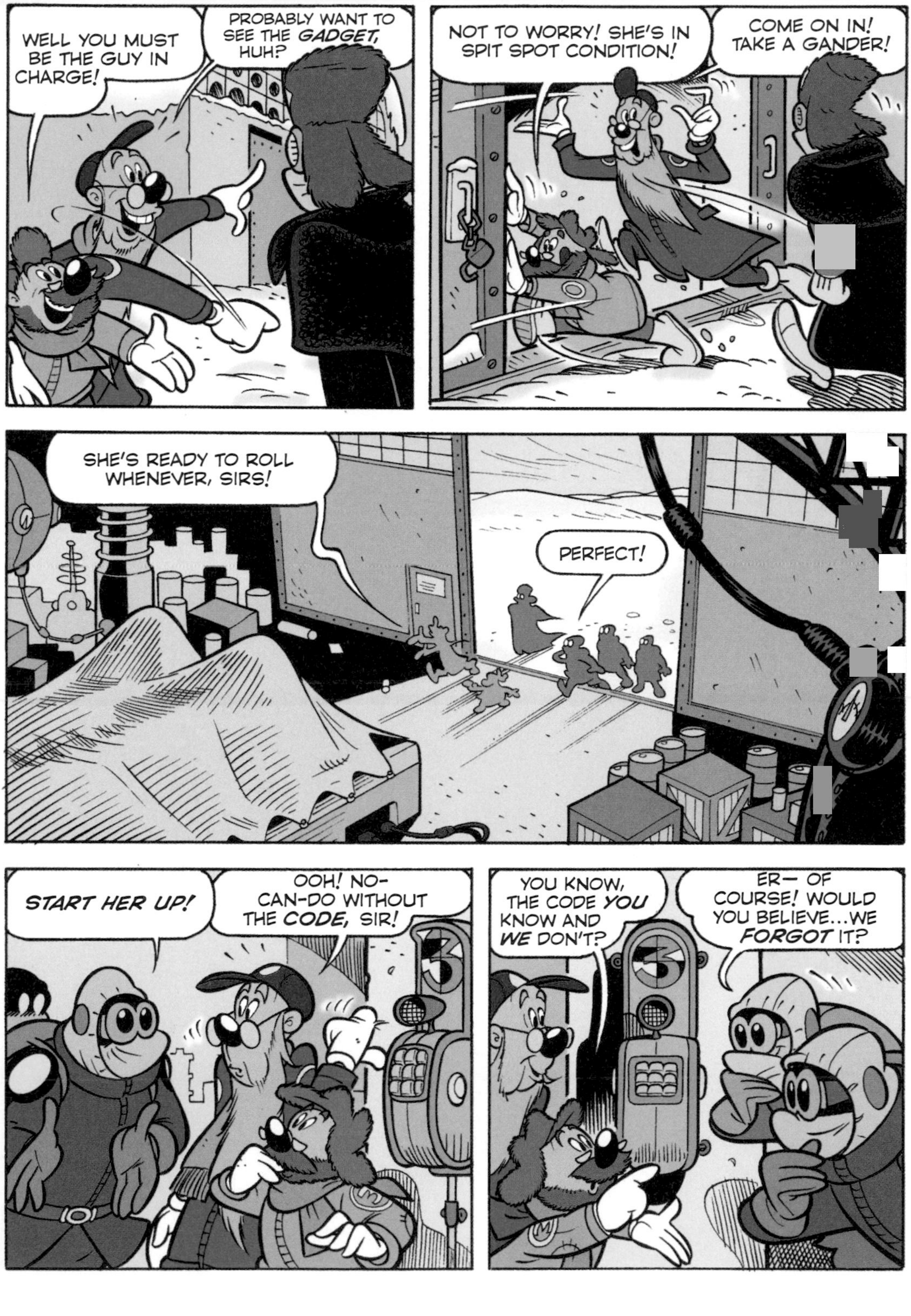
WELL YOU MUST BE THE GUY IN CHARGE!
PROBABLY WANT TO SEE THE GADGET, HUH?
NOT TO WORRY! SHE'S IN SPIT SPOT CONDITION!
COME ON IN! TAKE A GANDER!
SHE'S READY TO ROLL WHENEVER, SIRS!
PERFECT!
START HER UP!
OOH! NO-CAN-DO WITHOUT THE CODE, SIR!
YOU KNOW, THE CODE YOU KNOW AND WE DON'T?
ER— OF COURSE! WOULD YOU BELIEVE...WE FORGOT IT?

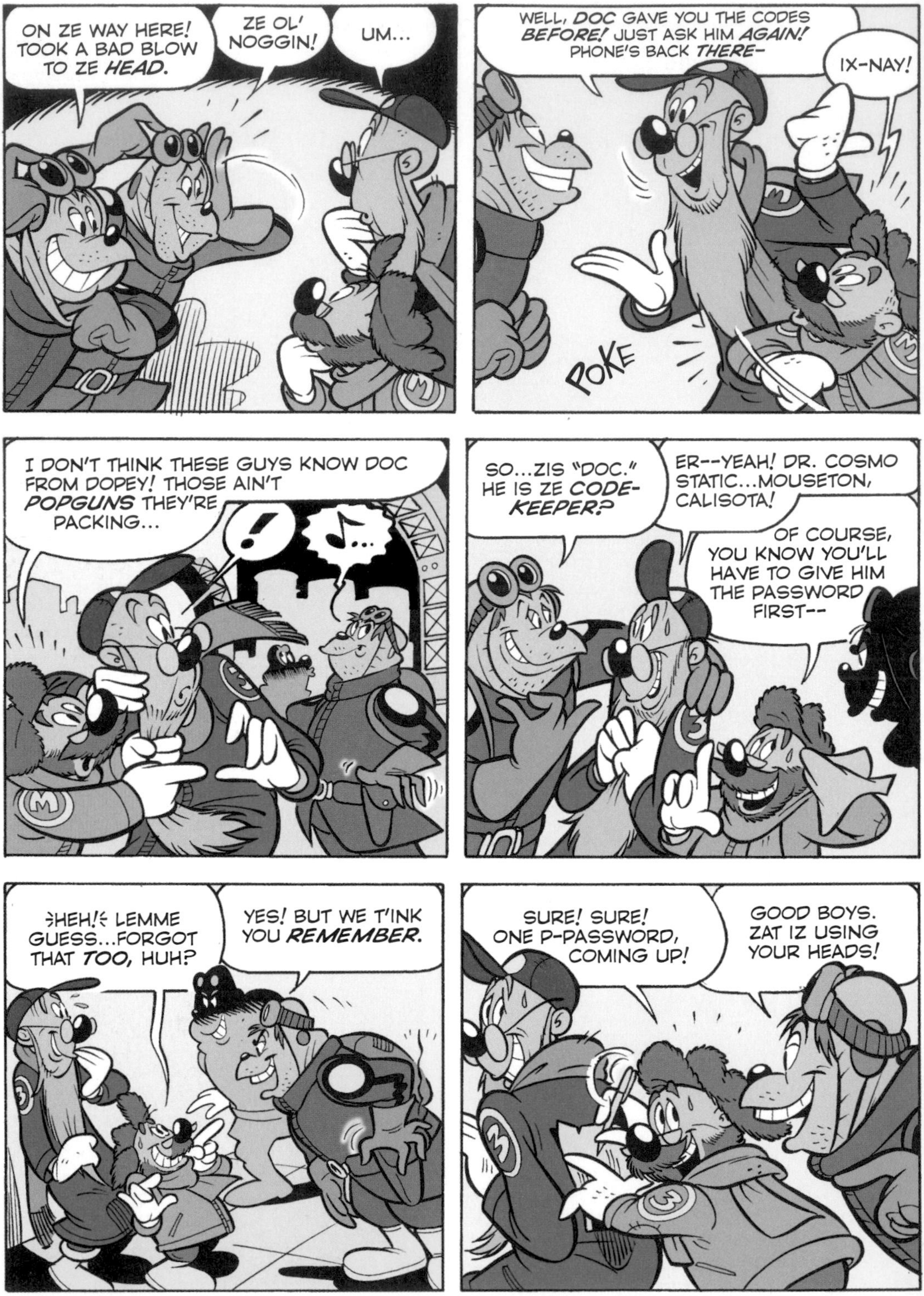
ON ZE WAY HERE! TOOK A BAD BLOW TO ZE HEAD.
ZE OL' NOGGIN!
UM...
WELL, DOC GAVE YOU THE CODES BEFORE! JUST ASK HIM AGAIN! PHONE'S BACK THERE–
IX-NAY!
POKE
I DON'T THINK THESE GUYS KNOW DOC FROM DOPEY! THOSE AIN'T POPGUNS THEY'RE PACKING...
!
♪...
SO...ZIS "DOC." HE IS ZE CODE-KEEPER?
ER--YEAH! DR. COSMO STATIC...MOUSETON, CALISOTA!
OF COURSE, YOU KNOW YOU'LL HAVE TO GIVE HIM THE PASSWORD FIRST--
HEH! LEMME GUESS...FORGOT THAT TOO, HUH?
YES! BUT WE T'INK YOU REMEMBER.
SURE! SURE! ONE P-PASSWORD, COMING UP!
GOOD BOYS. ZAT IZ USING YOUR HEADS!

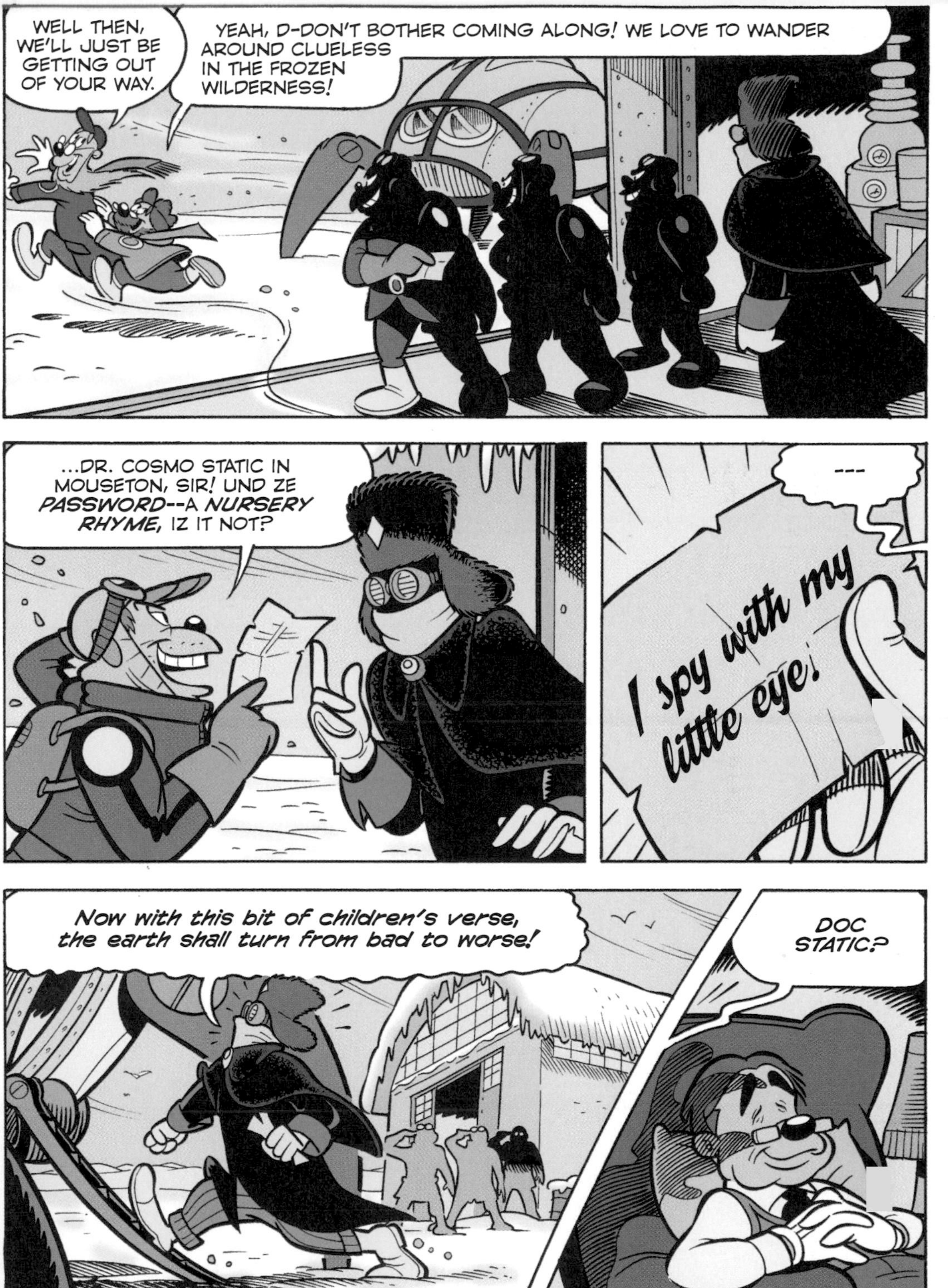

WELL THEN, WE'LL JUST BE GETTING OUT OF YOUR WAY.
YEAH, D-DON'T BOTHER COMING ALONG! WE LOVE TO WANDER AROUND CLUELESS IN THE FROZEN WILDERNESS!
...DR. COSMO STATIC IN MOUSETON, SIR! UND ZE PASSWORD--A NURSERY RHYME, IZ IT NOT?

I spy with my little eye!
Now with this bit of children's verse, the earth shall turn from bad to worse!
DOC STATIC?

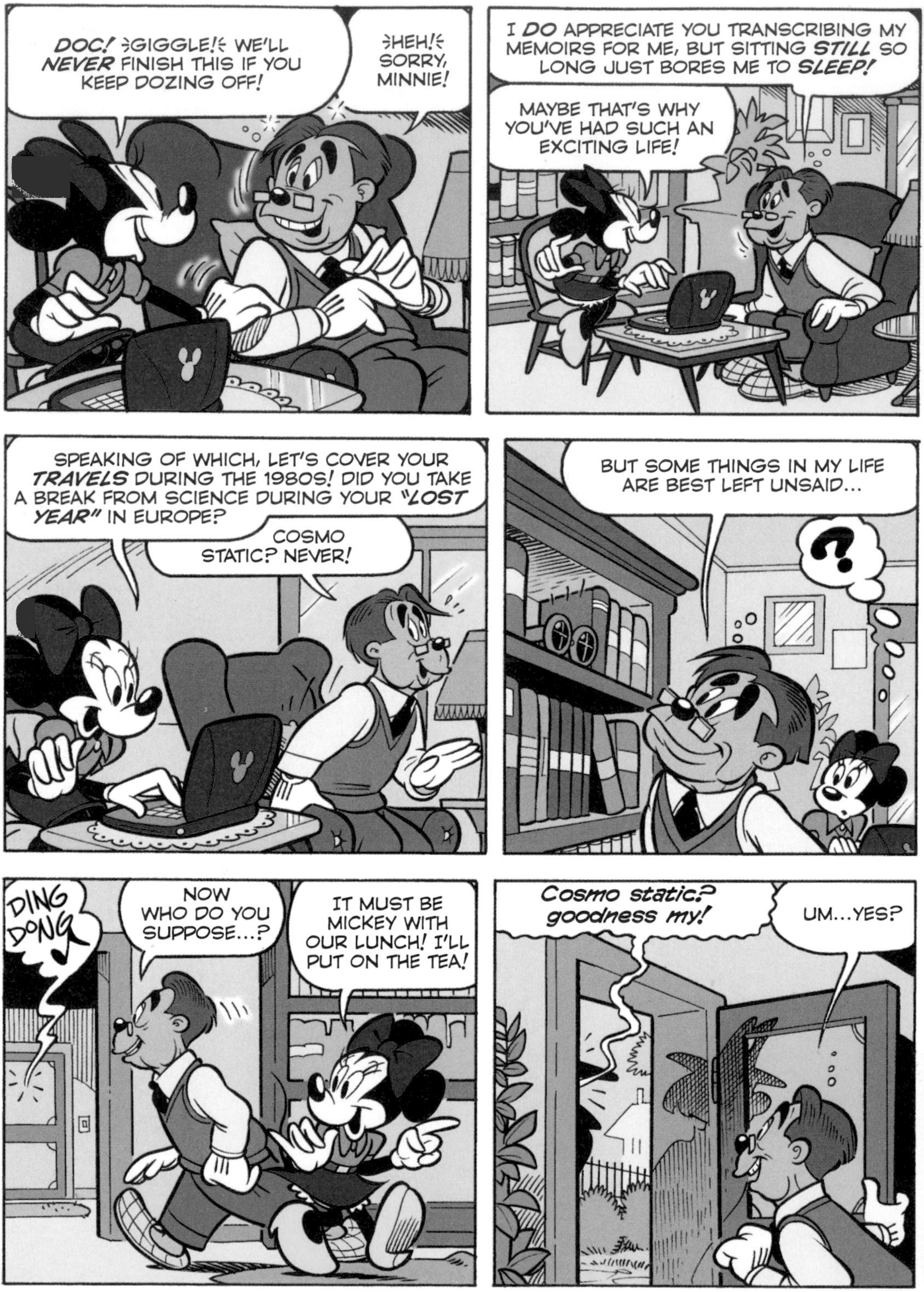
DOC! ⸗GIGGLE!⸗ WE'LL NEVER FINISH THIS IF YOU KEEP DOZING OFF!
⸗HEH!⸗ SORRY, MINNIE!
I DO APPRECIATE YOU TRANSCRIBING MY MEMOIRS FOR ME, BUT SITTING STILL SO LONG JUST BORES ME TO SLEEP!
MAYBE THAT'S WHY YOU'VE HAD SUCH AN EXCITING LIFE!
SPEAKING OF WHICH, LET'S COVER YOUR TRAVELS DURING THE 1980S! DID YOU TAKE A BREAK FROM SCIENCE DURING YOUR "LOST YEAR" IN EUROPE?
COSMO STATIC? NEVER!
BUT SOME THINGS IN MY LIFE ARE BEST LEFT UNSAID...
?
DING DONG
NOW WHO DO YOU SUPPOSE...?
IT MUST BE MICKEY WITH OUR LUNCH! I'LL PUT ON THE TEA!
Cosmo static? goodness my!
UM...YES?

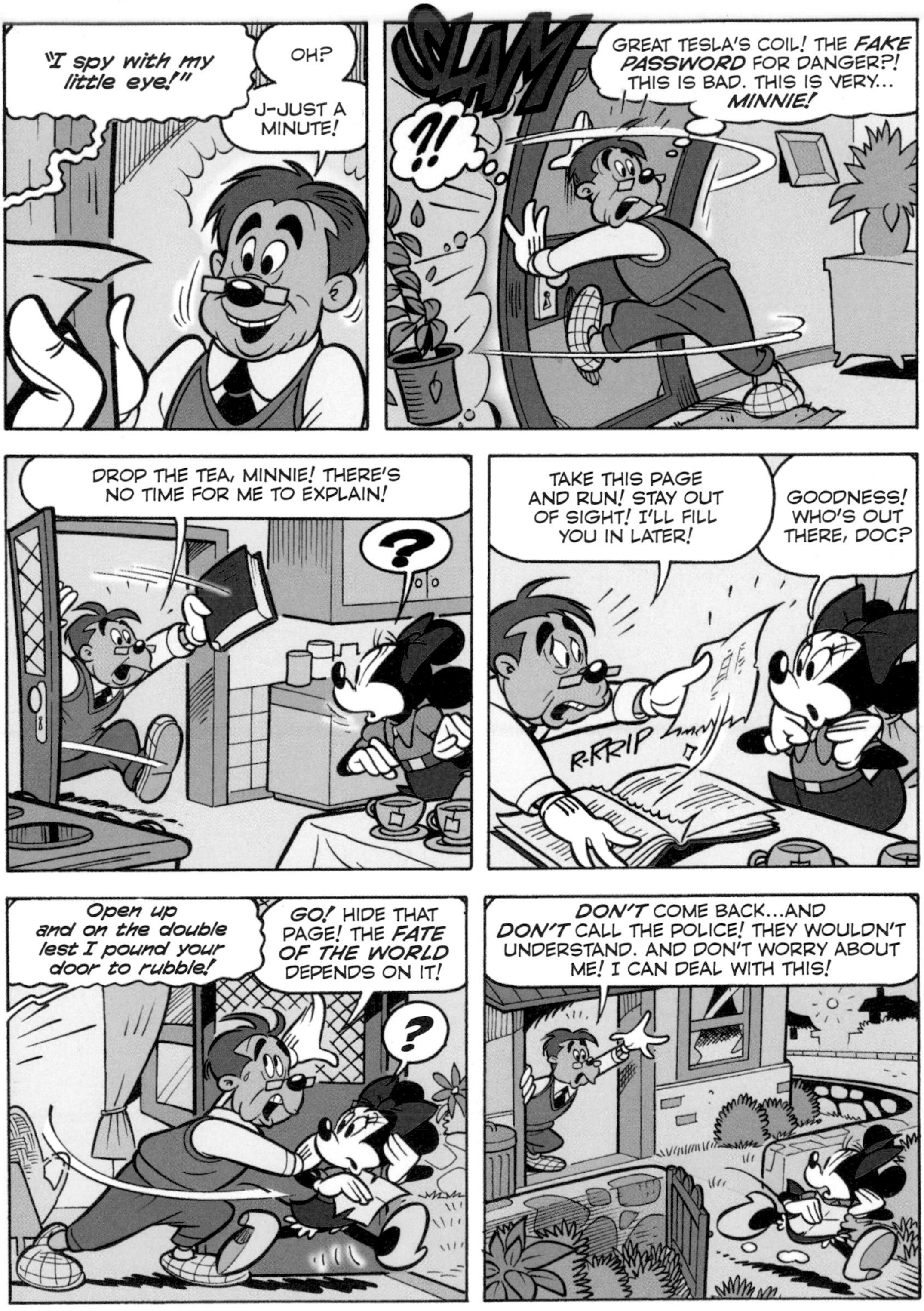
"I spy with my little eye!"
OH?
J-JUST A MINUTE!
SLAM
?!
GREAT TESLA'S COIL! THE FAKE PASSWORD FOR DANGER?! THIS IS BAD. THIS IS VERY... MINNIE!
DROP THE TEA, MINNIE! THERE'S NO TIME FOR ME TO EXPLAIN!
?
TAKE THIS PAGE AND RUN! STAY OUT OF SIGHT! I'LL FILL YOU IN LATER!
GOODNESS! WHO'S OUT THERE, DOC?
R-RRIP
Open up and on the double lest I pound your door to rubble!
GO! HIDE THAT PAGE! THE FATE OF THE WORLD DEPENDS ON IT!
?
DON'T COME BACK...AND DON'T CALL THE POLICE! THEY WOULDN'T UNDERSTAND. AND DON'T WORRY ABOUT ME! I CAN DEAL WITH THIS!

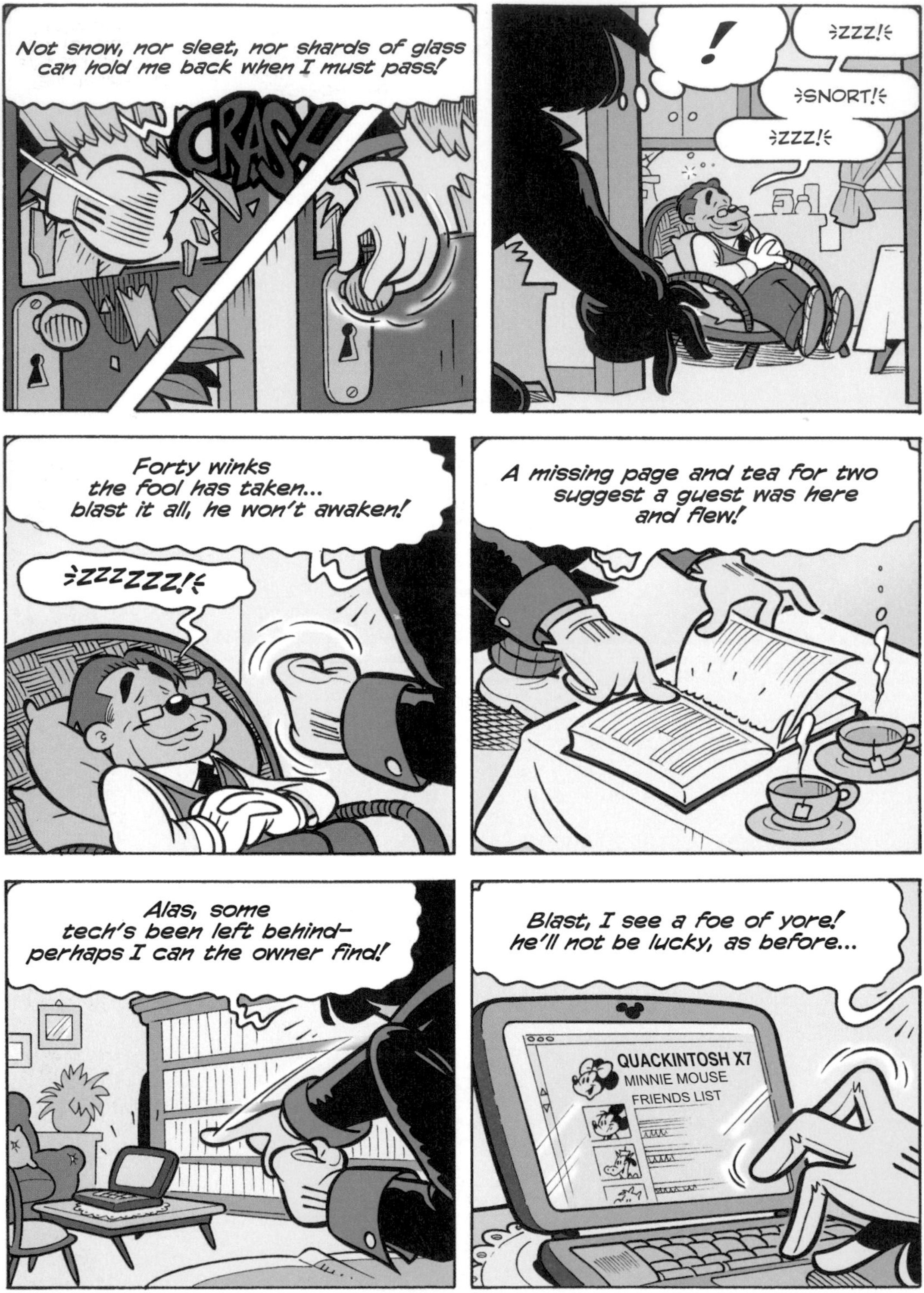

Not snow, nor sleet, nor shards of glass can hold me back when I must pass!
CRASH
!
ZZZ!
SNORT!
ZZZ!
Forty winks the fool has taken... blast it all, he won't awaken!
ZZZZZZ!
A missing page and tea for two suggest a guest was here and flew!
Alas, some tech's been left behind— perhaps I can the owner find!
Blast, I see a foe of yore! he'll not be lucky, as before...
QUACKINTOSH X7
MINNIE MOUSE
FRIENDS LIST

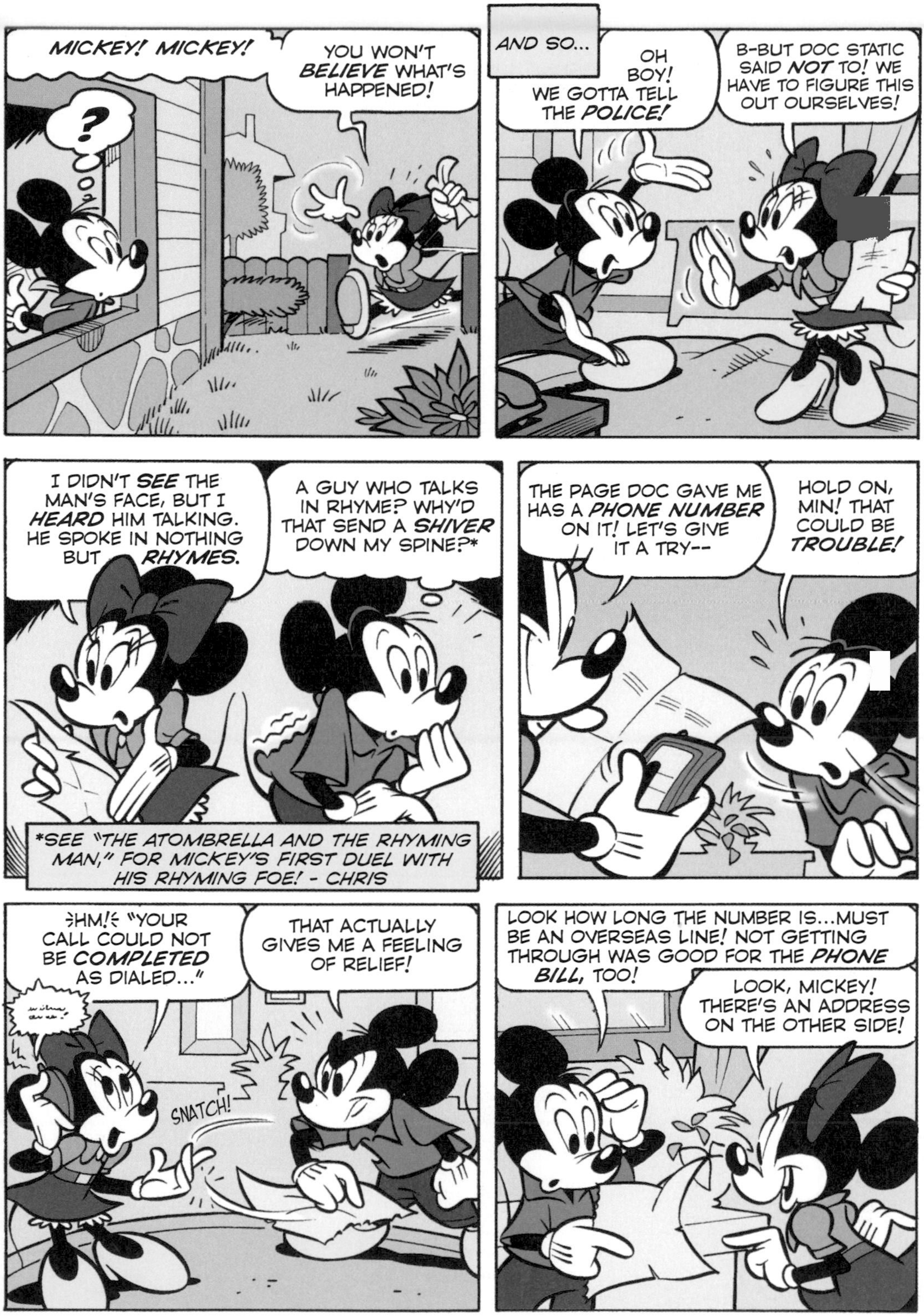
MICKEY! MICKEY!
YOU WON'T BELIEVE WHAT'S HAPPENED!
AND SO...
OH BOY! WE GOTTA TELL THE POLICE!
B-BUT DOC STATIC SAID NOT TO! WE HAVE TO FIGURE THIS OUT OURSELVES!
I DIDN'T SEE THE MAN'S FACE, BUT I HEARD HIM TALKING. HE SPOKE IN NOTHING BUT RHYMES.
A GUY WHO TALKS IN RHYME? WHY'D THAT SEND A SHIVER DOWN MY SPINE?*
*SEE "THE ATOMBRELLA AND THE RHYMING MAN," FOR MICKEY'S FIRST DUEL WITH HIS RHYMING FOE! - CHRIS
THE PAGE DOC GAVE ME HAS A PHONE NUMBER ON IT! LET'S GIVE IT A TRY--
HOLD ON, MIN! THAT COULD BE TROUBLE!
HM! "YOUR CALL COULD NOT BE COMPLETED AS DIALED..."
THAT ACTUALLY GIVES ME A FEELING OF RELIEF!
SNATCH!
LOOK HOW LONG THE NUMBER IS...MUST BE AN OVERSEAS LINE! NOT GETTING THROUGH WAS GOOD FOR THE PHONE BILL, TOO!
LOOK, MICKEY! THERE'S AN ADDRESS ON THE OTHER SIDE!

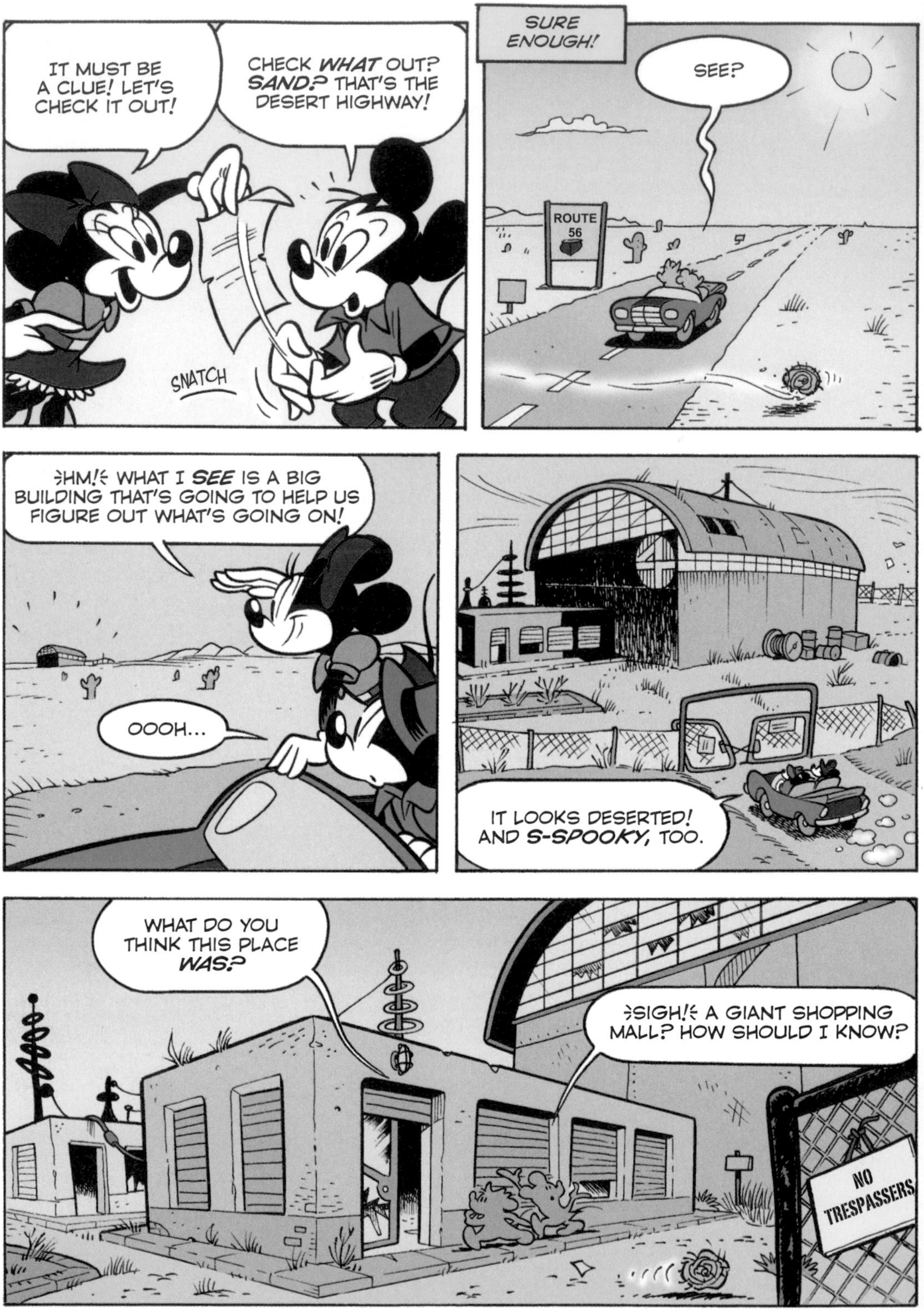
IT MUST BE A CLUE! LET'S CHECK IT OUT!
CHECK WHAT OUT? SAND? THAT'S THE DESERT HIGHWAY!
SNATCH
SURE ENOUGH!
SEE?
ROUTE 56
HM! WHAT I SEE IS A BIG BUILDING THAT'S GOING TO HELP US FIGURE OUT WHAT'S GOING ON!
OOOH...
IT LOOKS DESERTED! AND S-SPOOKY, TOO.
WHAT DO YOU THINK THIS PLACE WAS?
SIGH! A GIANT SHOPPING MALL? HOW SHOULD I KNOW?
NO TRESPASSERS

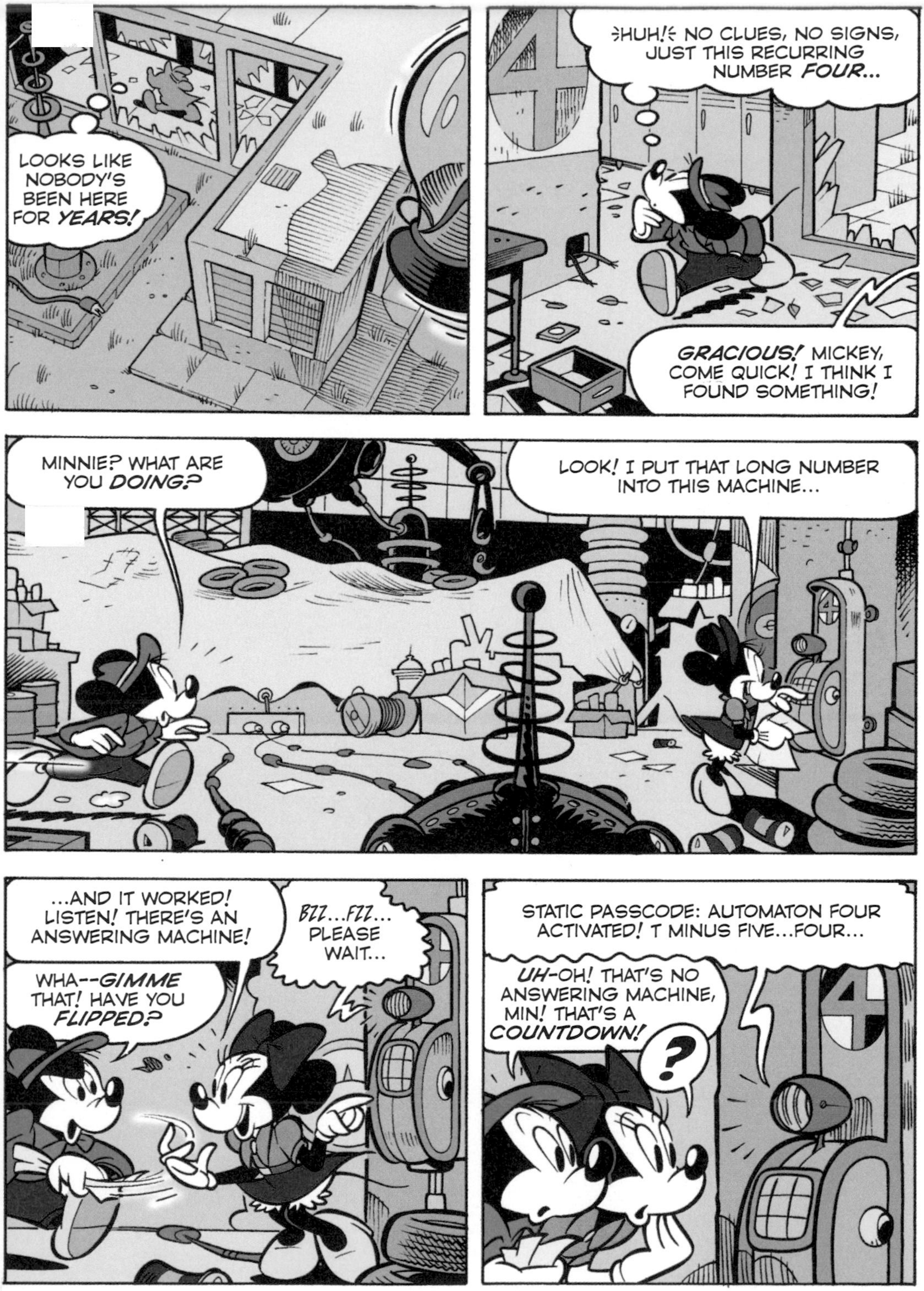
LOOKS LIKE NOBODY'S BEEN HERE FOR *YEARS!*
HUH! NO CLUES, NO SIGNS, JUST THIS RECURRING NUMBER *FOUR...*
GRACIOUS! MICKEY, COME QUICK! I THINK I FOUND SOMETHING!
MINNIE? WHAT ARE YOU *DOING?*
LOOK! I PUT THAT LONG NUMBER INTO THIS MACHINE...
...AND IT WORKED! LISTEN! THERE'S AN ANSWERING MACHINE!
BZZ...FZZ... PLEASE WAIT...
WHA--*GIMME* THAT! HAVE YOU *FLIPPED?*
STATIC PASSCODE: AUTOMATON FOUR ACTIVATED! T MINUS FIVE...FOUR...
UH-OH! THAT'S NO ANSWERING MACHINE, MIN! THAT'S A *COUNTDOWN!*
?

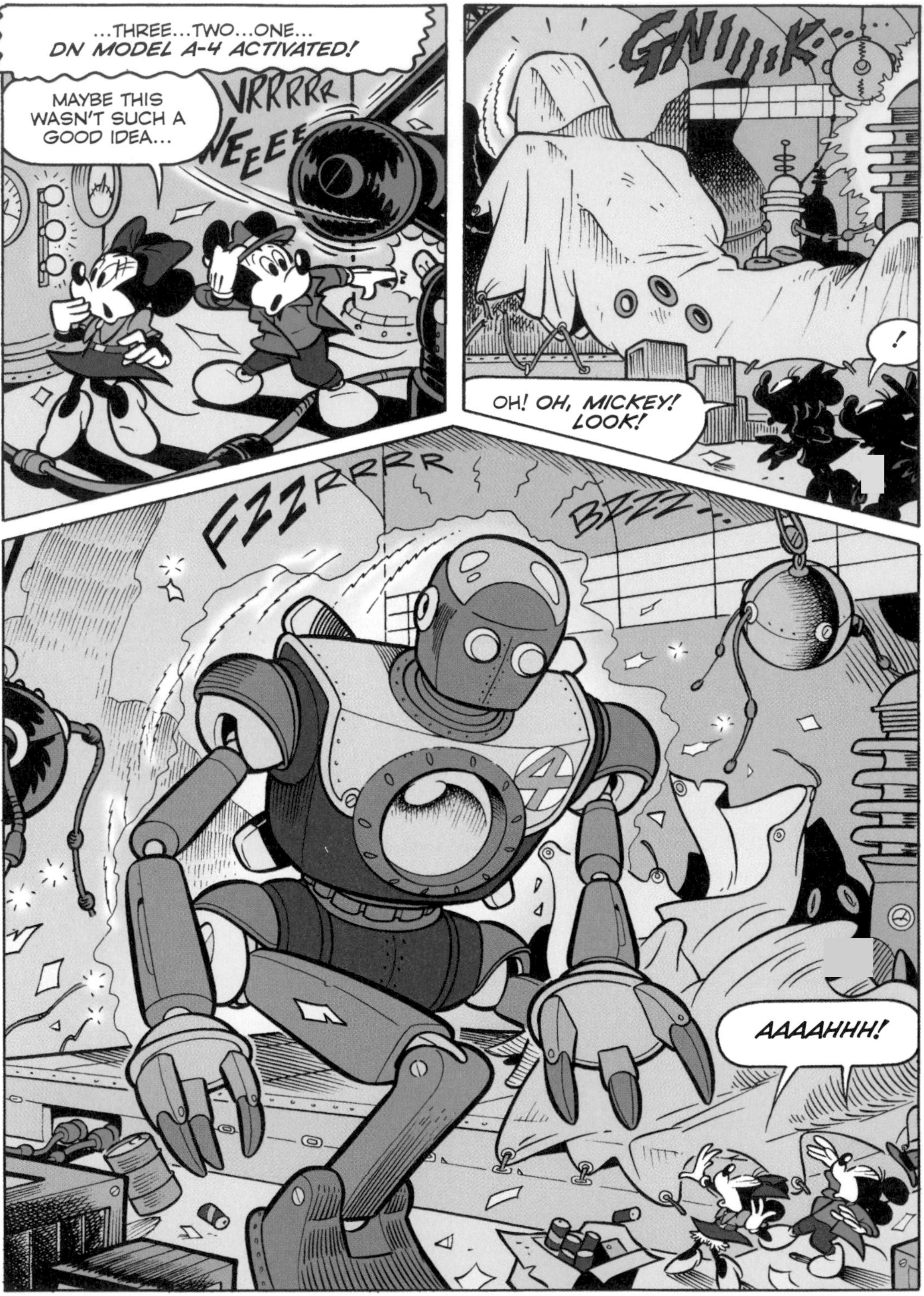
...THREE...TWO...ONE...
DN MODEL A-4 ACTIVATED!
MAYBE THIS WASN'T SUCH A GOOD IDEA...
VRRRRR
WEEEE
GNIIIIK
!
OH! OH, MICKEY! LOOK!
FZZRRRRR
BZZZ
AAAAHHH!

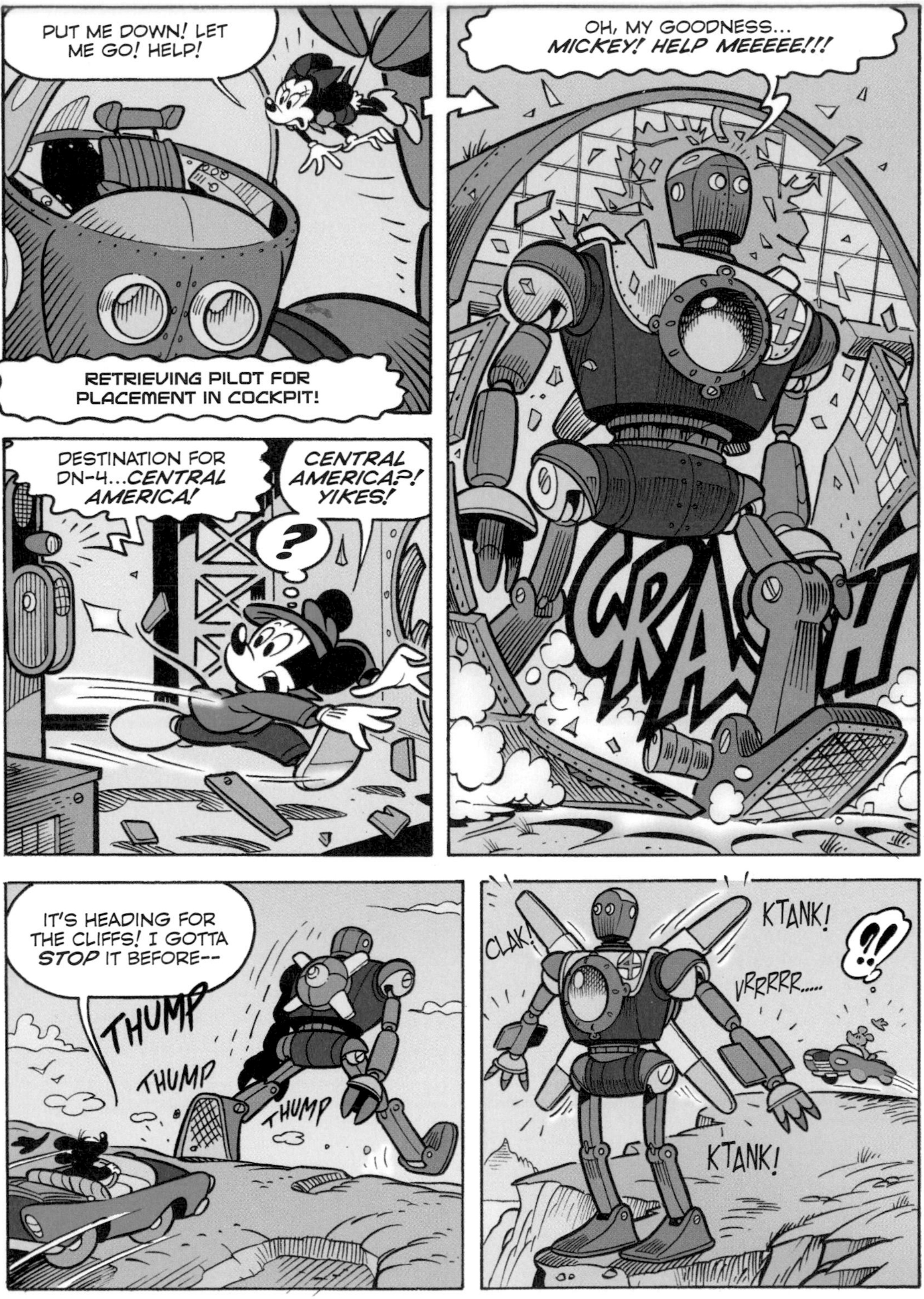
PUT ME DOWN! LET ME GO! HELP!
RETRIEVING PILOT FOR PLACEMENT IN COCKPIT!
OH, MY GOODNESS... *MICKEY! HELP MEEEEE!!!*
DESTINATION FOR DN-4...*CENTRAL AMERICA!*
CENTRAL AMERICA?! YIKES!
?
CRAASH
IT'S HEADING FOR THE CLIFFS! I GOTTA *STOP* IT BEFORE--
THUMP
THUMP
THUMP
CLAK!
KTANK!
!!
VRRRRR.....
KTANK!

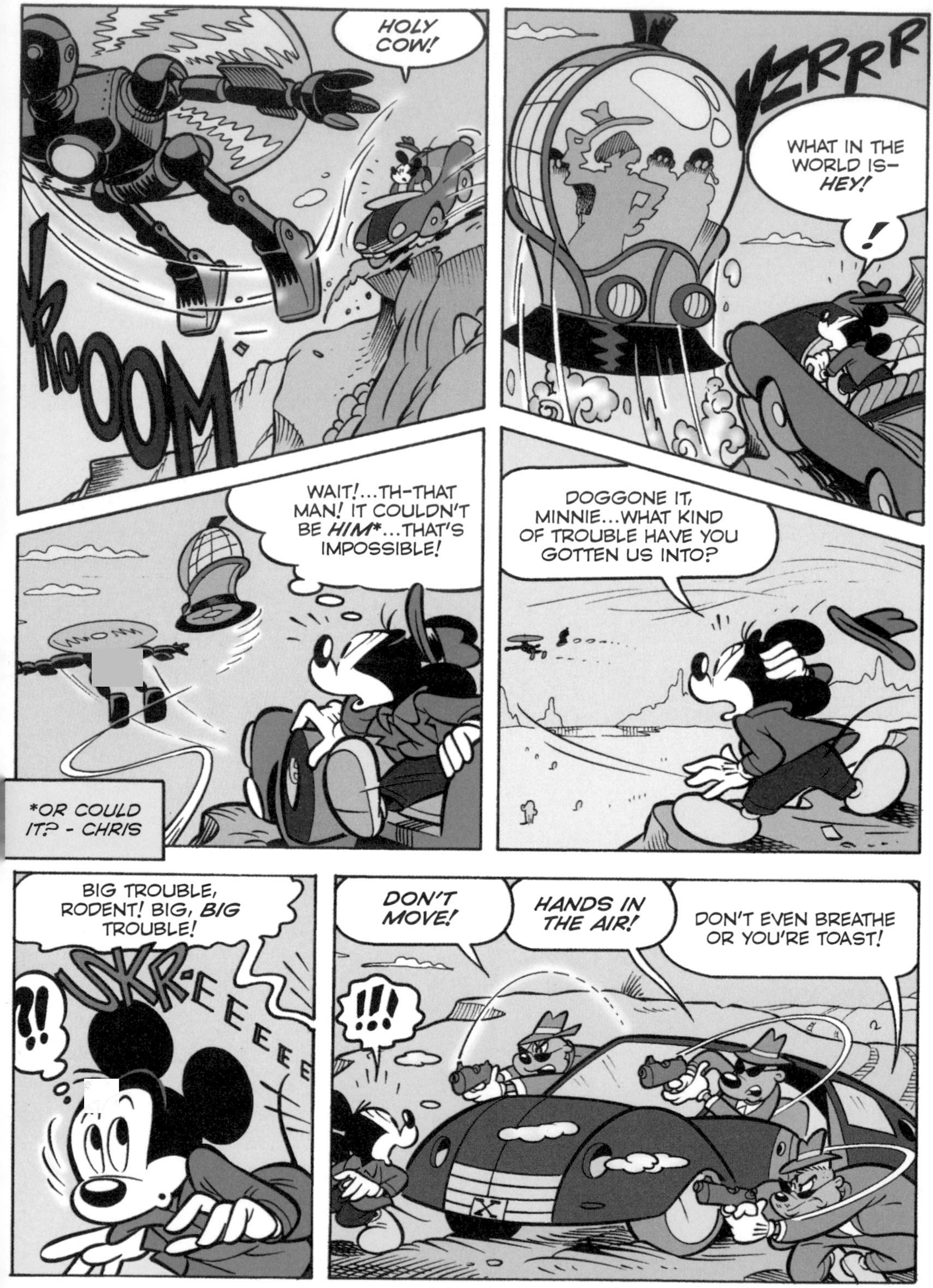
HOLY COW!
VROOOM
VZRRR
WHAT IN THE WORLD IS— HEY!
!
WAIT!...TH-THAT MAN! IT COULDN'T BE HIM*...THAT'S IMPOSSIBLE!
*OR COULD IT? - CHRIS
DOGGONE IT, MINNIE...WHAT KIND OF TROUBLE HAVE YOU GOTTEN US INTO?
BIG TROUBLE, RODENT! BIG, BIG TROUBLE!
SKR-EEEEE
?!
DON'T MOVE!
HANDS IN THE AIR!
DON'T EVEN BREATHE OR YOU'RE TOAST!
!!!

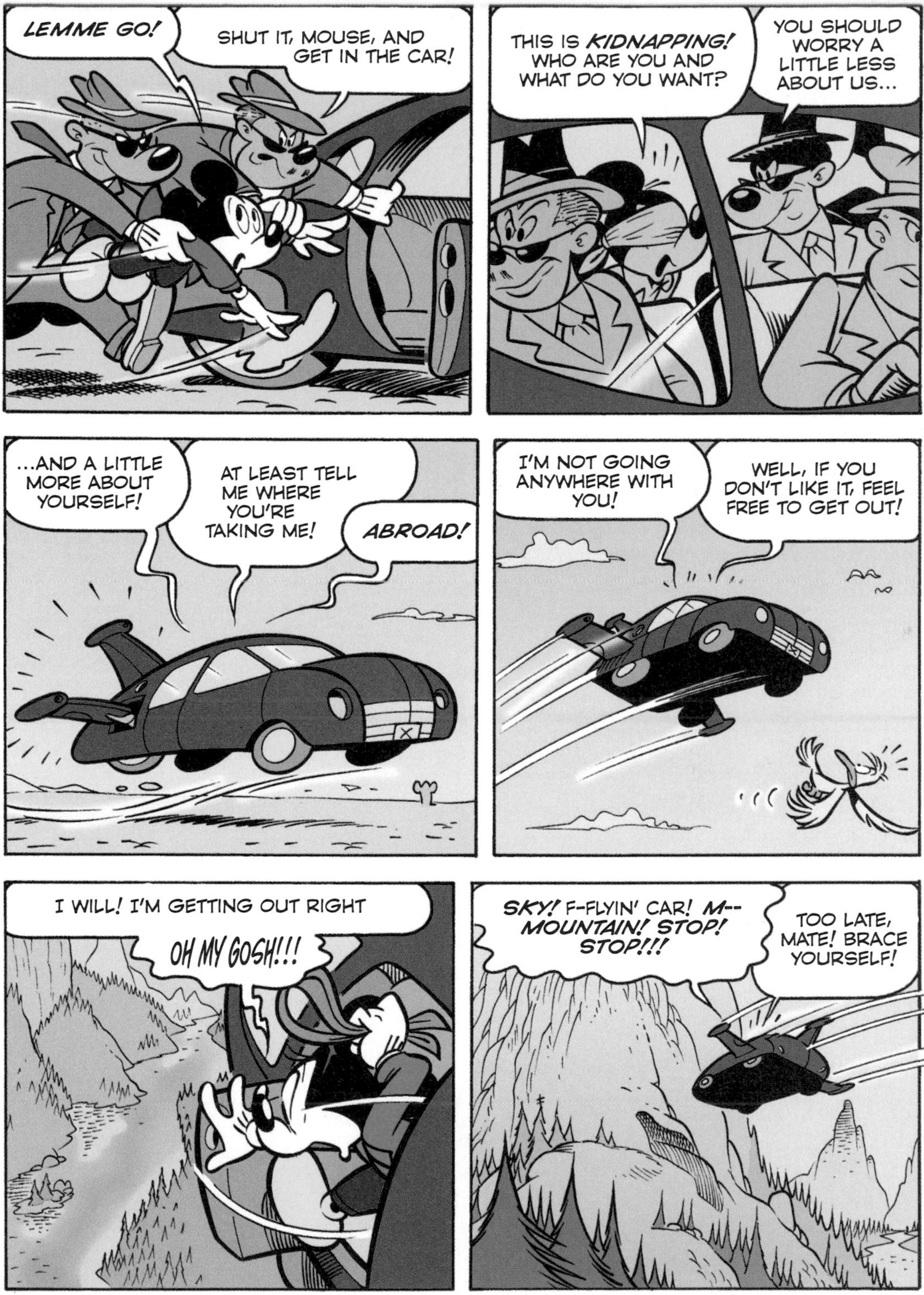

LEMME GO!
SHUT IT, MOUSE, AND GET IN THE CAR!
THIS IS KIDNAPPING! WHO ARE YOU AND WHAT DO YOU WANT?
YOU SHOULD WORRY A LITTLE LESS ABOUT US...
...AND A LITTLE MORE ABOUT YOURSELF!
AT LEAST TELL ME WHERE YOU'RE TAKING ME!
ABROAD!
I'M NOT GOING ANYWHERE WITH YOU!
WELL, IF YOU DON'T LIKE IT, FEEL FREE TO GET OUT!
I WILL! I'M GETTING OUT RIGHT
OH MY GOSH!!!
SKY! F-FLYIN' CAR! M--MOUNTAIN! STOP! STOP!!!
TOO LATE, MATE! BRACE YOURSELF!

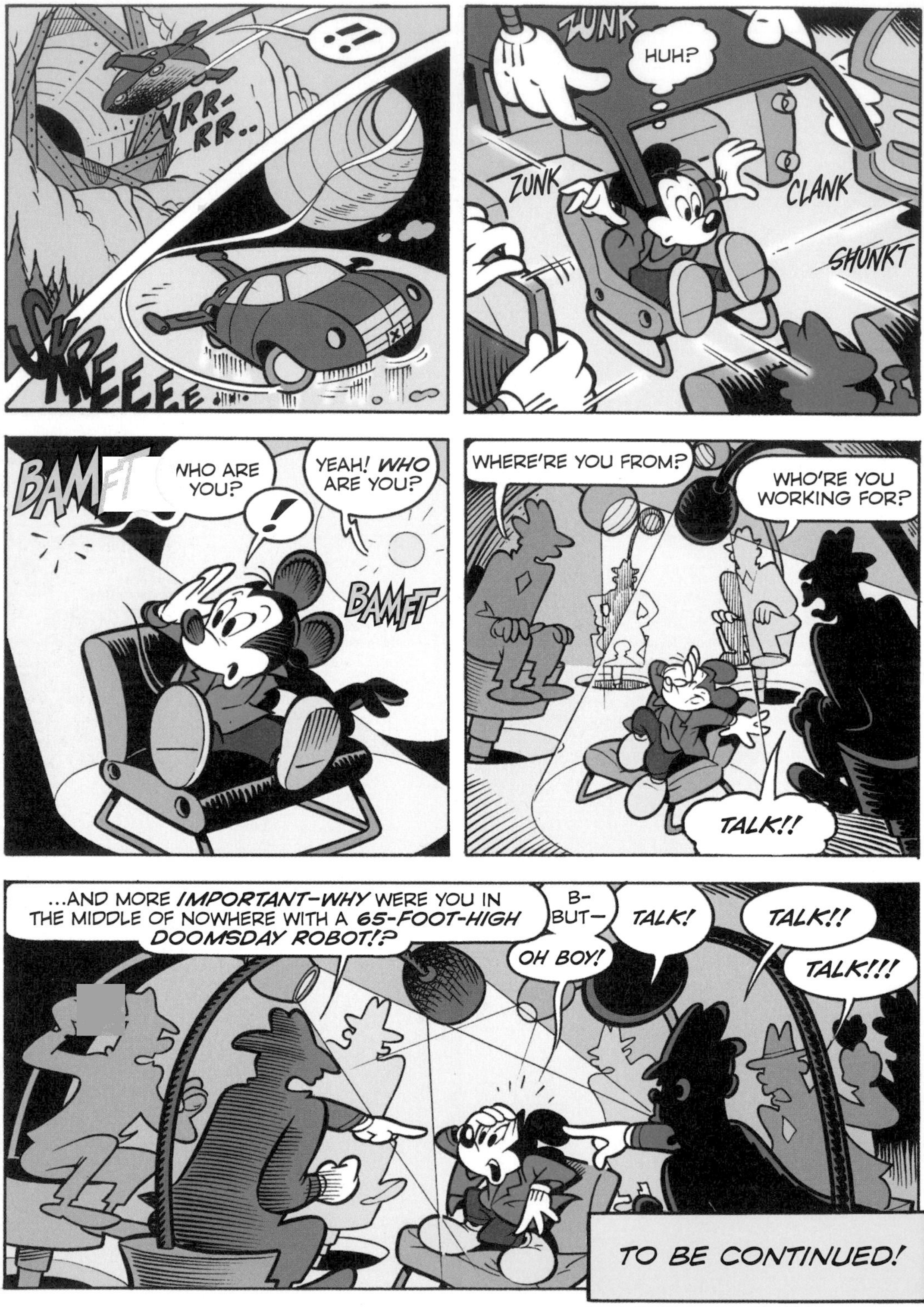
!!
VRR-RR..
ZUNK
HUH?
ZUNK
CLANK
SHUNKT
BAMFT
WHO ARE YOU?
YEAH! WHO ARE YOU?
!
BAMFT
WHERE'RE YOU FROM?
WHO'RE YOU WORKING FOR?
TALK!!
...AND MORE IMPORTANT—WHY WERE YOU IN THE MIDDLE OF NOWHERE WITH A 65-FOOT-HIGH DOOMSDAY ROBOT!?
B-BUT—
OH BOY!
TALK!
TALK!!
TALK!!!
TO BE CONTINUED!

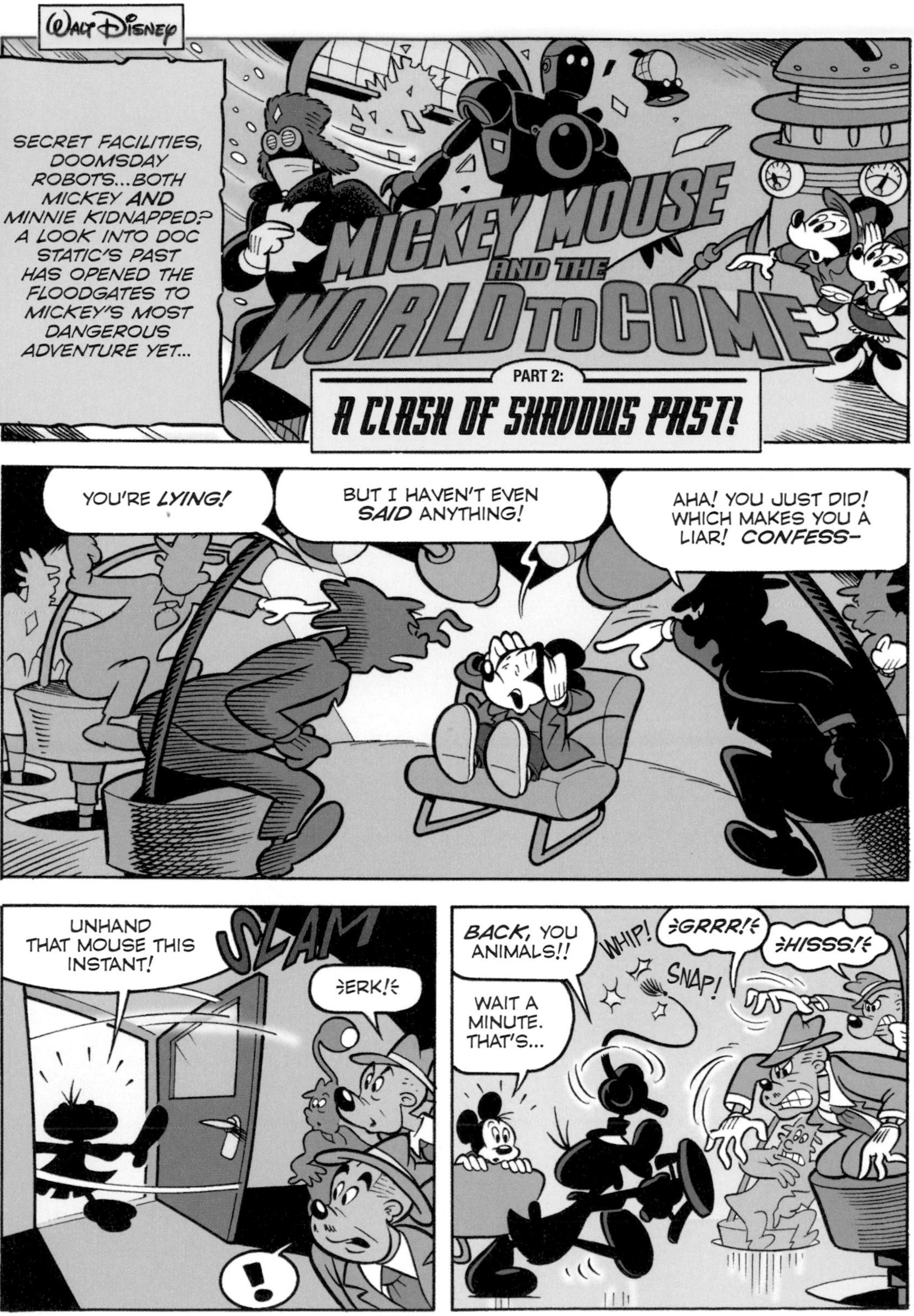
WALT DISNEY
SECRET FACILITIES, DOOMSDAY ROBOTS...BOTH MICKEY AND MINNIE KIDNAPPED? A LOOK INTO DOC STATIC'S PAST HAS OPENED THE FLOODGATES TO MICKEY'S MOST DANGEROUS ADVENTURE YET...
MICKEY MOUSE AND THE WORLD TO COME
PART 2:
A CLASH OF SHADOWS PAST!
YOU'RE LYING!
BUT I HAVEN'T EVEN SAID ANYTHING!
AHA! YOU JUST DID! WHICH MAKES YOU A LIAR! CONFESS–
UNHAND THAT MOUSE THIS INSTANT!
SLAM
ERK!
!
BACK, YOU ANIMALS!!
WHIP!
GRRR!
SNAP!
HISSS!
WAIT A MINUTE. THAT'S...

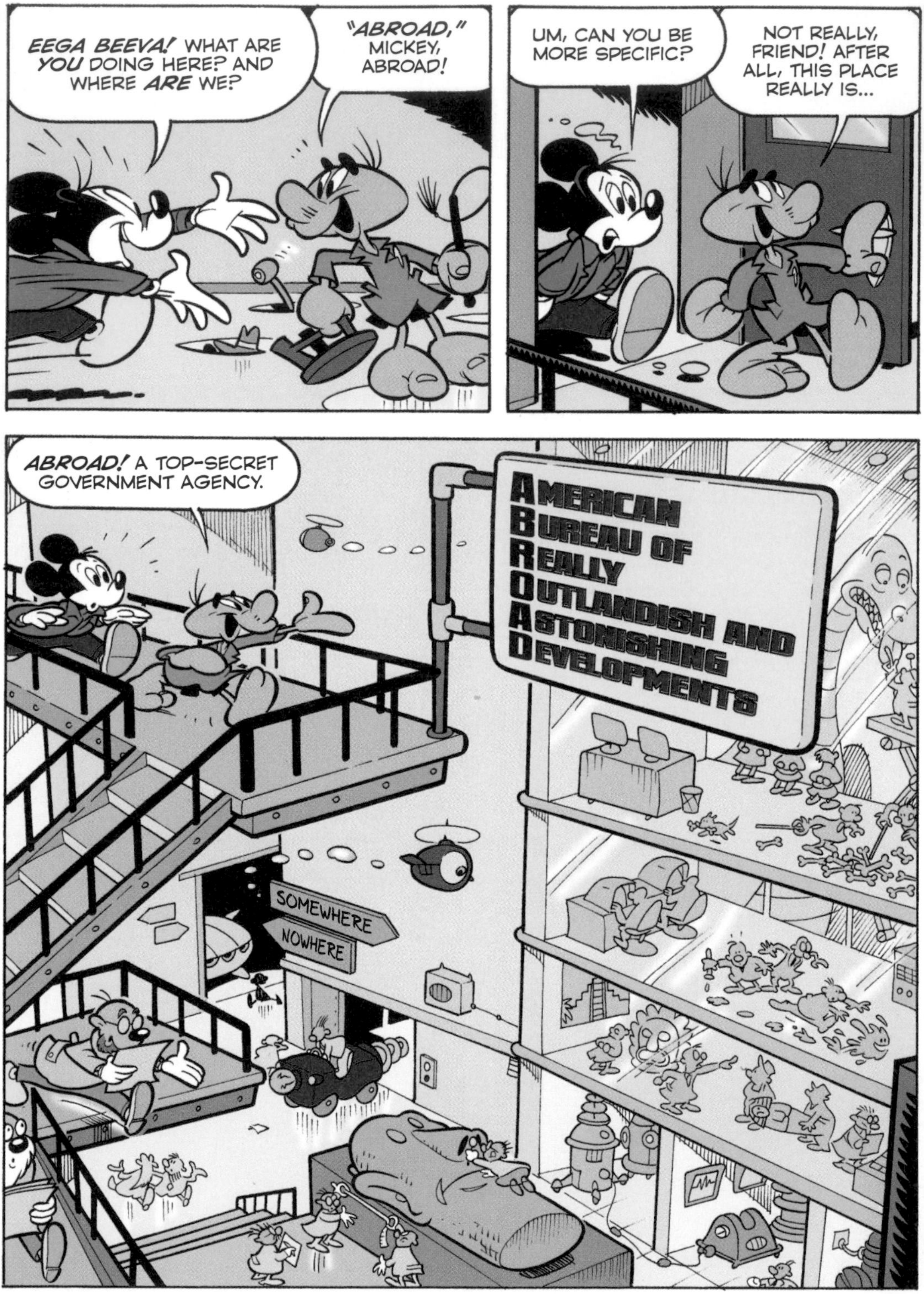
EEGA BEEVA! WHAT ARE YOU DOING HERE? AND WHERE ARE WE?
"ABROAD," MICKEY, ABROAD!
UM, CAN YOU BE MORE SPECIFIC?
NOT REALLY, FRIEND! AFTER ALL, THIS PLACE REALLY IS...
ABROAD! A TOP-SECRET GOVERNMENT AGENCY.
AMERICAN
BUREAU OF
REALLY
OUTLANDISH AND
ASTONISHING
DEVELOPMENTS
SOMEWHERE
NOWHERE

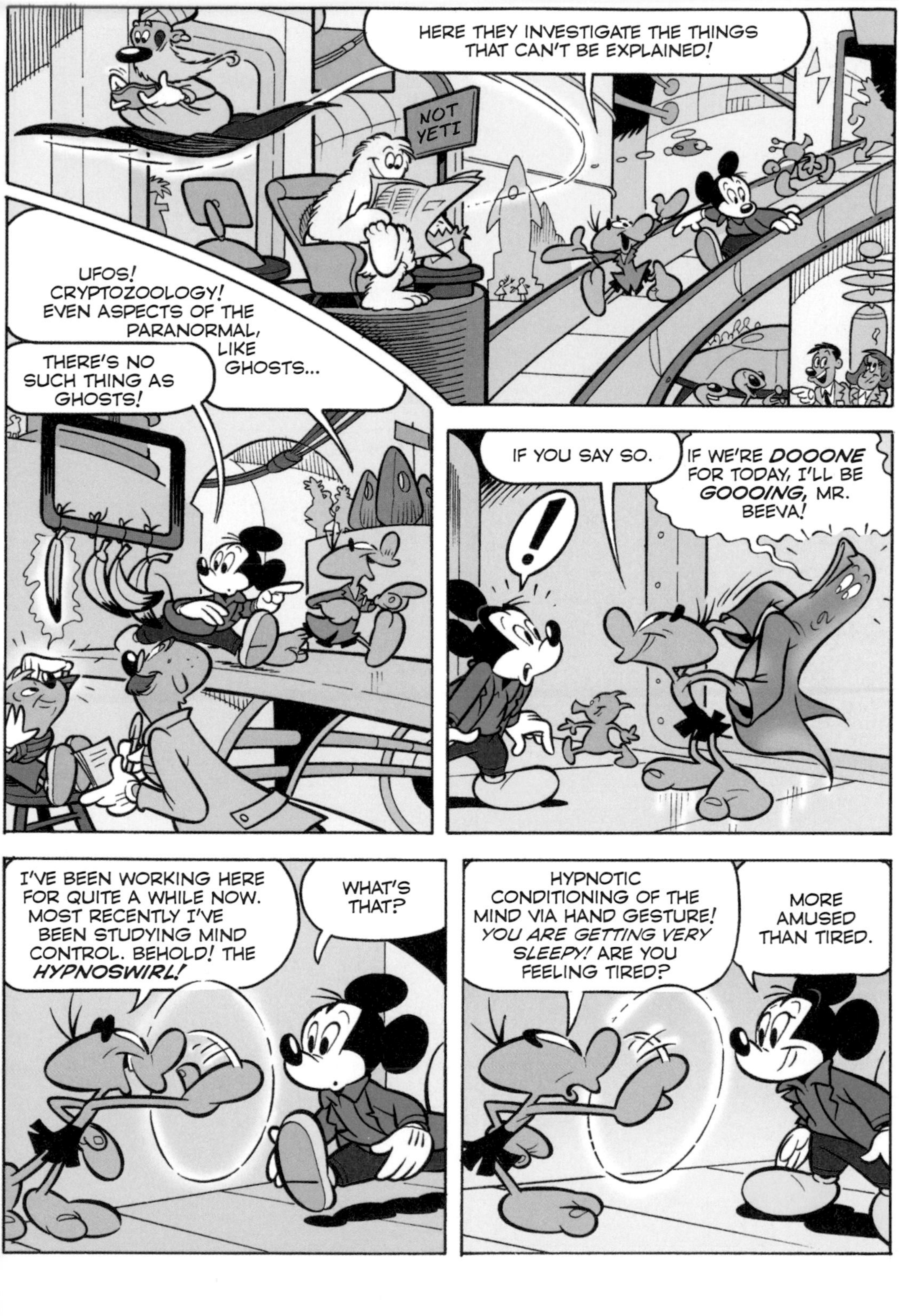
HERE THEY INVESTIGATE THE THINGS THAT CAN'T BE EXPLAINED!
NOT YETI
UFOS! CRYPTOZOOLOGY! EVEN ASPECTS OF THE PARANORMAL, LIKE GHOSTS...
THERE'S NO SUCH THING AS GHOSTS!
IF YOU SAY SO.
IF WE'RE DOOONE FOR TODAY, I'LL BE GOOOING, MR. BEEVA!
!
I'VE BEEN WORKING HERE FOR QUITE A WHILE NOW. MOST RECENTLY I'VE BEEN STUDYING MIND CONTROL. BEHOLD! THE HYPNOSWIRL!
WHAT'S THAT?
HYPNOTIC CONDITIONING OF THE MIND VIA HAND GESTURE! YOU ARE GETTING VERY SLEEPY! ARE YOU FEELING TIRED?
MORE AMUSED THAN TIRED.

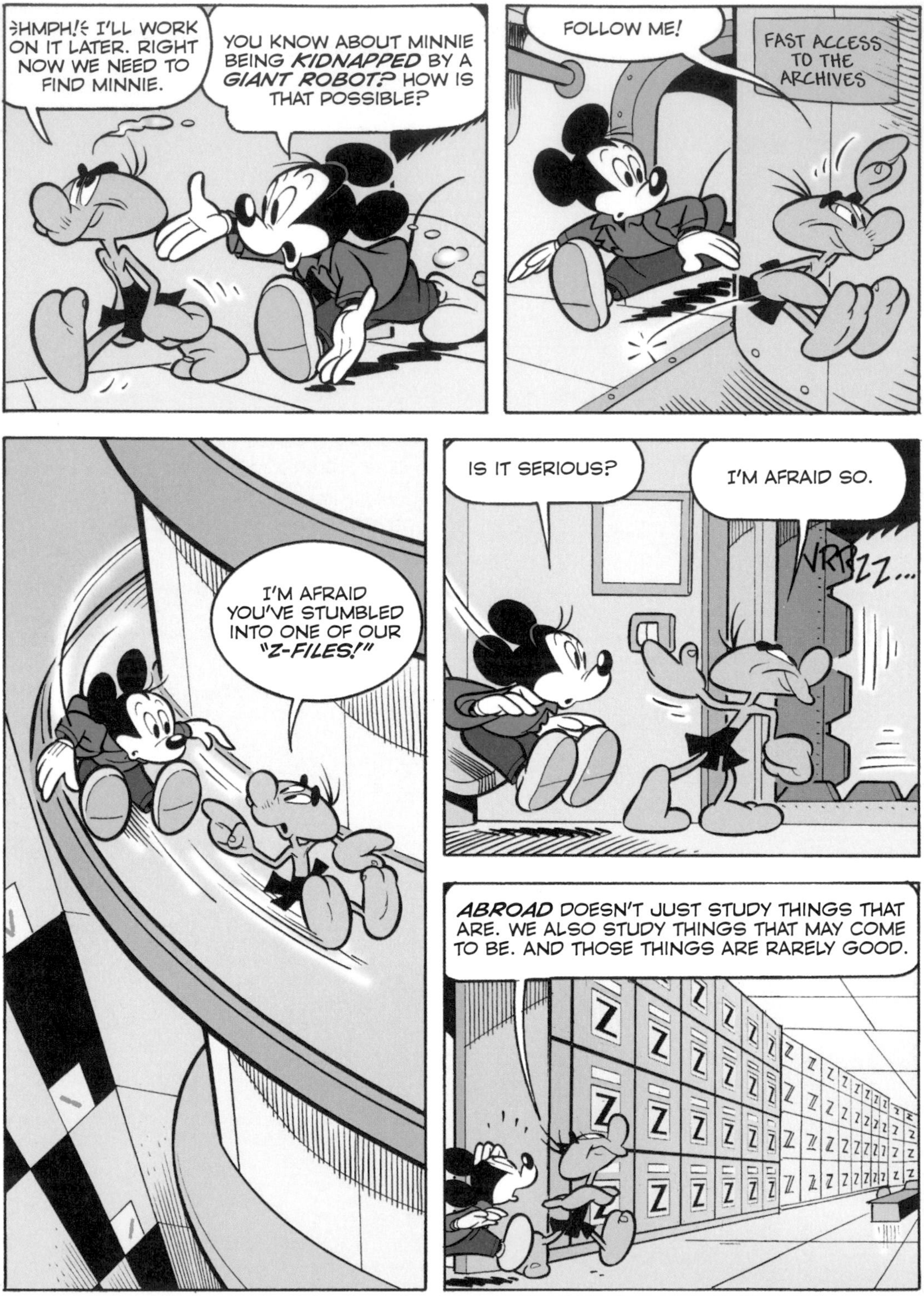

=HMPH!= I'LL WORK ON IT LATER. RIGHT NOW WE NEED TO FIND MINNIE.
YOU KNOW ABOUT MINNIE BEING KIDNAPPED BY A GIANT ROBOT? HOW IS THAT POSSIBLE?
FOLLOW ME!
FAST ACCESS TO THE ARCHIVES
I'M AFRAID YOU'VE STUMBLED INTO ONE OF OUR "Z-FILES!"
IS IT SERIOUS?
I'M AFRAID SO.
VRRZZ...
ABROAD DOESN'T JUST STUDY THINGS THAT ARE. WE ALSO STUDY THINGS THAT MAY COME TO BE. AND THOSE THINGS ARE RARELY GOOD.

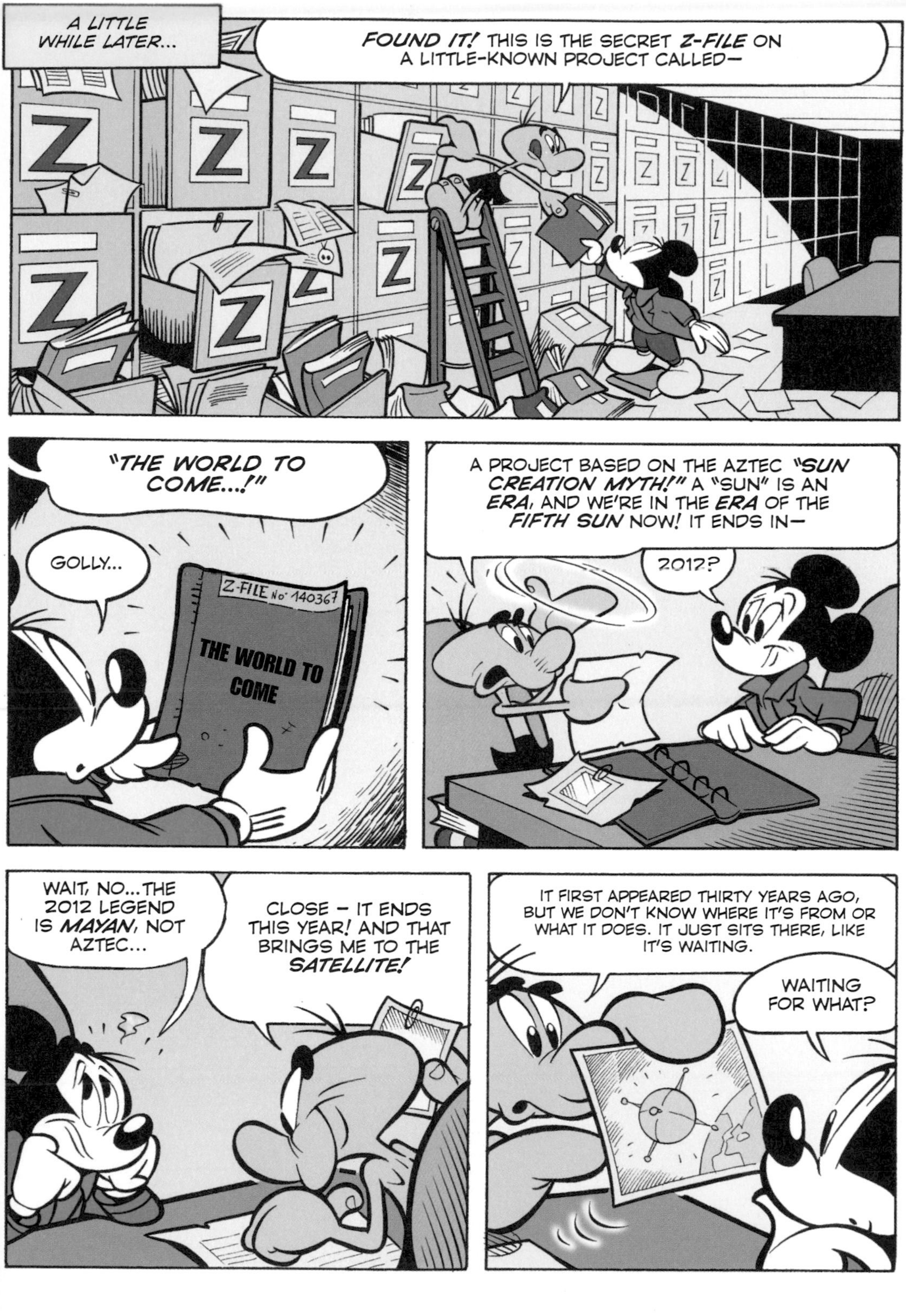

A LITTLE WHILE LATER...
FOUND IT! THIS IS THE SECRET Z-FILE ON A LITTLE-KNOWN PROJECT CALLED—
"THE WORLD TO COME...!"
GOLLY...
Z-FILE No 140367
THE WORLD TO COME
A PROJECT BASED ON THE AZTEC "SUN CREATION MYTH!" A "SUN" IS AN ERA, AND WE'RE IN THE ERA OF THE FIFTH SUN NOW! IT ENDS IN—
2012?
WAIT, NO...THE 2012 LEGEND IS MAYAN, NOT AZTEC...
CLOSE – IT ENDS THIS YEAR! AND THAT BRINGS ME TO THE SATELLITE!
IT FIRST APPEARED THIRTY YEARS AGO, BUT WE DON'T KNOW WHERE IT'S FROM OR WHAT IT DOES. IT JUST SITS THERE, LIKE IT'S WAITING.
WAITING FOR WHAT?

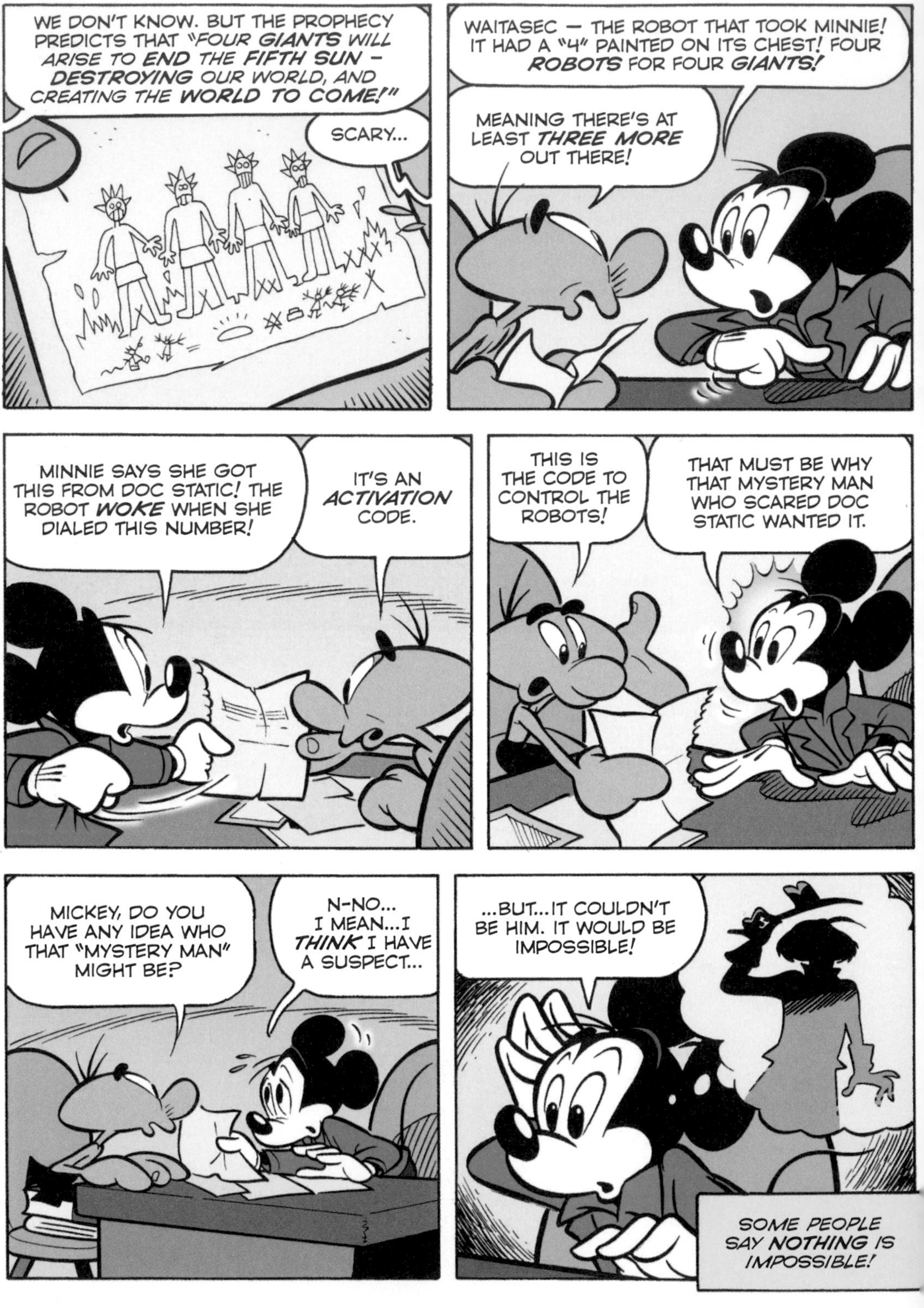
WE DON'T KNOW. BUT THE PROPHECY PREDICTS THAT "FOUR GIANTS WILL ARISE TO END THE FIFTH SUN – DESTROYING OUR WORLD, AND CREATING THE WORLD TO COME!"
SCARY...
WAITASEC — THE ROBOT THAT TOOK MINNIE! IT HAD A "4" PAINTED ON ITS CHEST! FOUR ROBOTS FOR FOUR GIANTS!
MEANING THERE'S AT LEAST THREE MORE OUT THERE!
MINNIE SAYS SHE GOT THIS FROM DOC STATIC! THE ROBOT WOKE WHEN SHE DIALED THIS NUMBER!
IT'S AN ACTIVATION CODE.
THIS IS THE CODE TO CONTROL THE ROBOTS!
THAT MUST BE WHY THAT MYSTERY MAN WHO SCARED DOC STATIC WANTED IT.
MICKEY, DO YOU HAVE ANY IDEA WHO THAT "MYSTERY MAN" MIGHT BE?
N-NO... I MEAN...I THINK I HAVE A SUSPECT...
...BUT...IT COULDN'T BE HIM. IT WOULD BE IMPOSSIBLE!
SOME PEOPLE SAY NOTHING IS IMPOSSIBLE!

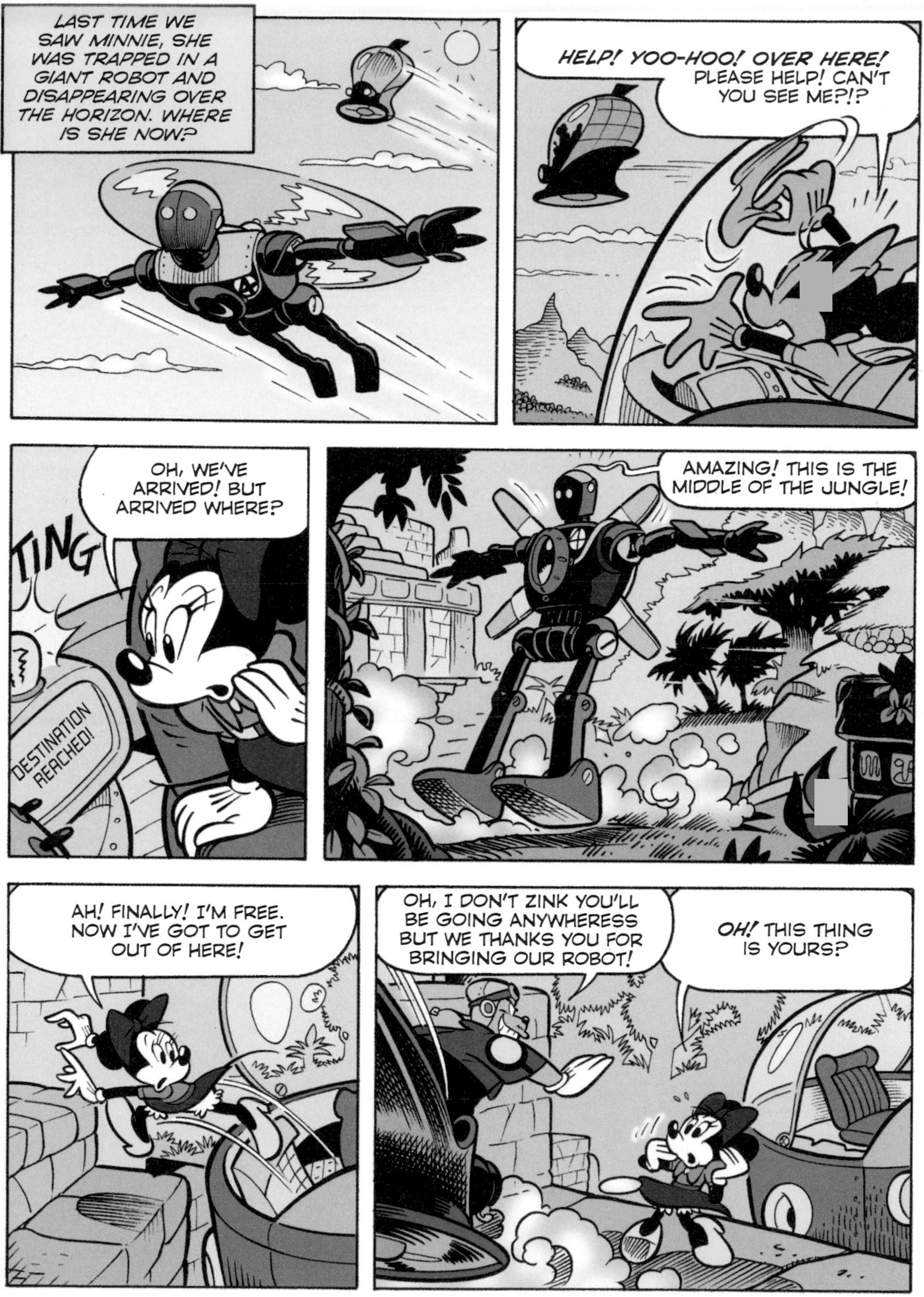
LAST TIME WE SAW MINNIE, SHE WAS TRAPPED IN A GIANT ROBOT AND DISAPPEARING OVER THE HORIZON. WHERE IS SHE NOW?
HELP! YOO-HOO! OVER HERE! PLEASE HELP! CAN'T YOU SEE ME?!?
OH, WE'VE ARRIVED! BUT ARRIVED WHERE?
TING
DESTINATION REACHED!
AMAZING! THIS IS THE MIDDLE OF THE JUNGLE!
AH! FINALLY! I'M FREE. NOW I'VE GOT TO GET OUT OF HERE!
OH, I DON'T ZINK YOU'LL BE GOING ANYWHERESS BUT WE THANKS YOU FOR BRINGING OUR ROBOT!
OH! THIS THING IS YOURS?

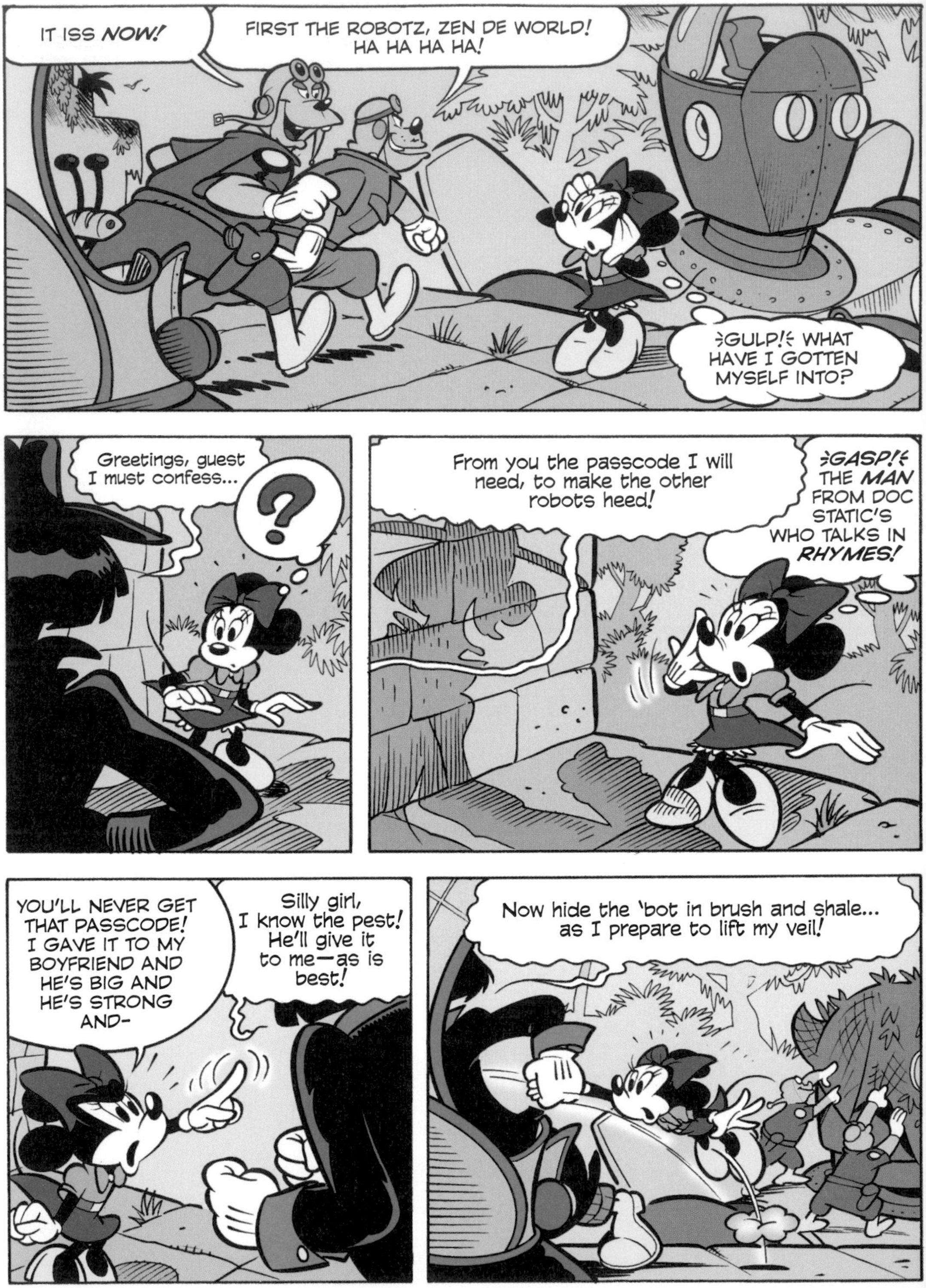
IT ISS *NOW!*
FIRST THE ROBOTZ, ZEN DE WORLD! HA HA HA HA!
GULP! WHAT HAVE I GOTTEN MYSELF INTO?
Greetings, guest I must confess...
?
From you the passcode I will need, to make the other robots heed!
GASP! THE *MAN* FROM DOC STATIC'S WHO TALKS IN *RHYMES!*
YOU'LL NEVER GET THAT PASSCODE! I GAVE IT TO MY BOYFRIEND AND HE'S BIG AND HE'S STRONG AND-
Silly girl, I know the pest! He'll give it to me—as is best!
Now hide the 'bot in brush and shale... as I prepare to lift my veil!

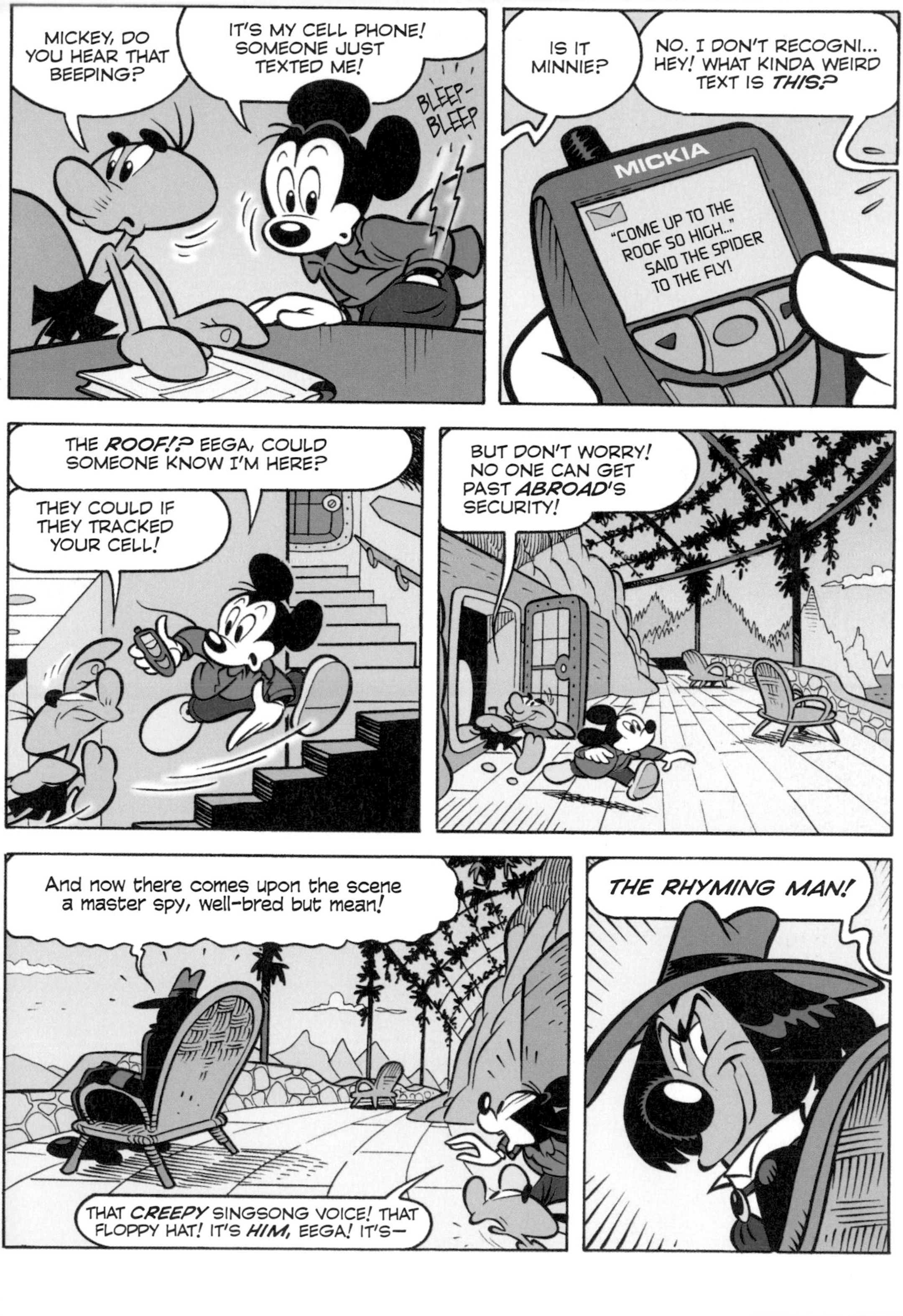
MICKEY, DO YOU HEAR THAT BEEPING?
IT'S MY CELL PHONE! SOMEONE JUST TEXTED ME!
BLEEP-BLEEP
IS IT MINNIE?
NO. I DON'T RECOGNI... HEY! WHAT KINDA WEIRD TEXT IS *THIS?*
MICKIA
"COME UP TO THE ROOF SO HIGH..." SAID THE SPIDER TO THE FLY!
THE *ROOF!?* EEGA, COULD SOMEONE KNOW I'M HERE?
THEY COULD IF THEY TRACKED YOUR CELL!
BUT DON'T WORRY! NO ONE CAN GET PAST *ABROAD*'S SECURITY!
And now there comes upon the scene a master spy, well-bred but mean!
THAT *CREEPY* SINGSONG VOICE! THAT FLOPPY HAT! IT'S *HIM,* EEGA! IT'S—
THE RHYMING MAN!

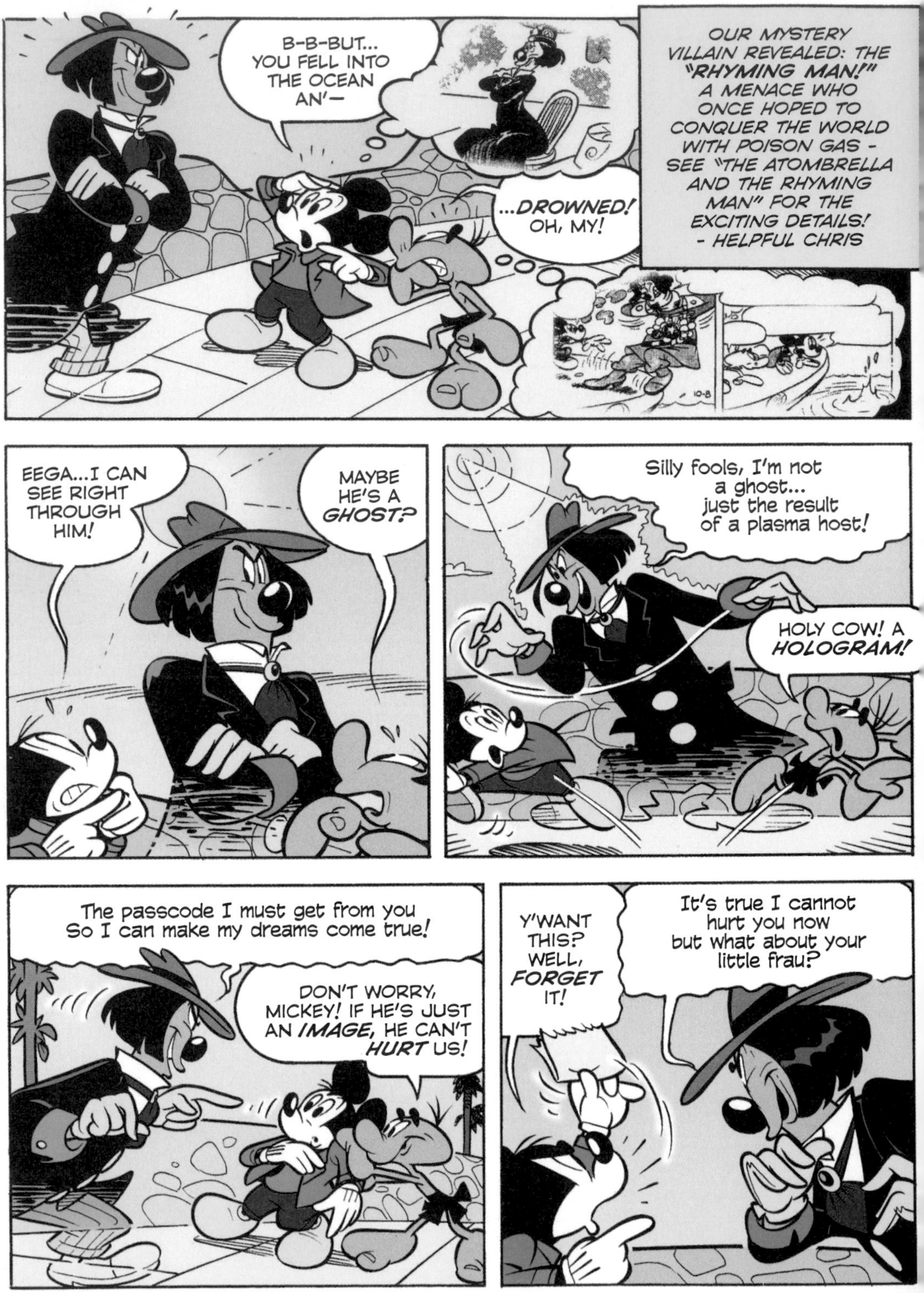

B-B-BUT... YOU FELL INTO THE OCEAN AN'—
OUR MYSTERY VILLAIN REVEALED: THE "RHYMING MAN!" A MENACE WHO ONCE HOPED TO CONQUER THE WORLD WITH POISON GAS - SEE "THE ATOMBRELLA AND THE RHYMING MAN" FOR THE EXCITING DETAILS! - HELPFUL CHRIS
...DROWNED! OH, MY!
10-8
EEGA...I CAN SEE RIGHT THROUGH HIM!
MAYBE HE'S A GHOST?
Silly fools, I'm not a ghost... just the result of a plasma host!
HOLY COW! A HOLOGRAM!
The passcode I must get from you So I can make my dreams come true!
DON'T WORRY, MICKEY! IF HE'S JUST AN IMAGE, HE CAN'T HURT US!
Y'WANT THIS? WELL, FORGET IT!
It's true I cannot hurt you now but what about your little frau?

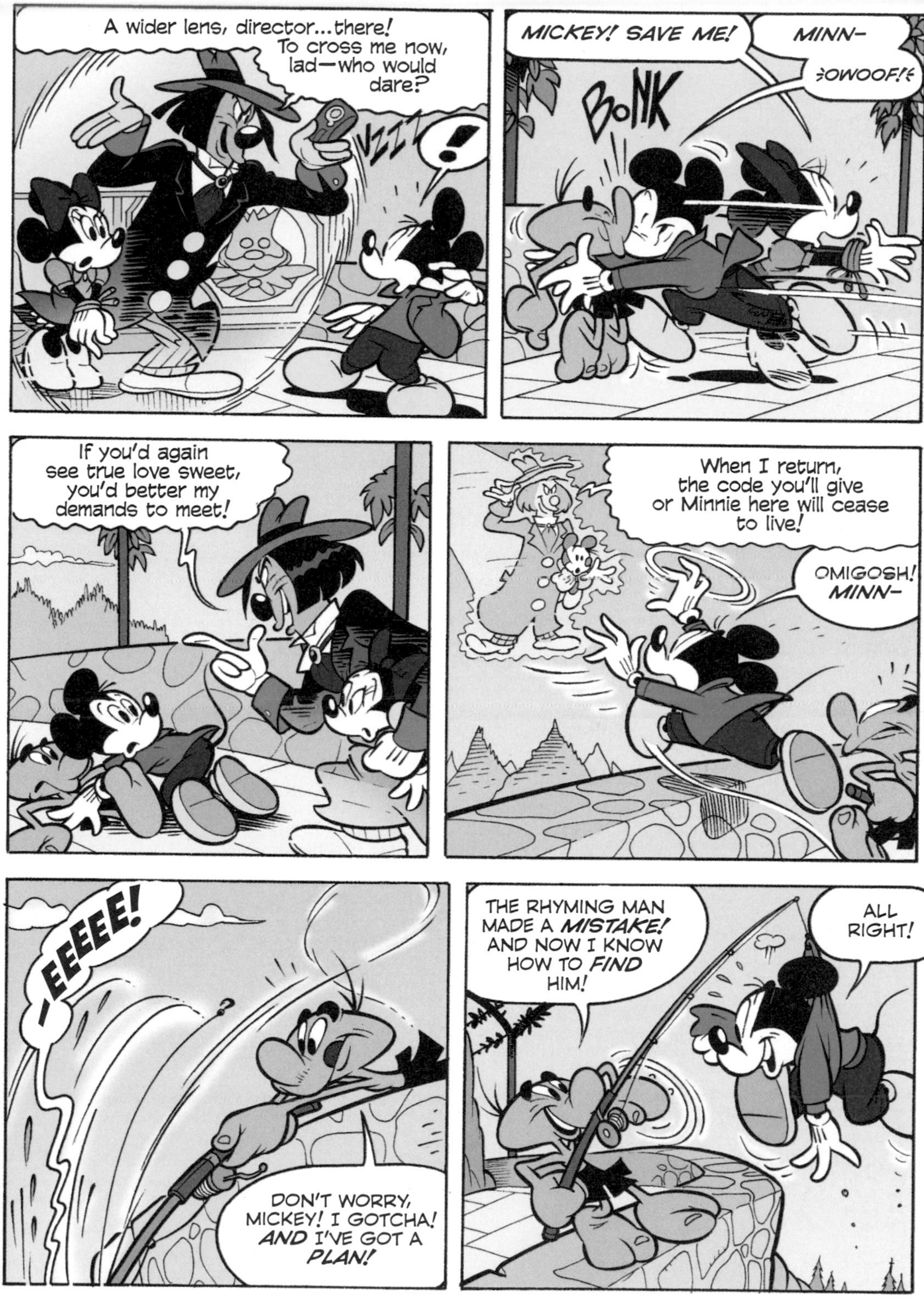
A wider lens, director...there!
To cross me now, lad—who would dare?
VZZT
!
MICKEY! SAVE ME!
MINN—
BONK
OWOOF!
If you'd again see true love sweet, you'd better my demands to meet!
When I return, the code you'll give or Minnie here will cease to live!
OMIGOSH! MINN—
—EEEEE!
DON'T WORRY, MICKEY! I GOTCHA! AND I'VE GOT A PLAN!
THE RHYMING MAN MADE A MISTAKE! AND NOW I KNOW HOW TO FIND HIM!
ALL RIGHT!

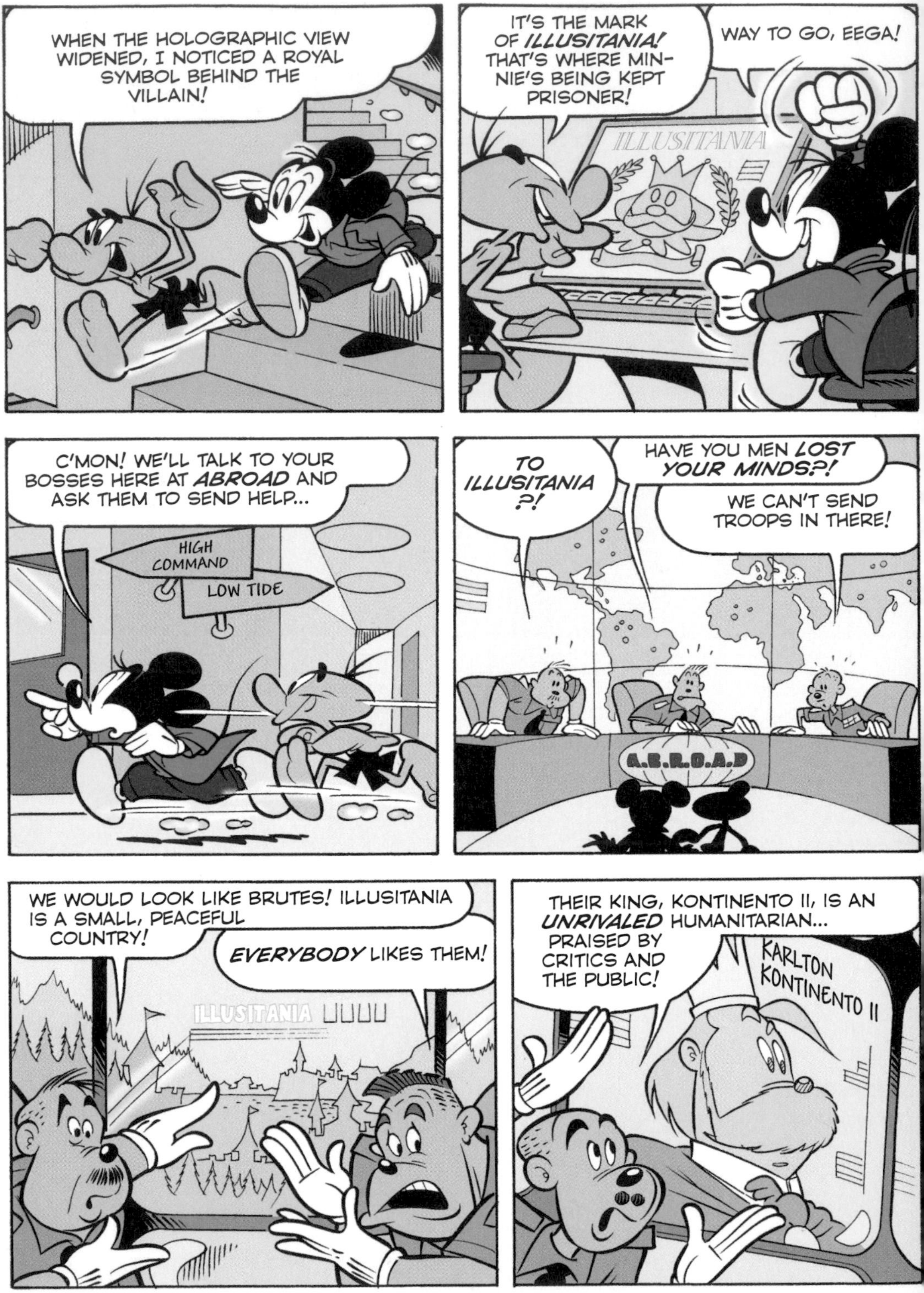
WHEN THE HOLOGRAPHIC VIEW WIDENED, I NOTICED A ROYAL SYMBOL BEHIND THE VILLAIN!
IT'S THE MARK OF ILLUSITANIA! THAT'S WHERE MIN-NIE'S BEING KEPT PRISONER!
WAY TO GO, EEGA!
ILLUSITANIA
C'MON! WE'LL TALK TO YOUR BOSSES HERE AT ABROAD AND ASK THEM TO SEND HELP...
HIGH COMMAND
LOW TIDE
TO ILLUSITANIA ?!
HAVE YOU MEN LOST YOUR MINDS?!
WE CAN'T SEND TROOPS IN THERE!
A.B.R.O.A.D
WE WOULD LOOK LIKE BRUTES! ILLUSITANIA IS A SMALL, PEACEFUL COUNTRY!
EVERYBODY LIKES THEM!
ILLUSITANIA
THEIR KING, KONTINENTO II, IS AN UNRIVALED HUMANITARIAN... PRAISED BY CRITICS AND THE PUBLIC!
KARLTON KONTINENTO II

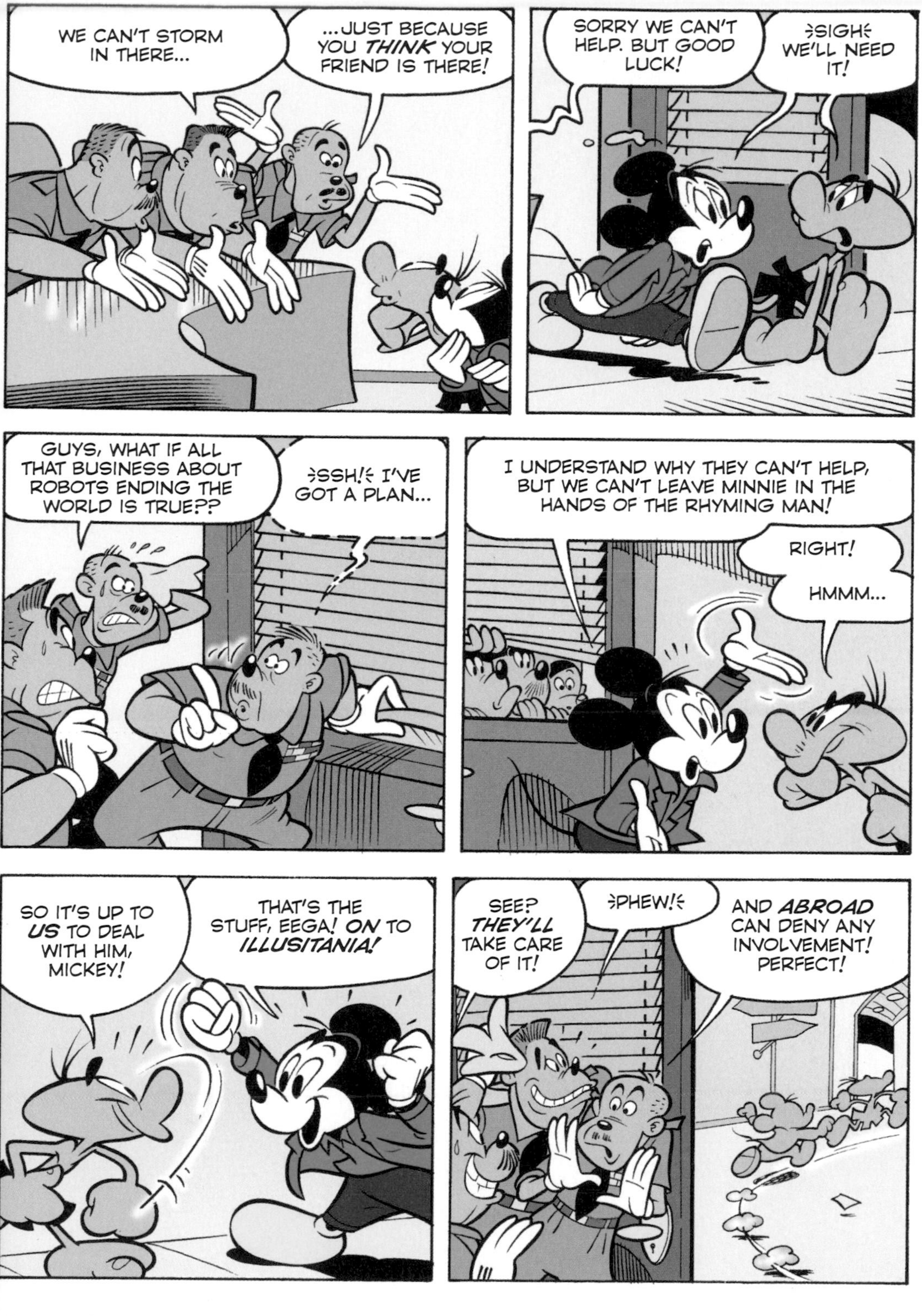
WE CAN'T STORM IN THERE...
...JUST BECAUSE YOU THINK YOUR FRIEND IS THERE!
SORRY WE CAN'T HELP. BUT GOOD LUCK!
SIGH WE'LL NEED IT!
GUYS, WHAT IF ALL THAT BUSINESS ABOUT ROBOTS ENDING THE WORLD IS TRUE??
SSH! I'VE GOT A PLAN...
I UNDERSTAND WHY THEY CAN'T HELP, BUT WE CAN'T LEAVE MINNIE IN THE HANDS OF THE RHYMING MAN!
RIGHT!
HMMM...
SO IT'S UP TO US TO DEAL WITH HIM, MICKEY!
THAT'S THE STUFF, EEGA! ON TO ILLUSITANIA!
SEE? THEY'LL TAKE CARE OF IT!
PHEW!
AND ABROAD CAN DENY ANY INVOLVEMENT! PERFECT!

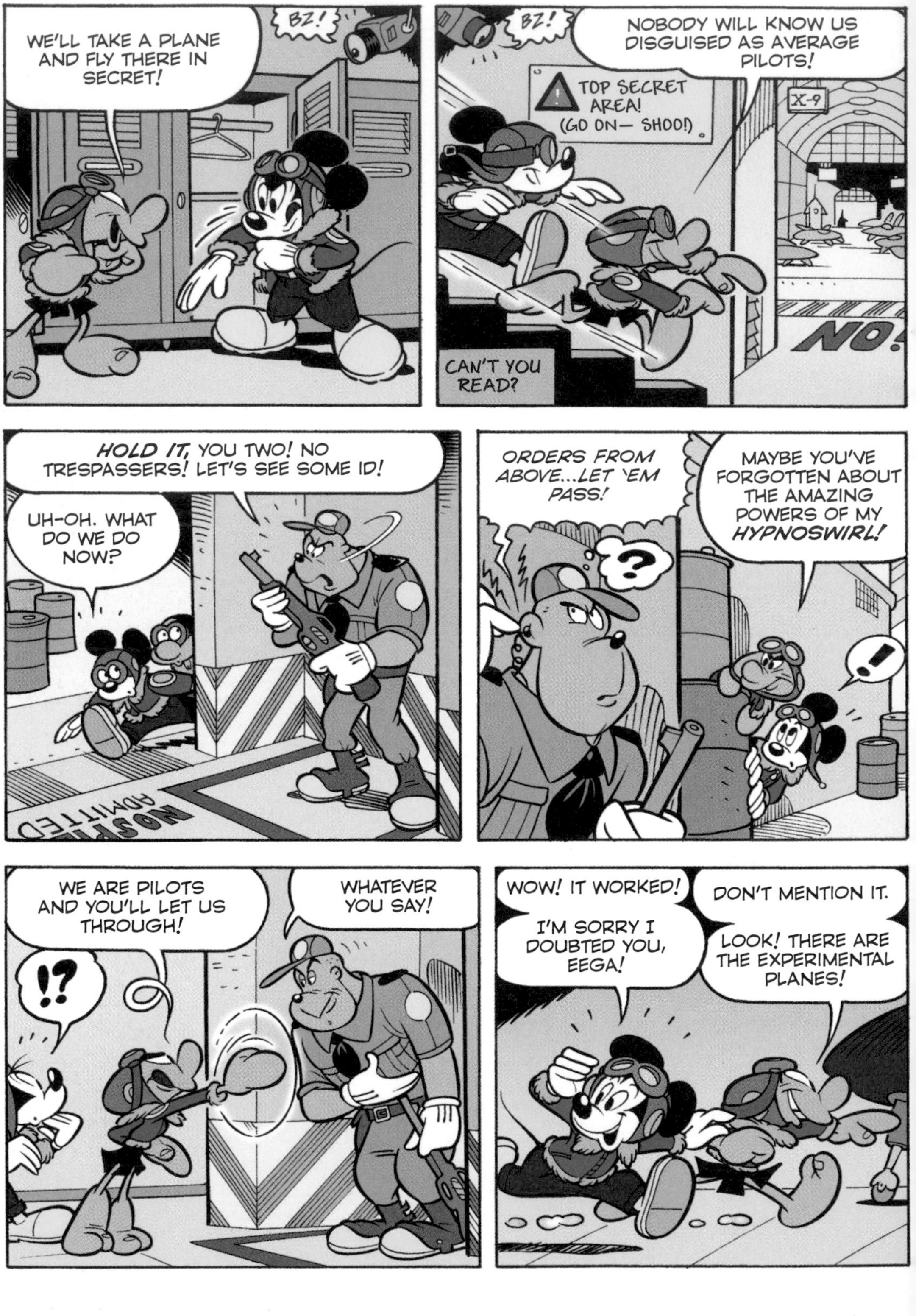
WE'LL TAKE A PLANE AND FLY THERE IN SECRET!
BZ!
BZ!
NOBODY WILL KNOW US DISGUISED AS AVERAGE PILOTS!
TOP SECRET AREA! (GO ON— SHOO!)
X-9
NO!
CAN'T YOU READ?
HOLD IT, YOU TWO! NO TRESPASSERS! LET'S SEE SOME ID!
UH-OH. WHAT DO WE DO NOW?
NOSPIED ADMITTED
ORDERS FROM ABOVE...LET 'EM PASS!
?
MAYBE YOU'VE FORGOTTEN ABOUT THE AMAZING POWERS OF MY HYPNOSWIRL!
!
WE ARE PILOTS AND YOU'LL LET US THROUGH!
WHATEVER YOU SAY!
!?
WOW! IT WORKED!
I'M SORRY I DOUBTED YOU, EEGA!
DON'T MENTION IT.
LOOK! THERE ARE THE EXPERIMENTAL PLANES!

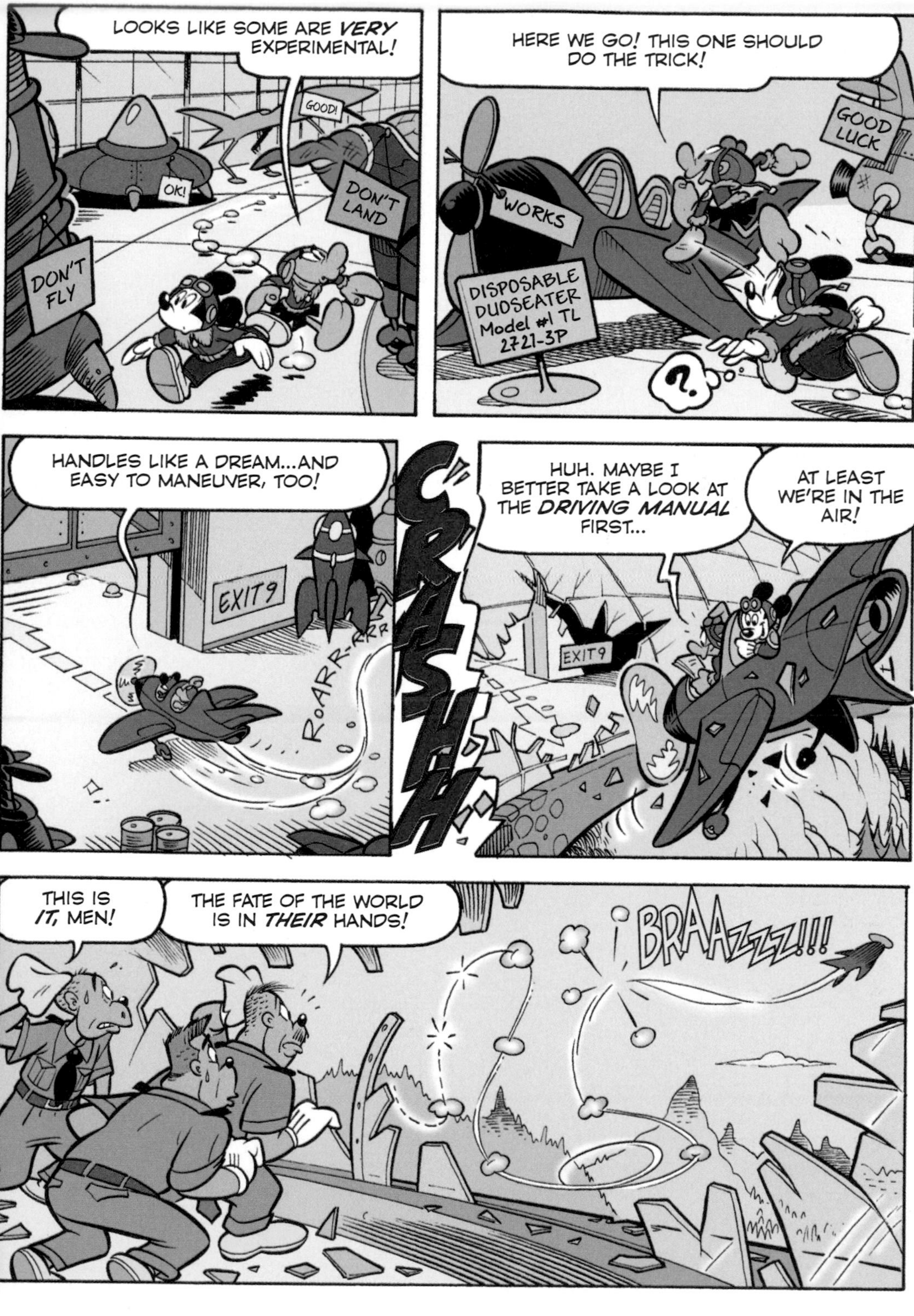

LOOKS LIKE SOME ARE *VERY* EXPERIMENTAL!
GOOD!
OK!
DON'T LAND
DON'T FLY
HERE WE GO! THIS ONE SHOULD DO THE TRICK!
GOOD LUCK
WORKS
DISPOSABLE DUOSEATER Model #1 TL 2721-3P
?
HANDLES LIKE A DREAM...AND EASY TO MANEUVER, TOO!
EXIT 9
RoARR-RRR
CRASHHH
HUH. MAYBE I BETTER TAKE A LOOK AT THE *DRIVING MANUAL* FIRST...
AT LEAST WE'RE IN THE AIR!
EXIT 9
THIS IS *IT,* MEN!
THE FATE OF THE WORLD IS IN *THEIR* HANDS!
¡BRAAzzzz!!!

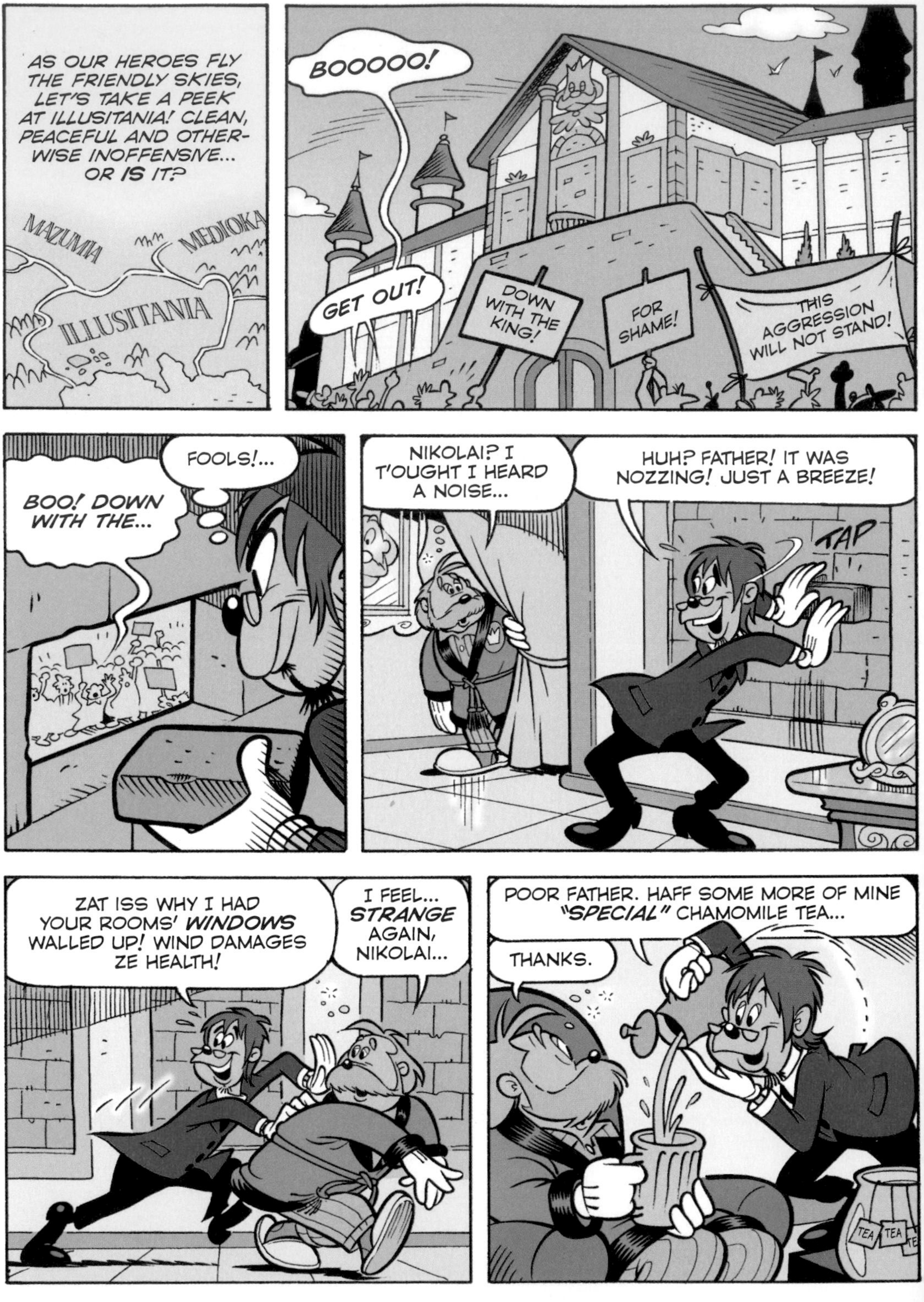

AS OUR HEROES FLY THE FRIENDLY SKIES, LET'S TAKE A PEEK AT ILLUSITANIA! CLEAN, PEACEFUL AND OTHER-WISE INOFFENSIVE... OR IS IT?
MAZUMIA
MEDIOKA
ILLUSITANIA
BOOOOO!
GET OUT!
DOWN WITH THE KING!
FOR SHAME!
THIS AGGRESSION WILL NOT STAND!
FOOLS!...
BOO! DOWN WITH THE...
NIKOLAI? I T'OUGHT I HEARD A NOISE...
HUH? FATHER! IT WAS NOZZING! JUST A BREEZE!
TAP
ZAT ISS WHY I HAD YOUR ROOMS' WINDOWS WALLED UP! WIND DAMAGES ZE HEALTH!
I FEEL... STRANGE AGAIN, NIKOLAI...
POOR FATHER. HAFF SOME MORE OF MINE "SPECIAL" CHAMOMILE TEA...
THANKS.
TEA
TEA

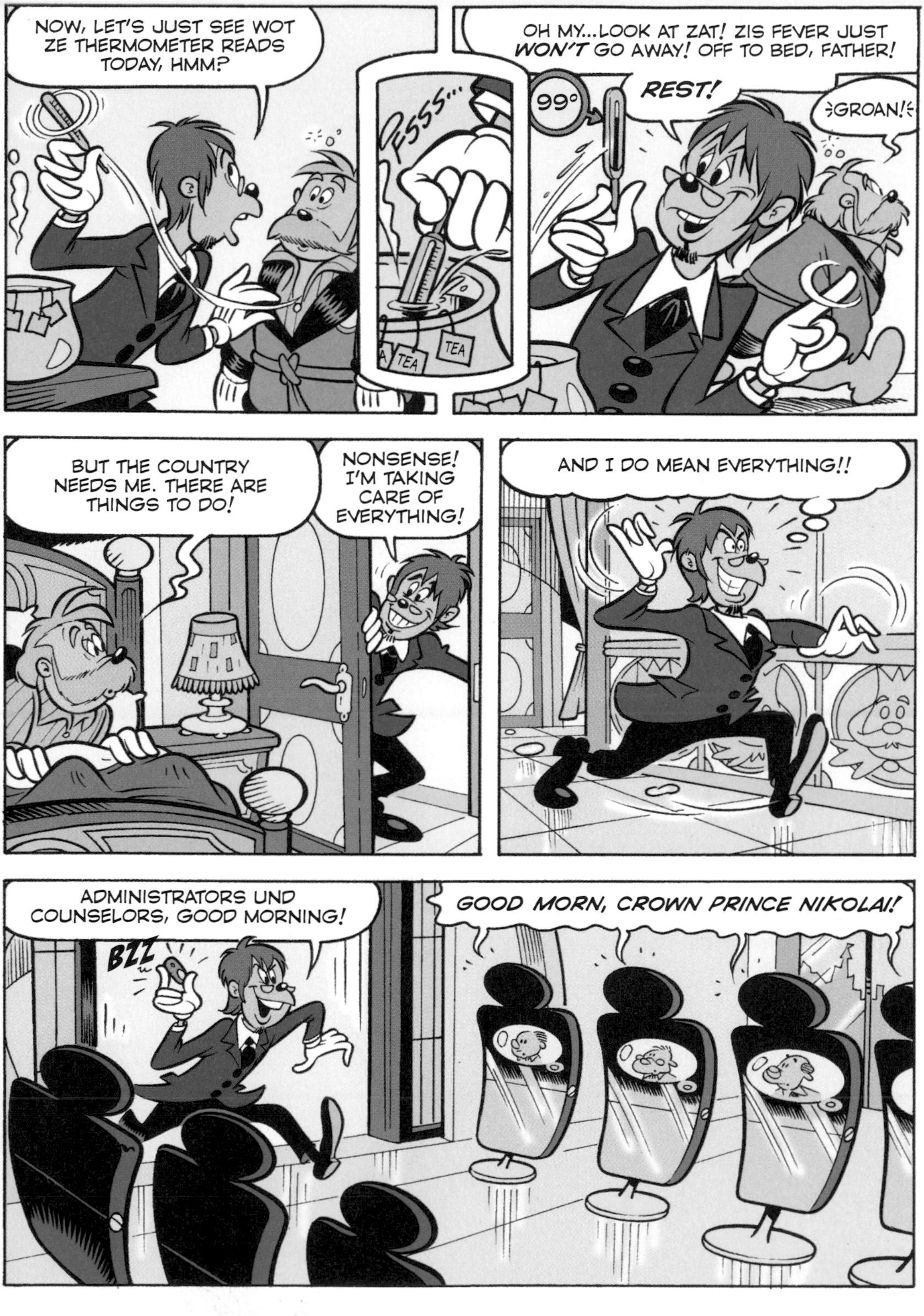
NOW, LET'S JUST SEE WOT ZE THERMOMETER READS TODAY, HMM?
FSSS...
TEA
TEA
OH MY...LOOK AT ZAT! ZIS FEVER JUST *WON'T* GO AWAY! OFF TO BED, FATHER!
99°
REST!
GROAN!
BUT THE COUNTRY NEEDS ME. THERE ARE THINGS TO DO!
NONSENSE! I'M TAKING CARE OF EVERYTHING!
AND I DO MEAN EVERYTHING!!
ADMINISTRATORS UND COUNSELORS, GOOD MORNING!
BZZ
GOOD MORN, CROWN PRINCE NIKOLAI!

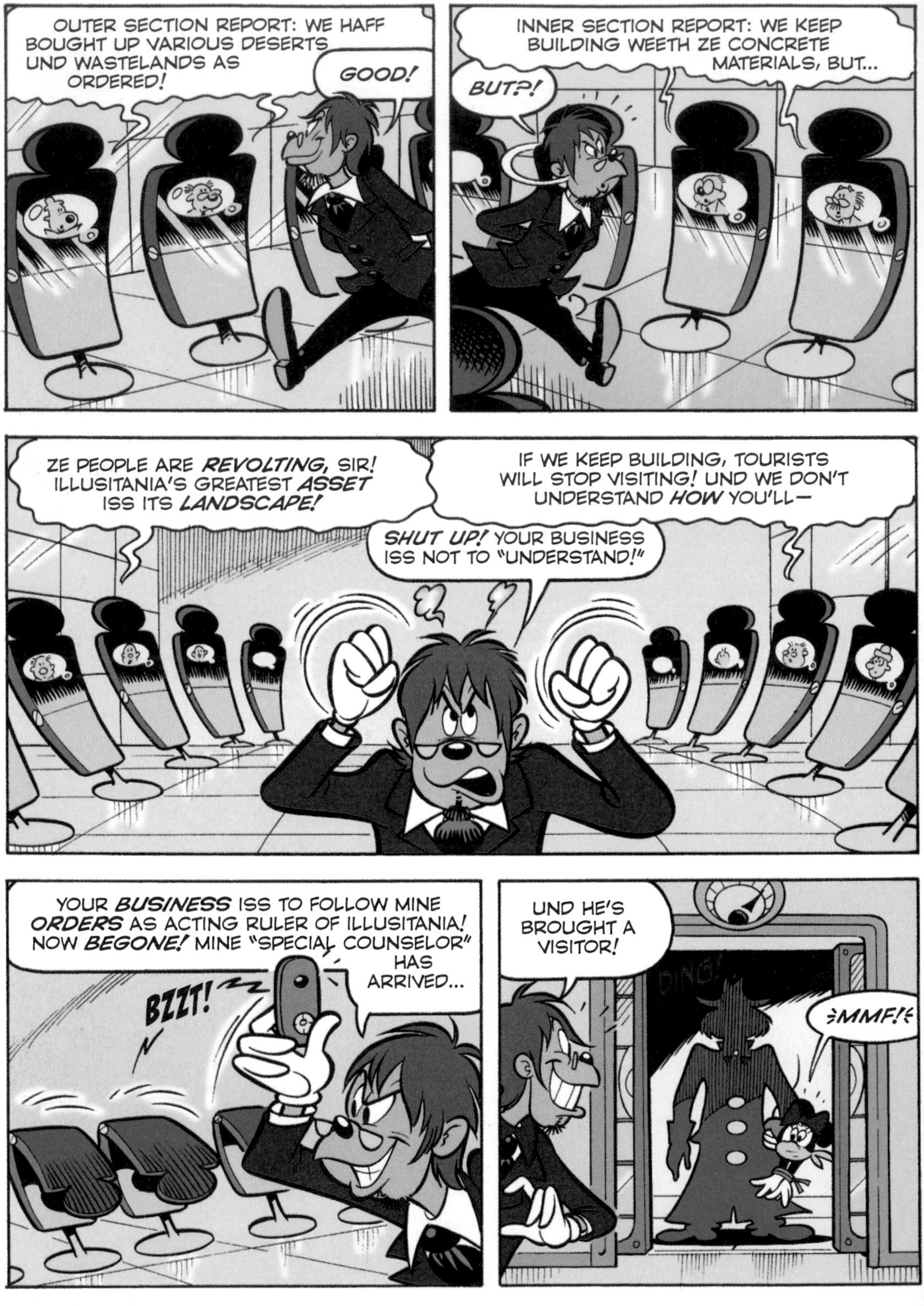
OUTER SECTION REPORT: WE HAFF BOUGHT UP VARIOUS DESERTS UND WASTELANDS AS ORDERED!
GOOD!
INNER SECTION REPORT: WE KEEP BUILDING WEETH ZE CONCRETE MATERIALS, BUT...
BUT?!
ZE PEOPLE ARE REVOLTING, SIR! ILLUSITANIA'S GREATEST ASSET ISS ITS LANDSCAPE!
IF WE KEEP BUILDING, TOURISTS WILL STOP VISITING! UND WE DON'T UNDERSTAND HOW YOU'LL—
SHUT UP! YOUR BUSINESS ISS NOT TO "UNDERSTAND!"
YOUR BUSINESS ISS TO FOLLOW MINE ORDERS AS ACTING RULER OF ILLUSITANIA! NOW BEGONE! MINE "SPECIAL COUNSELOR" HAS ARRIVED...
BZZT!
UND HE'S BROUGHT A VISITOR!
DING!
MMF!

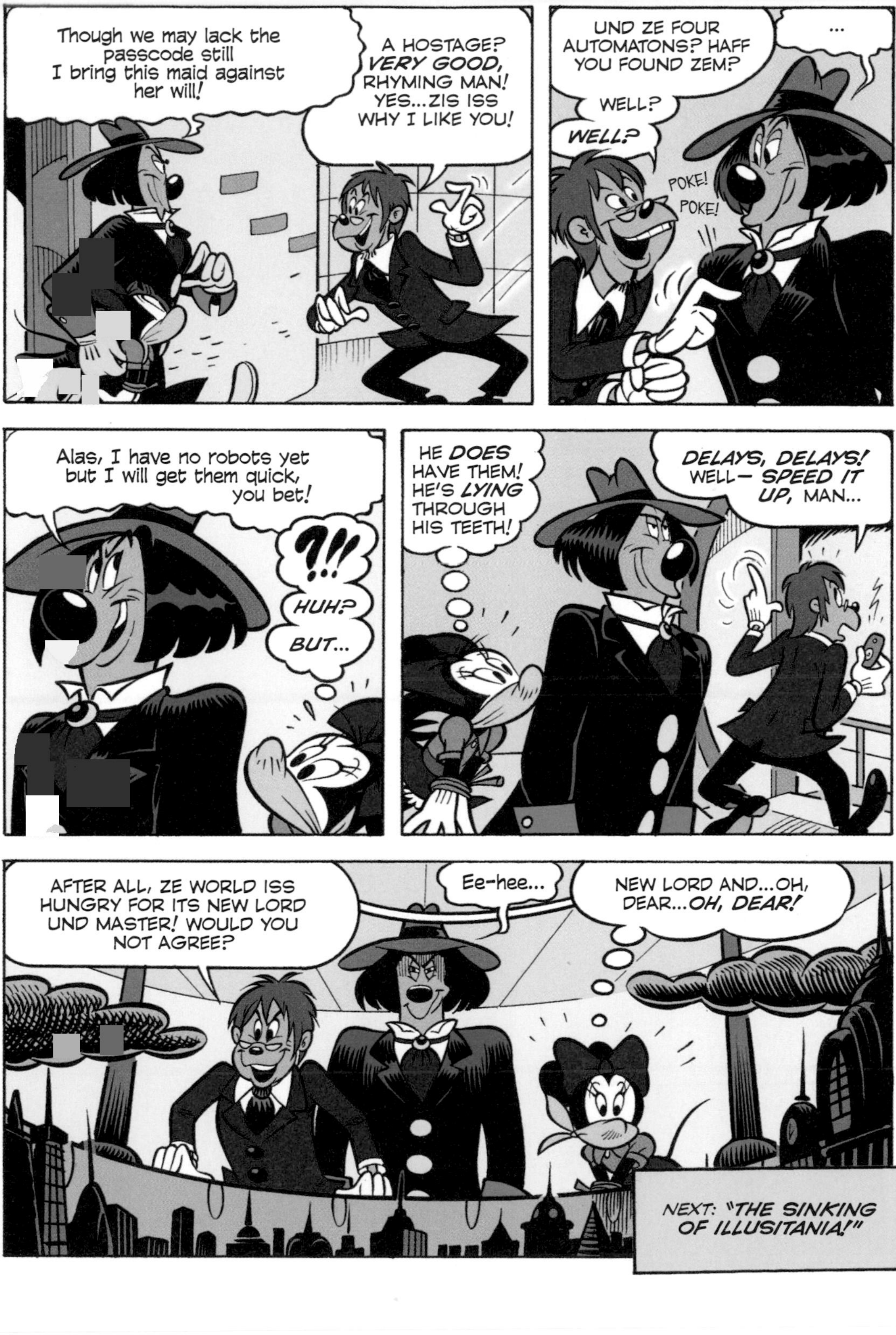

Though we may lack the passcode still I bring this maid against her will!
A HOSTAGE? VERY GOOD, RHYMING MAN! YES...ZIS ISS WHY I LIKE YOU!
UND ZE FOUR AUTOMATONS? HAFF YOU FOUND ZEM?
...
WELL?
WELL?
POKE!
POKE!
Alas, I have no robots yet but I will get them quick, you bet!
?!!
HUH?
BUT...
HE DOES HAVE THEM! HE'S LYING THROUGH HIS TEETH!
DELAYS, DELAYS! WELL— SPEED IT UP, MAN...
AFTER ALL, ZE WORLD ISS HUNGRY FOR ITS NEW LORD UND MASTER! WOULD YOU NOT AGREE?
Ee-hee...
NEW LORD AND...OH, DEAR...OH, DEAR!
NEXT: "THE SINKING OF ILLUSITANIA!"

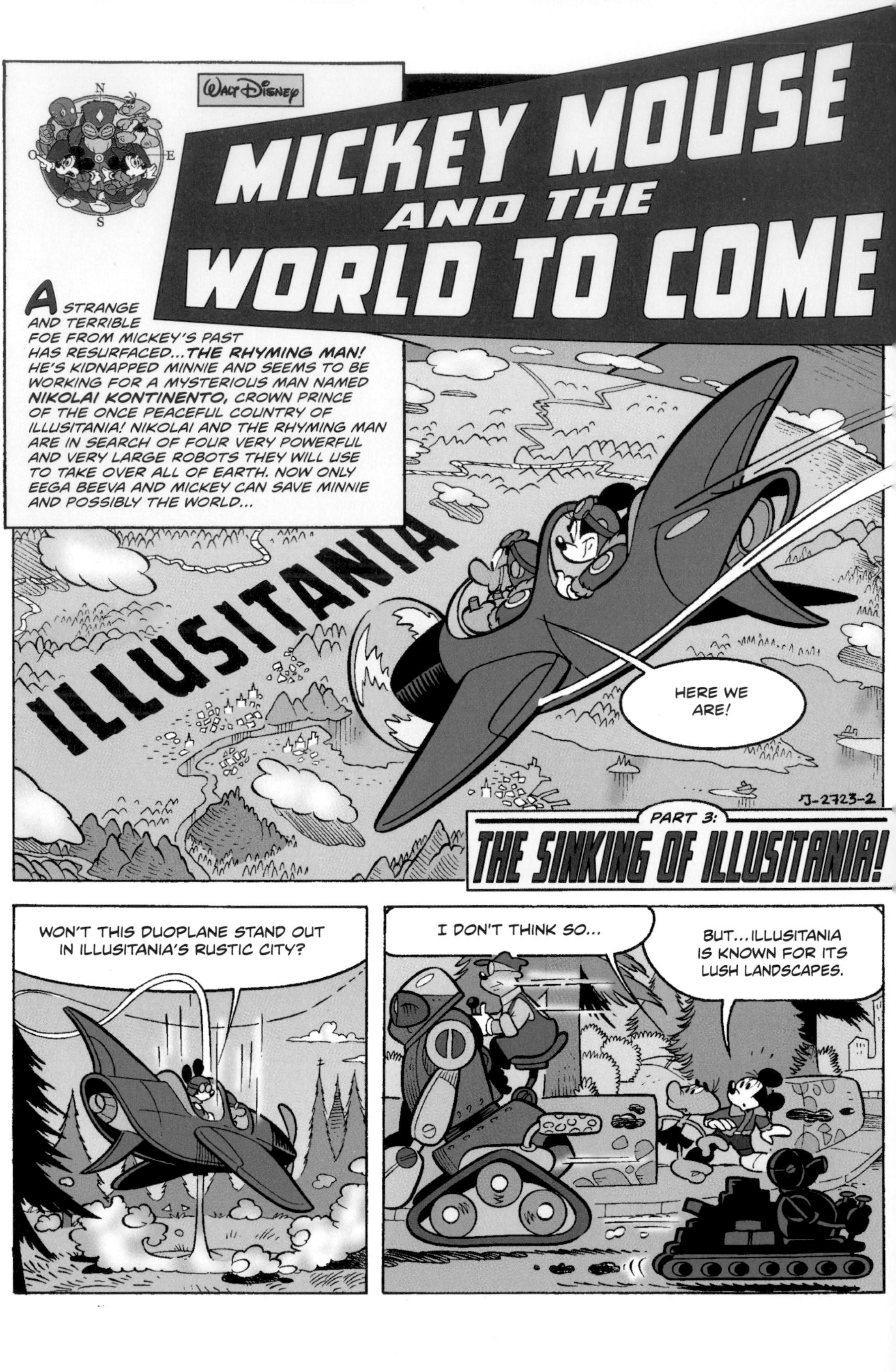
Walt Disney
MICKEY MOUSE AND THE WORLD TO COME
A STRANGE AND TERRIBLE FOE FROM MICKEY'S PAST HAS RESURFACED...THE RHYMING MAN! HE'S KIDNAPPED MINNIE AND SEEMS TO BE WORKING FOR A MYSTERIOUS MAN NAMED NIKOLAI KONTINENTO, CROWN PRINCE OF THE ONCE PEACEFUL COUNTRY OF ILLUSITANIA! NIKOLAI AND THE RHYMING MAN ARE IN SEARCH OF FOUR VERY POWERFUL AND VERY LARGE ROBOTS THEY WILL USE TO TAKE OVER ALL OF EARTH. NOW ONLY EEGA BEEVA AND MICKEY CAN SAVE MINNIE AND POSSIBLY THE WORLD...
ILLUSITANIA
HERE WE ARE!
J-2723-2
PART 3:
THE SINKING OF ILLUSITANIA!
WON'T THIS DUOPLANE STAND OUT IN ILLUSITANIA'S RUSTIC CITY?
I DON'T THINK SO...
BUT...ILLUSITANIA IS KNOWN FOR ITS LUSH LANDSCAPES.

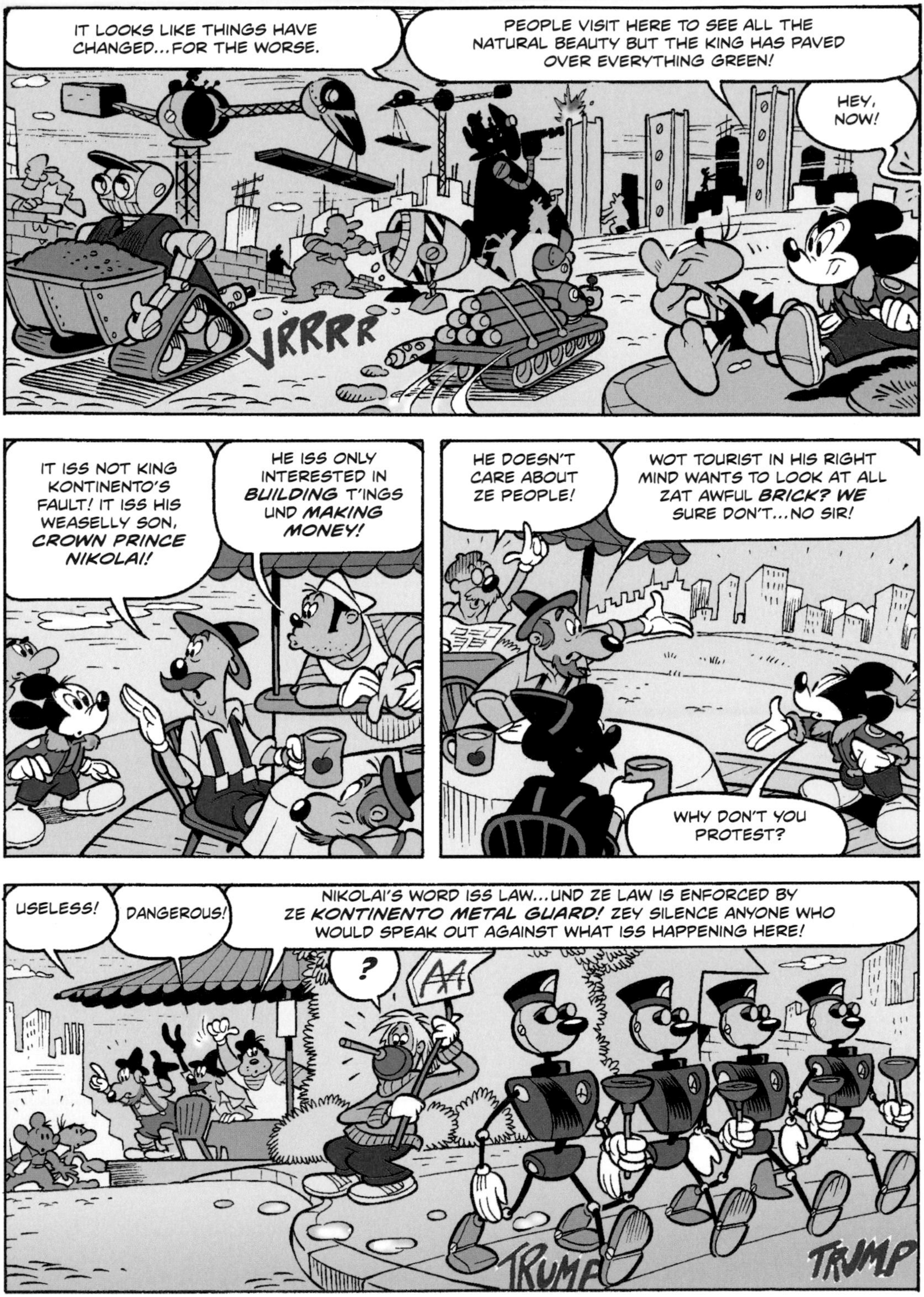
IT LOOKS LIKE THINGS HAVE CHANGED...FOR THE WORSE.
PEOPLE VISIT HERE TO SEE ALL THE NATURAL BEAUTY BUT THE KING HAS PAVED OVER EVERYTHING GREEN!
HEY, NOW!
VRRRR
IT ISS NOT KING KONTINENTO'S FAULT! IT ISS HIS WEASELLY SON, CROWN PRINCE NIKOLAI!
HE ISS ONLY INTERESTED IN BUILDING T'INGS UND MAKING MONEY!
HE DOESN'T CARE ABOUT ZE PEOPLE!
WOT TOURIST IN HIS RIGHT MIND WANTS TO LOOK AT ALL ZAT AWFUL BRICK? WE SURE DON'T...NO SIR!
WHY DON'T YOU PROTEST?
USELESS!
DANGEROUS!
NIKOLAI'S WORD ISS LAW...UND ZE LAW IS ENFORCED BY ZE KONTINENTO METAL GUARD! ZEY SILENCE ANYONE WHO WOULD SPEAK OUT AGAINST WHAT ISS HAPPENING HERE!
?
TRUMP
TRUMP

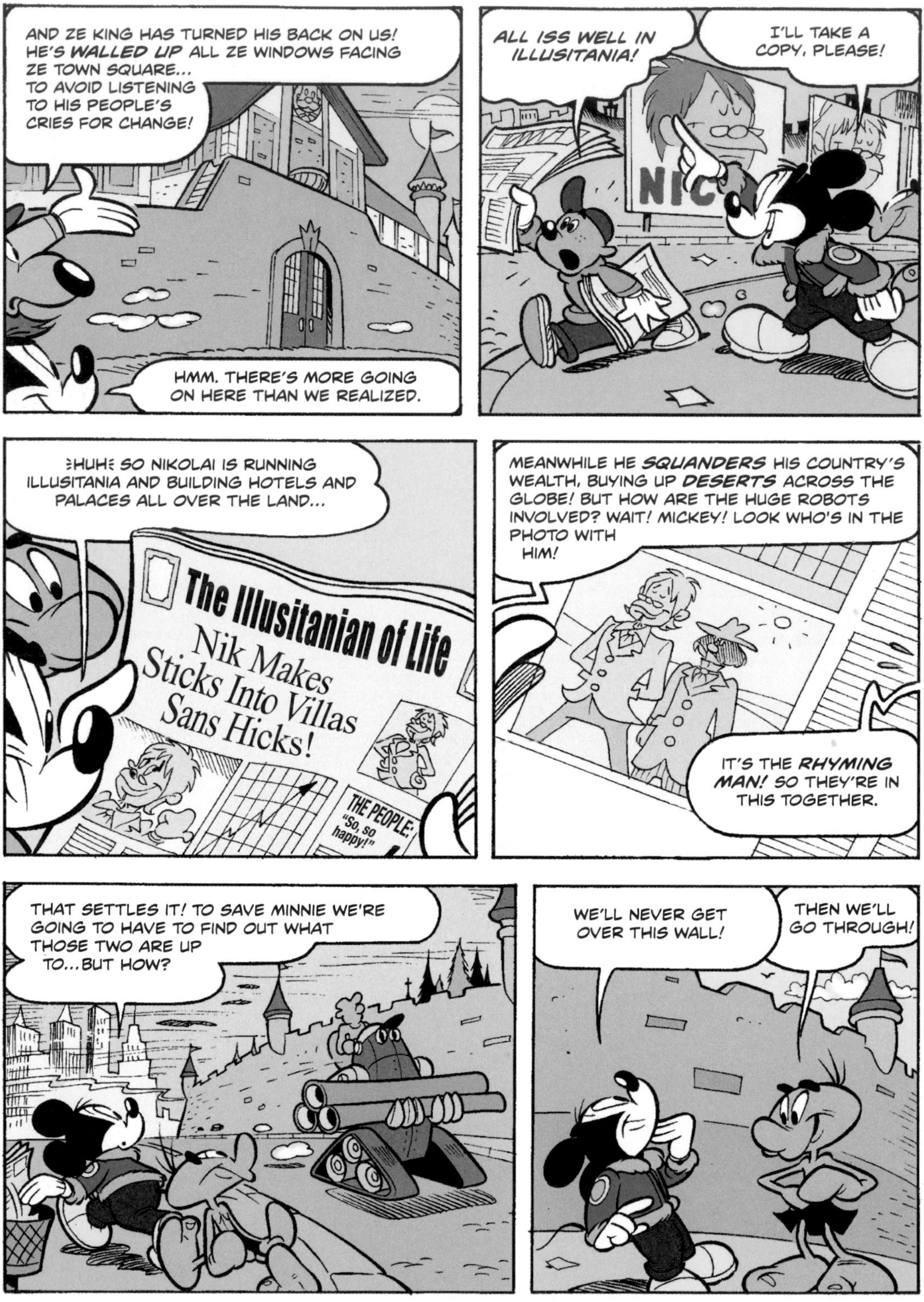

AND ZE KING HAS TURNED HIS BACK ON US! HE'S WALLED UP ALL ZE WINDOWS FACING ZE TOWN SQUARE... TO AVOID LISTENING TO HIS PEOPLE'S CRIES FOR CHANGE!
HMM. THERE'S MORE GOING ON HERE THAN WE REALIZED.
ALL ISS WELL IN ILLUSITANIA!
I'LL TAKE A COPY, PLEASE!
NIC
HUH SO NIKOLAI IS RUNNING ILLUSITANIA AND BUILDING HOTELS AND PALACES ALL OVER THE LAND...
The Illusitanian of Life
Nik Makes Sticks Into Villas Sans Hicks!
THE PEOPLE: "So, so happy!"
MEANWHILE HE SQUANDERS HIS COUNTRY'S WEALTH, BUYING UP DESERTS ACROSS THE GLOBE! BUT HOW ARE THE HUGE ROBOTS INVOLVED? WAIT! MICKEY! LOOK WHO'S IN THE PHOTO WITH HIM!
IT'S THE RHYMING MAN! SO THEY'RE IN THIS TOGETHER.
THAT SETTLES IT! TO SAVE MINNIE WE'RE GOING TO HAVE TO FIND OUT WHAT THOSE TWO ARE UP TO...BUT HOW?
WE'LL NEVER GET OVER THIS WALL!
THEN WE'LL GO THROUGH!

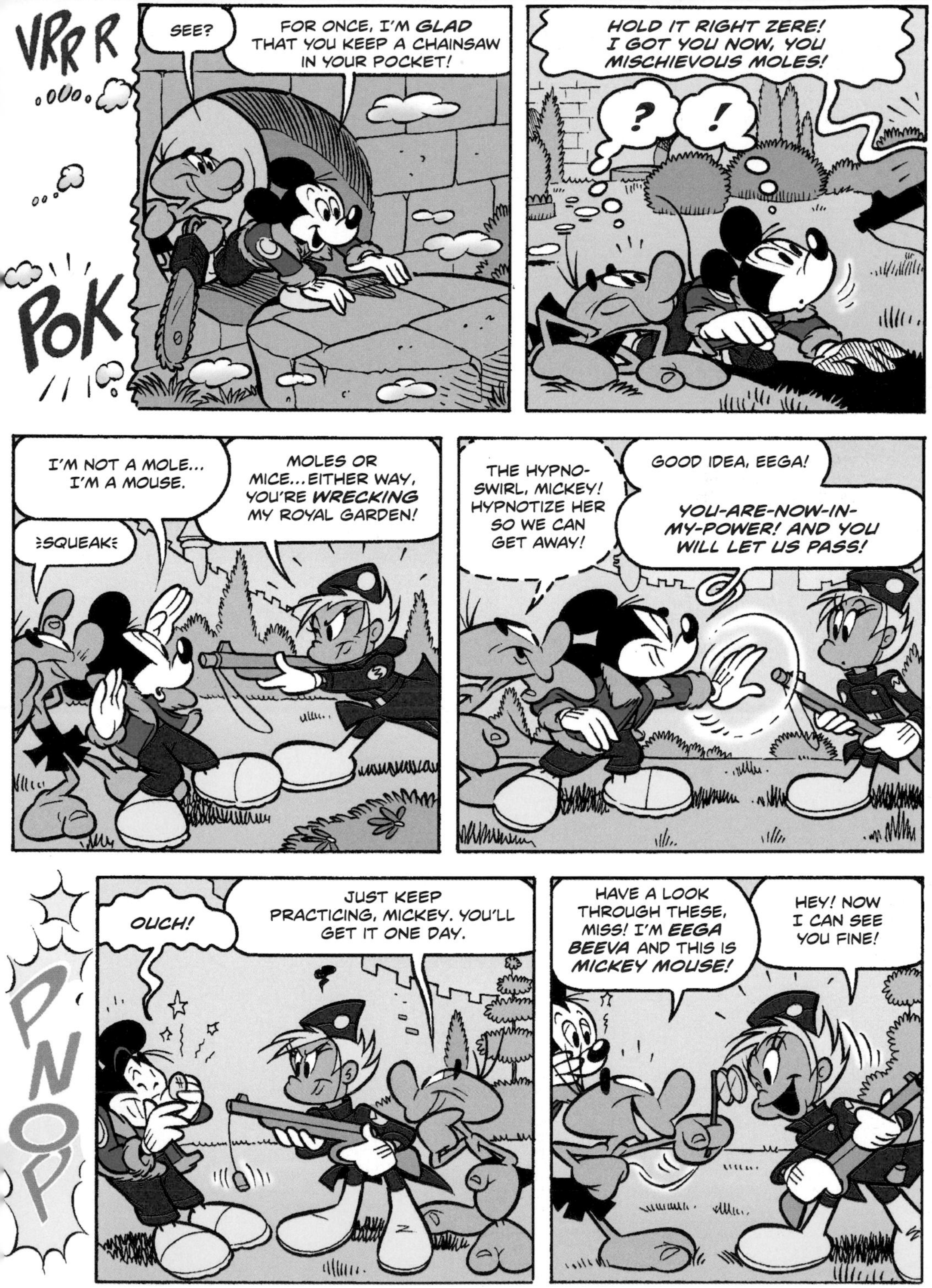
VRRR
POK
SEE?
FOR ONCE, I'M GLAD THAT YOU KEEP A CHAINSAW IN YOUR POCKET!
HOLD IT RIGHT ZERE! I GOT YOU NOW, YOU MISCHIEVOUS MOLES!
?
!
I'M NOT A MOLE... I'M A MOUSE.
SQUEAK
MOLES OR MICE...EITHER WAY, YOU'RE WRECKING MY ROYAL GARDEN!
THE HYPNO-SWIRL, MICKEY! HYPNOTIZE HER SO WE CAN GET AWAY!
GOOD IDEA, EEGA!
YOU-ARE-NOW-IN-MY-POWER! AND YOU WILL LET US PASS!
PNOP
OUCH!
JUST KEEP PRACTICING, MICKEY. YOU'LL GET IT ONE DAY.
HAVE A LOOK THROUGH THESE, MISS! I'M EEGA BEEVA AND THIS IS MICKEY MOUSE!
HEY! NOW I CAN SEE YOU FINE!

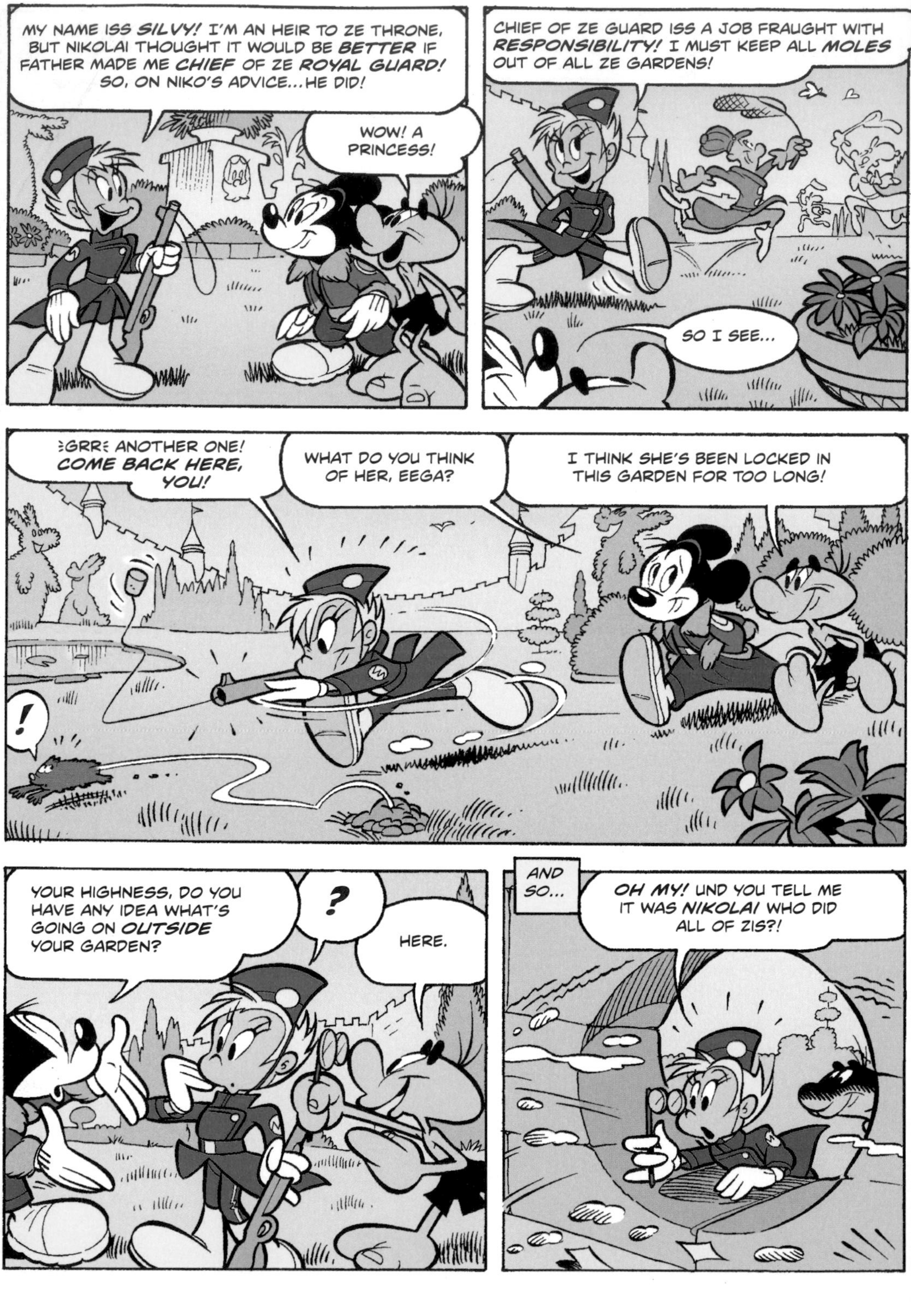
MY NAME ISS SILVY! I'M AN HEIR TO ZE THRONE, BUT NIKOLAI THOUGHT IT WOULD BE BETTER IF FATHER MADE ME CHIEF OF ZE ROYAL GUARD! SO, ON NIKO'S ADVICE... HE DID!
WOW! A PRINCESS!
CHIEF OF ZE GUARD ISS A JOB FRAUGHT WITH RESPONSIBILITY! I MUST KEEP ALL MOLES OUT OF ALL ZE GARDENS!
SO I SEE...
GRR ANOTHER ONE! COME BACK HERE, YOU!
WHAT DO YOU THINK OF HER, EEGA?
I THINK SHE'S BEEN LOCKED IN THIS GARDEN FOR TOO LONG!
!
YOUR HIGHNESS, DO YOU HAVE ANY IDEA WHAT'S GOING ON OUTSIDE YOUR GARDEN?
?
HERE.
AND SO...
OH MY! UND YOU TELL ME IT WAS NIKOLAI WHO DID ALL OF ZIS?!

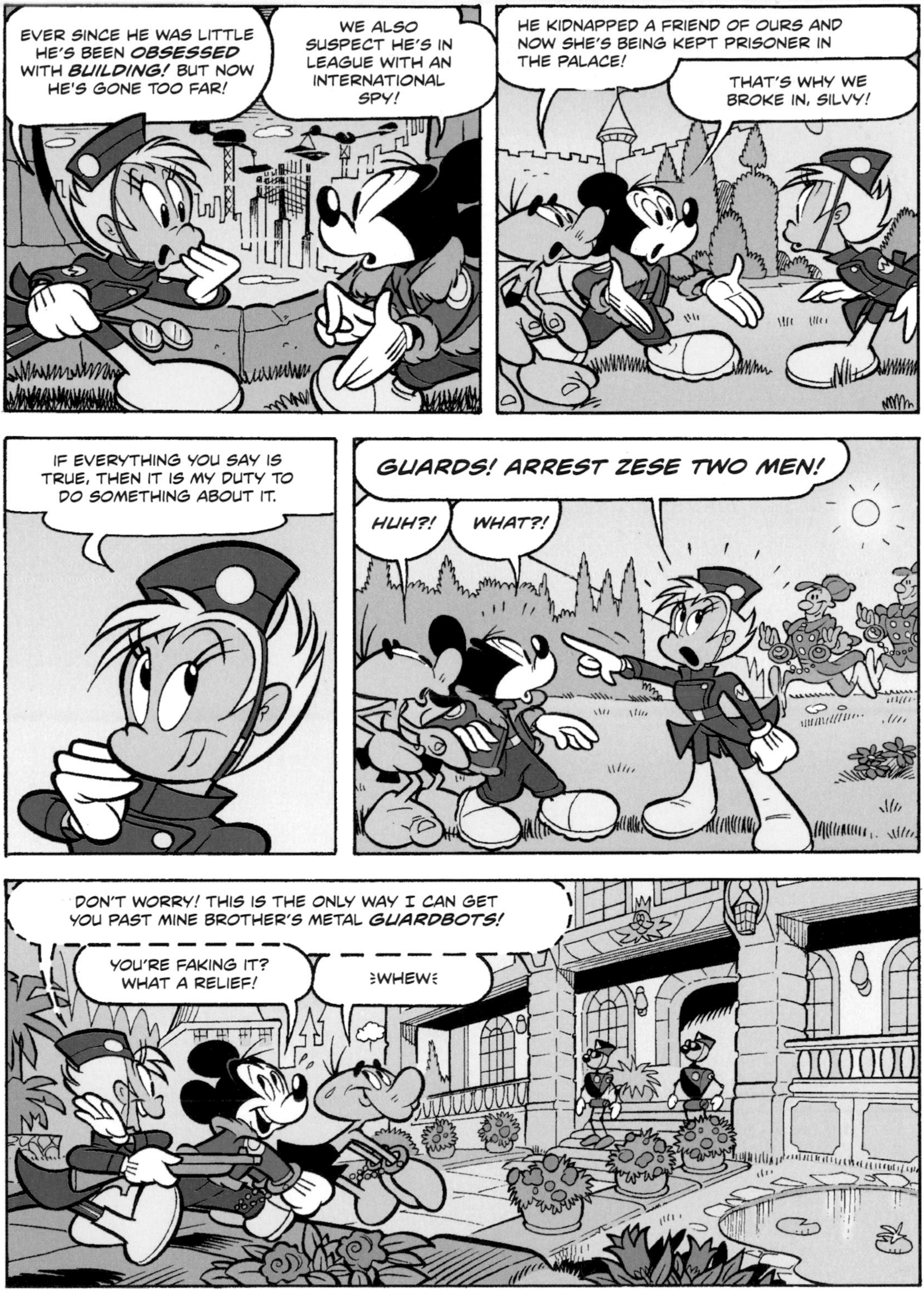
EVER SINCE HE WAS LITTLE HE'S BEEN OBSESSED WITH BUILDING! BUT NOW HE'S GONE TOO FAR!
WE ALSO SUSPECT HE'S IN LEAGUE WITH AN INTERNATIONAL SPY!
HE KIDNAPPED A FRIEND OF OURS AND NOW SHE'S BEING KEPT PRISONER IN THE PALACE!
THAT'S WHY WE BROKE IN, SILVY!
IF EVERYTHING YOU SAY IS TRUE, THEN IT IS MY DUTY TO DO SOMETHING ABOUT IT.
GUARDS! ARREST ZESE TWO MEN!
HUH?!
WHAT?!
DON'T WORRY! THIS IS THE ONLY WAY I CAN GET YOU PAST MINE BROTHER'S METAL GUARDBOTS!
YOU'RE FAKING IT? WHAT A RELIEF!
WHEW

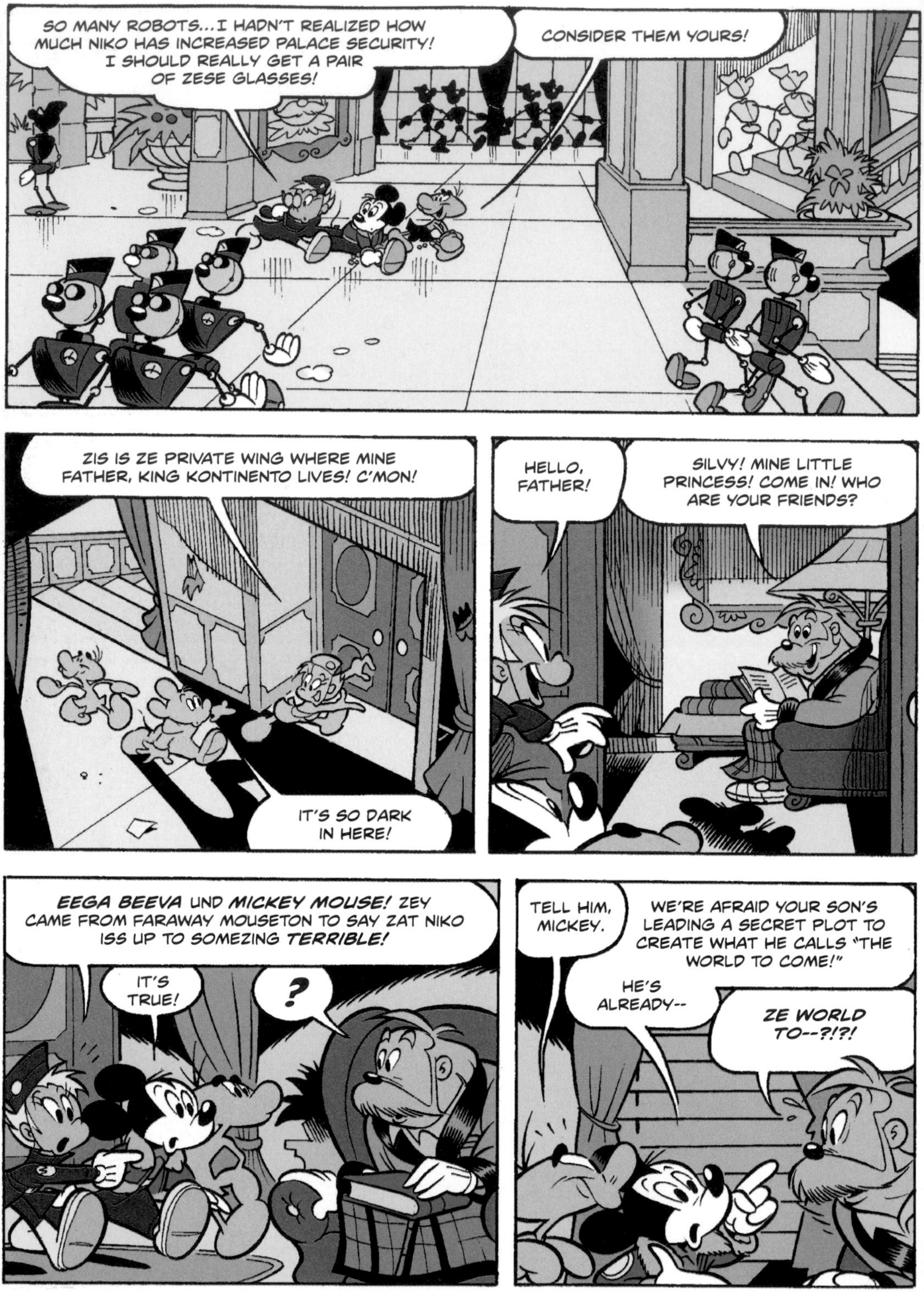
SO MANY ROBOTS...I HADN'T REALIZED HOW MUCH NIKO HAS INCREASED PALACE SECURITY! I SHOULD REALLY GET A PAIR OF ZESE GLASSES!
CONSIDER THEM YOURS!
ZIS IS ZE PRIVATE WING WHERE MINE FATHER, KING KONTINENTO LIVES! C'MON!
IT'S SO DARK IN HERE!
HELLO, FATHER!
SILVY! MINE LITTLE PRINCESS! COME IN! WHO ARE YOUR FRIENDS?
EEGA BEEVA UND MICKEY MOUSE! ZEY CAME FROM FARAWAY MOUSETON TO SAY ZAT NIKO ISS UP TO SOMEZING TERRIBLE!
IT'S TRUE!
?
TELL HIM, MICKEY.
WE'RE AFRAID YOUR SON'S LEADING A SECRET PLOT TO CREATE WHAT HE CALLS "THE WORLD TO COME!"
HE'S ALREADY--
ZE WORLD TO--?!?!

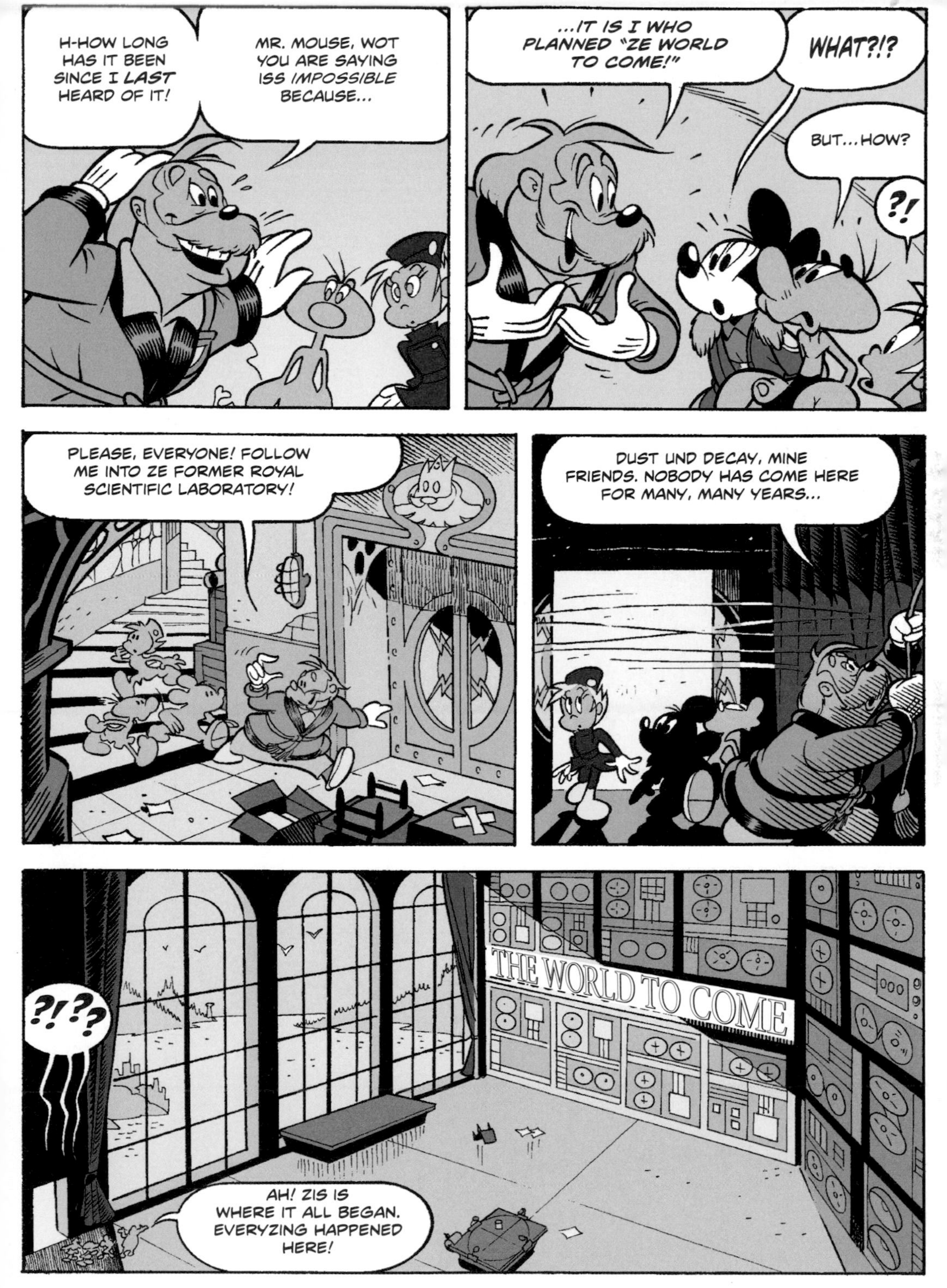
H-HOW LONG HAS IT BEEN SINCE I *LAST* HEARD OF IT!
MR. MOUSE, WOT YOU ARE SAYING ISS *IMPOSSIBLE* BECAUSE...
...IT IS I WHO PLANNED "ZE WORLD TO COME!"
WHAT?!?
BUT...HOW?
?!
PLEASE, EVERYONE! FOLLOW ME INTO ZE FORMER ROYAL SCIENTIFIC LABORATORY!
DUST UND DECAY, MINE FRIENDS. NOBODY HAS COME HERE FOR MANY, MANY YEARS...
?!??
THE WORLD TO COME
AH! ZIS IS WHERE IT ALL BEGAN. EVERYZING HAPPENED HERE!

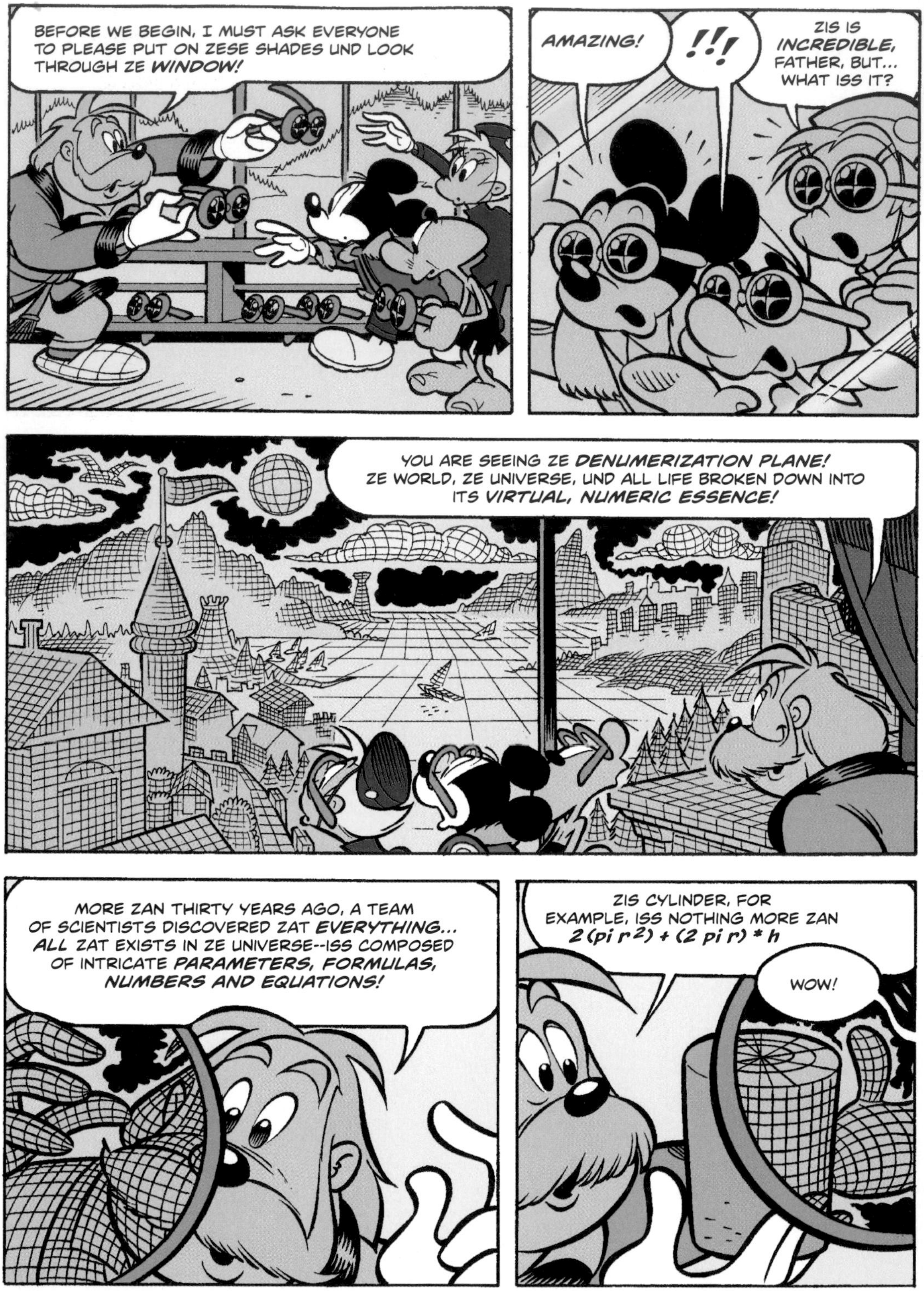
BEFORE WE BEGIN, I MUST ASK EVERYONE TO PLEASE PUT ON ZESE SHADES UND LOOK THROUGH ZE *WINDOW!*
AMAZING!
!!!
ZIS IS *INCREDIBLE,* FATHER, BUT... WHAT ISS IT?
YOU ARE SEEING ZE *DENUMERIZATION PLANE!* ZE WORLD, ZE UNIVERSE, UND ALL LIFE BROKEN DOWN INTO ITS *VIRTUAL, NUMERIC ESSENCE!*
MORE ZAN THIRTY YEARS AGO, A TEAM OF SCIENTISTS DISCOVERED ZAT *EVERYTHING... ALL* ZAT EXISTS IN ZE UNIVERSE--ISS COMPOSED OF INTRICATE *PARAMETERS, FORMULAS, NUMBERS AND EQUATIONS!*
ZIS CYLINDER, FOR EXAMPLE, ISS NOTHING MORE ZAN $2(\pi r^2) + (2 \pi r) * h$
WOW!

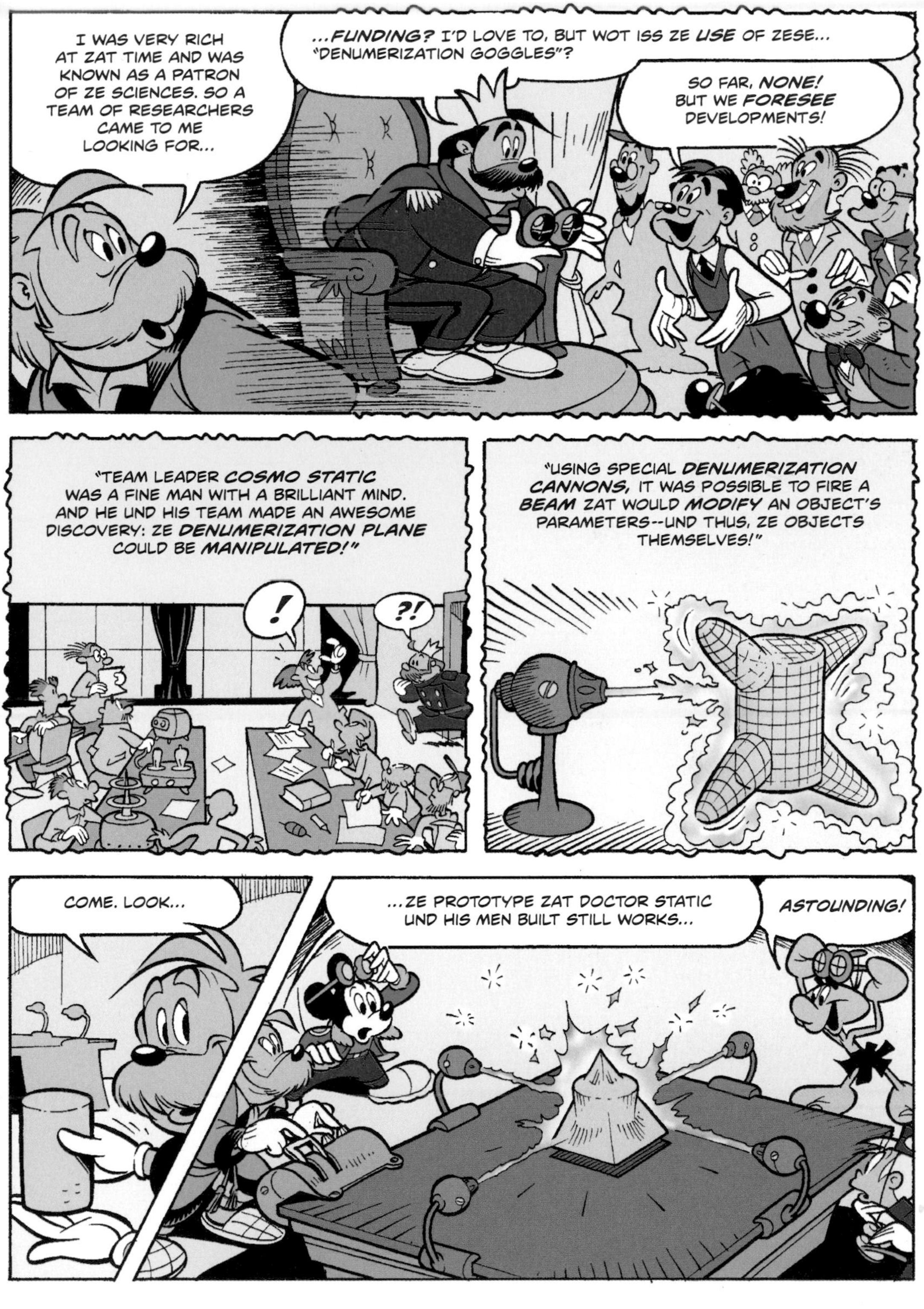
I WAS VERY RICH AT ZAT TIME AND WAS KNOWN AS A PATRON OF ZE SCIENCES. SO A TEAM OF RESEARCHERS CAME TO ME LOOKING FOR...
...FUNDING? I'D LOVE TO, BUT WOT ISS ZE USE OF ZESE... "DENUMERIZATION GOGGLES"?
SO FAR, NONE! BUT WE FORESEE DEVELOPMENTS!
"TEAM LEADER COSMO STATIC WAS A FINE MAN WITH A BRILLIANT MIND. AND HE UND HIS TEAM MADE AN AWESOME DISCOVERY: ZE DENUMERIZATION PLANE COULD BE MANIPULATED!"
!
?!
"USING SPECIAL DENUMERIZATION CANNONS, IT WAS POSSIBLE TO FIRE A BEAM ZAT WOULD MODIFY AN OBJECT'S PARAMETERS--UND THUS, ZE OBJECTS THEMSELVES!"
COME. LOOK...
...ZE PROTOTYPE ZAT DOCTOR STATIC UND HIS MEN BUILT STILL WORKS...
ASTOUNDING!

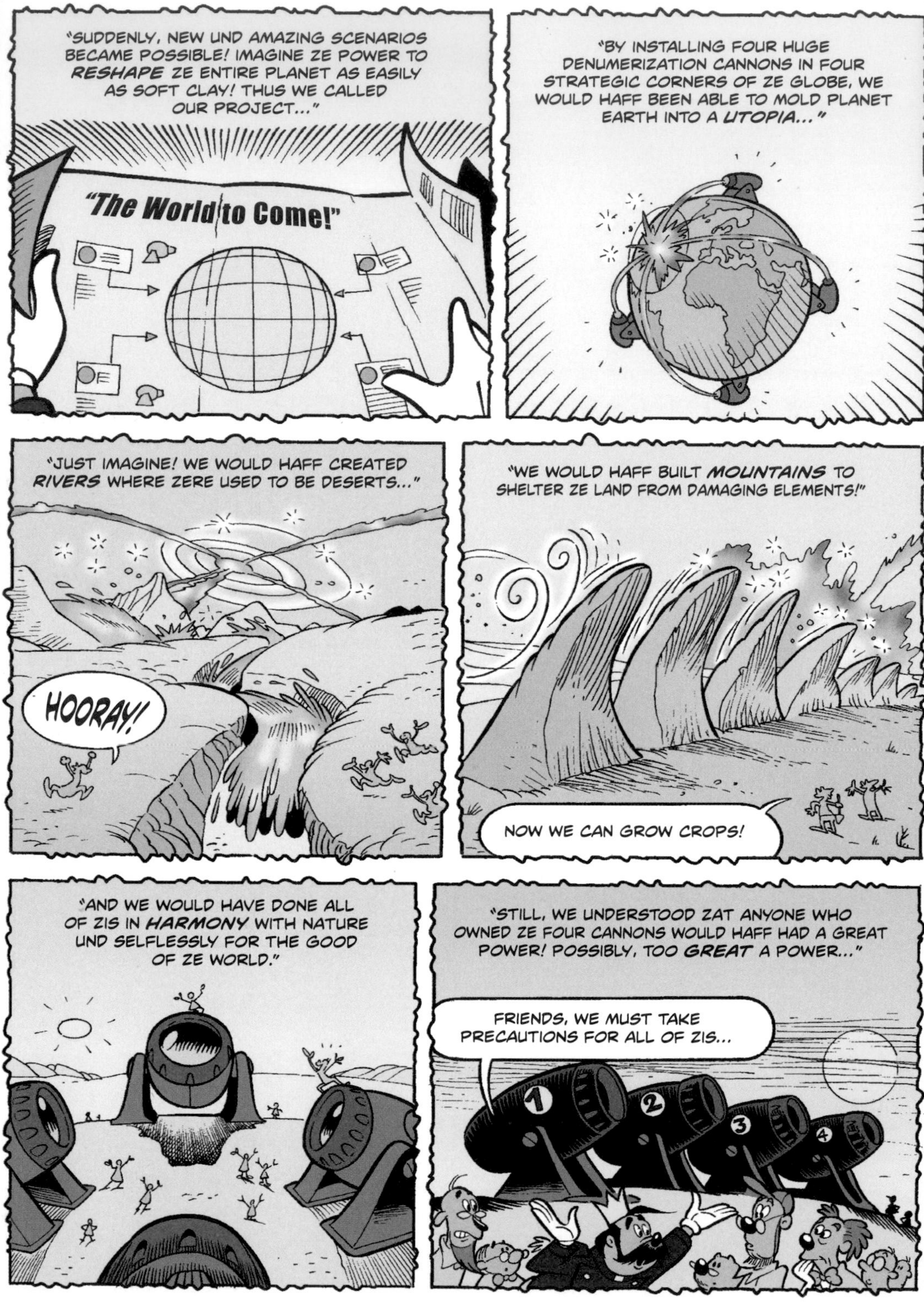
"SUDDENLY, NEW UND AMAZING SCENARIOS BECAME POSSIBLE! IMAGINE ZE POWER TO RESHAPE ZE ENTIRE PLANET AS EASILY AS SOFT CLAY! THUS WE CALLED OUR PROJECT..."
"The World to Come!"
"BY INSTALLING FOUR HUGE DENUMERIZATION CANNONS IN FOUR STRATEGIC CORNERS OF ZE GLOBE, WE WOULD HAFF BEEN ABLE TO MOLD PLANET EARTH INTO A UTOPIA..."
"JUST IMAGINE! WE WOULD HAFF CREATED RIVERS WHERE ZERE USED TO BE DESERTS..."
HOORAY!
"WE WOULD HAFF BUILT MOUNTAINS TO SHELTER ZE LAND FROM DAMAGING ELEMENTS!"
NOW WE CAN GROW CROPS!
"AND WE WOULD HAVE DONE ALL OF ZIS IN HARMONY WITH NATURE UND SELFLESSLY FOR THE GOOD OF ZE WORLD."
"STILL, WE UNDERSTOOD ZAT ANYONE WHO OWNED ZE FOUR CANNONS WOULD HAFF HAD A GREAT POWER! POSSIBLY, TOO GREAT A POWER..."
FRIENDS, WE MUST TAKE PRECAUTIONS FOR ALL OF ZIS...
1
2
3
4

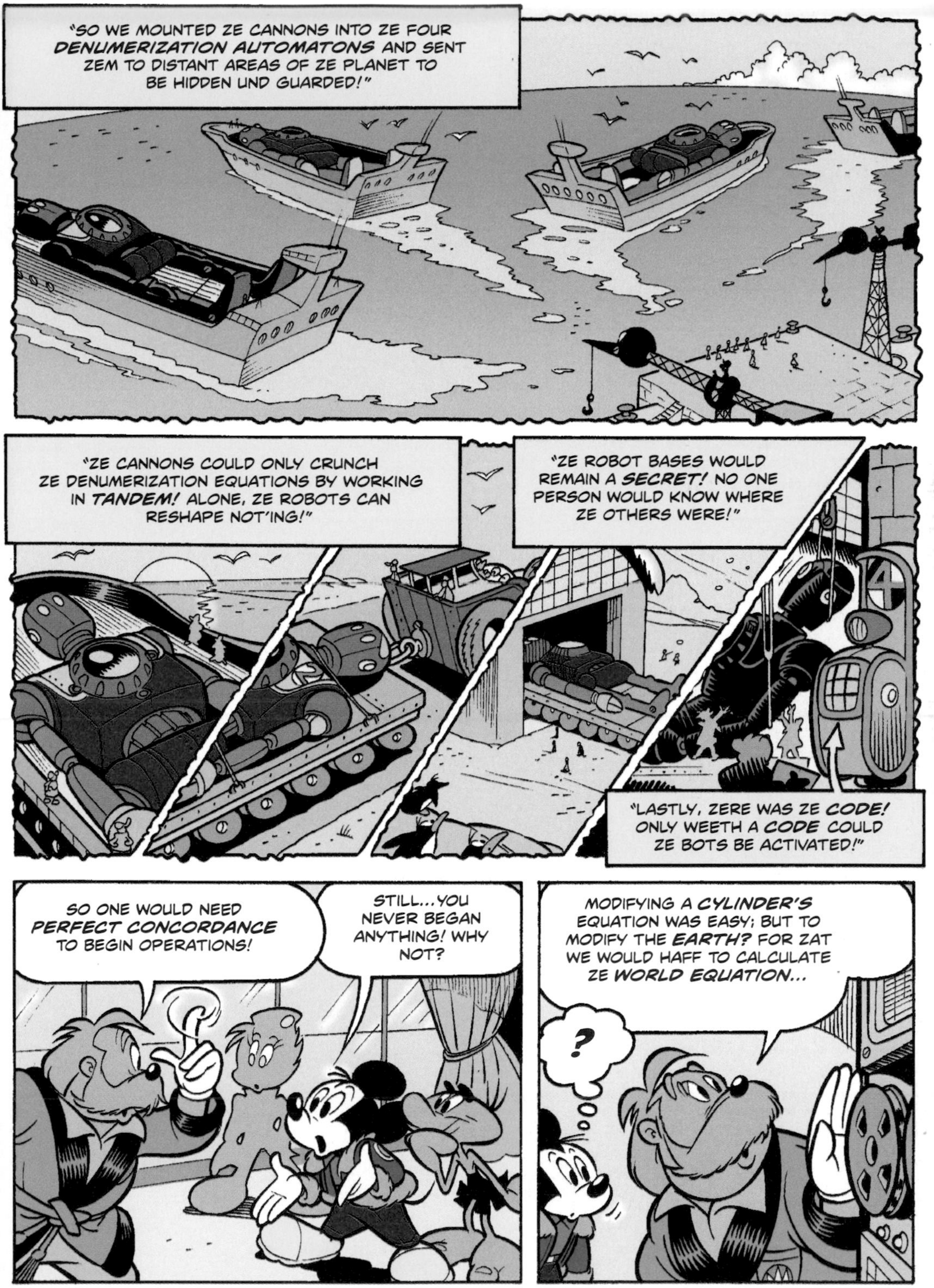
"SO WE MOUNTED ZE CANNONS INTO ZE FOUR DENUMERIZATION AUTOMATONS AND SENT ZEM TO DISTANT AREAS OF ZE PLANET TO BE HIDDEN UND GUARDED!"
"ZE CANNONS COULD ONLY CRUNCH ZE DENUMERIZATION EQUATIONS BY WORKING IN TANDEM! ALONE, ZE ROBOTS CAN RESHAPE NOT'ING!"
"ZE ROBOT BASES WOULD REMAIN A SECRET! NO ONE PERSON WOULD KNOW WHERE ZE OTHERS WERE!"
4
"LASTLY, ZERE WAS ZE CODE! ONLY WEETH A CODE COULD ZE BOTS BE ACTIVATED!"
SO ONE WOULD NEED PERFECT CONCORDANCE TO BEGIN OPERATIONS!
STILL...YOU NEVER BEGAN ANYTHING! WHY NOT?
MODIFYING A CYLINDER'S EQUATION WAS EASY; BUT TO MODIFY THE EARTH? FOR ZAT WE WOULD HAFF TO CALCULATE ZE WORLD EQUATION...
?

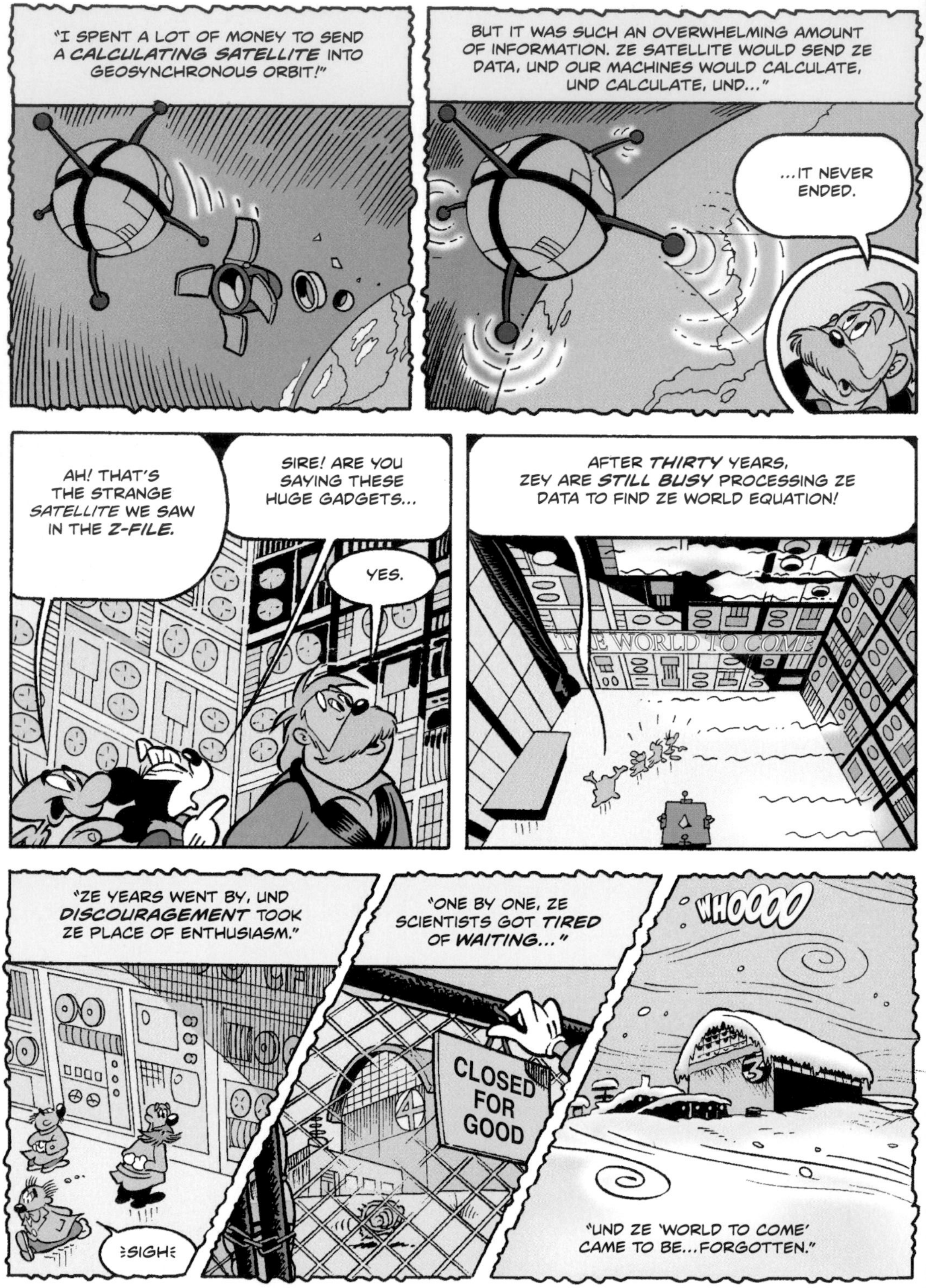
"I SPENT A LOT OF MONEY TO SEND A CALCULATING SATELLITE INTO GEOSYNCHRONOUS ORBIT!"
BUT IT WAS SUCH AN OVERWHELMING AMOUNT OF INFORMATION. ZE SATELLITE WOULD SEND ZE DATA, UND OUR MACHINES WOULD CALCULATE, UND CALCULATE, UND..."
...IT NEVER ENDED.
AH! THAT'S THE STRANGE SATELLITE WE SAW IN THE Z-FILE.
SIRE! ARE YOU SAYING THESE HUGE GADGETS...
YES.
AFTER THIRTY YEARS, ZEY ARE STILL BUSY PROCESSING ZE DATA TO FIND ZE WORLD EQUATION!
THE WORLD TO COME
"ZE YEARS WENT BY, UND DISCOURAGEMENT TOOK ZE PLACE OF ENTHUSIASM."
SIGH
"ONE BY ONE, ZE SCIENTISTS GOT TIRED OF WAITING..."
CLOSED FOR GOOD
WHOOOO
"UND ZE 'WORLD TO COME' CAME TO BE...FORGOTTEN."

BUT SIR, ONE OF THE DENUMERIZATION ROBOTS HAS BEEN *ACTIVATED* NOW!

ZAT *ISS* TERRIBLE, BUT...AS I POINTED OUT: ZE FOUR GIANTS ARE *USELESS* WITHOUT ZE *EQUATION* TO--

THUMP

OOPS!

I REALLY NEED TO START WEARING THOSE GLASSES ALL ZE TIME! I DIDN'T NOTICE ZIS *WIRE*, UND I ALMOST TRIPPED OVER IT!

ZAT WIRE IS NEW TO ME! WHAT DOES IT GO TO?

LET'S FOLLOW IT!

C'MON GANG! IT GOES UP THESE DARK STAIRS!

OH, NO!

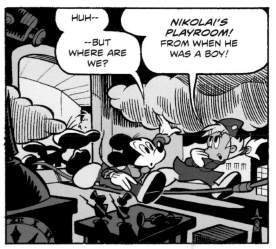

HUH--

--BUT WHERE ARE WE?

NIKOLAI'S PLAYROOM! FROM WHEN HE WAS A BOY!

WHO'S PLAYING IN IT NOW?

STILL ME!

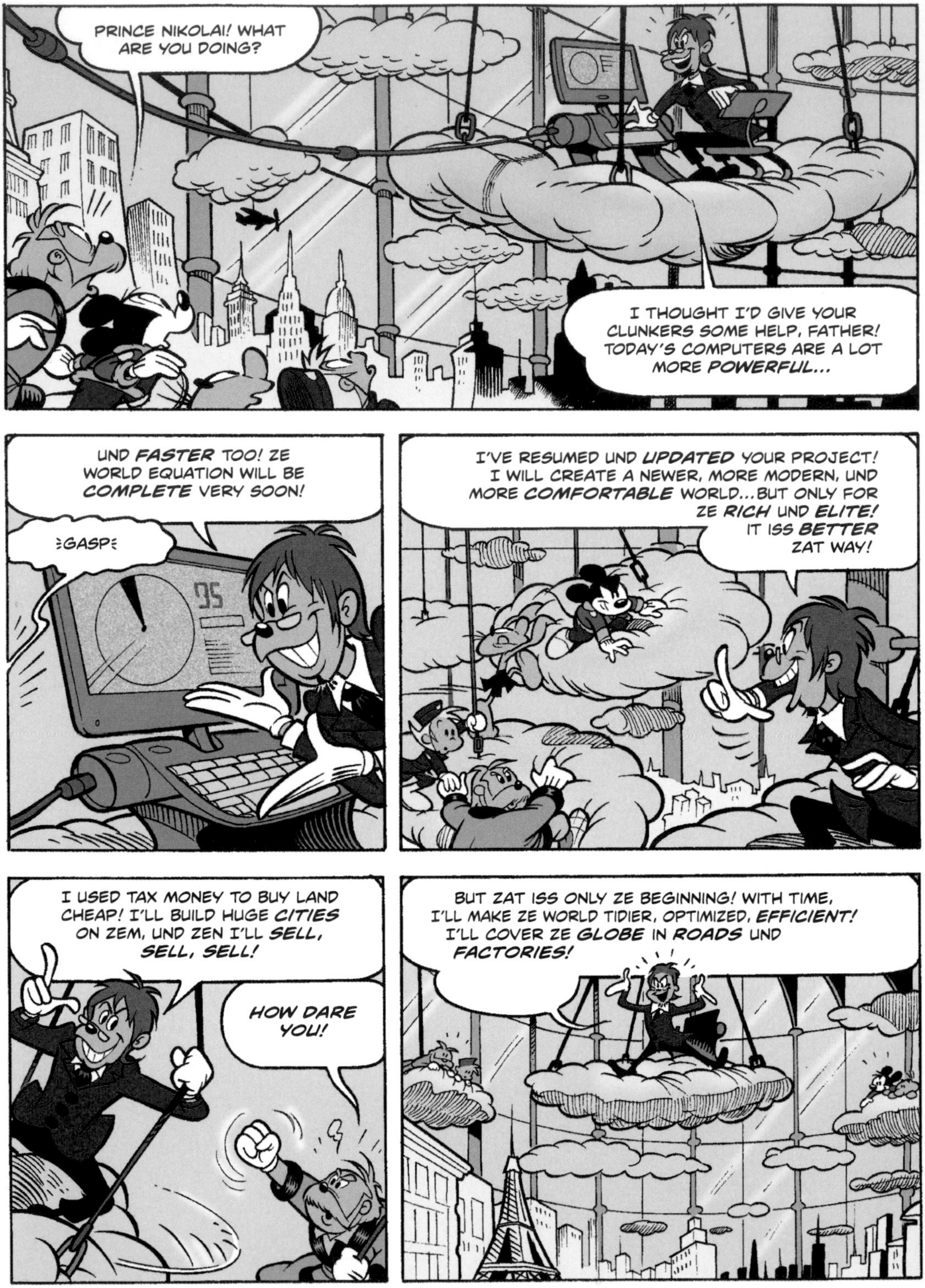
PRINCE NIKOLAI! WHAT ARE YOU DOING?
I THOUGHT I'D GIVE YOUR CLUNKERS SOME HELP, FATHER! TODAY'S COMPUTERS ARE A LOT MORE POWERFUL...
UND FASTER TOO! ZE WORLD EQUATION WILL BE COMPLETE VERY SOON!
GASP
95
I'VE RESUMED UND UPDATED YOUR PROJECT! I WILL CREATE A NEWER, MORE MODERN, UND MORE COMFORTABLE WORLD...BUT ONLY FOR ZE RICH UND ELITE! IT ISS BETTER ZAT WAY!
I USED TAX MONEY TO BUY LAND CHEAP! I'LL BUILD HUGE CITIES ON ZEM, UND ZEN I'LL SELL, SELL, SELL!
HOW DARE YOU!
BUT ZAT ISS ONLY ZE BEGINNING! WITH TIME, I'LL MAKE ZE WORLD TIDIER, OPTIMIZED, EFFICIENT! I'LL COVER ZE GLOBE IN ROADS UND FACTORIES!

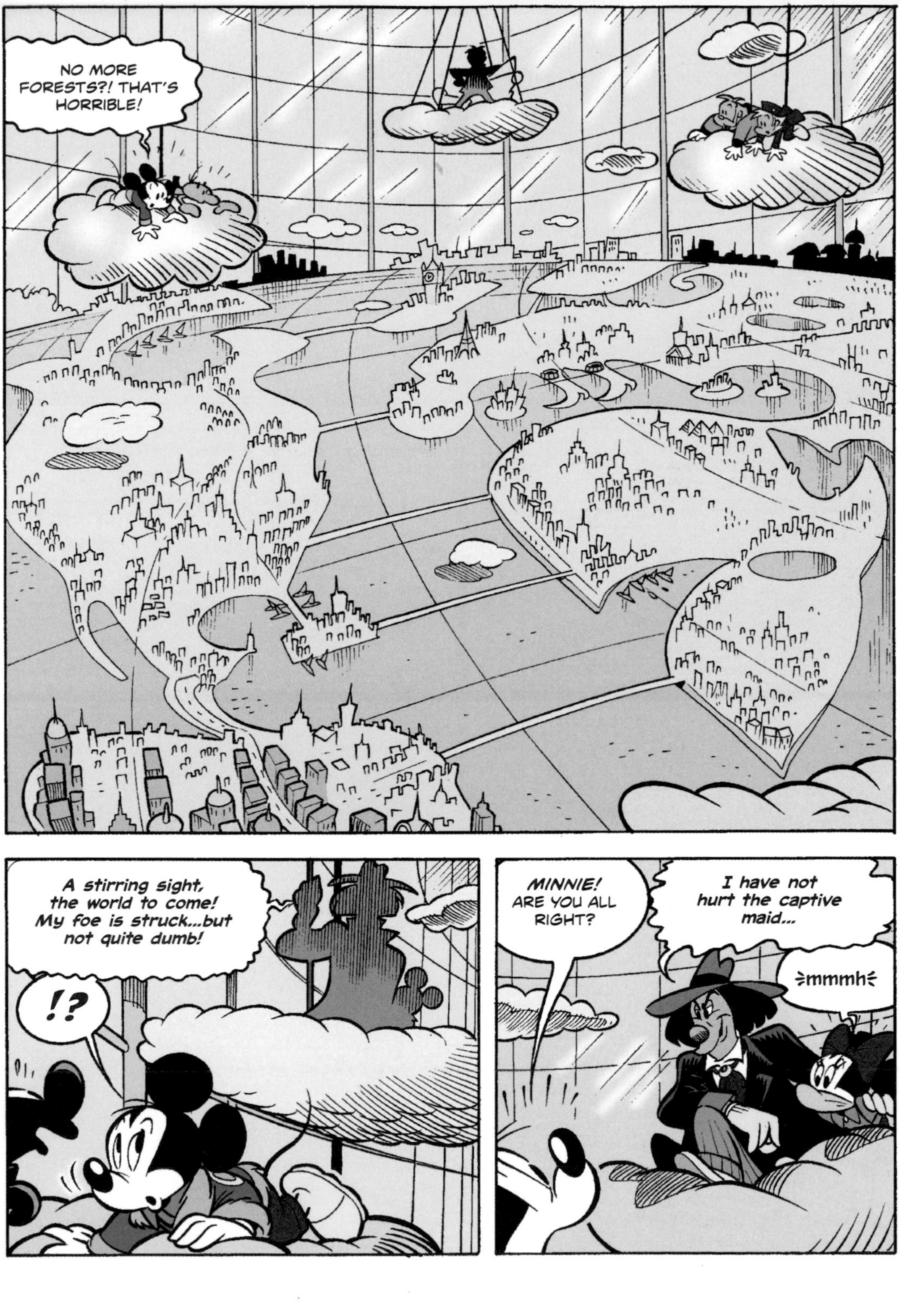
NO MORE FORESTS?! THAT'S HORRIBLE!
A stirring sight, the world to come! My foe is struck...but not quite dumb!
!?
MINNIE! ARE YOU ALL RIGHT?
I have not hurt the captive maid...
mmmh

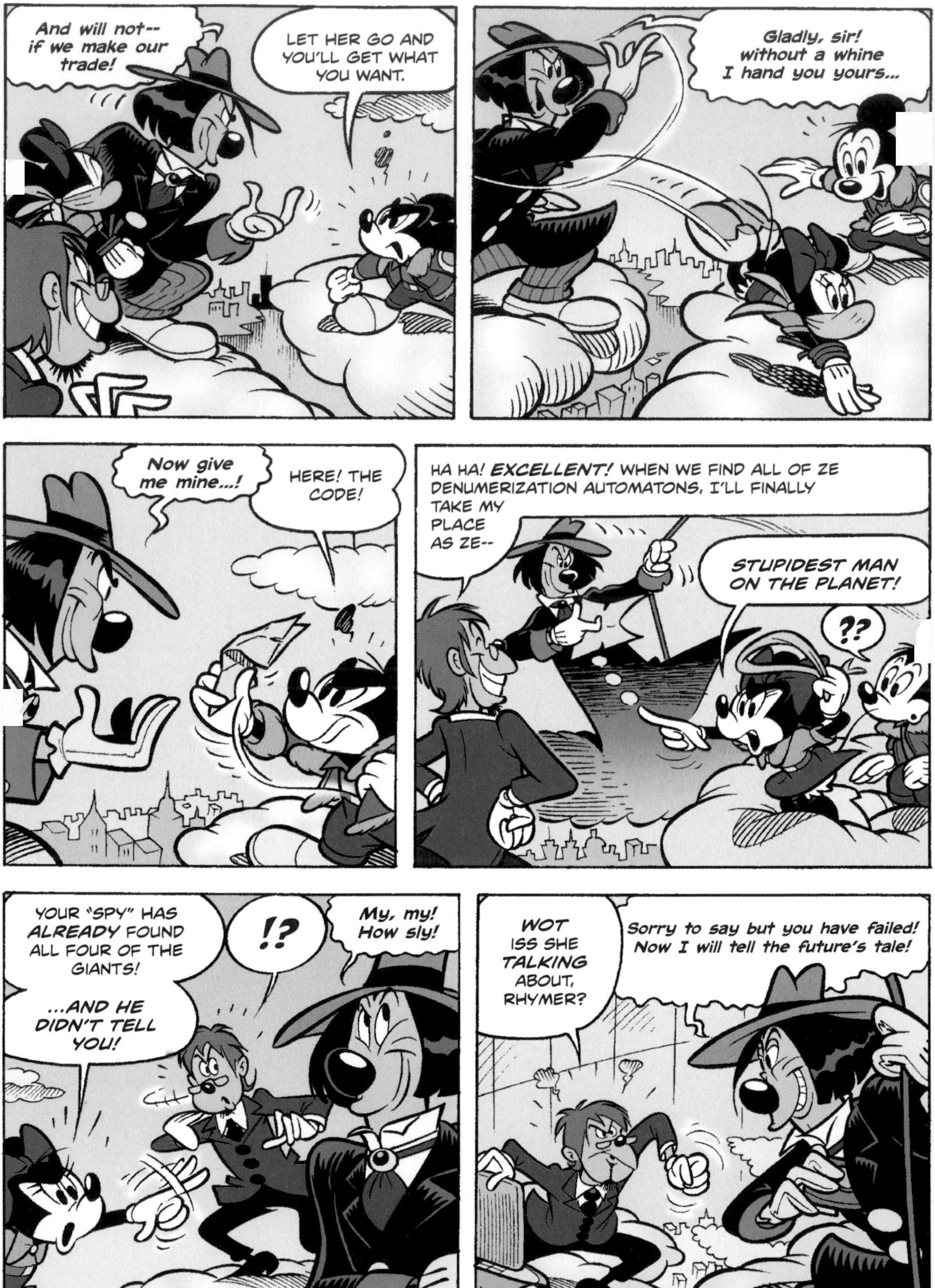

And will not-- if we make our trade!
LET HER GO AND YOU'LL GET WHAT YOU WANT.
Gladly, sir! without a whine I hand you yours...
Now give me mine...!
HERE! THE CODE!
HA HA! EXCELLENT! WHEN WE FIND ALL OF ZE DENUMERIZATION AUTOMATONS, I'LL FINALLY TAKE MY PLACE AS ZE--
STUPIDEST MAN ON THE PLANET!
??
YOUR "SPY" HAS ALREADY FOUND ALL FOUR OF THE GIANTS!
...AND HE DIDN'T TELL YOU!
!?
My, my! How sly!
WOT ISS SHE TALKING ABOUT, RHYMER?
Sorry to say but you have failed! Now I will tell the future's tale!

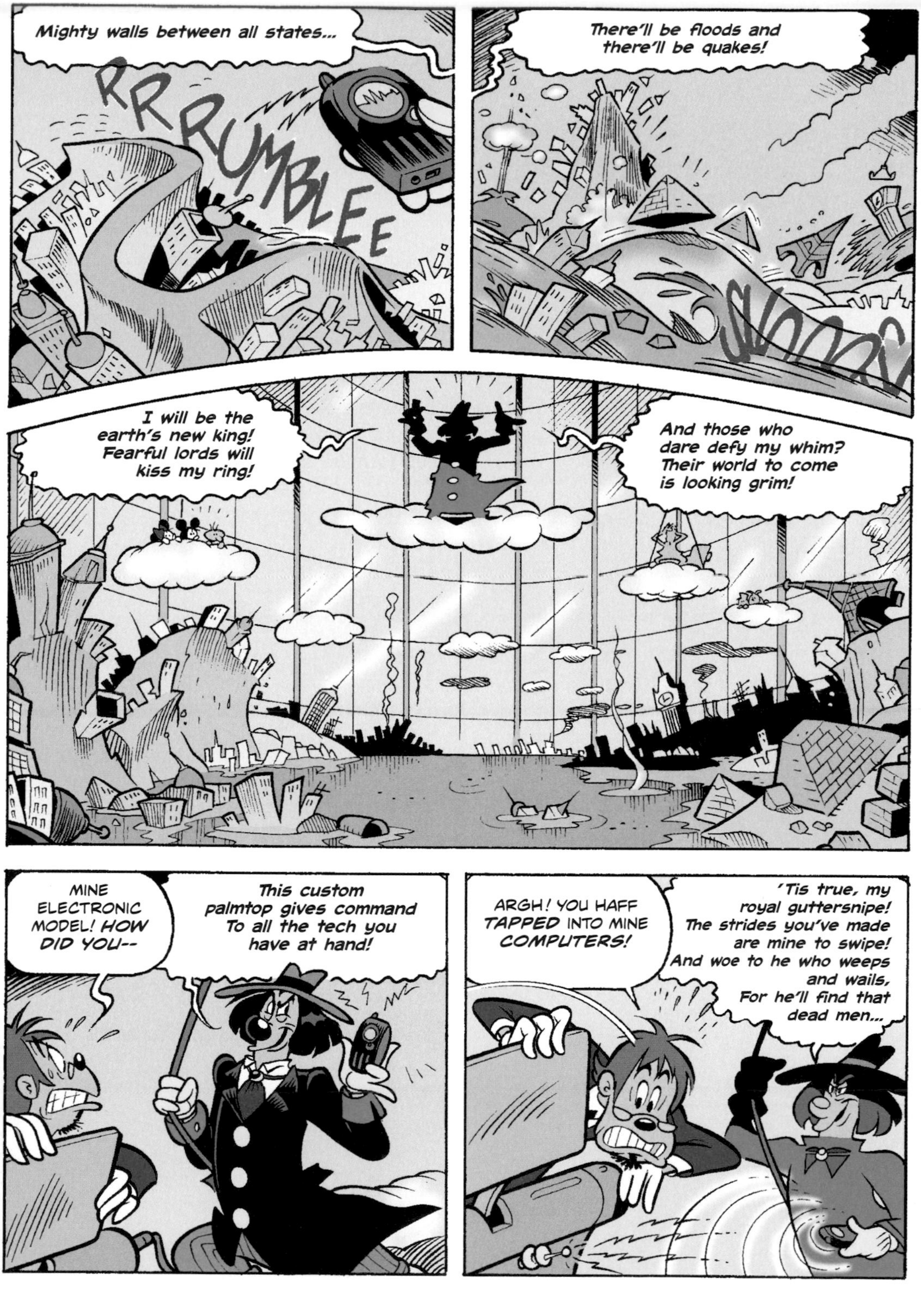
Mighty walls between all states...
RRRUMBLEE
There'll be floods and there'll be quakes!
I will be the earth's new king! Fearful lords will kiss my ring!
And those who dare defy my whim? Their world to come is looking grim!
MINE ELECTRONIC MODEL! HOW DID YOU--
This custom palmtop gives command To all the tech you have at hand!
ARGH! YOU HAFF TAPPED INTO MINE COMPUTERS!
'Tis true, my royal guttersnipe! The strides you've made are mine to swipe! And woe to he who weeps and wails, For he'll find that dead men...

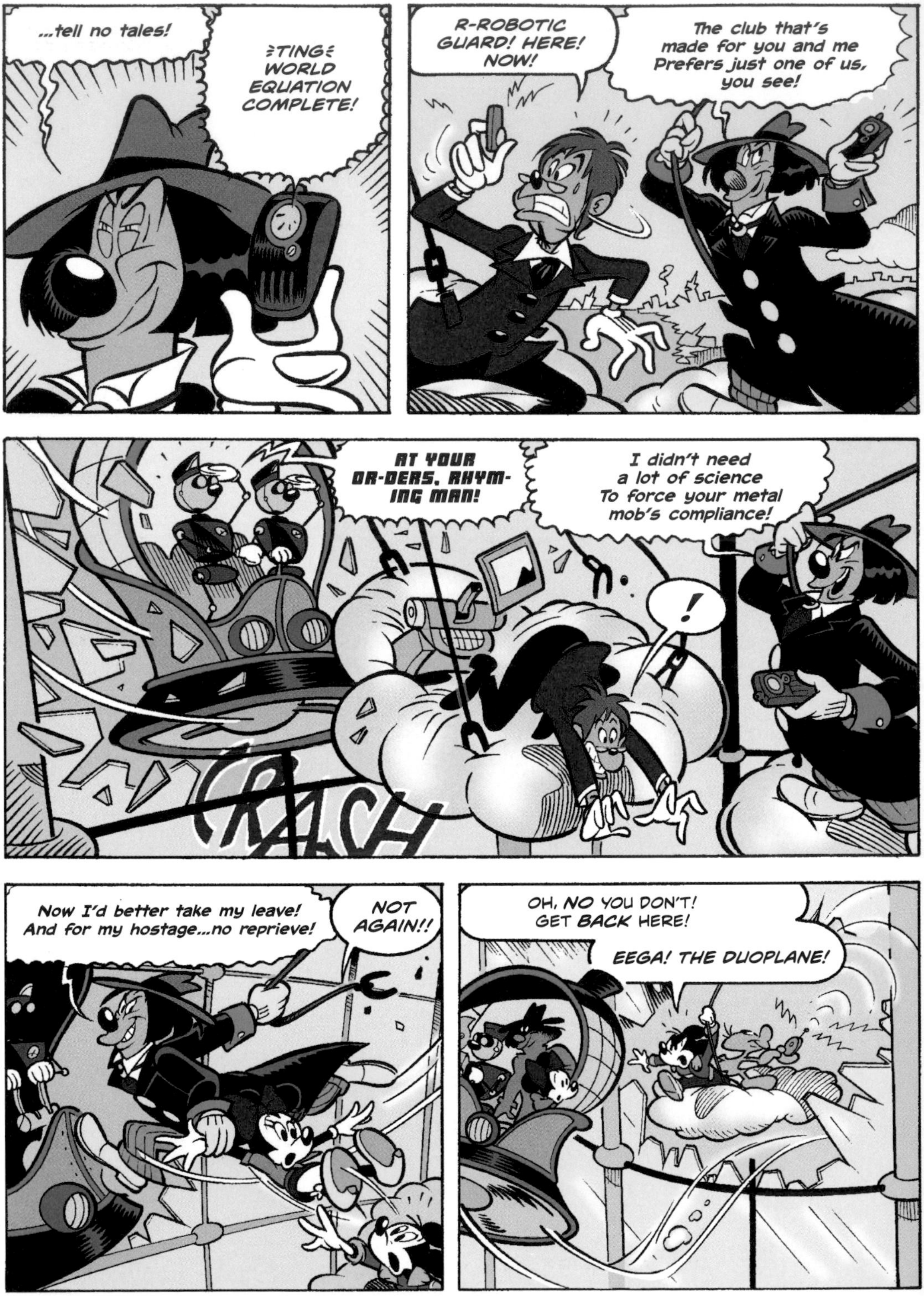
...tell no tales!
≡TING≡ WORLD EQUATION COMPLETE!
R-ROBOTIC GUARD! HERE! NOW!
The club that's made for you and me Prefers just one of us, you see!
AT YOUR OR-DERS, RHYM-ING MAN!
I didn't need a lot of science To force your metal mob's compliance!
!
CRASH
Now I'd better take my leave! And for my hostage...no reprieve!
NOT AGAIN!!
OH, NO YOU DON'T! GET BACK HERE!
EEGA! THE DUOPLANE!

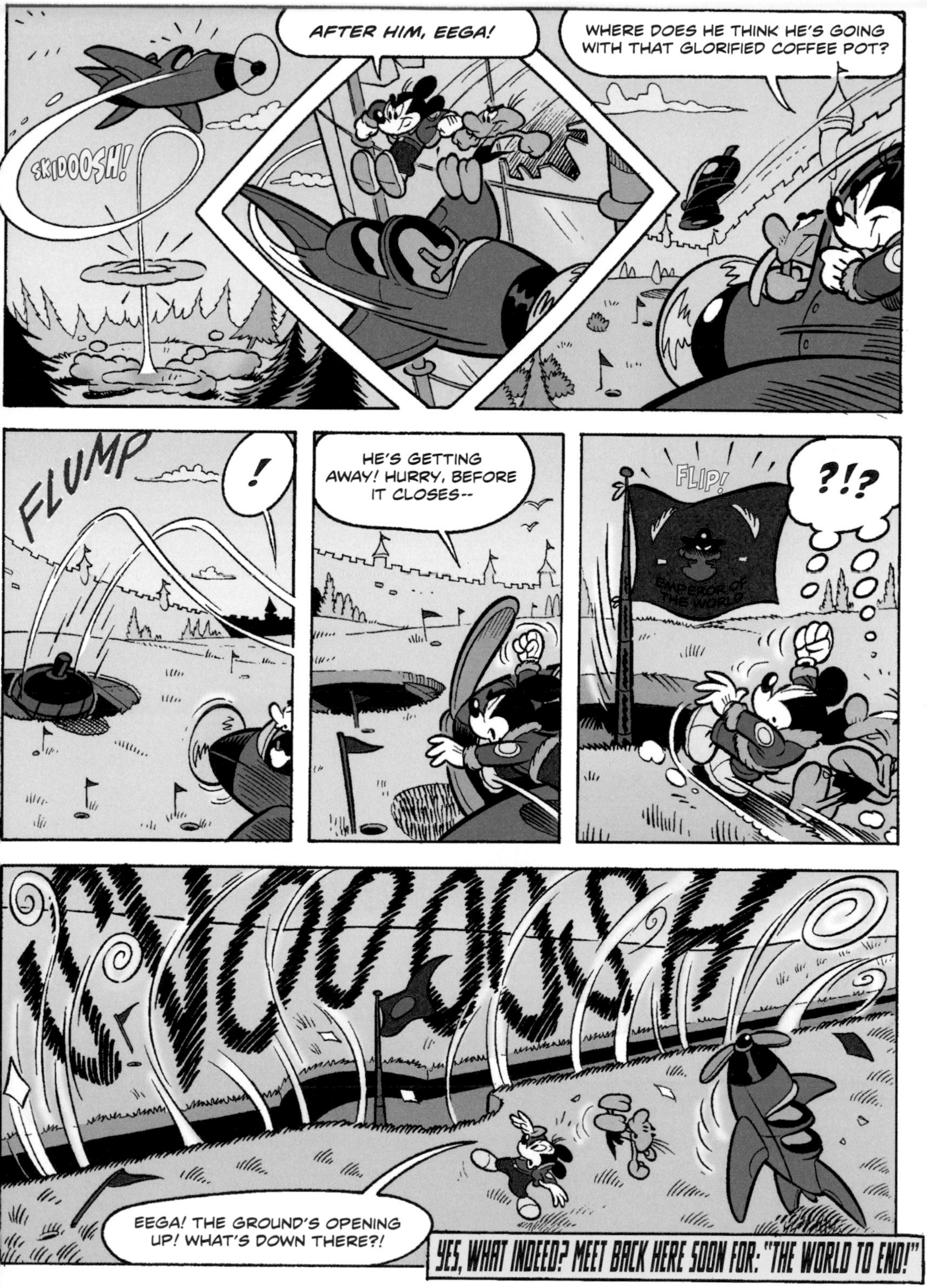
SKIDOOSH!
AFTER HIM, EEGA!
WHERE DOES HE THINK HE'S GOING WITH THAT GLORIFIED COFFEE POT?
FLUMP
!
HE'S GETTING AWAY! HURRY, BEFORE IT CLOSES--
FLIP!
EMPEROR OF THE WORLD
?!?
SHWOOOSH
EEGA! THE GROUND'S OPENING UP! WHAT'S DOWN THERE?!
YES, WHAT INDEED? MEET BACK HERE SOON FOR: "THE WORLD TO END!"

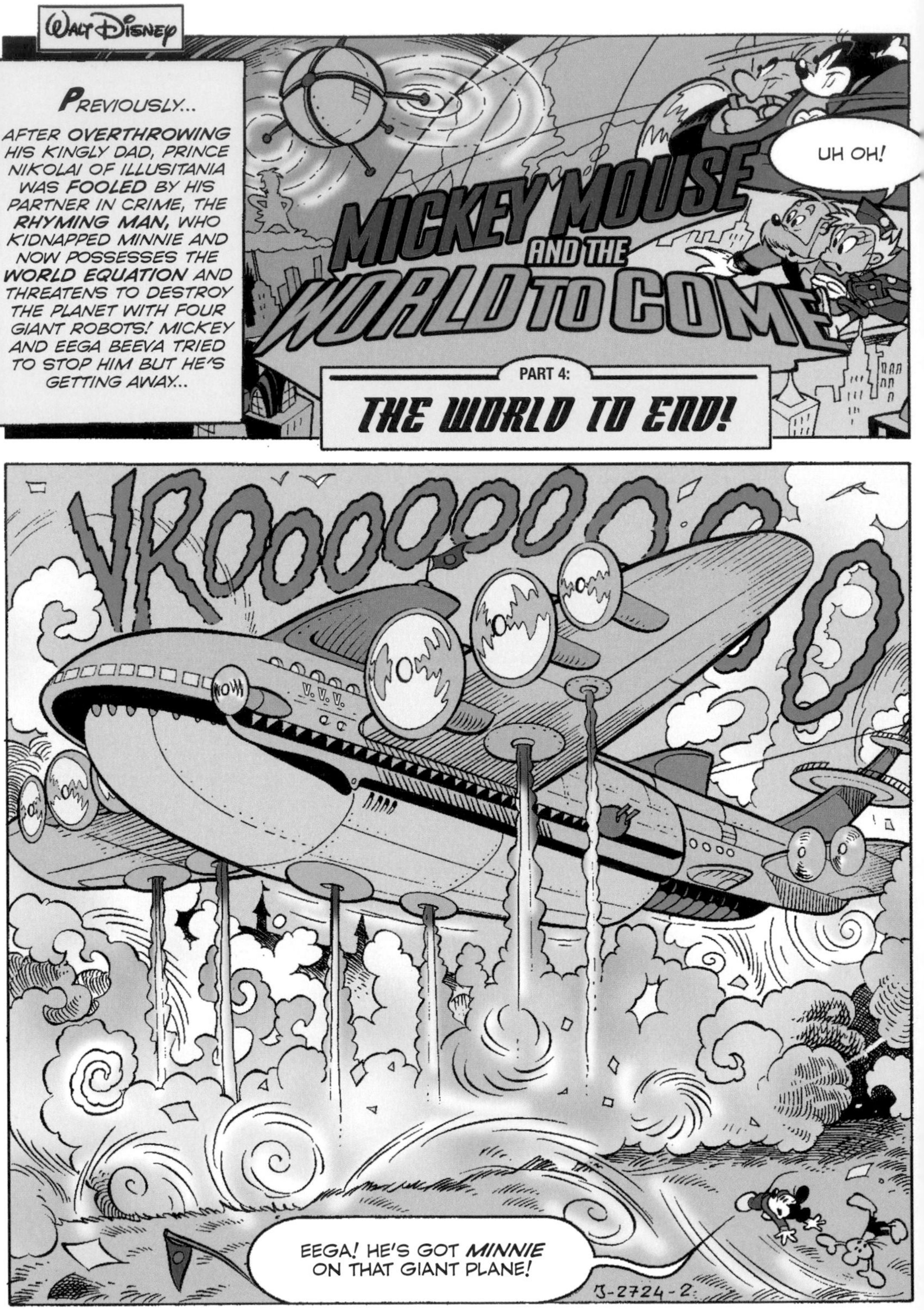
WALT DISNEY
PREVIOUSLY...
AFTER OVERTHROWING HIS KINGLY DAD, PRINCE NIKOLAI OF ILLUSITANIA WAS FOOLED BY HIS PARTNER IN CRIME, THE RHYMING MAN, WHO KIDNAPPED MINNIE AND NOW POSSESSES THE WORLD EQUATION AND THREATENS TO DESTROY THE PLANET WITH FOUR GIANT ROBOTS! MICKEY AND EEGA BEEVA TRIED TO STOP HIM BUT HE'S GETTING AWAY...
MICKEY MOUSE AND THE WORLD TO COME
UH OH!
PART 4:
THE WORLD TO END!
VROOOOOOOOOO
V.V.V.
EEGA! HE'S GOT MINNIE ON THAT GIANT PLANE!
I-2724-2

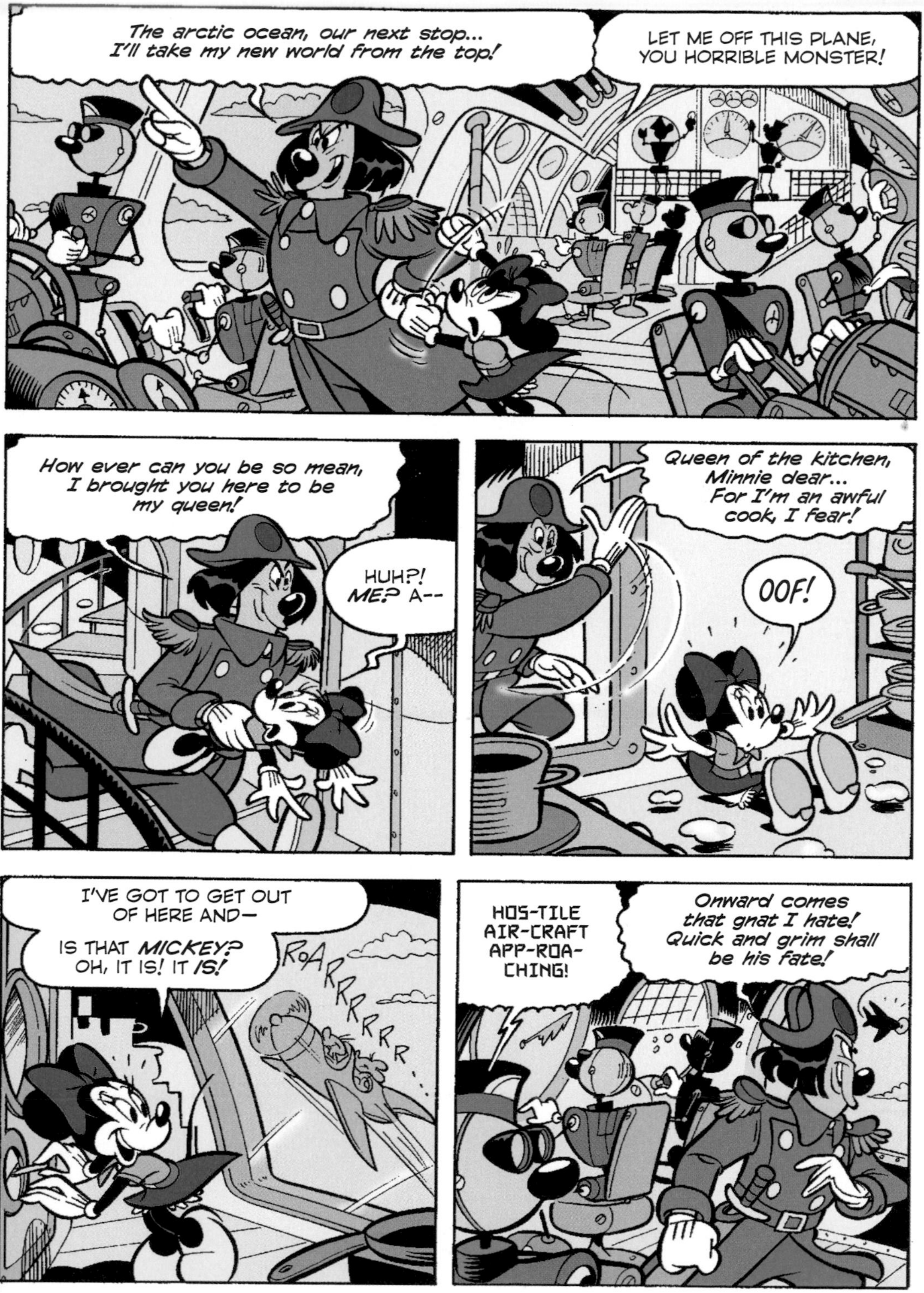

The arctic ocean, our next stop... I'll take my new world from the top!
LET ME OFF THIS PLANE, YOU HORRIBLE MONSTER!
How ever can you be so mean, I brought you here to be my queen!
HUH?! ME? A--
Queen of the kitchen, Minnie dear... For I'm an awful cook, I fear!
OOF!
I'VE GOT TO GET OUT OF HERE AND—
IS THAT MICKEY? OH, IT IS! IT IS!
ROARRRRRRR
HOS-TILE AIR-CRAFT APP-ROA-CHING!
Onward comes that gnat I hate! Quick and grim shall be his fate!

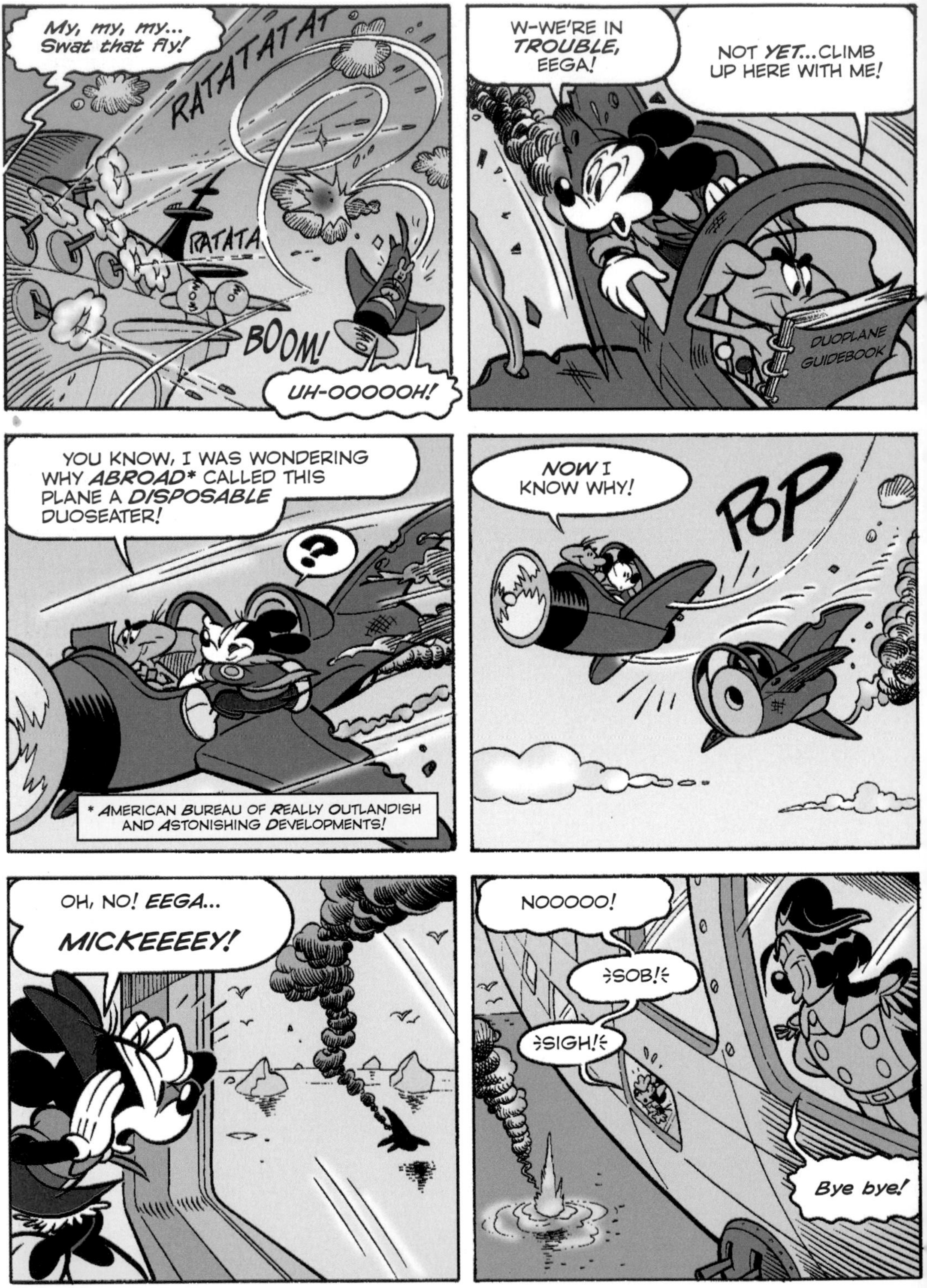

My, my, my... Swat that fly!
RATATATAT
RATATA
BOOM!
UH-OOOOOH!
W-WE'RE IN TROUBLE, EEGA!
NOT YET...CLIMB UP HERE WITH ME!
DUOPLANE GUIDEBOOK
YOU KNOW, I WAS WONDERING WHY ABROAD* CALLED THIS PLANE A DISPOSABLE DUOSEATER!
?
* AMERICAN BUREAU OF REALLY OUTLANDISH AND ASTONISHING DEVELOPMENTS!
NOW I KNOW WHY!
POP
OH, NO! EEGA... MICKEEEEY!
NOOOOO!
SOB!
SIGH!
Bye bye!

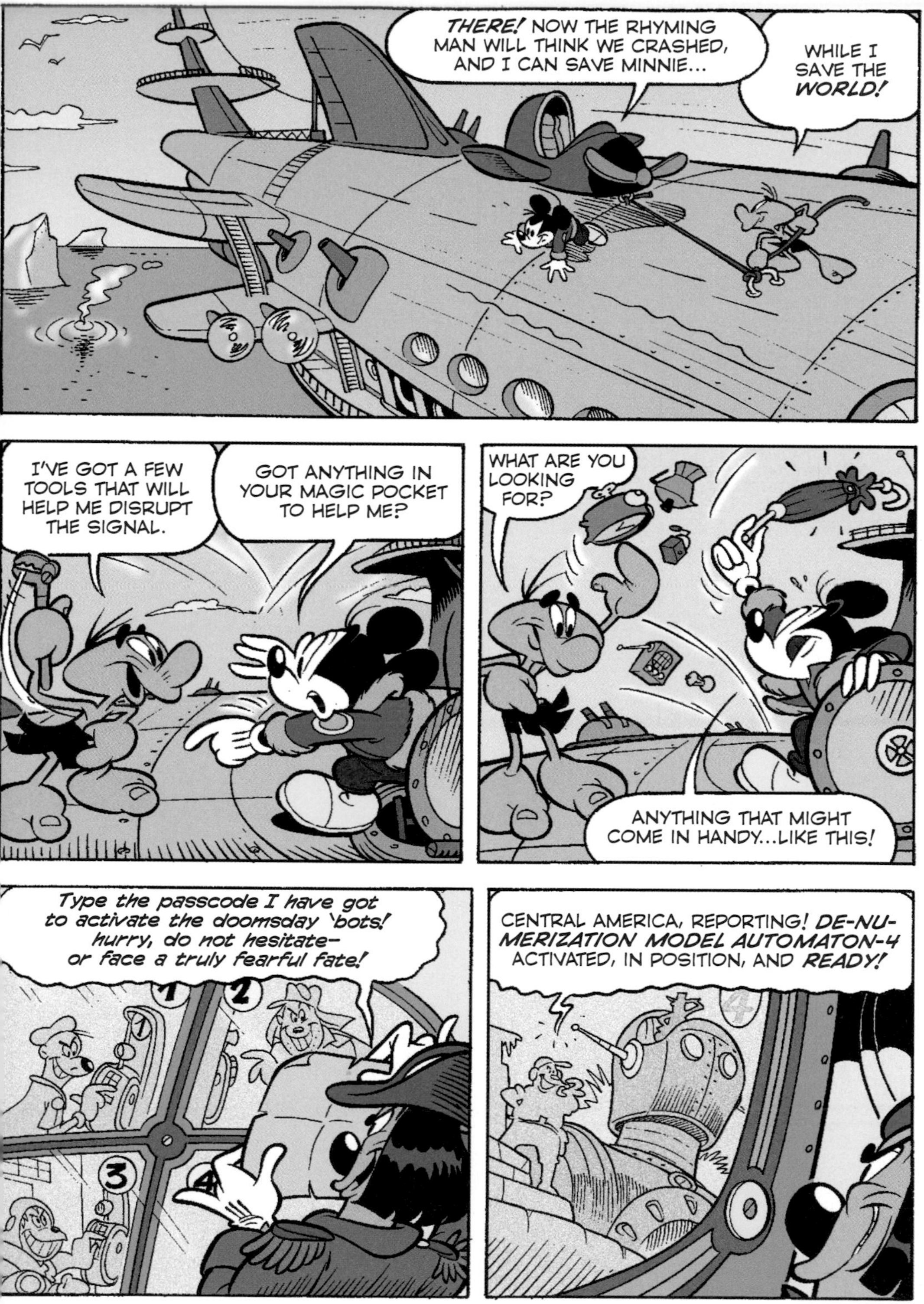
THERE! NOW THE RHYMING MAN WILL THINK WE CRASHED, AND I CAN SAVE MINNIE...
WHILE I SAVE THE WORLD!
I'VE GOT A FEW TOOLS THAT WILL HELP ME DISRUPT THE SIGNAL.
GOT ANYTHING IN YOUR MAGIC POCKET TO HELP ME?
WHAT ARE YOU LOOKING FOR?
ANYTHING THAT MIGHT COME IN HANDY...LIKE THIS!
Type the passcode I have got to activate the doomsday 'bots! hurry, do not hesitate— or face a truly fearful fate!
1
2
3
4
CENTRAL AMERICA, REPORTING! DE-NUMERIZATION MODEL AUTOMATON-4 ACTIVATED, IN POSITION, AND READY!
4

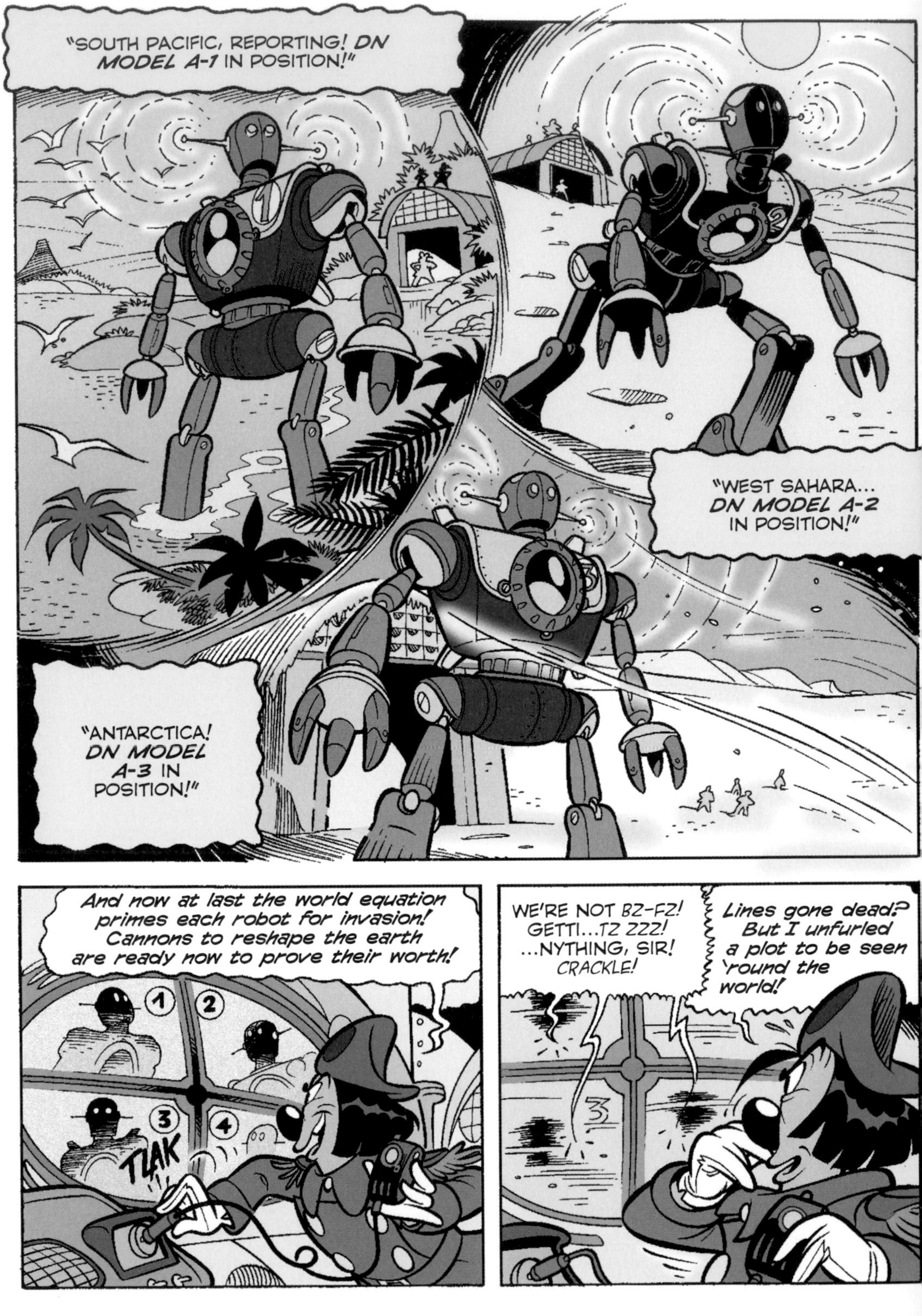
"SOUTH PACIFIC, REPORTING! DN MODEL A-1 IN POSITION!"
"WEST SAHARA... DN MODEL A-2 IN POSITION!"
"ANTARCTICA! DN MODEL A-3 IN POSITION!"
And now at last the world equation primes each robot for invasion! Cannons to reshape the earth are ready now to prove their worth!
TLAK
WE'RE NOT BZ-FZ! GETTI...TZ ZZZ! ...NYTHING, SIR! CRACKLE!
Lines gone dead? But I unfurled a plot to be seen 'round the world!

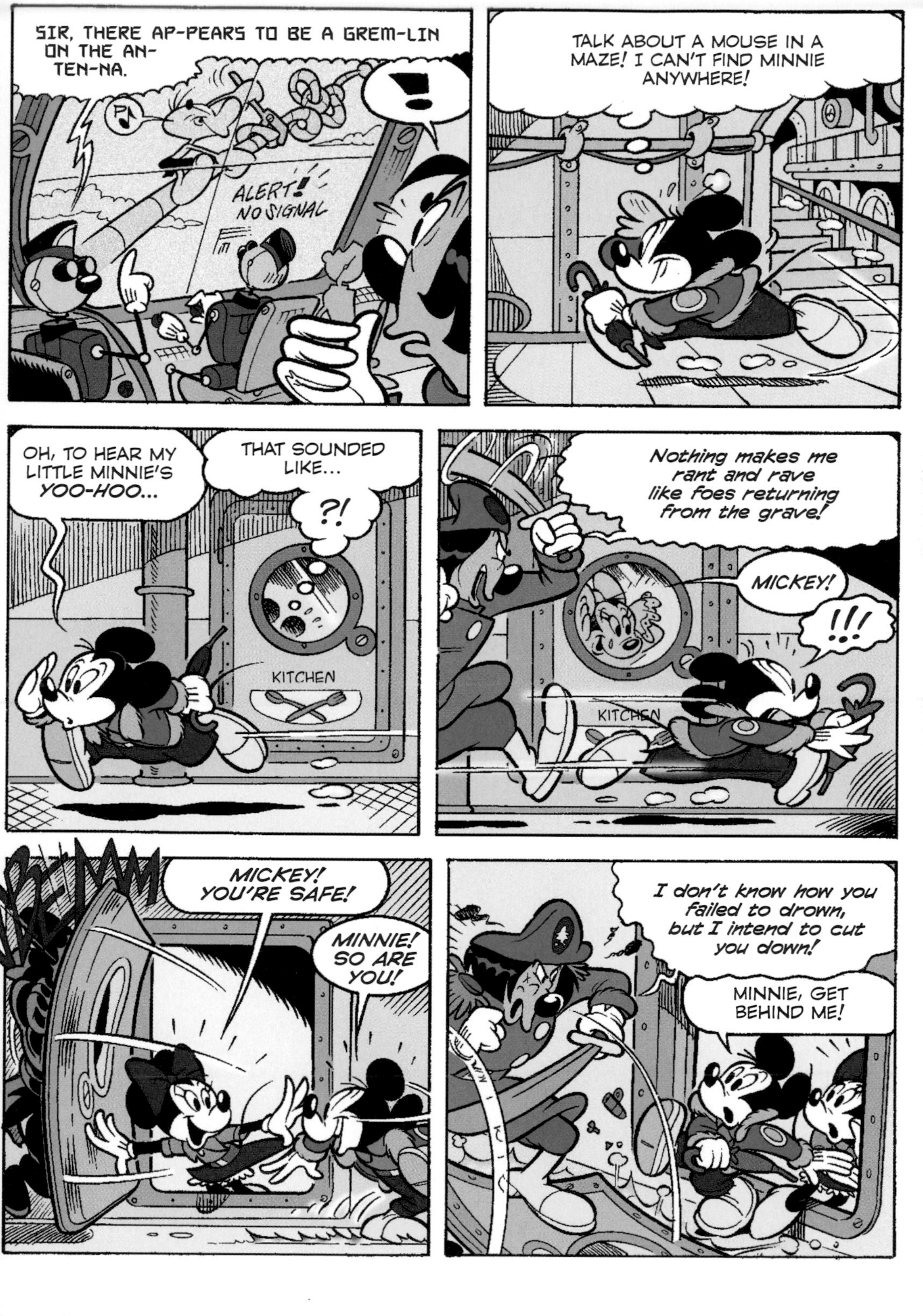
SIR, THERE AP-PEARS TO BE A GREM-LIN ON THE AN-TEN-NA.
PA
ALERT! NO SIGNAL
!
TALK ABOUT A MOUSE IN A MAZE! I CAN'T FIND MINNIE ANYWHERE!
OH, TO HEAR MY LITTLE MINNIE'S YOO-HOO...
THAT SOUNDED LIKE...
?!
KITCHEN
Nothing makes me rant and rave like foes returning from the grave!
MICKEY!
!!!
KITCHEN
BEMM
MICKEY! YOU'RE SAFE!
MINNIE! SO ARE YOU!
I don't know how you failed to drown, but I intend to cut you down!
MINNIE, GET BEHIND ME!

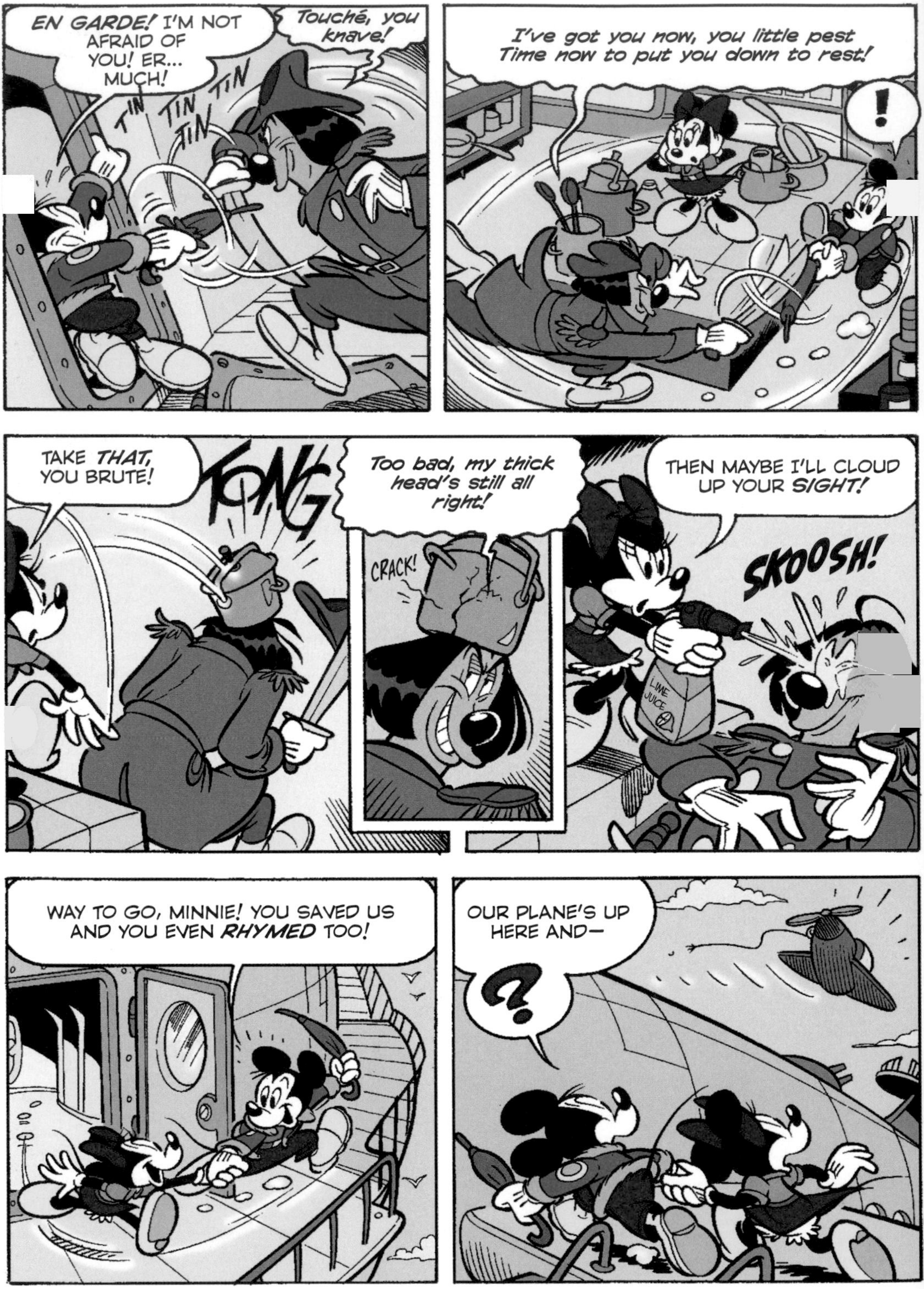
EN GARDE! I'M NOT AFRAID OF YOU! ER... MUCH!
Touché, you knave!
TIN TIN TIN TIN
I've got you now, you little pest
Time now to put you down to rest!
!
TAKE THAT, YOU BRUTE!
TONG
Too bad, my thick head's still all right!
CRACK!
THEN MAYBE I'LL CLOUD UP YOUR SIGHT!
SKOOSH!
LIME JUICE
WAY TO GO, MINNIE! YOU SAVED US AND YOU EVEN RHYMED TOO!
OUR PLANE'S UP HERE AND—
?

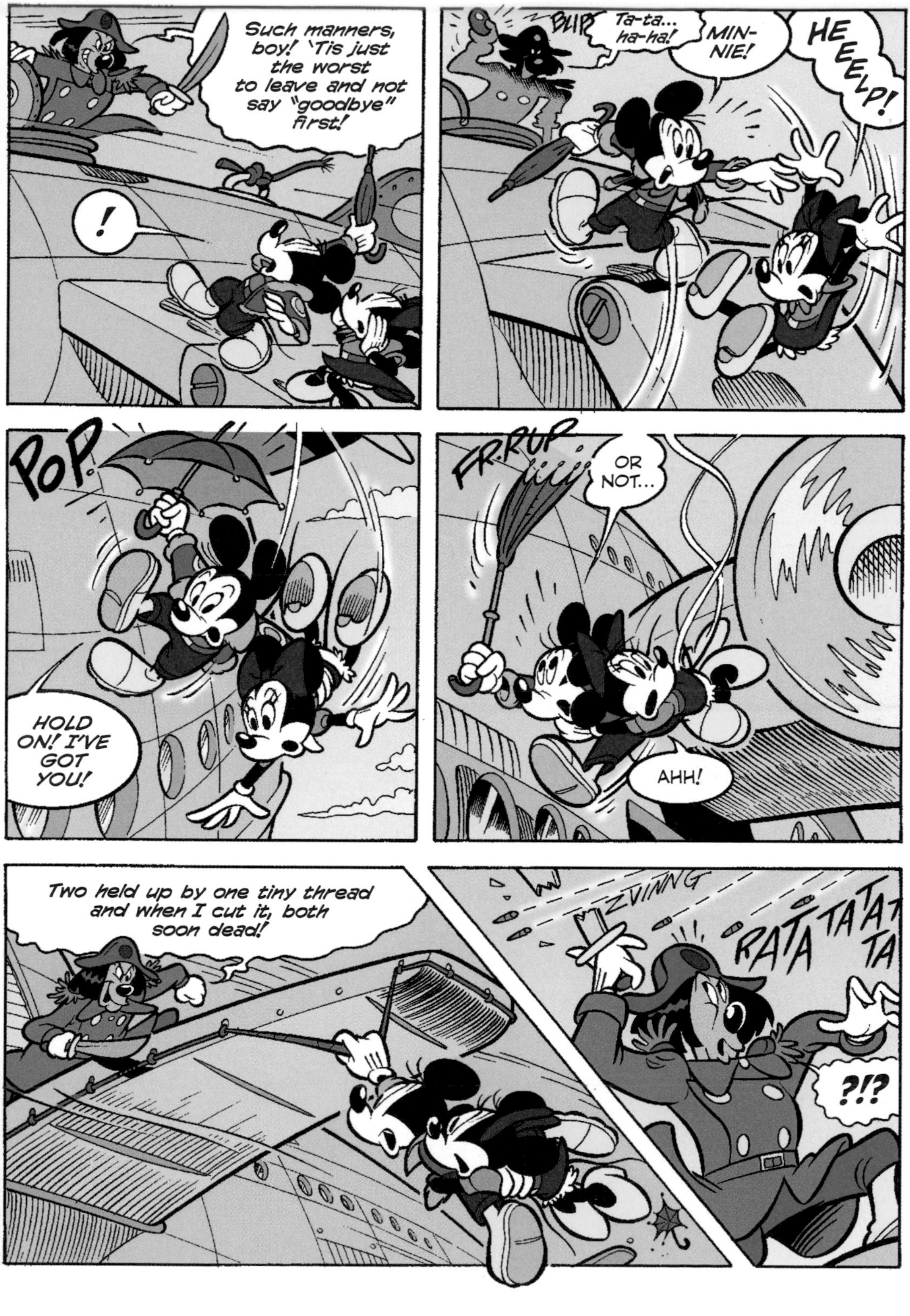
Such manners, boy! 'Tis just the worst to leave and not say "goodbye" first!
!
BLIP
Ta-ta... ha-ha!
MIN-NIE!
HEEELP!
POP
HOLD ON! I'VE GOT YOU!
FRRUP
OR NOT...
AHH!
Two held up by one tiny thread and when I cut it, both soon dead!
ZVINNG
RATATATATA
?!?

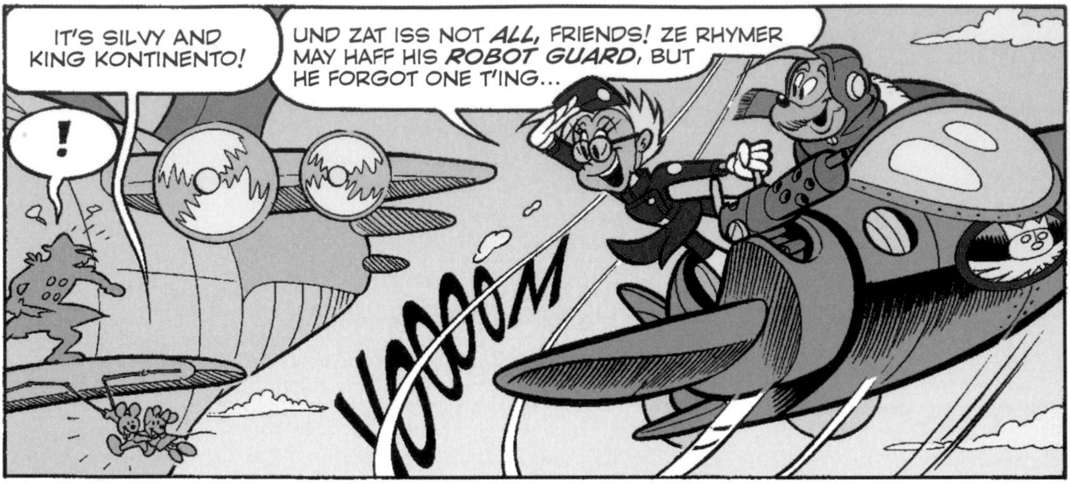

IT'S SILVY AND KING KONTINENTO!
UND ZAT ISS NOT ALL, FRIENDS! ZE RHYMER MAY HAFF HIS ROBOT GUARD, BUT HE FORGOT ONE T'ING...
!
VOOOOM

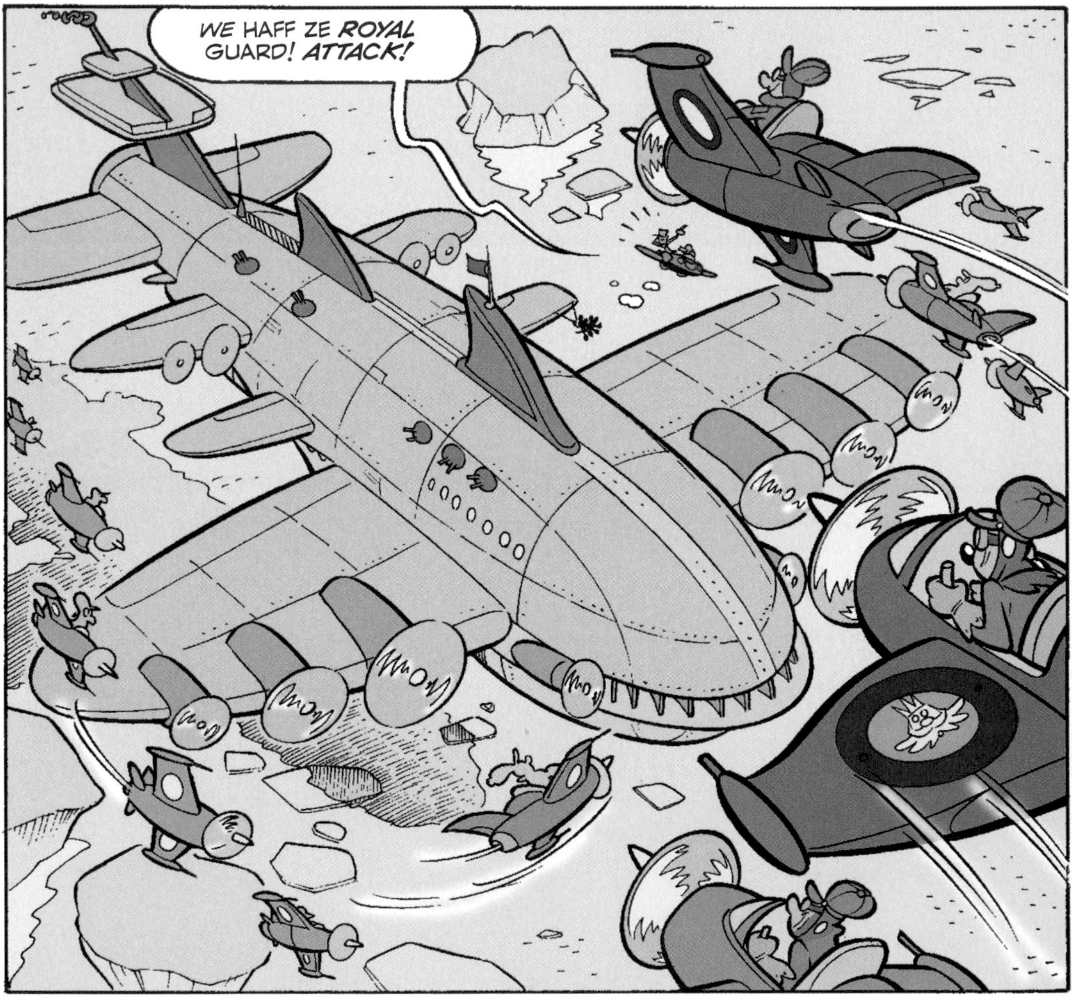

WE HAFF ZE ROYAL GUARD! ATTACK!

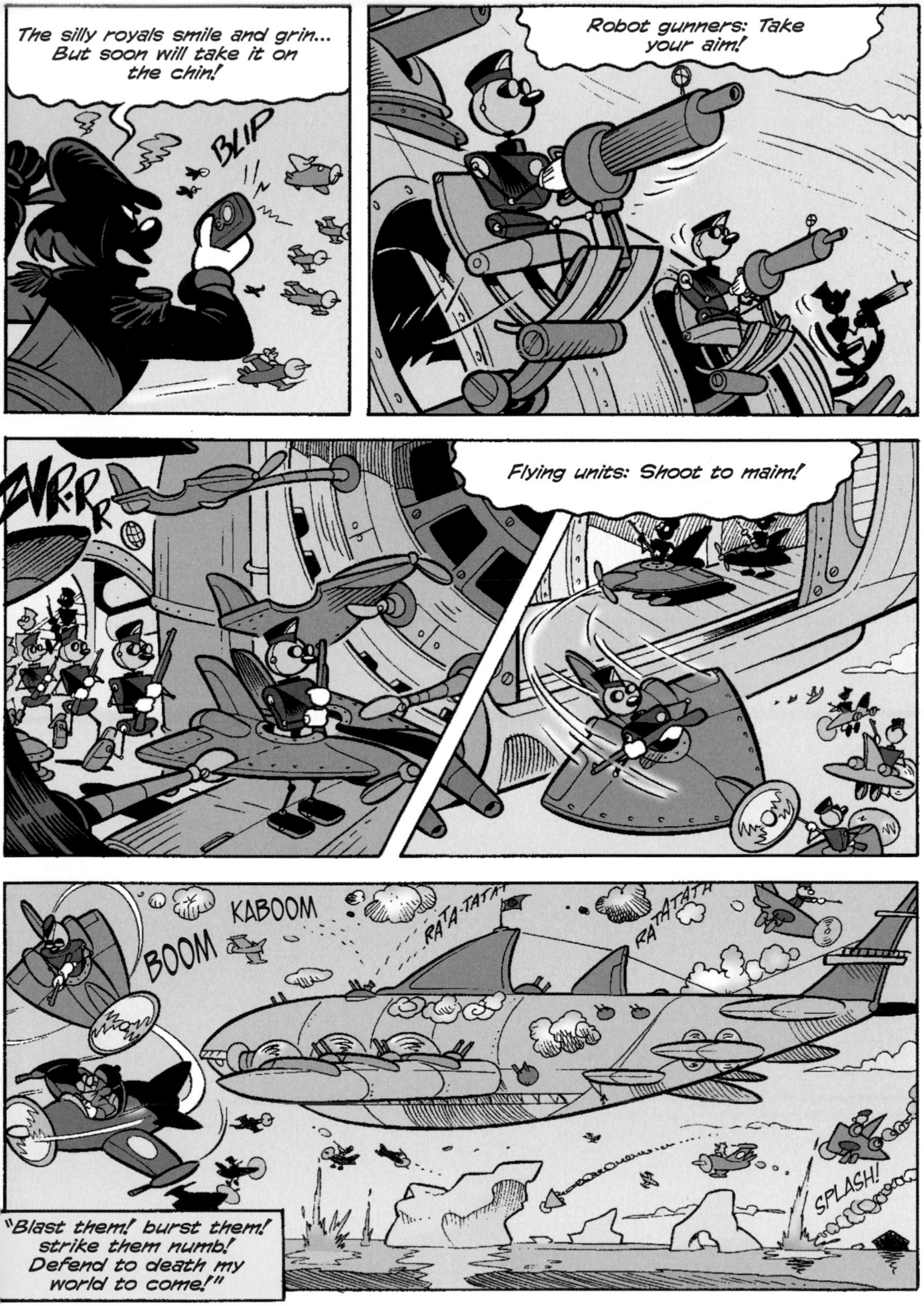
The silly royals smile and grin... But soon will take it on the chin!
BLIP
Robot gunners: Take your aim!
ZVR-R-R
Flying units: Shoot to maim!
BOOM
KABOOM
RA-TA-TATAT
RATATATH
SPLASH!
"Blast them! burst them! strike them numb! Defend to death my world to come!"

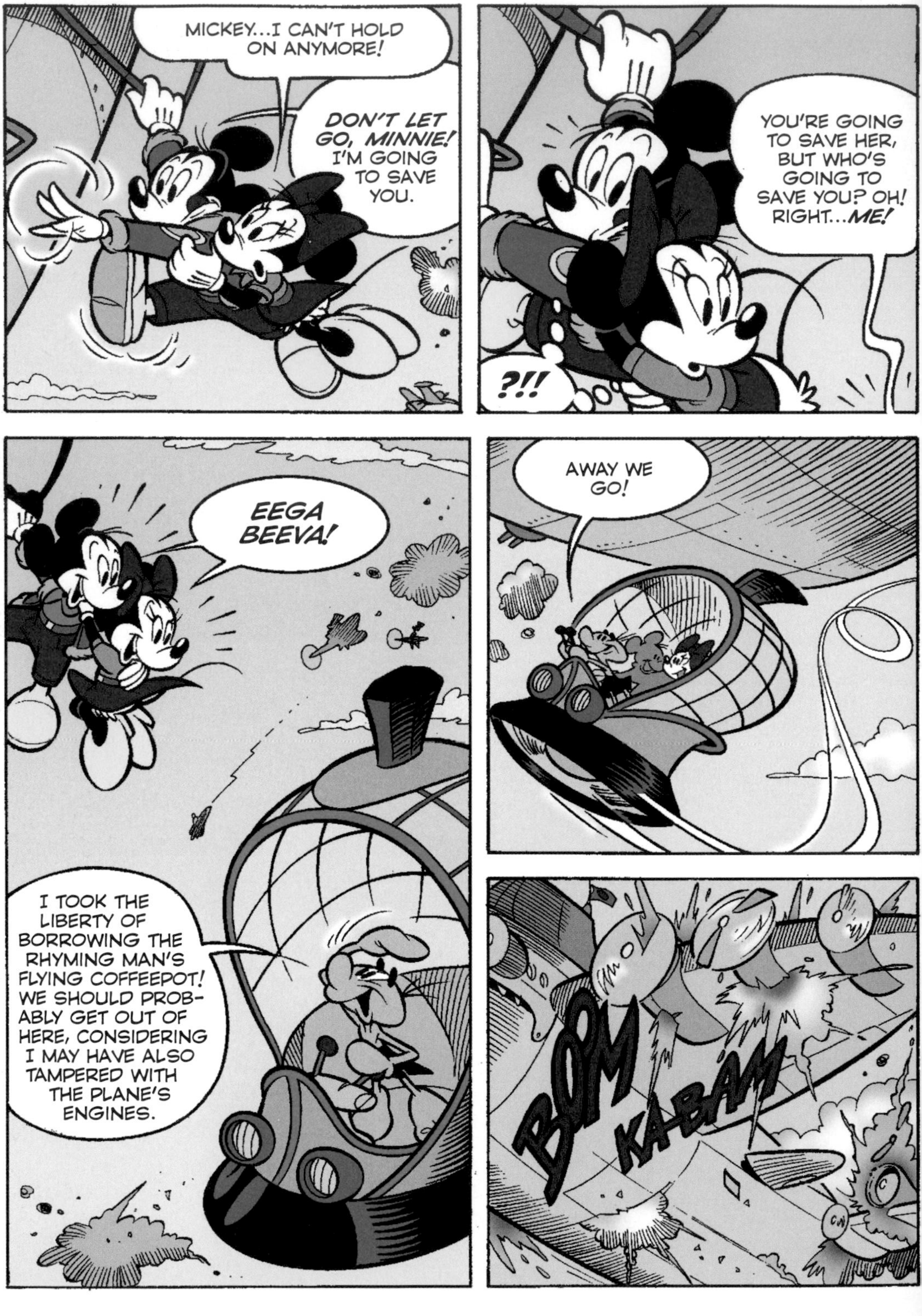
MICKEY...I CAN'T HOLD ON ANYMORE!
DON'T LET GO, MINNIE! I'M GOING TO SAVE YOU.
YOU'RE GOING TO SAVE HER, BUT WHO'S GOING TO SAVE YOU? OH! RIGHT...ME!
?!!
EEGA BEEVA!
I TOOK THE LIBERTY OF BORROWING THE RHYMING MAN'S FLYING COFFEEPOT! WE SHOULD PROBABLY GET OUT OF HERE, CONSIDERING I MAY HAVE ALSO TAMPERED WITH THE PLANE'S ENGINES.
AWAY WE GO!
BOOM
KA-BAM

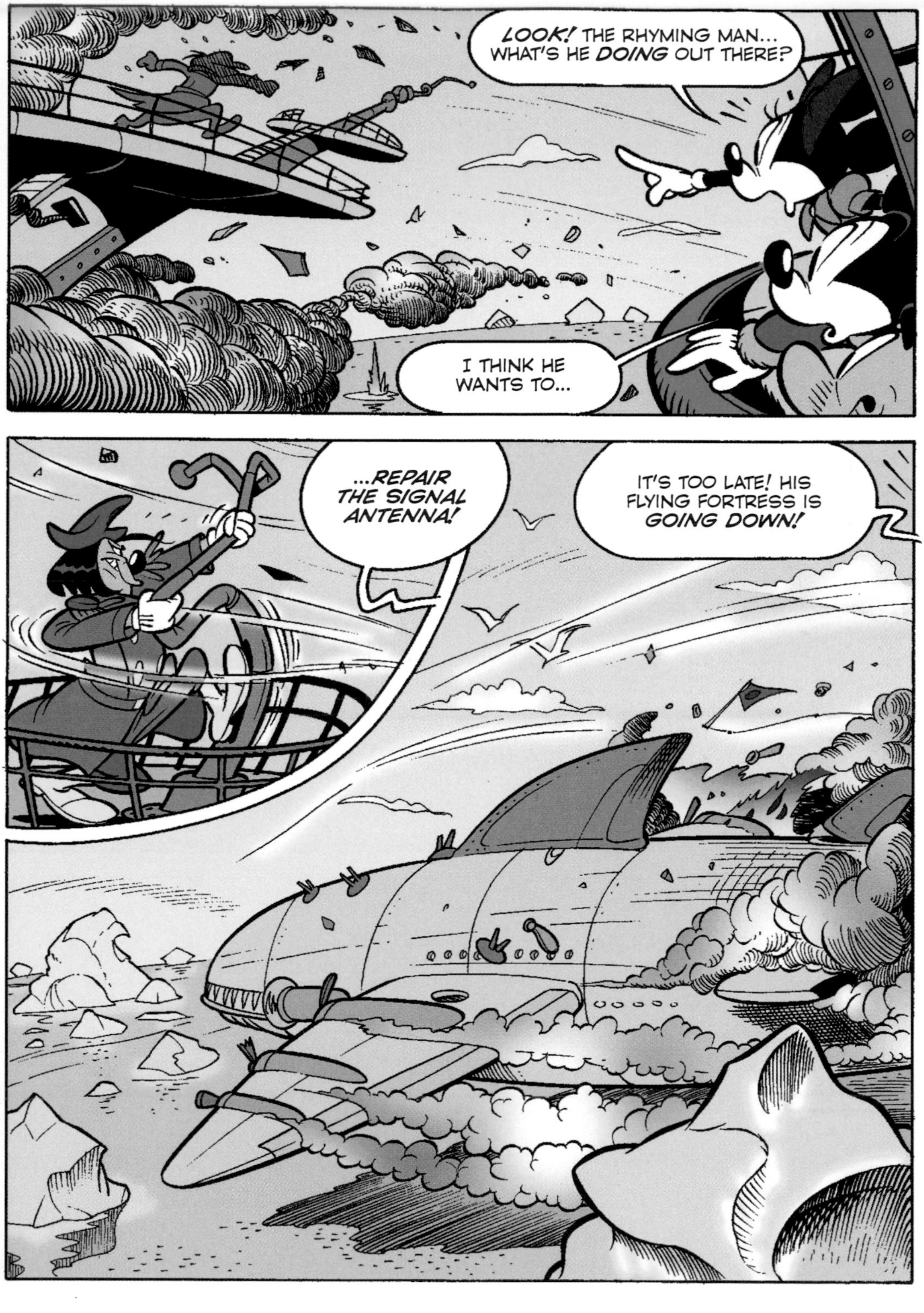
LOOK! THE RHYMING MAN... WHAT'S HE DOING OUT THERE?
I THINK HE WANTS TO...
...REPAIR THE SIGNAL ANTENNA!
IT'S TOO LATE! HIS FLYING FORTRESS IS GOING DOWN!

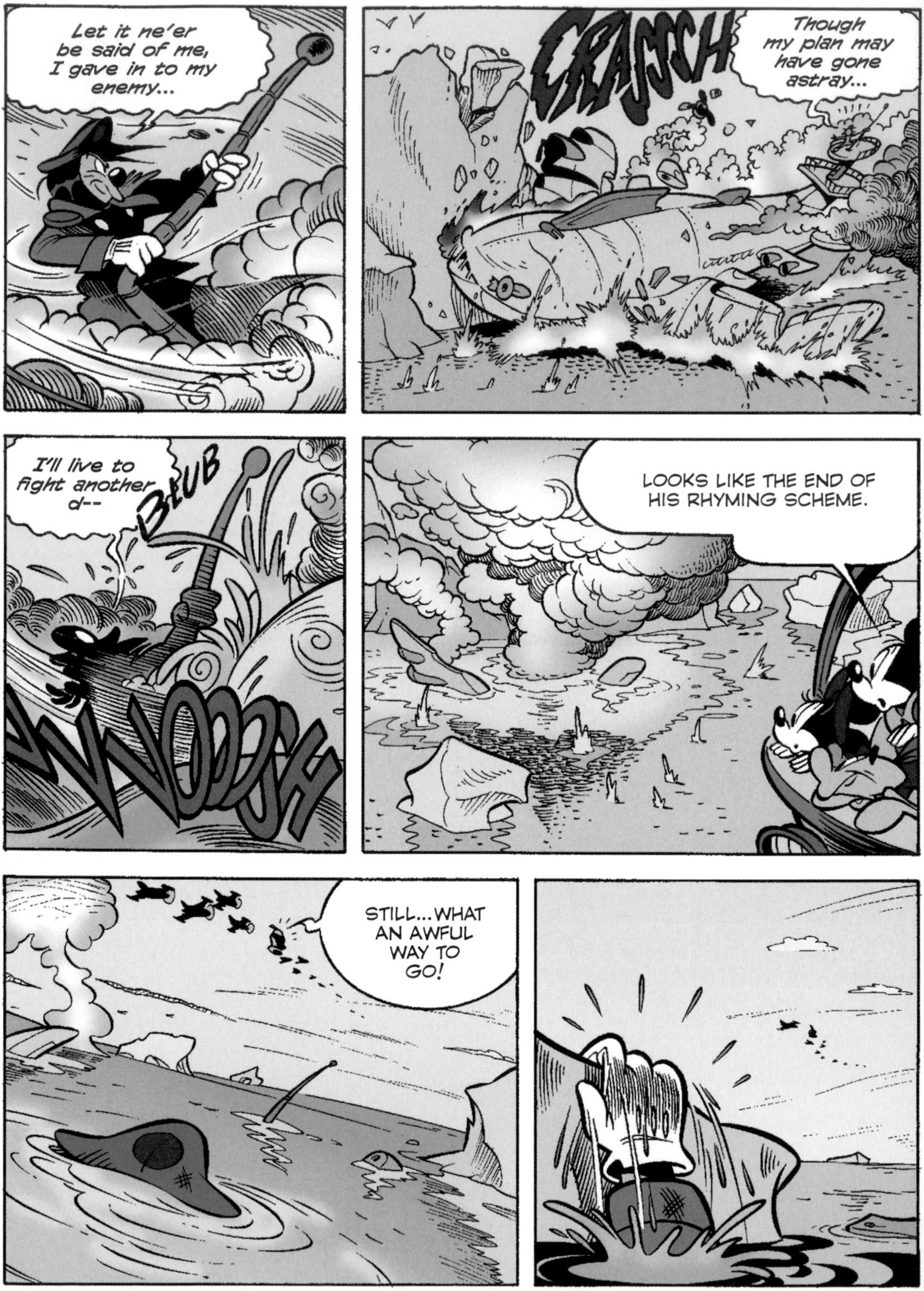
Let it ne'er be said of me, I gave in to my enemy...
CRASSCH
Though my plan may have gone astray...
I'll live to fight another d--
BLUB
WOOOSH
LOOKS LIKE THE END OF HIS RHYMING SCHEME.
STILL...WHAT AN AWFUL WAY TO GO!

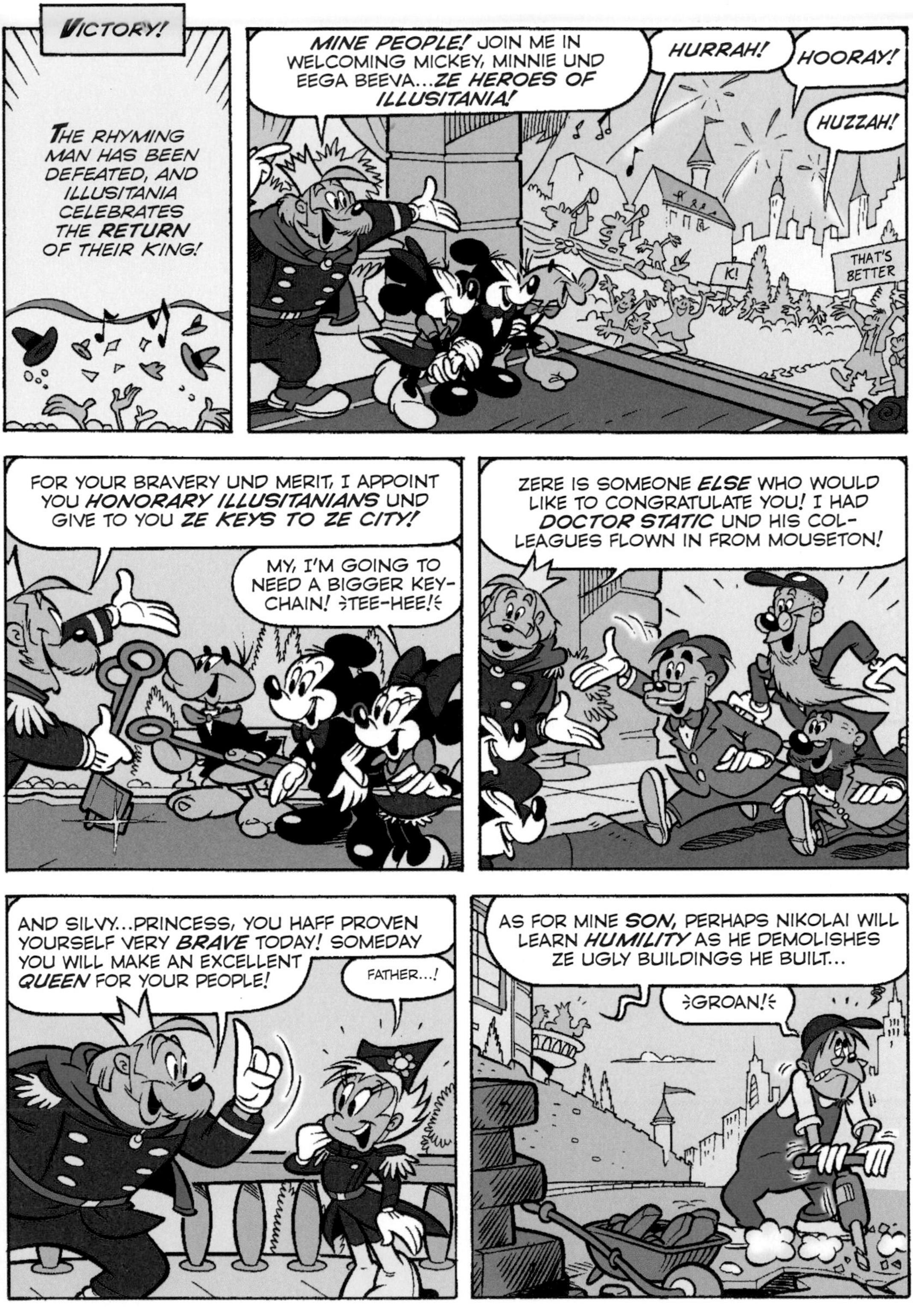

VICTORY!
THE RHYMING MAN HAS BEEN DEFEATED, AND ILLUSITANIA CELEBRATES THE RETURN OF THEIR KING!
MINE PEOPLE! JOIN ME IN WELCOMING MICKEY, MINNIE UND EEGA BEEVA...ZE HEROES OF ILLUSITANIA!
HURRAH!
HOORAY!
HUZZAH!
K!
THAT'S BETTER
FOR YOUR BRAVERY UND MERIT, I APPOINT YOU HONORARY ILLUSITANIANS UND GIVE TO YOU ZE KEYS TO ZE CITY!
MY, I'M GOING TO NEED A BIGGER KEY-CHAIN! TEE-HEE!
ZERE IS SOMEONE ELSE WHO WOULD LIKE TO CONGRATULATE YOU! I HAD DOCTOR STATIC UND HIS COL-LEAGUES FLOWN IN FROM MOUSETON!
AND SILVY...PRINCESS, YOU HAFF PROVEN YOURSELF VERY BRAVE TODAY! SOMEDAY YOU WILL MAKE AN EXCELLENT QUEEN FOR YOUR PEOPLE!
FATHER...!
AS FOR MINE SON, PERHAPS NIKOLAI WILL LEARN HUMILITY AS HE DEMOLISHES ZE UGLY BUILDINGS HE BUILT...
GROAN!

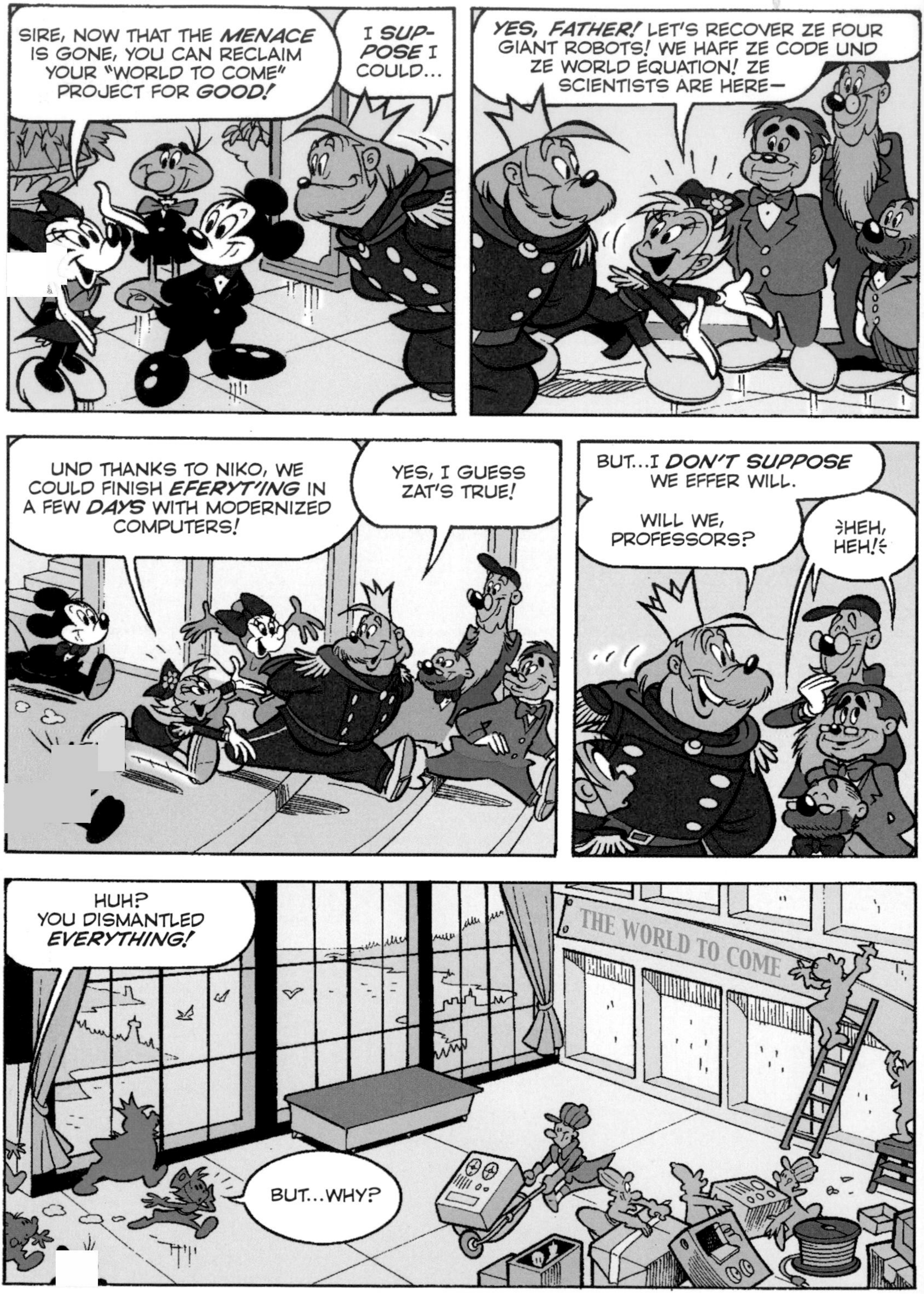
SIRE, NOW THAT THE MENACE IS GONE, YOU CAN RECLAIM YOUR "WORLD TO COME" PROJECT FOR GOOD!
I SUPPOSE I COULD...
YES, FATHER! LET'S RECOVER ZE FOUR GIANT ROBOTS! WE HAFF ZE CODE UND ZE WORLD EQUATION! ZE SCIENTISTS ARE HERE—
UND THANKS TO NIKO, WE COULD FINISH EFERYT'ING IN A FEW DAYS WITH MODERNIZED COMPUTERS!
YES, I GUESS ZAT'S TRUE!
BUT...I DON'T SUPPOSE WE EFFER WILL.
WILL WE, PROFESSORS?
HEH, HEH!
HUH? YOU DISMANTLED EVERYTHING!
THE WORLD TO COME
BUT...WHY?

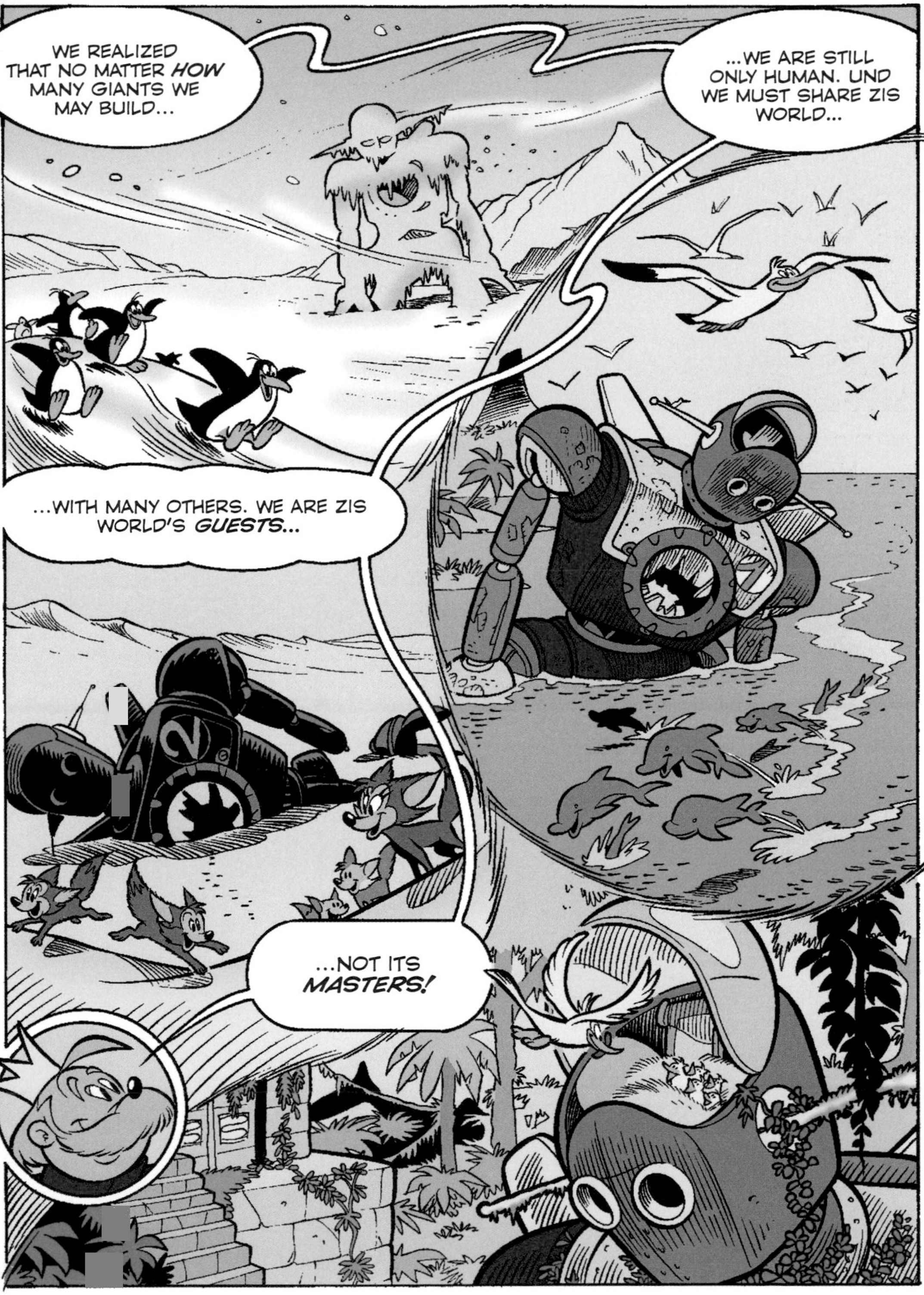
WE REALIZED THAT NO MATTER *HOW* MANY GIANTS WE MAY BUILD...
...WE ARE STILL ONLY HUMAN. UND WE MUST SHARE ZIS WORLD...
...WITH MANY OTHERS. WE ARE ZIS WORLD'S *GUESTS*...
...NOT ITS *MASTERS!*

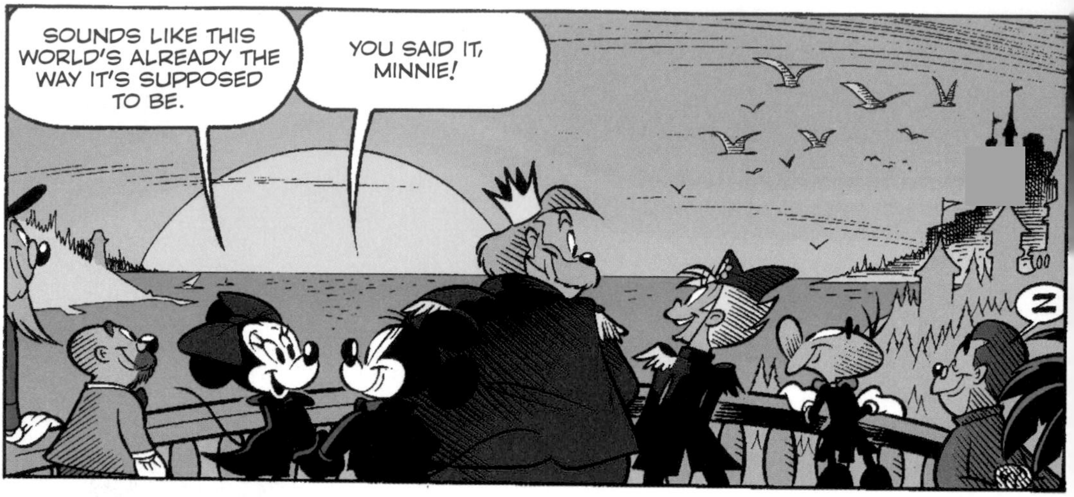
SOUNDS LIKE THIS WORLD'S ALREADY THE WAY IT'S SUPPOSED TO BE.
YOU SAID IT, MINNIE!
Z

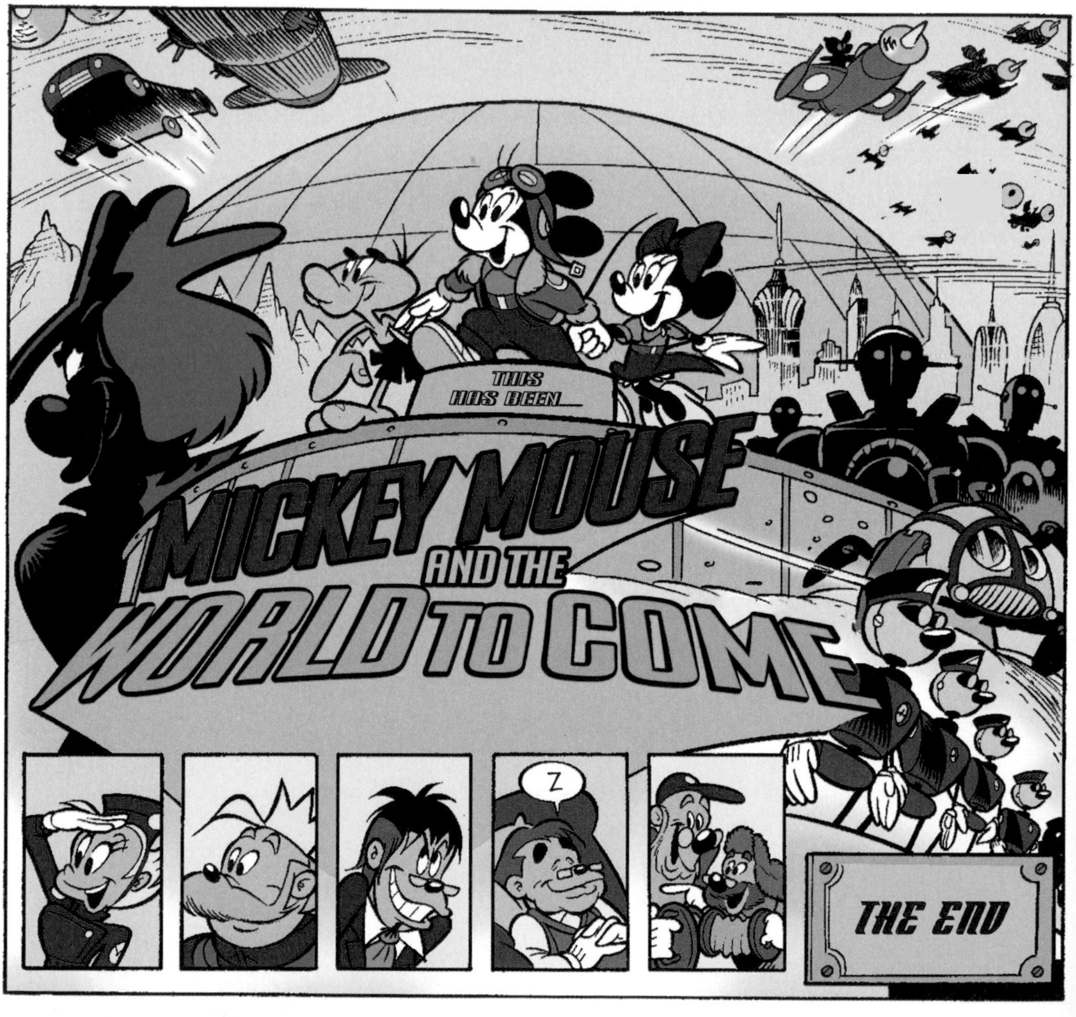
THIS HAS BEEN...
MICKEY MOUSE AND THE WORLD TO COME
Z
THE END

WHEN THE MOUSE IS AWAY, THE CAT WILL PLAY! WITH MICKEY OTHERWISE OCCUPIED, WHO WILL KEEP MOUSETON SAFE FROM THE SINISTER MACHINATIONS OF PEG-LEG PETE? WHAT IS THE CONNIVING CAT UP TO? WELL, WONDER NO FURTHER, DISNEY FANS...BECAUSE PETE'S ADVENTURE BEGINS NOW!

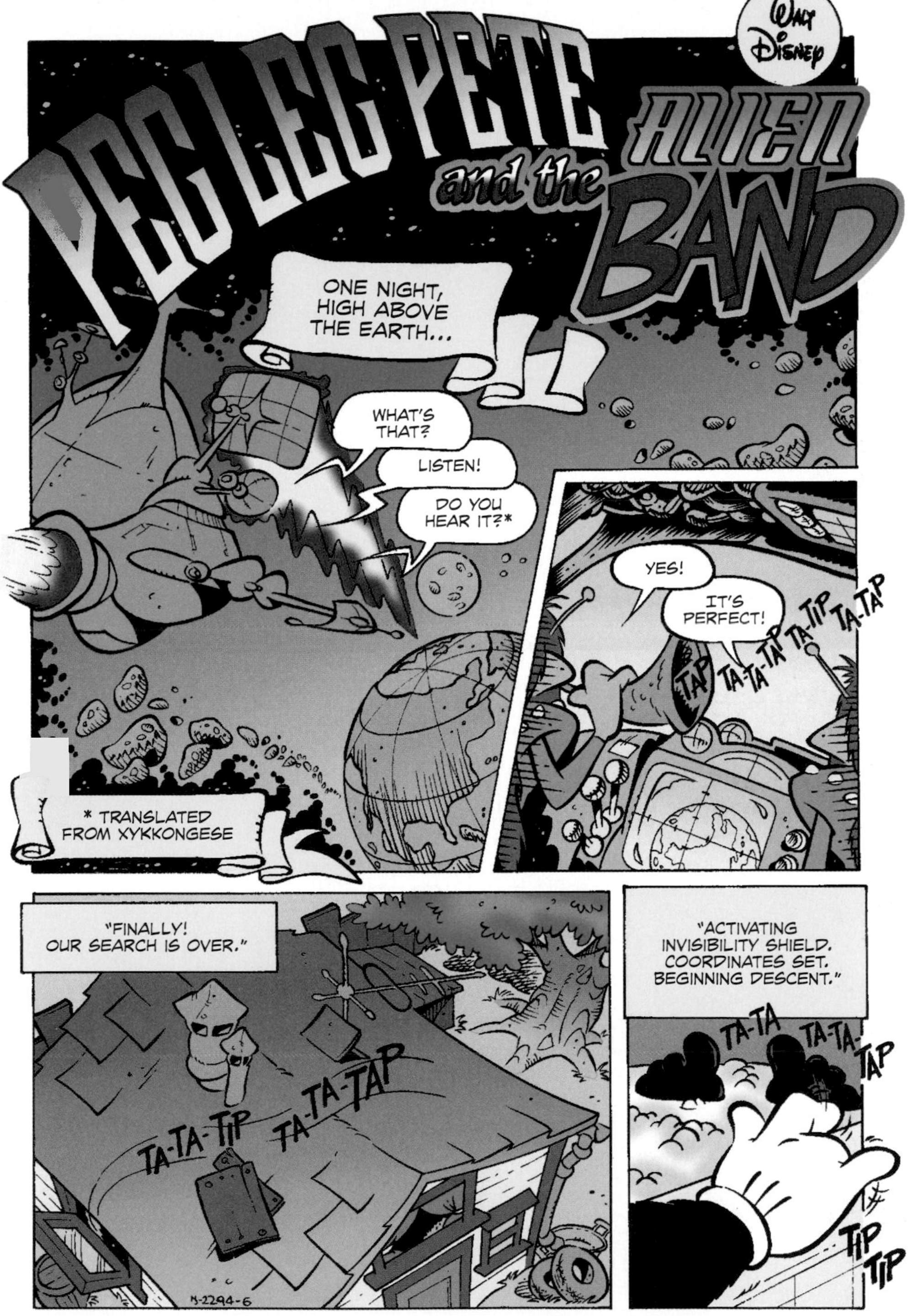

WALT DISNEY
PEG LEG PETE and the ALIEN BAND
ONE NIGHT, HIGH ABOVE THE EARTH...
WHAT'S THAT?
LISTEN!
DO YOU HEAR IT?*
* TRANSLATED FROM XYKKONGESE
YES!
IT'S PERFECT!
TAP TA-TA-TAP TA-TIP TA-TAP
"FINALLY! OUR SEARCH IS OVER."
TA-TA-TIP TA-TA-TAP
PETE
M-2294-6
"ACTIVATING INVISIBILITY SHIELD. COORDINATES SET. BEGINNING DESCENT."
TA-TA TA-TA-TAP
TIP TIP

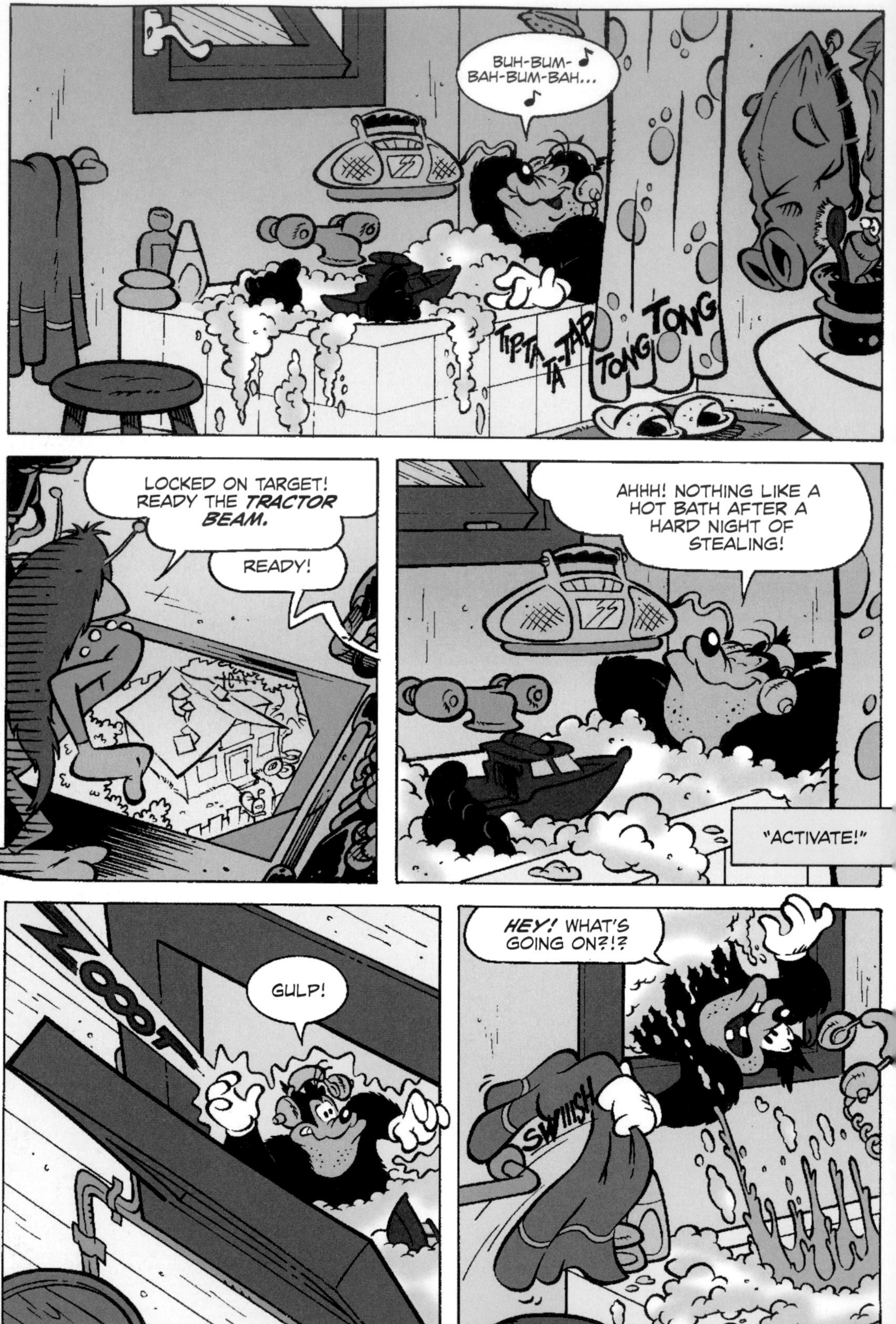
BUH-BUM-
BAH-BUM-BAH...
TIP TA TA-TAP
TONG TONG TONG
LOCKED ON TARGET! READY THE *TRACTOR BEAM.*
READY!
AHHH! NOTHING LIKE A HOT BATH AFTER A HARD NIGHT OF STEALING!
"ACTIVATE!"
ZOOOT
GULP!
HEY! WHAT'S GOING ON?!?
SWIIISH

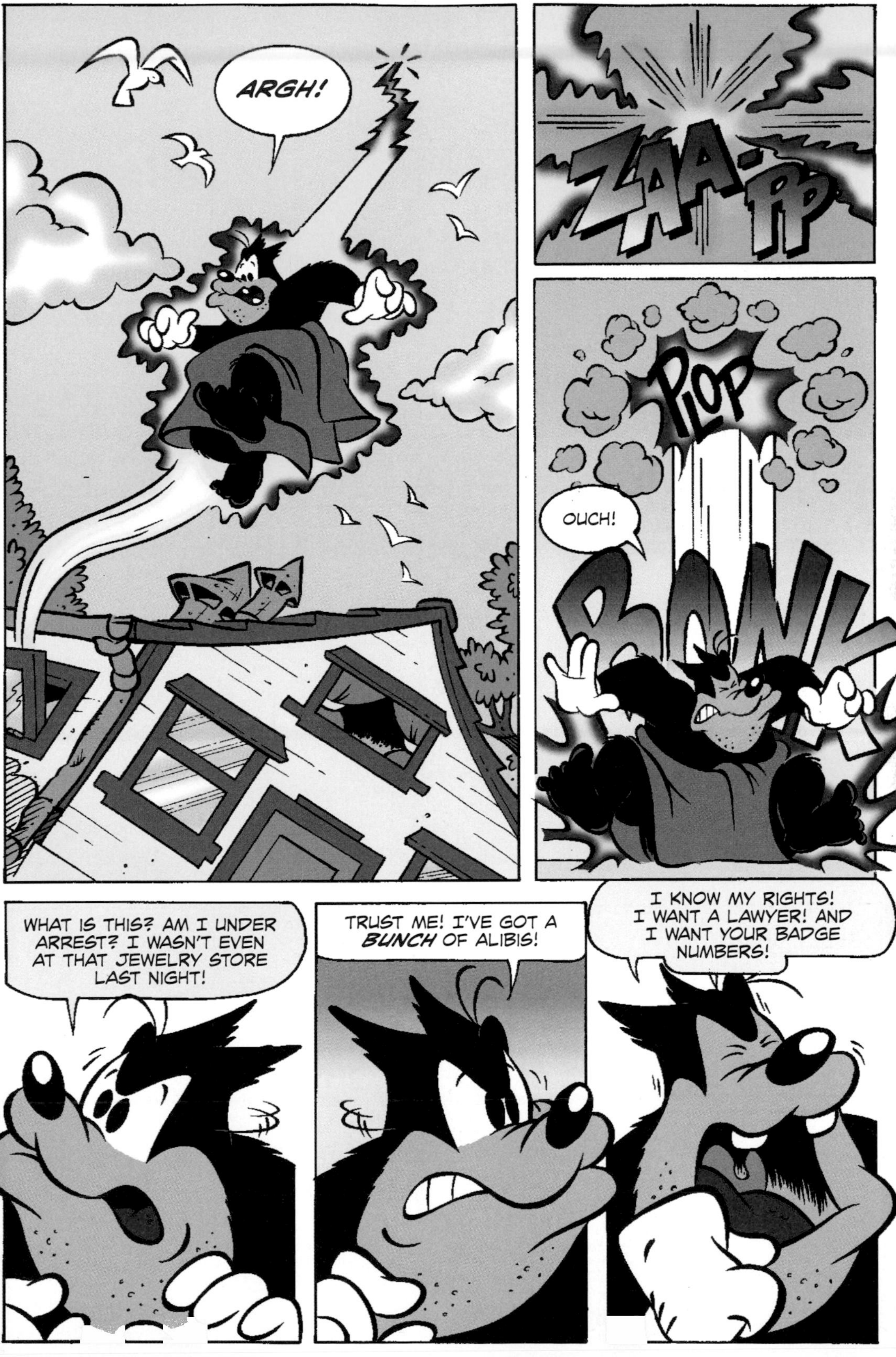
ARGH!
ZAA-PP
PLOP
OUCH!
BONK
WHAT IS THIS? AM I UNDER ARREST? I WASN'T EVEN AT THAT JEWELRY STORE LAST NIGHT!
TRUST ME! I'VE GOT A *BUNCH* OF ALIBIS!
I KNOW MY RIGHTS! I WANT A LAWYER! AND I WANT YOUR BADGE NUMBERS!

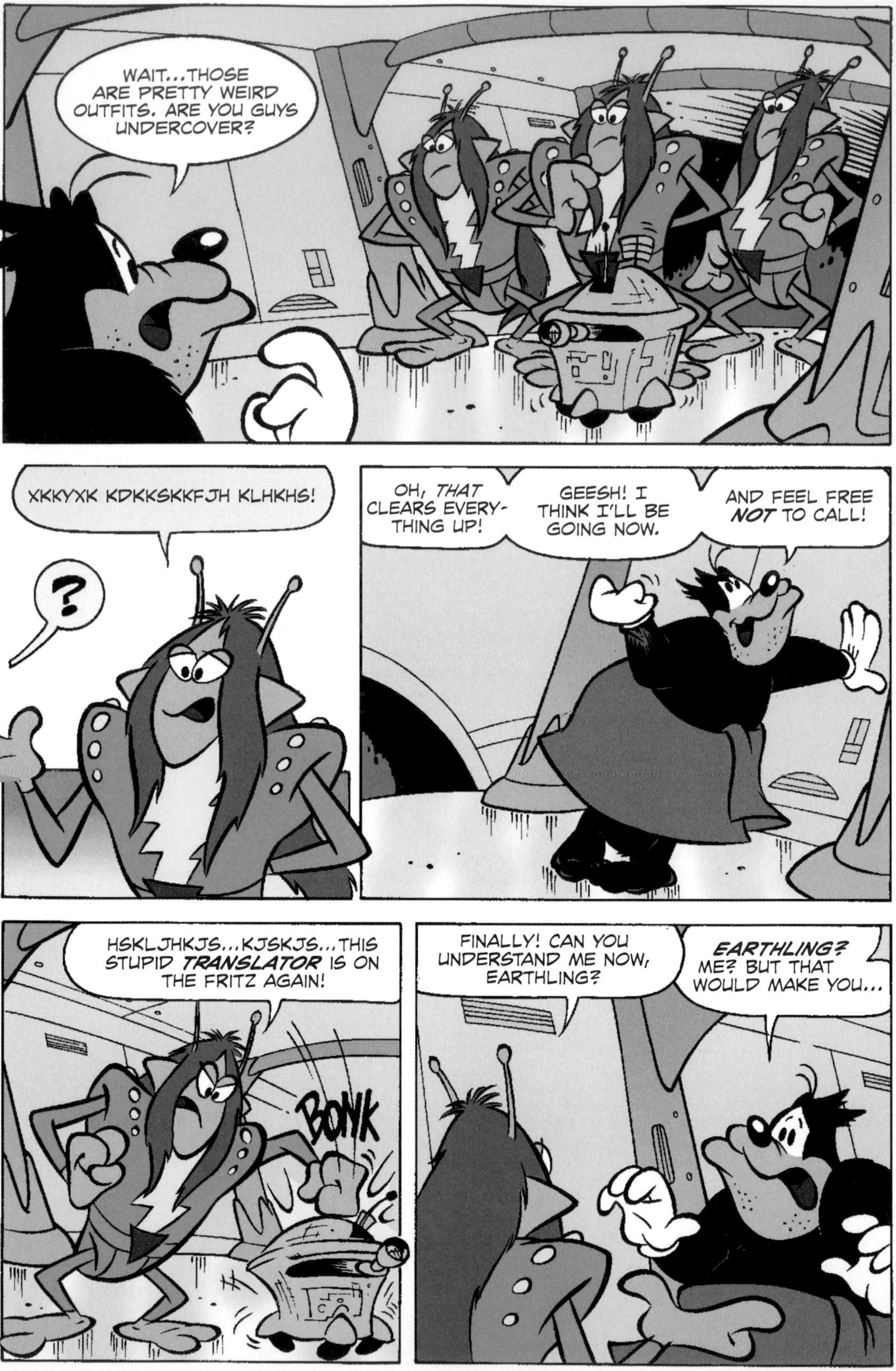
WAIT...THOSE ARE PRETTY WEIRD OUTFITS. ARE YOU GUYS UNDERCOVER?
XKKYXK KDKKSKKFJH KLHKHS!
?
OH, *THAT* CLEARS EVERY-THING UP!
GEESH! I THINK I'LL BE GOING NOW.
AND FEEL FREE *NOT* TO CALL!
HSKLJHKJS...KJSKJS...THIS STUPID *TRANSLATOR* IS ON THE FRITZ AGAIN!
BONK
FINALLY! CAN YOU UNDERSTAND ME NOW, EARTHLING?
EARTHLING? ME? BUT THAT WOULD MAKE YOU...

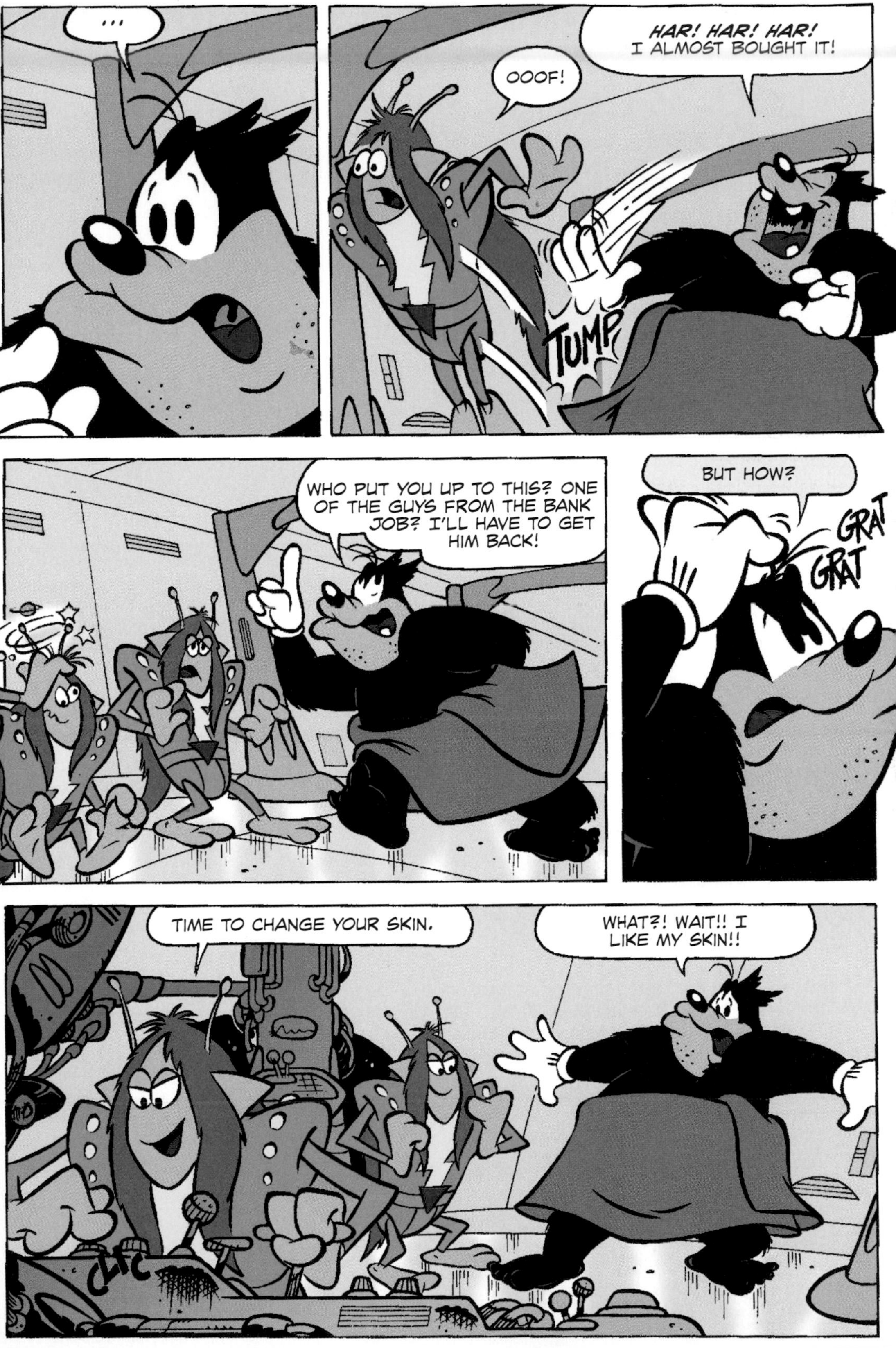
...
OOOF!
HAR! HAR! HAR! I ALMOST BOUGHT IT!
TUMP
WHO PUT YOU UP TO THIS? ONE OF THE GUYS FROM THE BANK JOB? I'LL HAVE TO GET HIM BACK!
BUT HOW?
GRAT GRAT
TIME TO CHANGE YOUR SKIN.
WHAT?! WAIT!! I LIKE MY SKIN!!
CLIC

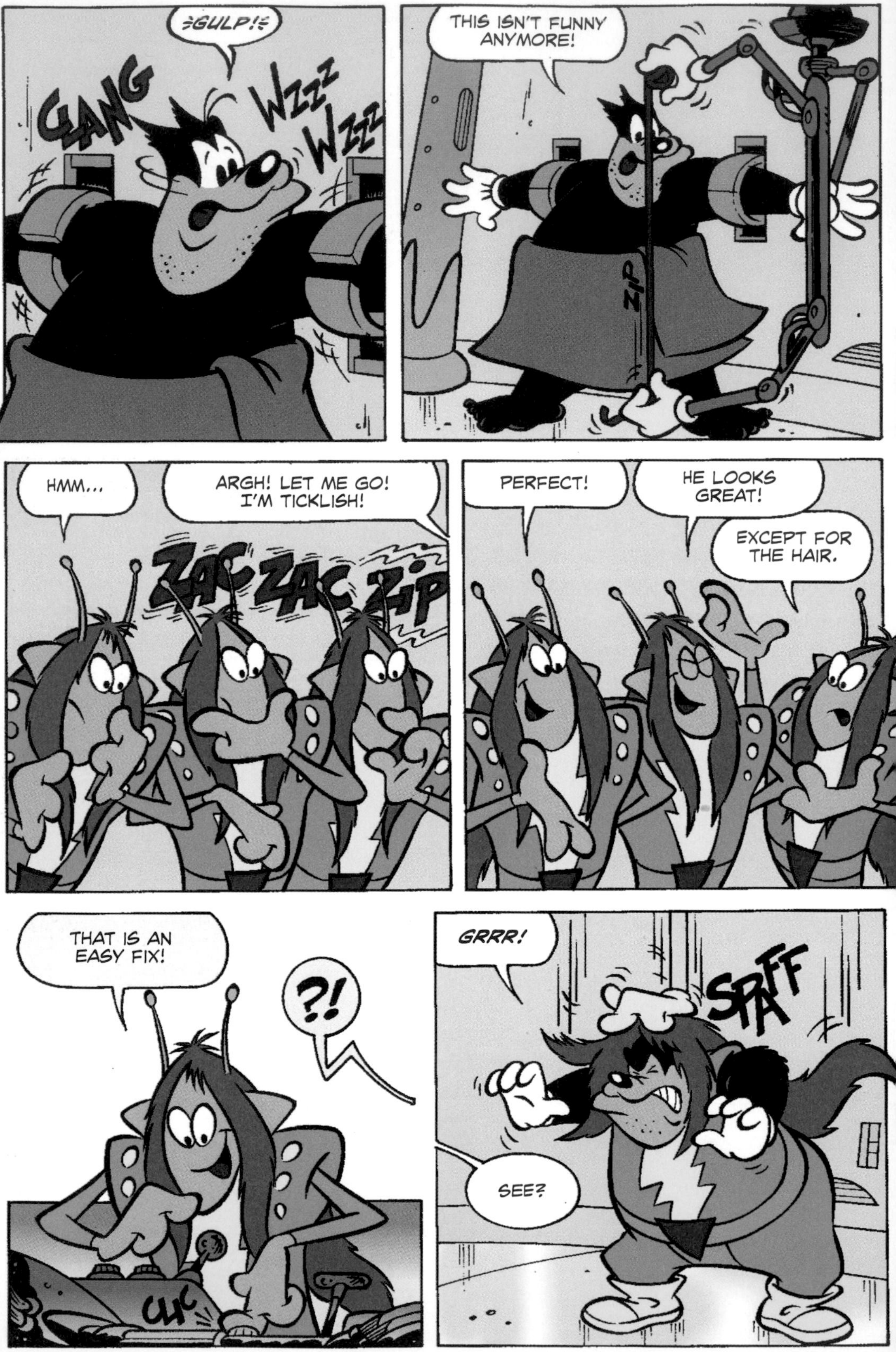
GULP!
GANG
WZZZ WZZZ
THIS ISN'T FUNNY ANYMORE!
ZIP
HMM...
ARGH! LET ME GO! I'M TICKLISH!
ZAC ZAC ZIP
PERFECT!
HE LOOKS GREAT!
EXCEPT FOR THE HAIR.
THAT IS AN EASY FIX!
?!
CLIC
GRRR!
SPAFF
SEE?

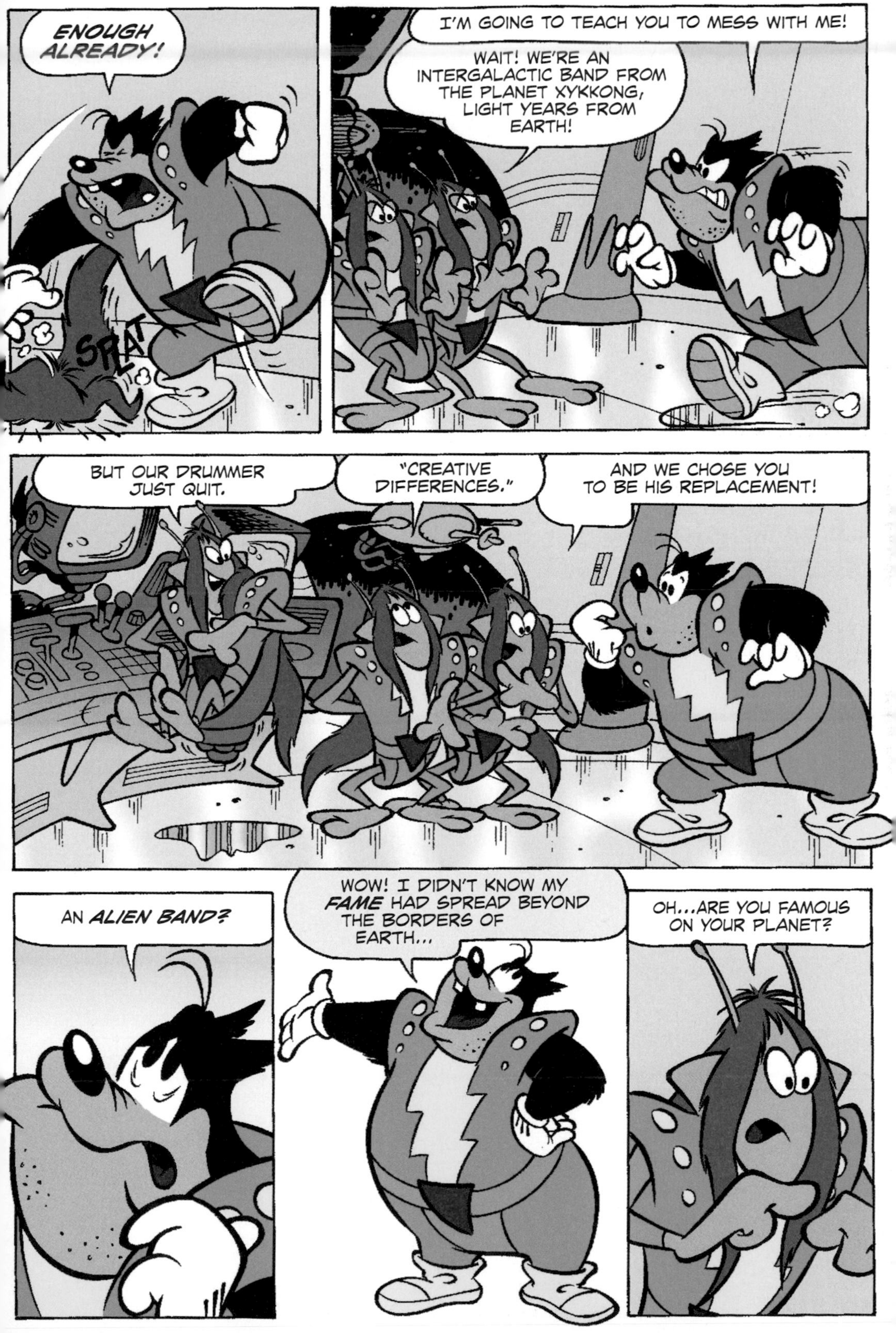
ENOUGH ALREADY!
SPLAT
I'M GOING TO TEACH YOU TO MESS WITH ME!
WAIT! WE'RE AN INTERGALACTIC BAND FROM THE PLANET XYKKONG, LIGHT YEARS FROM EARTH!
BUT OUR DRUMMER JUST QUIT.
"CREATIVE DIFFERENCES."
AND WE CHOSE YOU TO BE HIS REPLACEMENT!
AN ALIEN BAND?
WOW! I DIDN'T KNOW MY FAME HAD SPREAD BEYOND THE BORDERS OF EARTH...
OH...ARE YOU FAMOUS ON YOUR PLANET?

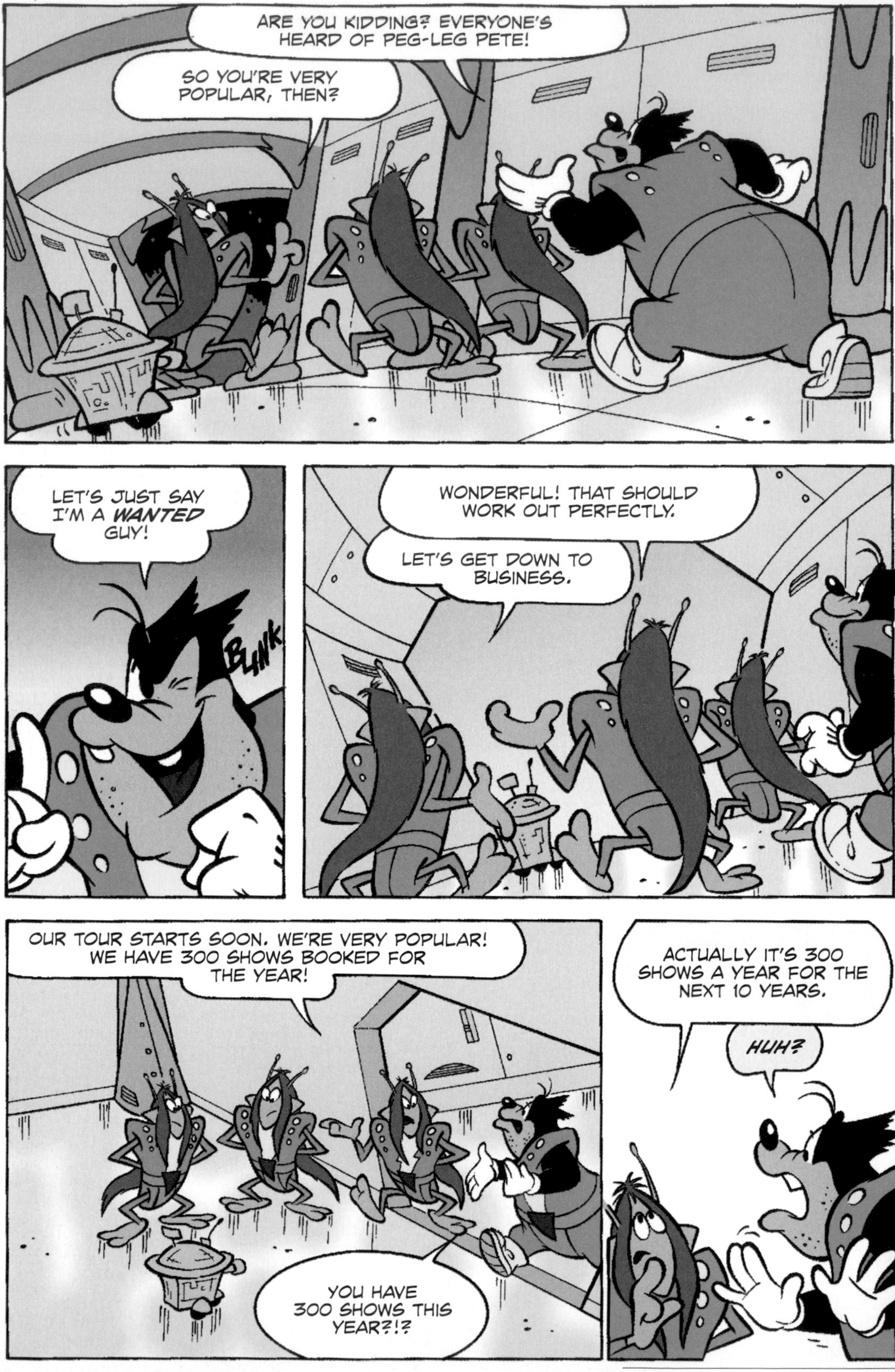
SO YOU'RE VERY POPULAR, THEN?
ARE YOU KIDDING? EVERYONE'S HEARD OF PEG-LEG PETE!
LET'S JUST SAY I'M A *WANTED* GUY!
BLINK
WONDERFUL! THAT SHOULD WORK OUT PERFECTLY.
LET'S GET DOWN TO BUSINESS.
OUR TOUR STARTS SOON. WE'RE VERY POPULAR! WE HAVE 300 SHOWS BOOKED FOR THE YEAR!
YOU HAVE 300 SHOWS THIS YEAR?!?
ACTUALLY IT'S 300 SHOWS A YEAR FOR THE NEXT 10 YEARS.
HUH?

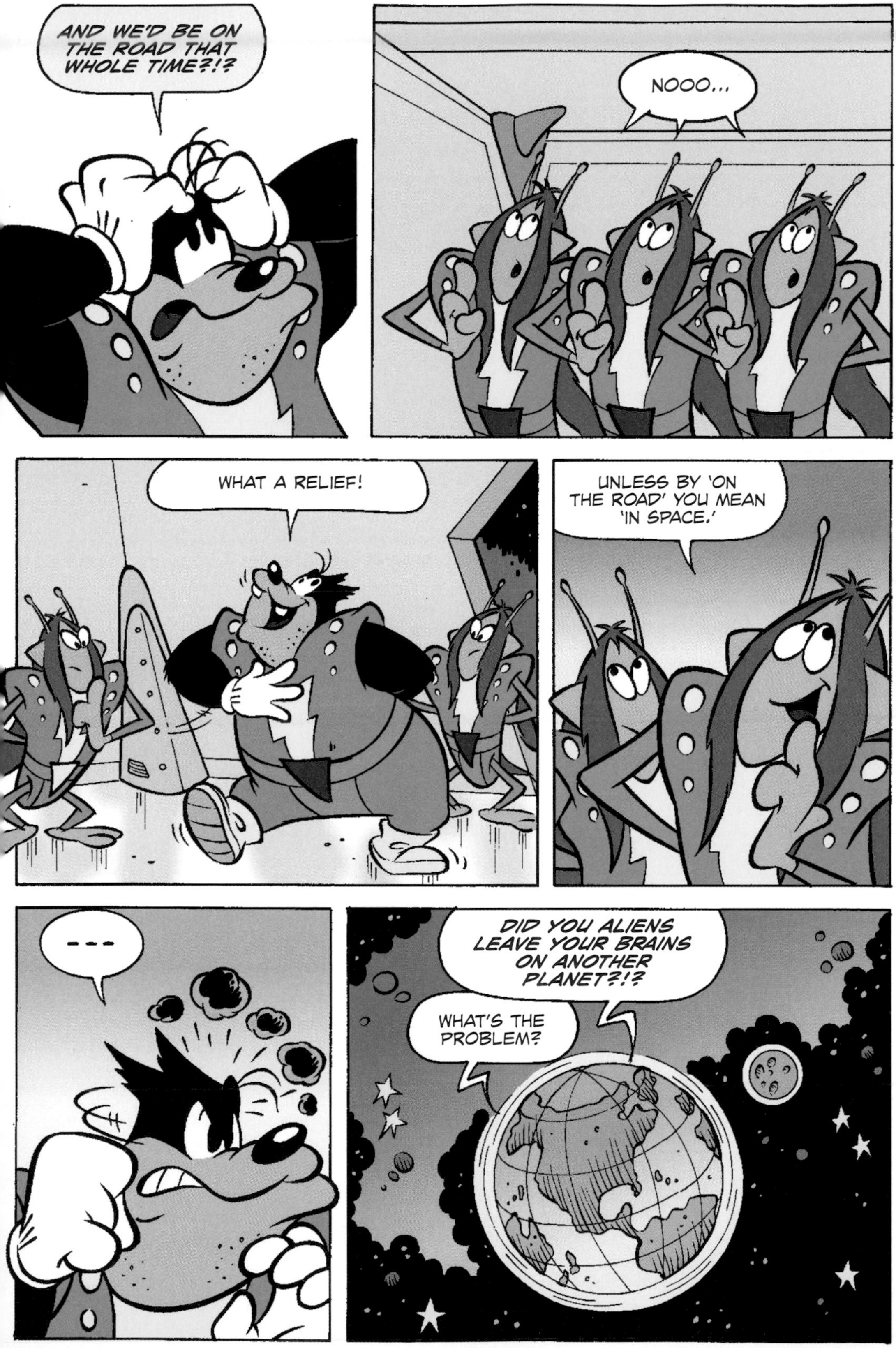
AND WE'D BE ON THE ROAD THAT WHOLE TIME?!?
NOOO...
WHAT A RELIEF!
UNLESS BY 'ON THE ROAD' YOU MEAN 'IN SPACE.'
- - -
DID YOU ALIENS LEAVE YOUR BRAINS ON ANOTHER PLANET?!?
WHAT'S THE PROBLEM?

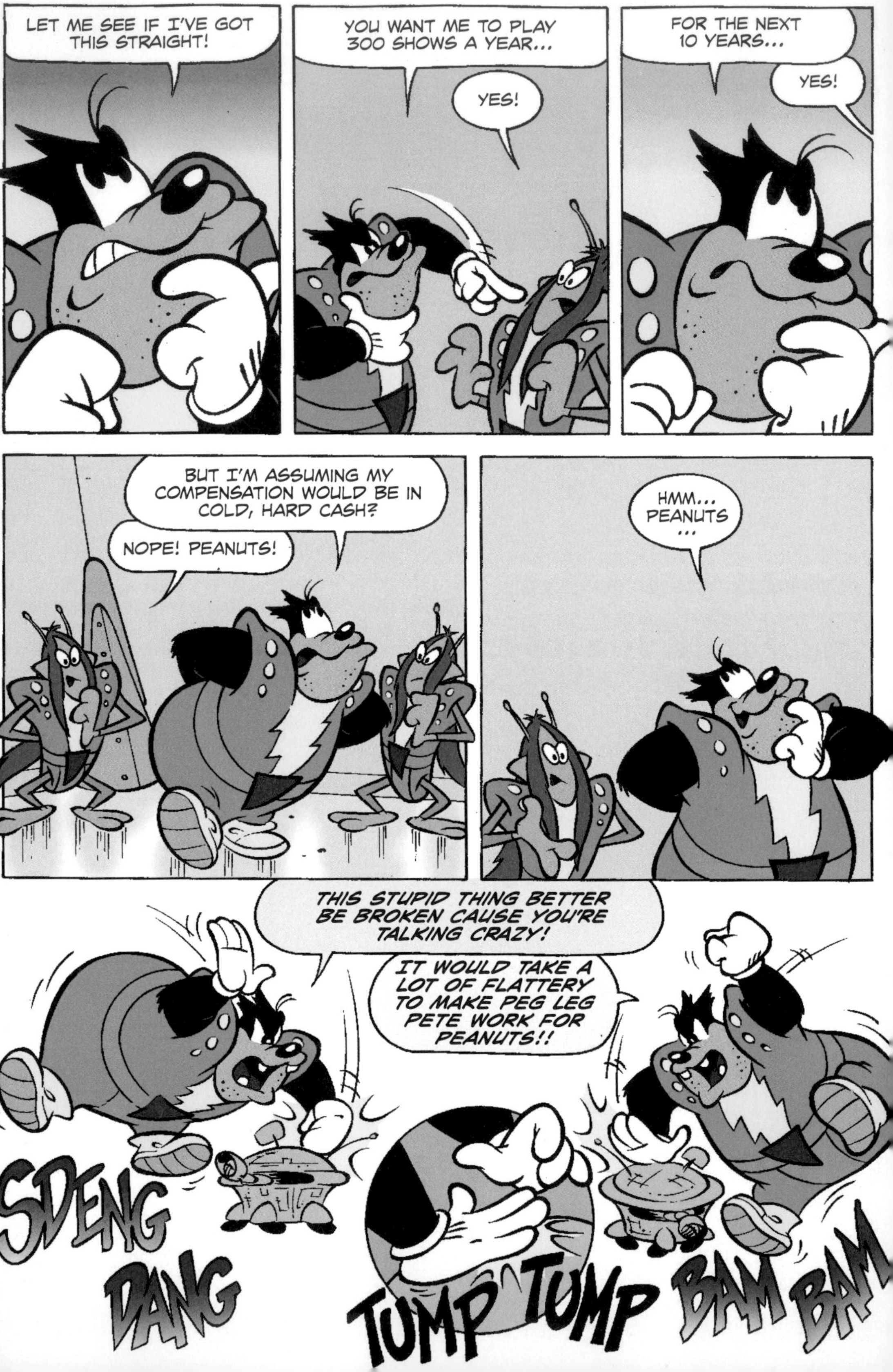
LET ME SEE IF I'VE GOT THIS STRAIGHT!
YOU WANT ME TO PLAY 300 SHOWS A YEAR...
YES!
FOR THE NEXT 10 YEARS...
YES!
BUT I'M ASSUMING MY COMPENSATION WOULD BE IN COLD, HARD CASH?
NOPE! PEANUTS!
HMM... PEANUTS ...
THIS STUPID THING BETTER BE BROKEN CAUSE YOU'RE TALKING CRAZY!
IT WOULD TAKE A LOT OF FLATTERY TO MAKE PEG LEG PETE WORK FOR PEANUTS!!
SDENG
DANG
TUMP TUMP
BAM BAM

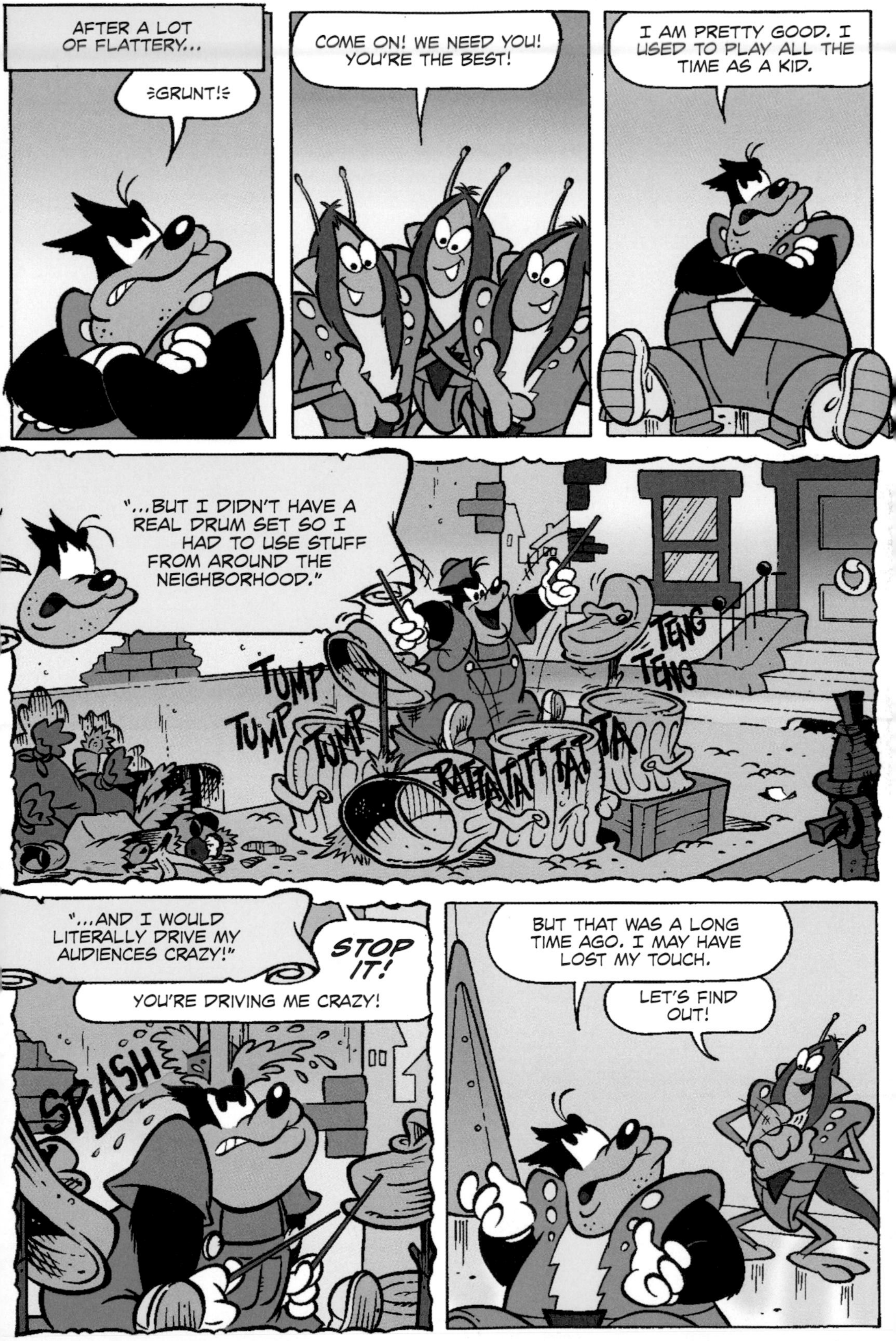
AFTER A LOT OF FLATTERY...
GRUNT!
COME ON! WE NEED YOU! YOU'RE THE BEST!
I AM PRETTY GOOD. I USED TO PLAY ALL THE TIME AS A KID.
"...BUT I DIDN'T HAVE A REAL DRUM SET SO I HAD TO USE STUFF FROM AROUND THE NEIGHBORHOOD."
TUMP
TUMP
TUMP
RATTATATT TAT TA
TENG
TENG
"...AND I WOULD LITERALLY DRIVE MY AUDIENCES CRAZY!"
STOP IT!
YOU'RE DRIVING ME CRAZY!
SPLASH
BUT THAT WAS A LONG TIME AGO. I MAY HAVE LOST MY TOUCH.
LET'S FIND OUT!

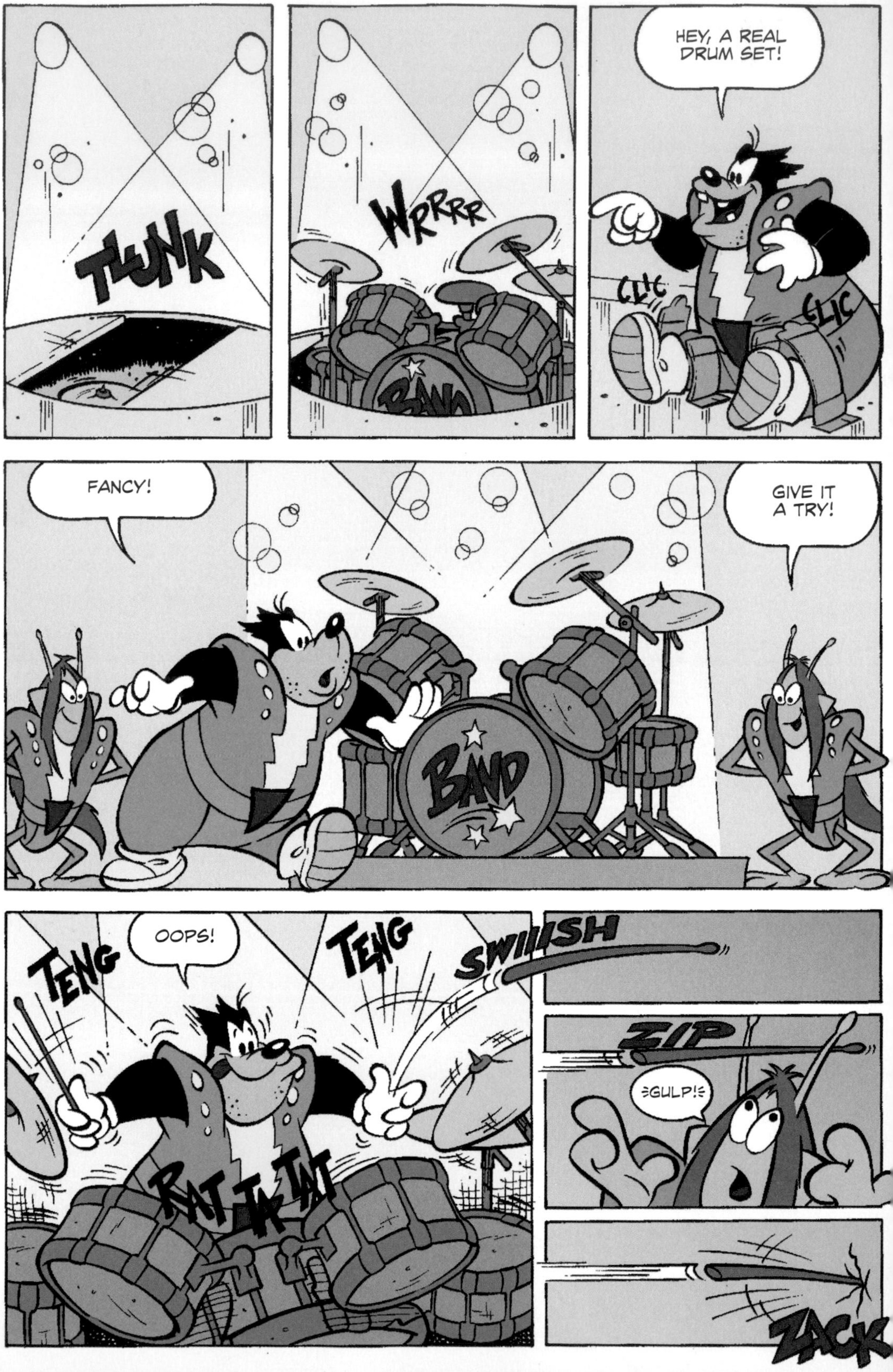

TLUNK
WRRRR
BAND
HEY, A REAL DRUM SET!
CLIC
CLIC
FANCY!
GIVE IT A TRY!
BAND
TENG
OOPS!
TENG
SWIIISH
RAT TA TAT
ZIP
GULP!
ZACK

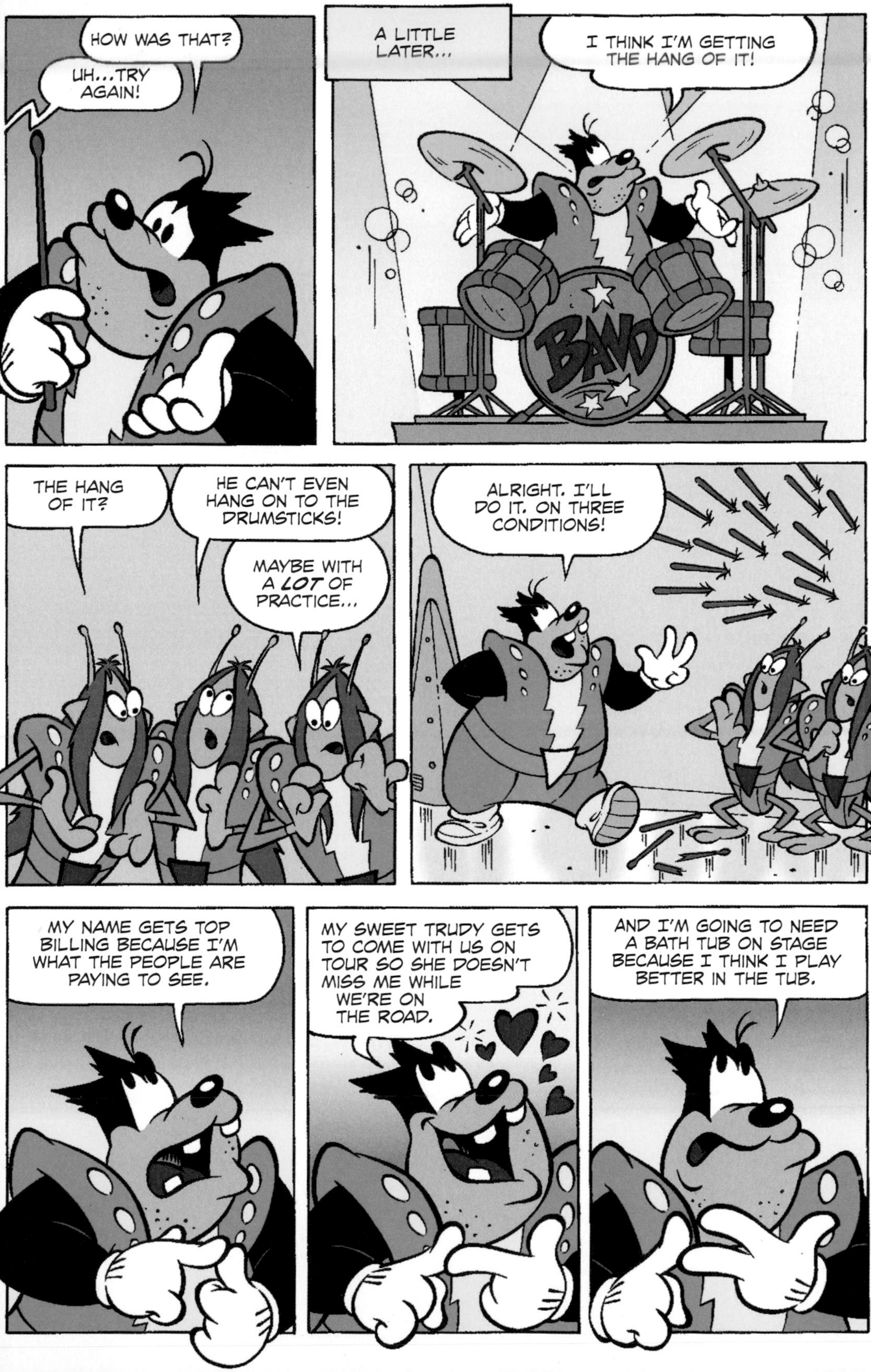

HOW WAS THAT?
UH...TRY AGAIN!
A LITTLE LATER...
I THINK I'M GETTING THE HANG OF IT!
BAND
THE HANG OF IT?
HE CAN'T EVEN HANG ON TO THE DRUMSTICKS!
MAYBE WITH A *LOT* OF PRACTICE...
ALRIGHT. I'LL DO IT. ON THREE CONDITIONS!
MY NAME GETS TOP BILLING BECAUSE I'M WHAT THE PEOPLE ARE PAYING TO SEE.
MY SWEET TRUDY GETS TO COME WITH US ON TOUR SO SHE DOESN'T MISS ME WHILE WE'RE ON THE ROAD.
AND I'M GOING TO NEED A BATH TUB ON STAGE BECAUSE I THINK I PLAY BETTER IN THE TUB.

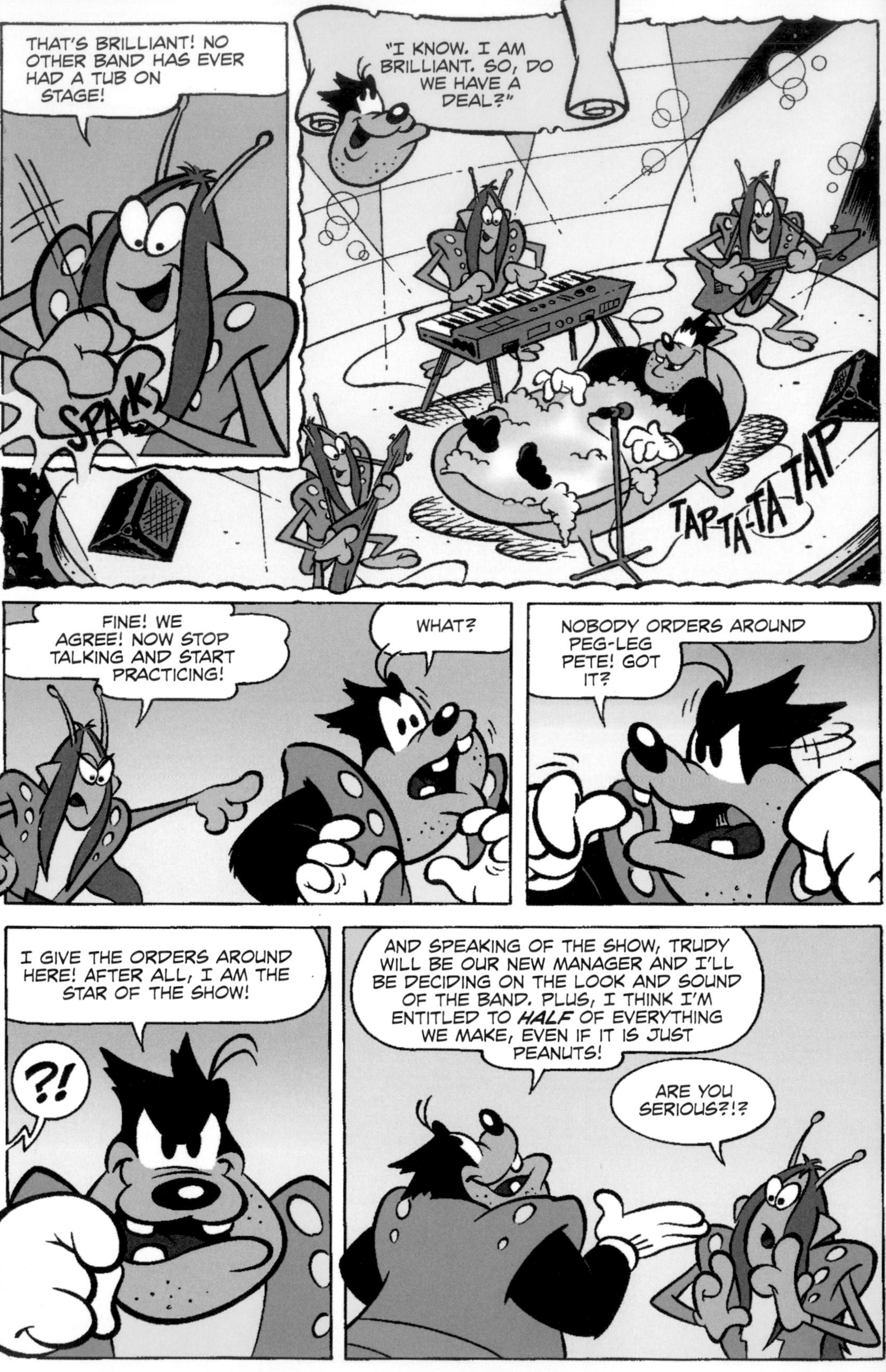
THAT'S BRILLIANT! NO OTHER BAND HAS EVER HAD A TUB ON STAGE!
SPACK
"I KNOW. I AM BRILLIANT. SO, DO WE HAVE A DEAL?"
TAP-TA-TA TAP
FINE! WE AGREE! NOW STOP TALKING AND START PRACTICING!
WHAT?
NOBODY ORDERS AROUND PEG-LEG PETE! GOT IT?
I GIVE THE ORDERS AROUND HERE! AFTER ALL, I AM THE STAR OF THE SHOW!
?!
AND SPEAKING OF THE SHOW, TRUDY WILL BE OUR NEW MANAGER AND I'LL BE DECIDING ON THE LOOK AND SOUND OF THE BAND. PLUS, I THINK I'M ENTITLED TO *HALF* OF EVERYTHING WE MAKE, EVEN IF IT IS JUST PEANUTS!
ARE YOU SERIOUS?!?

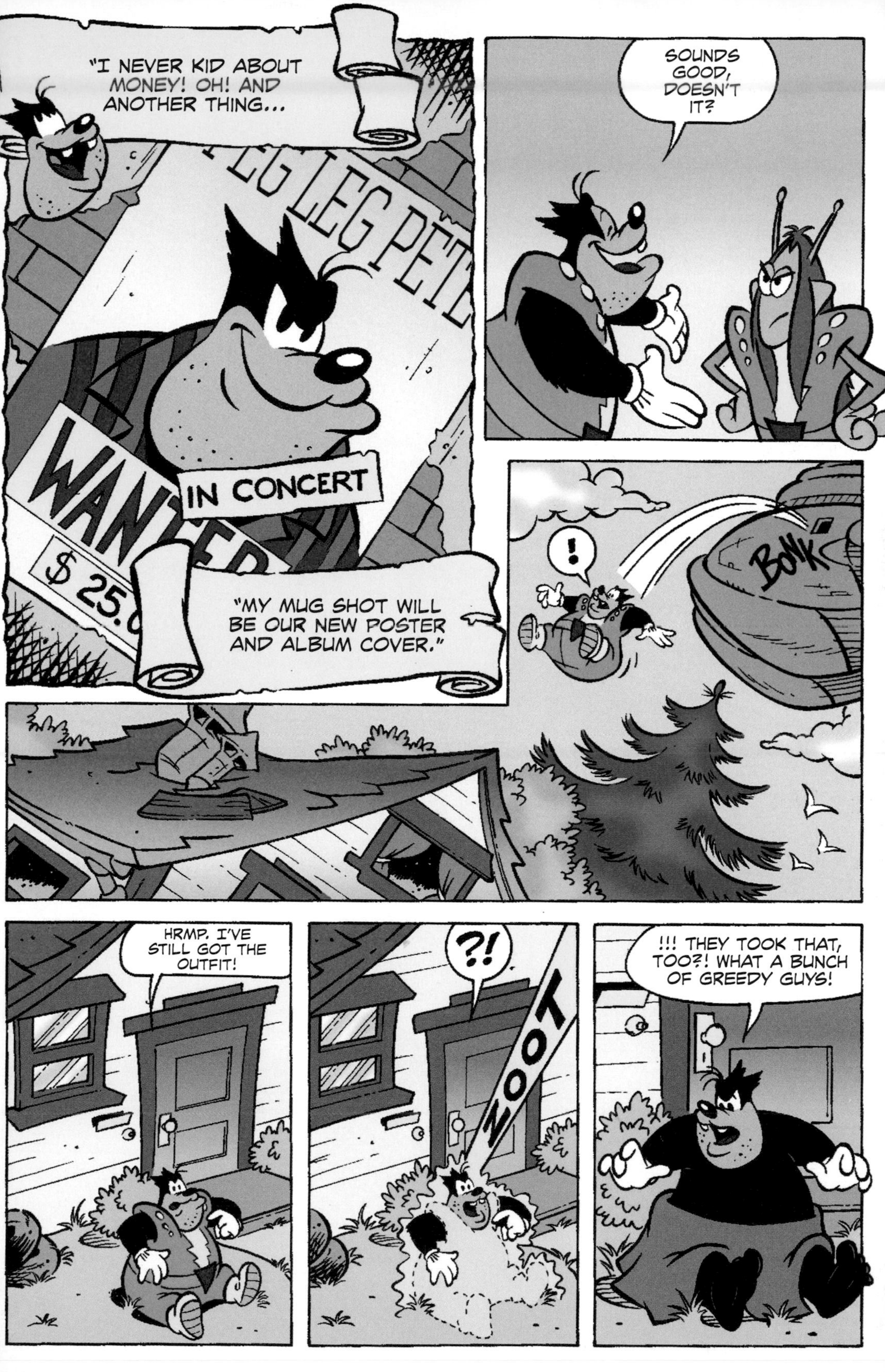
"I NEVER KID ABOUT MONEY! OH! AND ANOTHER THING...
PEG LEG PETE
WANTED
$ 25.0
IN CONCERT
"MY MUG SHOT WILL BE OUR NEW POSTER AND ALBUM COVER."
SOUNDS GOOD, DOESN'T IT?
!
BONK
HRMP. I'VE STILL GOT THE OUTFIT!
?!
ZOOT
!!! THEY TOOK THAT, TOO?! WHAT A BUNCH OF GREEDY GUYS!

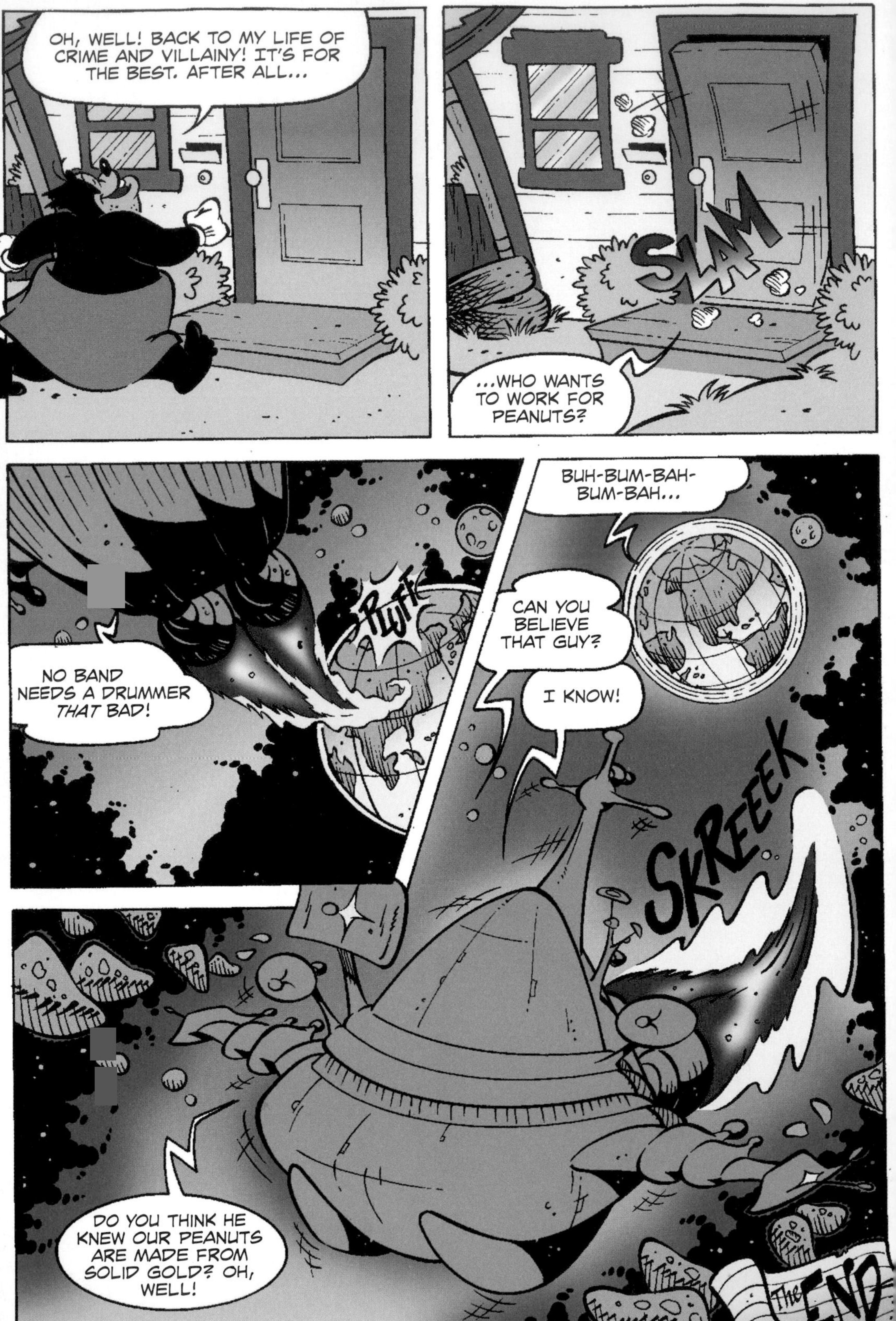
OH, WELL! BACK TO MY LIFE OF CRIME AND VILLAINY! IT'S FOR THE BEST. AFTER ALL...
SLAM
...WHO WANTS TO WORK FOR PEANUTS?
PLUFF
NO BAND NEEDS A DRUMMER *THAT* BAD!
BUH-BUM-BAH-BUM-BAH...
CAN YOU BELIEVE THAT GUY?
I KNOW!
SKREEEK
DO YOU THINK HE KNEW OUR PEANUTS ARE MADE FROM SOLID GOLD? OH, WELL!
THE END

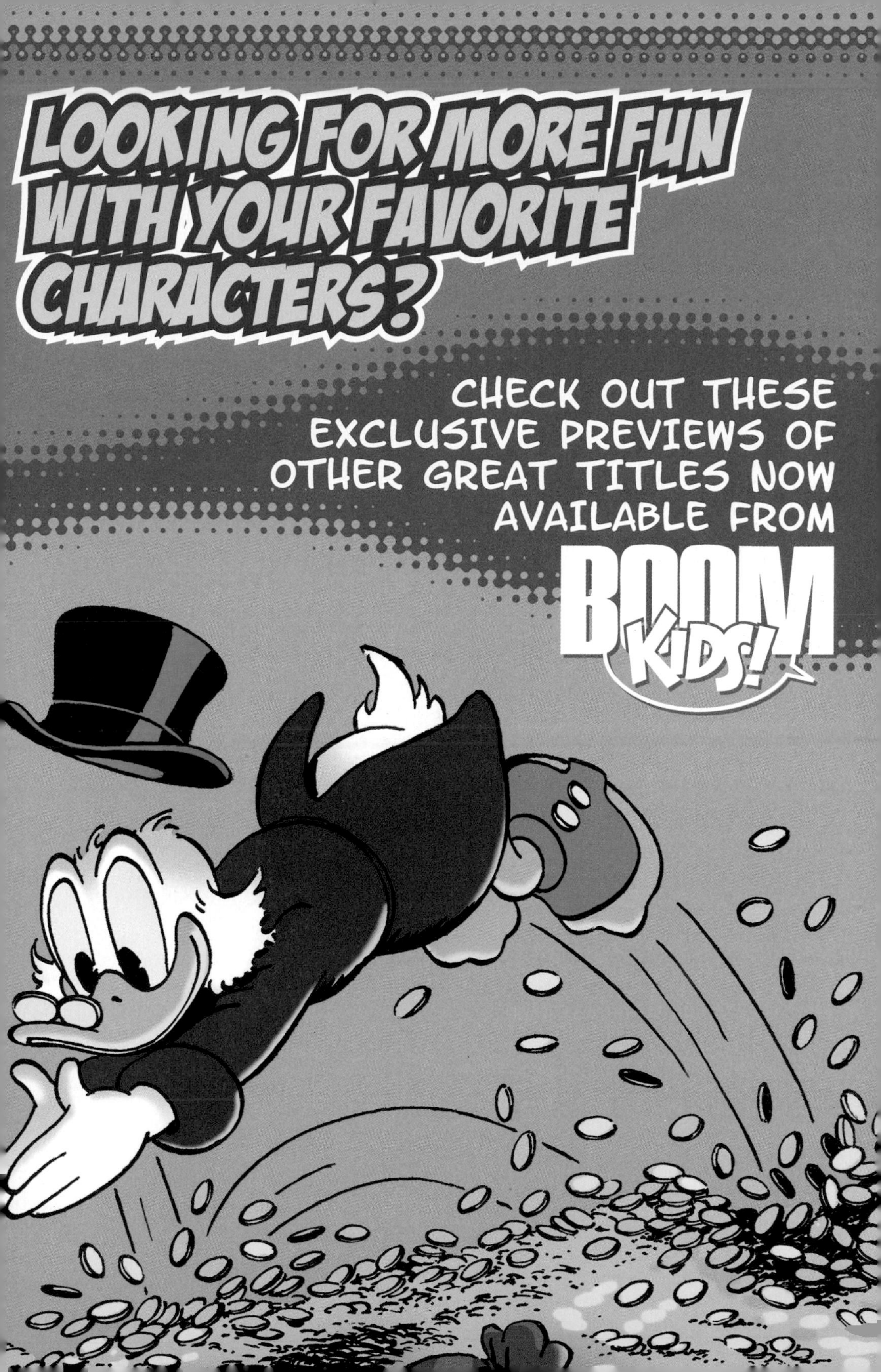

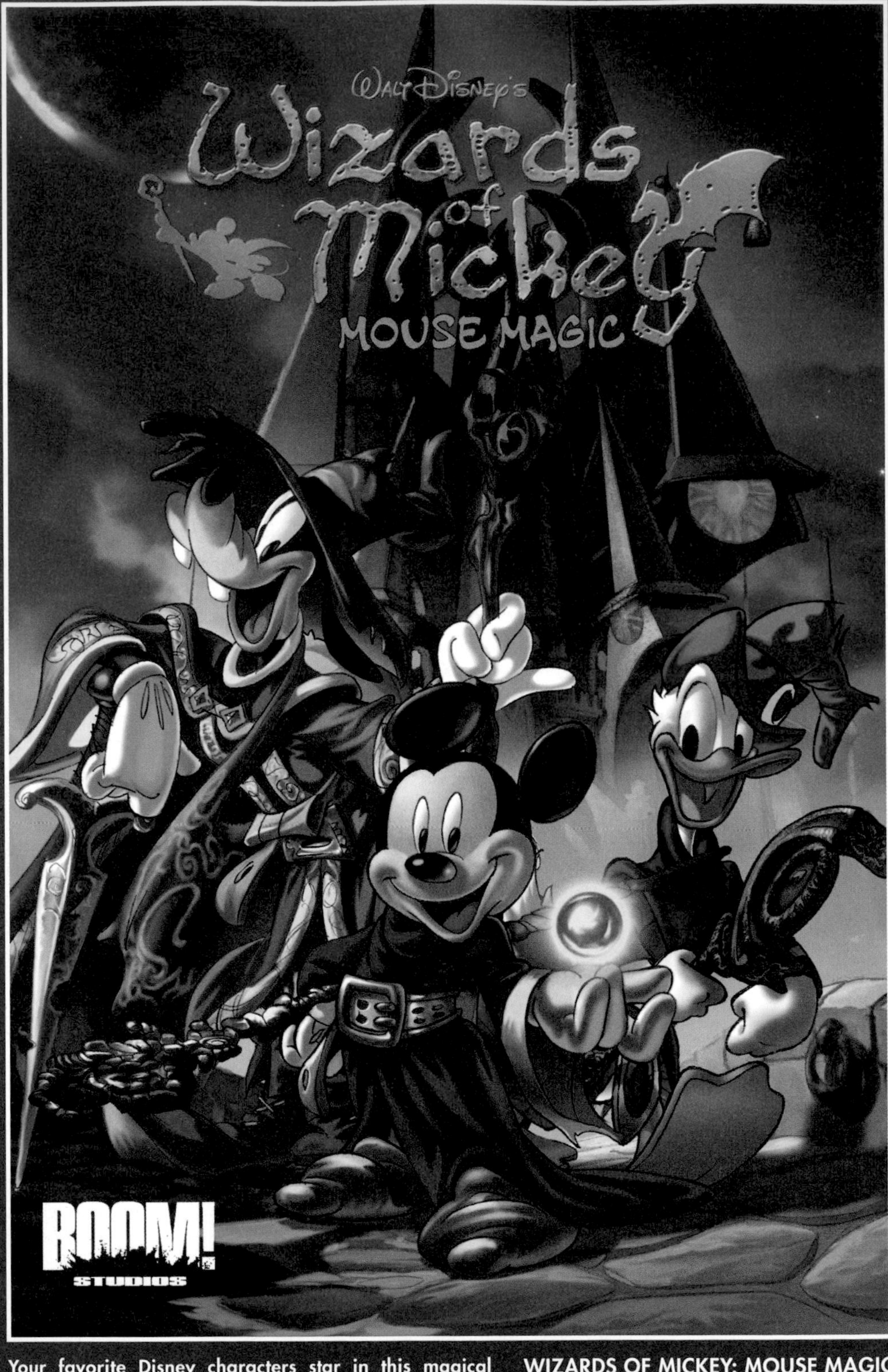
WALT DISNEY'S
Wizards of Mickey
MOUSE MAGIC
BOOM! STUDIOS

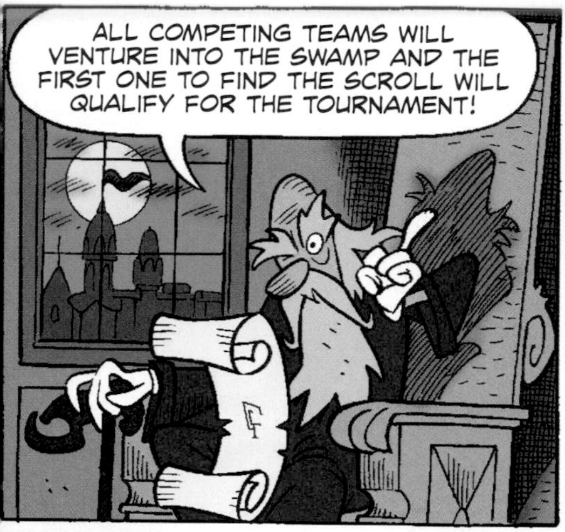
ALL COMPETING TEAMS WILL VENTURE INTO THE SWAMP AND THE FIRST ONE TO FIND THE SCROLL WILL QUALIFY FOR THE TOURNAMENT!

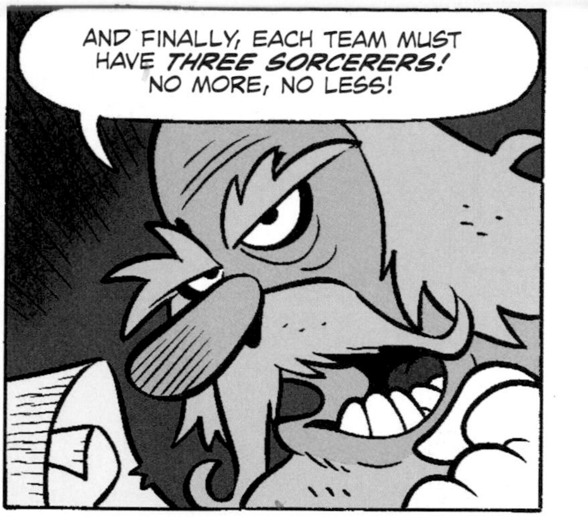
AND FINALLY, EACH TEAM MUST HAVE *THREE SORCERERS!* NO MORE, NO LESS!

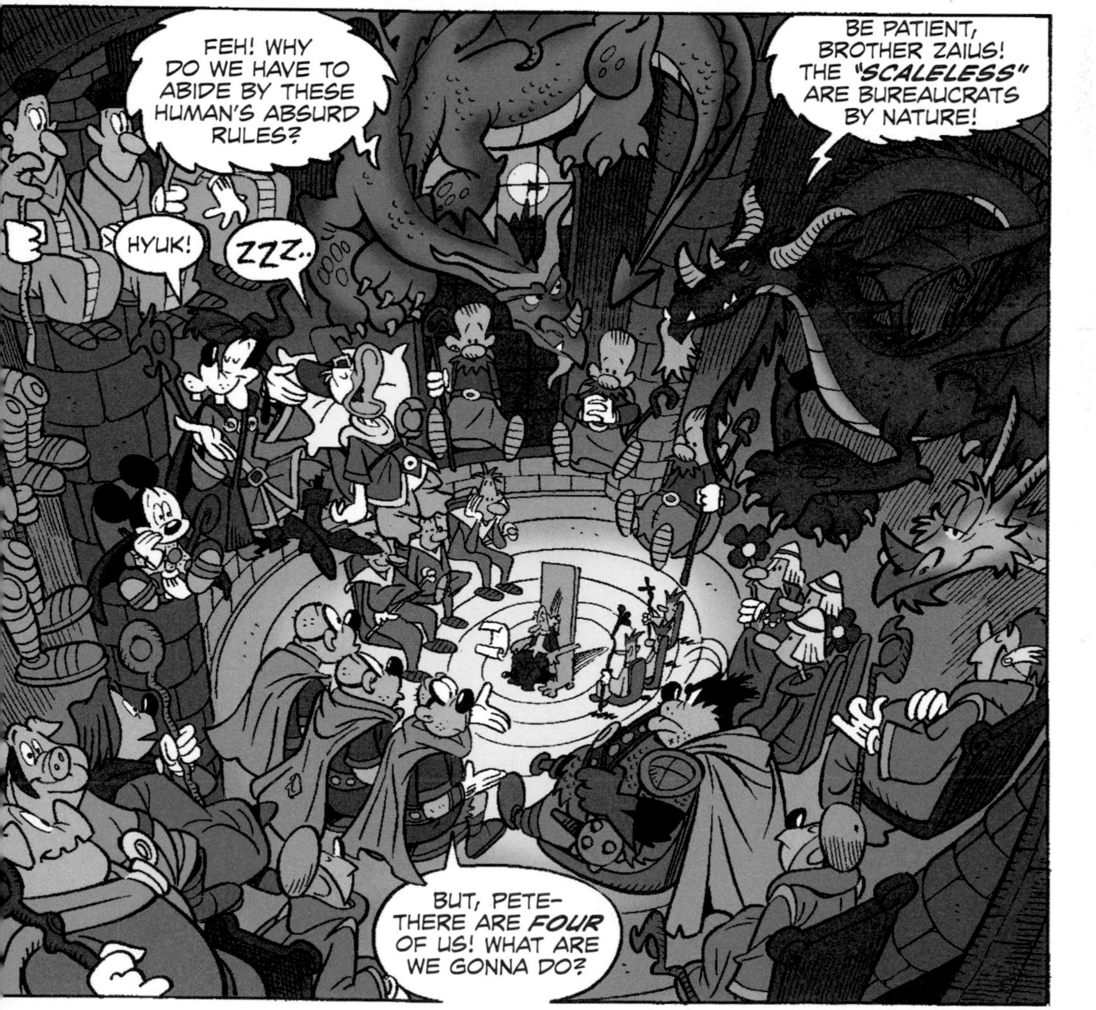
FEH! WHY DO WE HAVE TO ABIDE BY THESE HUMAN'S ABSURD RULES?
BE PATIENT, BROTHER ZAIUS! THE *"SCALELESS"* ARE BUREAUCRATS BY NATURE!
HYUK!
ZZZ..
BUT, PETE- THERE ARE *FOUR* OF US! WHAT ARE WE GONNA DO?

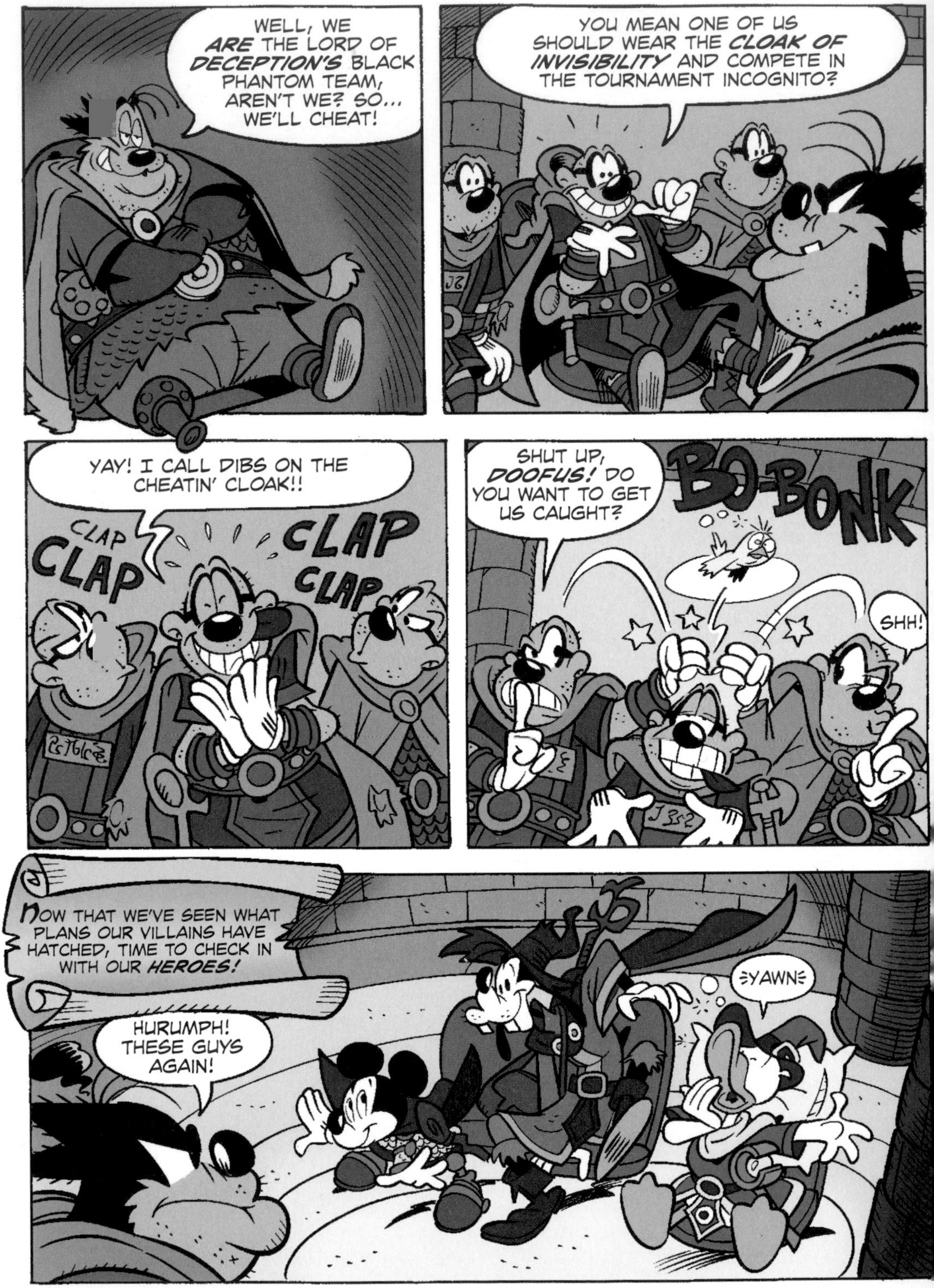

WELL, WE *ARE* THE LORD OF *DECEPTION'S* BLACK PHANTOM TEAM, AREN'T WE? SO... WE'LL CHEAT!
YOU MEAN ONE OF US SHOULD WEAR THE *CLOAK OF INVISIBILITY* AND COMPETE IN THE TOURNAMENT INCOGNITO?
YAY! I CALL DIBS ON THE CHEATIN' CLOAK!!
CLAP CLAP
CLAP CLAP
SHUT UP, *DOOFUS!* DO YOU WANT TO GET US CAUGHT?
BO-BONK
SHH!
NOW THAT WE'VE SEEN WHAT PLANS OUR VILLAINS HAVE HATCHED, TIME TO CHECK IN WITH OUR *HEROES!*
HURUMPH! THESE GUYS AGAIN!
YAWN

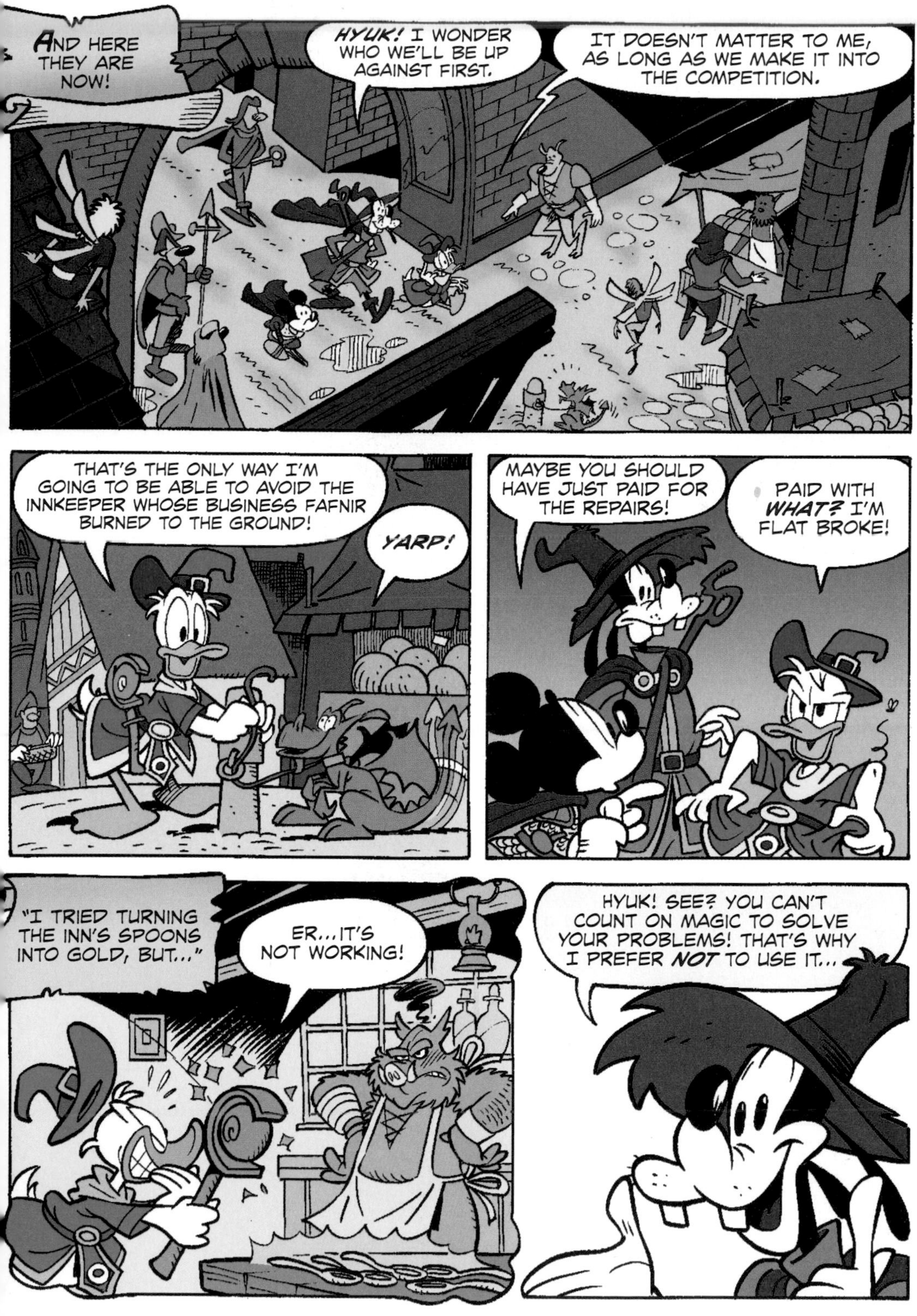
AND HERE THEY ARE NOW!
HYUK! I WONDER WHO WE'LL BE UP AGAINST FIRST.
IT DOESN'T MATTER TO ME, AS LONG AS WE MAKE IT INTO THE COMPETITION.
THAT'S THE ONLY WAY I'M GOING TO BE ABLE TO AVOID THE INNKEEPER WHOSE BUSINESS FAFNIR BURNED TO THE GROUND!
YARP!
MAYBE YOU SHOULD HAVE JUST PAID FOR THE REPAIRS!
PAID WITH WHAT? I'M FLAT BROKE!
"I TRIED TURNING THE INN'S SPOONS INTO GOLD, BUT..."
ER...IT'S NOT WORKING!
HYUK! SEE? YOU CAN'T COUNT ON MAGIC TO SOLVE YOUR PROBLEMS! THAT'S WHY I PREFER NOT TO USE IT...

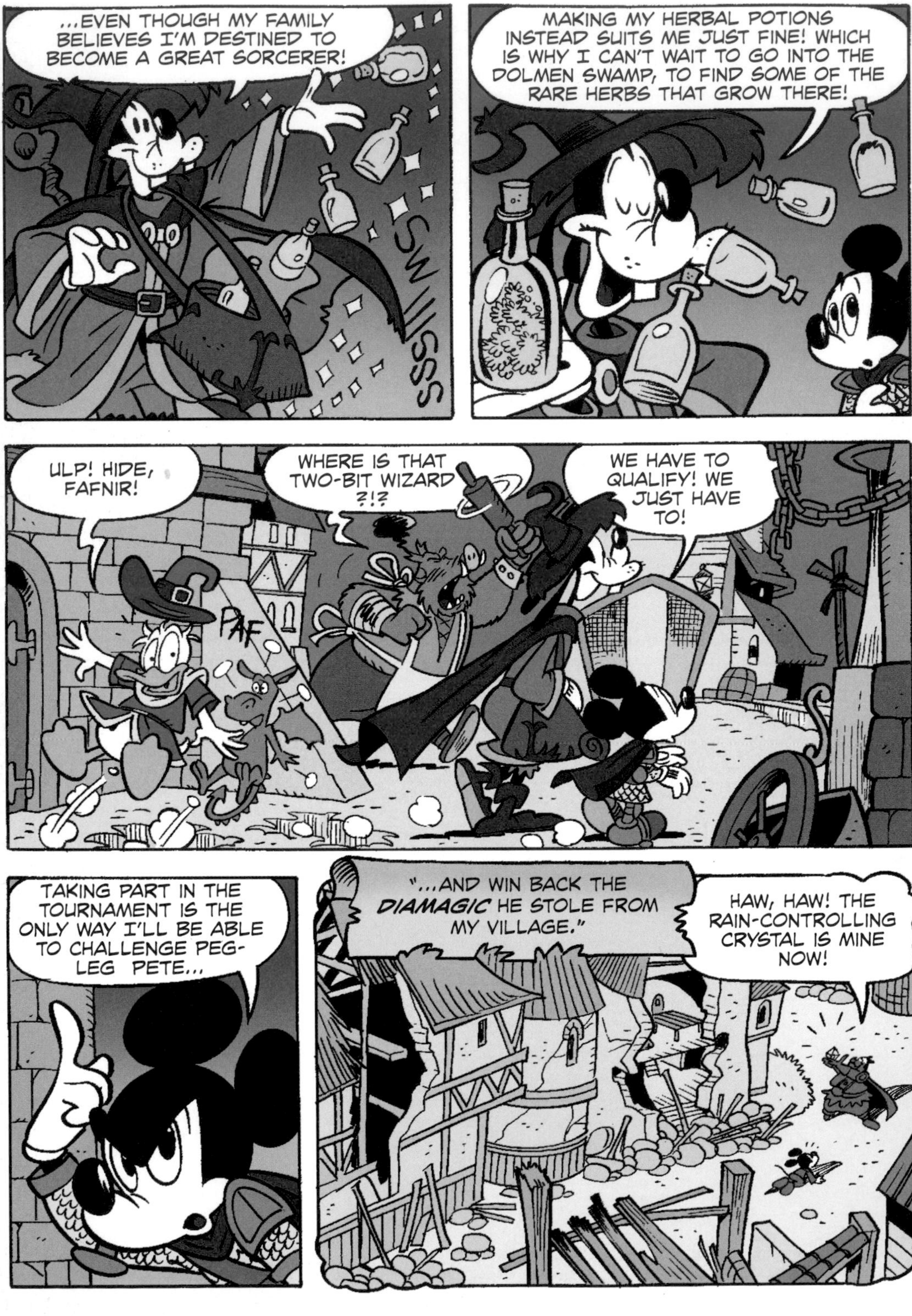
...EVEN THOUGH MY FAMILY BELIEVES I'M DESTINED TO BECOME A GREAT SORCERER!
SWISSS
MAKING MY HERBAL POTIONS INSTEAD SUITS ME JUST FINE! WHICH IS WHY I CAN'T WAIT TO GO INTO THE DOLMEN SWAMP, TO FIND SOME OF THE RARE HERBS THAT GROW THERE!
ULP! HIDE, FAFNIR!
WHERE IS THAT TWO-BIT WIZARD ?!?
WE HAVE TO QUALIFY! WE JUST HAVE TO!
PAF
TAKING PART IN THE TOURNAMENT IS THE ONLY WAY I'LL BE ABLE TO CHALLENGE PEG-LEG PETE...
"...AND WIN BACK THE DIAMAGIC HE STOLE FROM MY VILLAGE."
HAW, HAW! THE RAIN-CONTROLLING CRYSTAL IS MINE NOW!

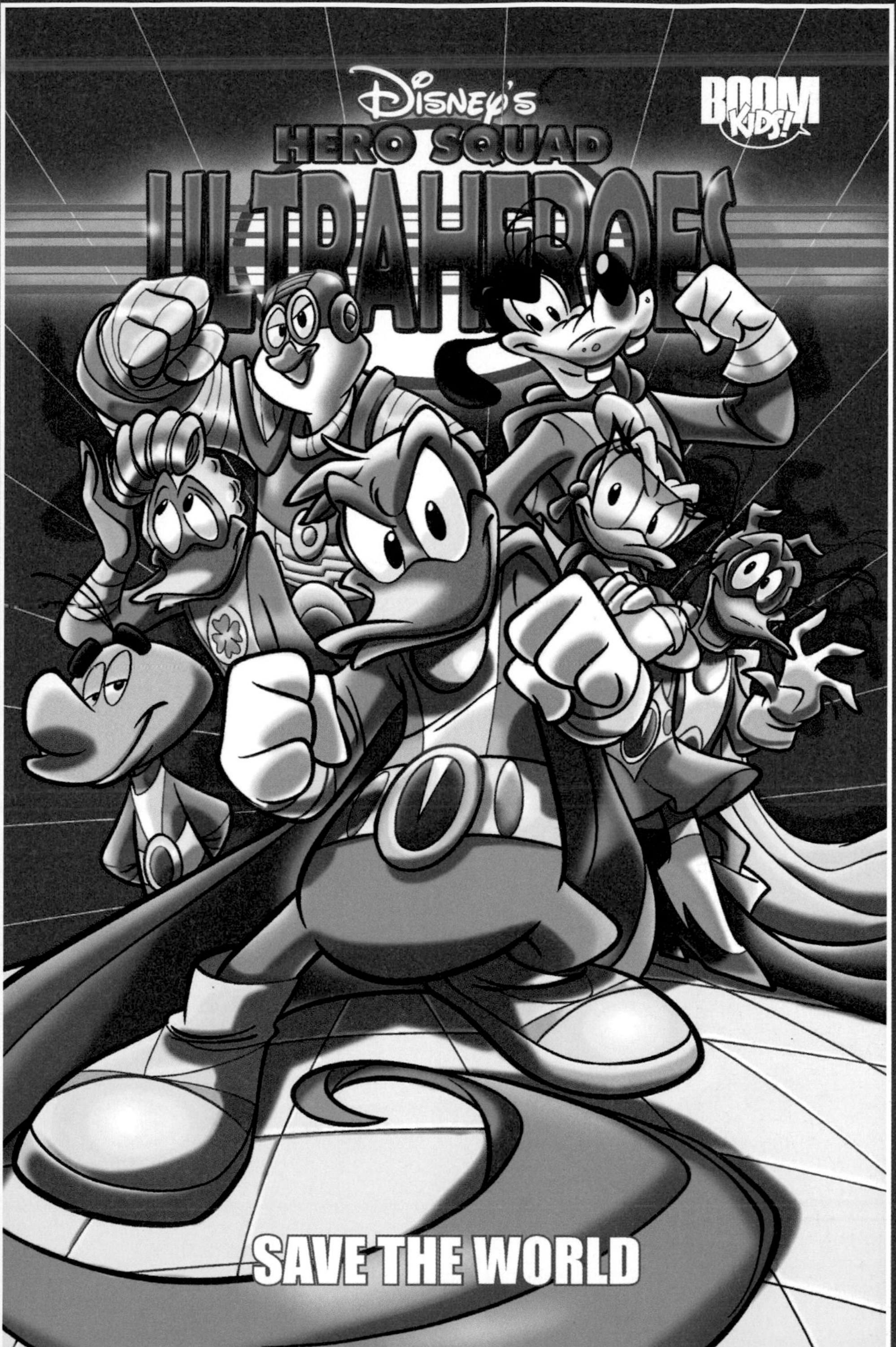
DISNEY'S
HERO SQUAD
ULTRAHEROES
BOOM KIDS!
SAVE THE WORLD

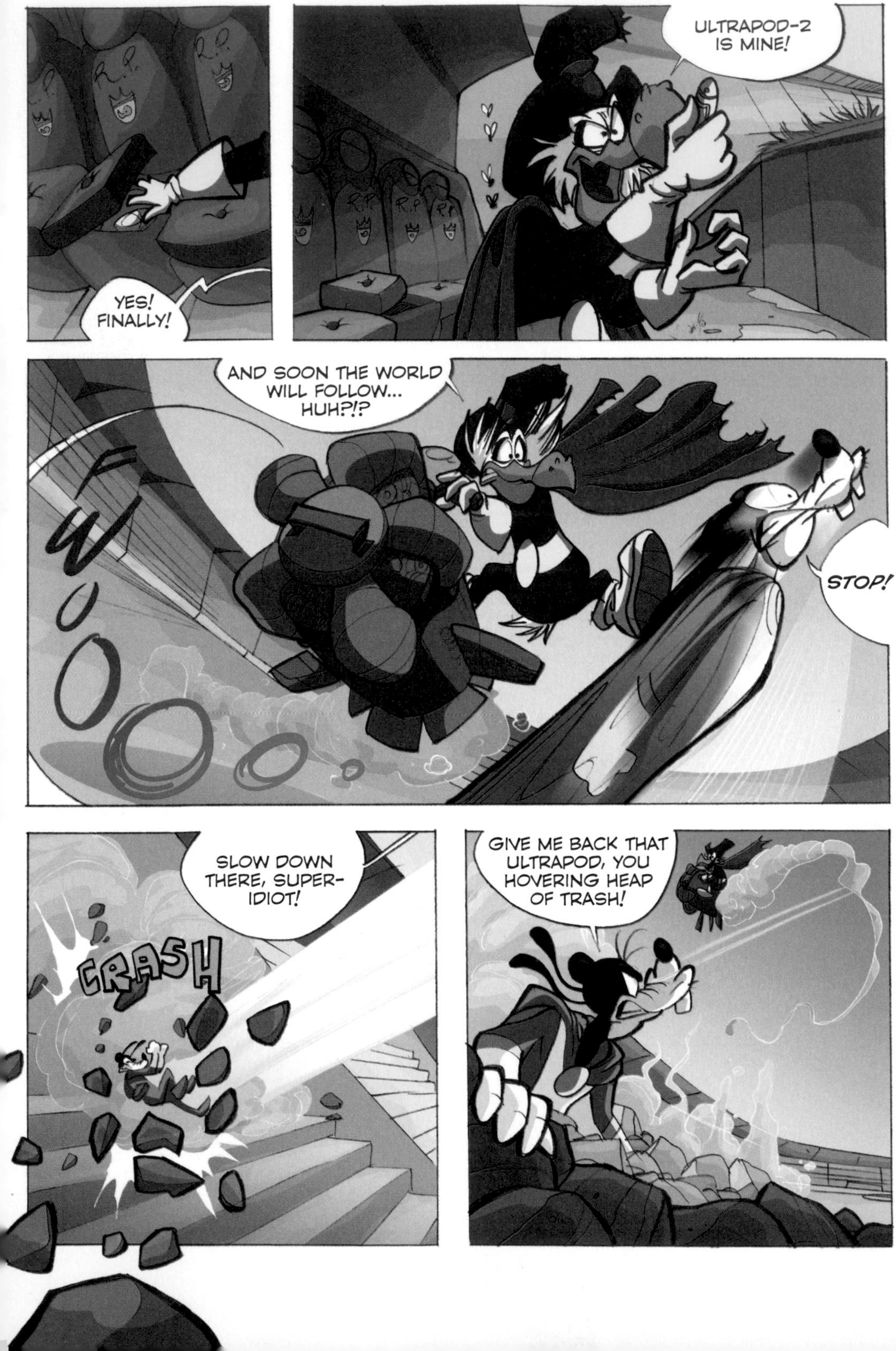
YES! FINALLY!
ULTRAPOD-2 IS MINE!
AND SOON THE WORLD WILL FOLLOW... HUH?!?
STOP!
SLOW DOWN THERE, SUPER-IDIOT!
CRASH
GIVE ME BACK THAT ULTRAPOD, YOU HOVERING HEAP OF TRASH!

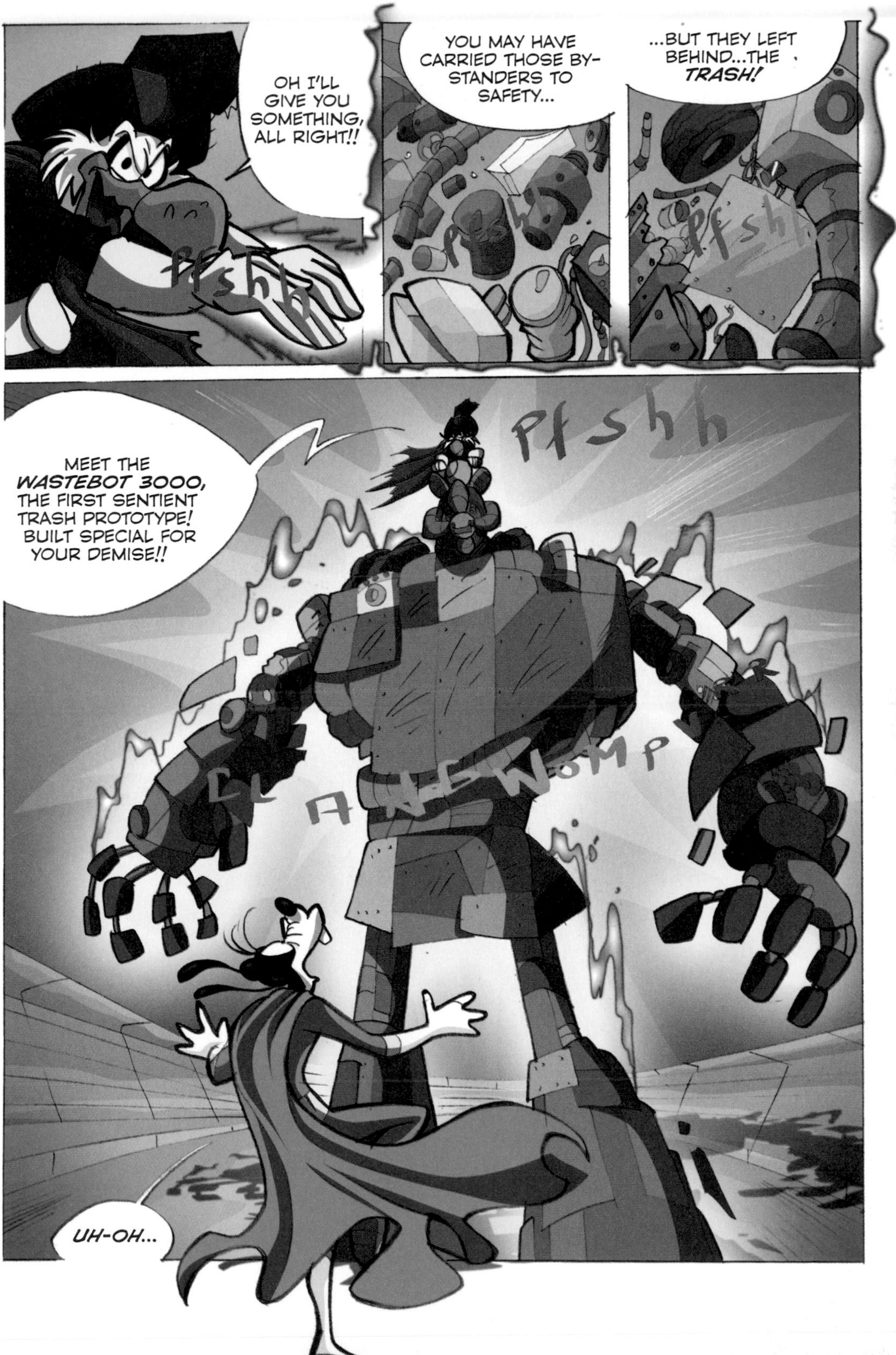
OH I'LL GIVE YOU SOMETHING, ALL RIGHT!!
Pfshh
YOU MAY HAVE CARRIED THOSE BY-STANDERS TO SAFETY...
Pfshh
...BUT THEY LEFT BEHIND...THE *TRASH!*
Pfshh
MEET THE *WASTEBOT 3000,* THE FIRST SENTIENT TRASH PROTOTYPE! BUILT SPECIAL FOR YOUR DEMISE!!
Pfshh
CLANGWOMP
UH-OH...

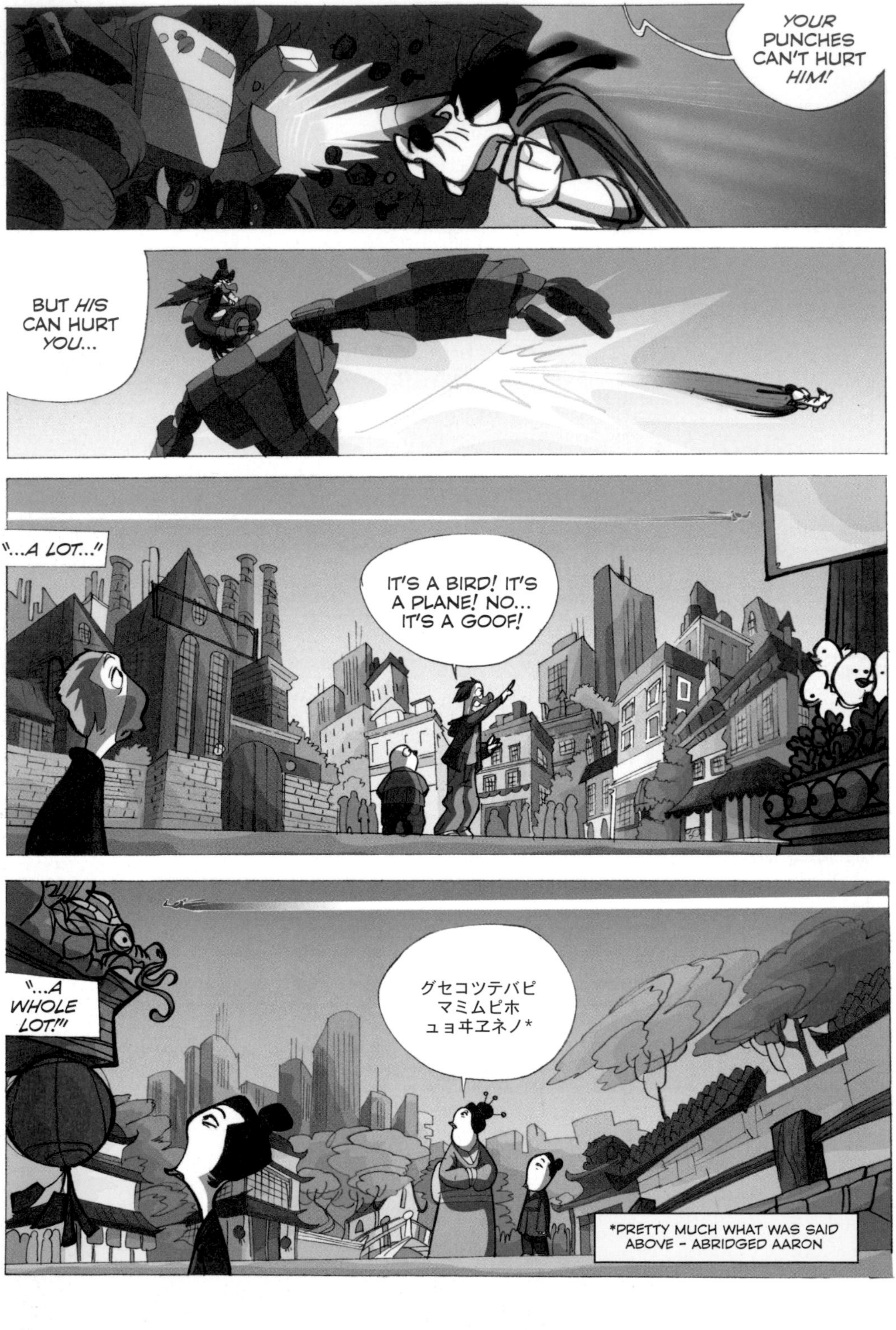
YOUR PUNCHES CAN'T HURT HIM!
BUT HIS CAN HURT YOU...
"...A LOT..."
IT'S A BIRD! IT'S A PLANE! NO... IT'S A GOOF!
"...A WHOLE LOT!"
グセコツテバピ
マミムピホ
ュヨ丮ヱネノ*
*PRETTY MUCH WHAT WAS SAID ABOVE - ABRIDGED AARON

WALT DISNEY's
DONALD DUCK
AND FRIENDS

DOUBLE DUCK

DISNEY'S SECRET AGENT!

Donald Duck...as a secret agent? Villainous
fiends beware as the world of super-sleuthing
and espionage will never be the same! This is
Donald Duck like you've never seen him!

DONALD DUCK AND FRIENDS: DOUBLE DUCK
DIAMOND CODE: DEC090752
SC $9.99 ISBN 978160886545
HC $24.99 ISBN 978160886551

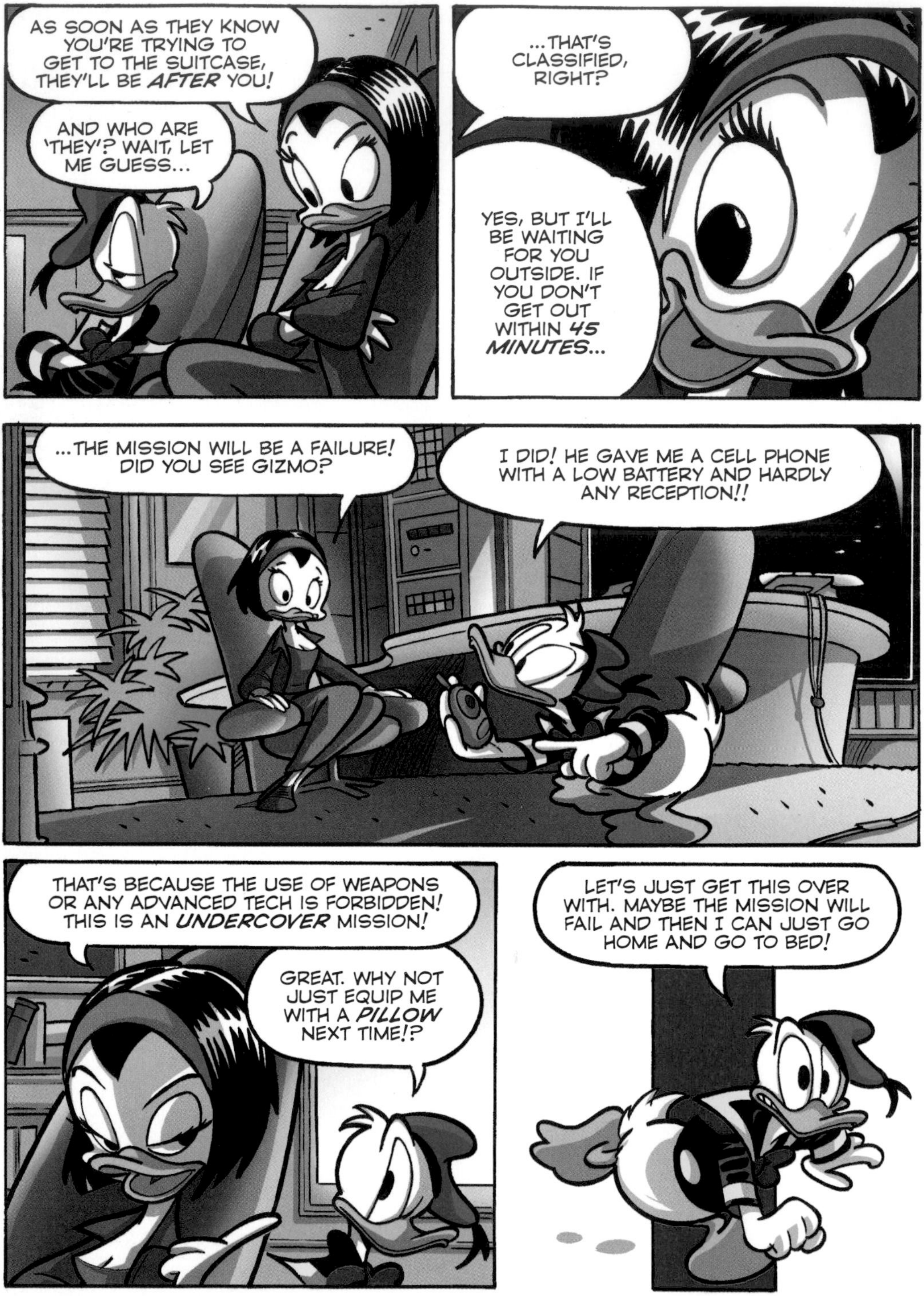
AS SOON AS THEY KNOW YOU'RE TRYING TO GET TO THE SUITCASE, THEY'LL BE *AFTER* YOU!
AND WHO ARE 'THEY'? WAIT, LET ME GUESS...
...THAT'S CLASSIFIED, RIGHT?
YES, BUT I'LL BE WAITING FOR YOU OUTSIDE. IF YOU DON'T GET OUT WITHIN *45 MINUTES*...
...THE MISSION WILL BE A FAILURE! DID YOU SEE GIZMO?
I DID! HE GAVE ME A CELL PHONE WITH A LOW BATTERY AND HARDLY ANY RECEPTION!!
THAT'S BECAUSE THE USE OF WEAPONS OR ANY ADVANCED TECH IS FORBIDDEN! THIS IS AN *UNDERCOVER* MISSION!
GREAT. WHY NOT JUST EQUIP ME WITH A *PILLOW* NEXT TIME!?
LET'S JUST GET THIS OVER WITH. MAYBE THE MISSION WILL FAIL AND THEN I CAN JUST GO HOME AND GO TO BED!

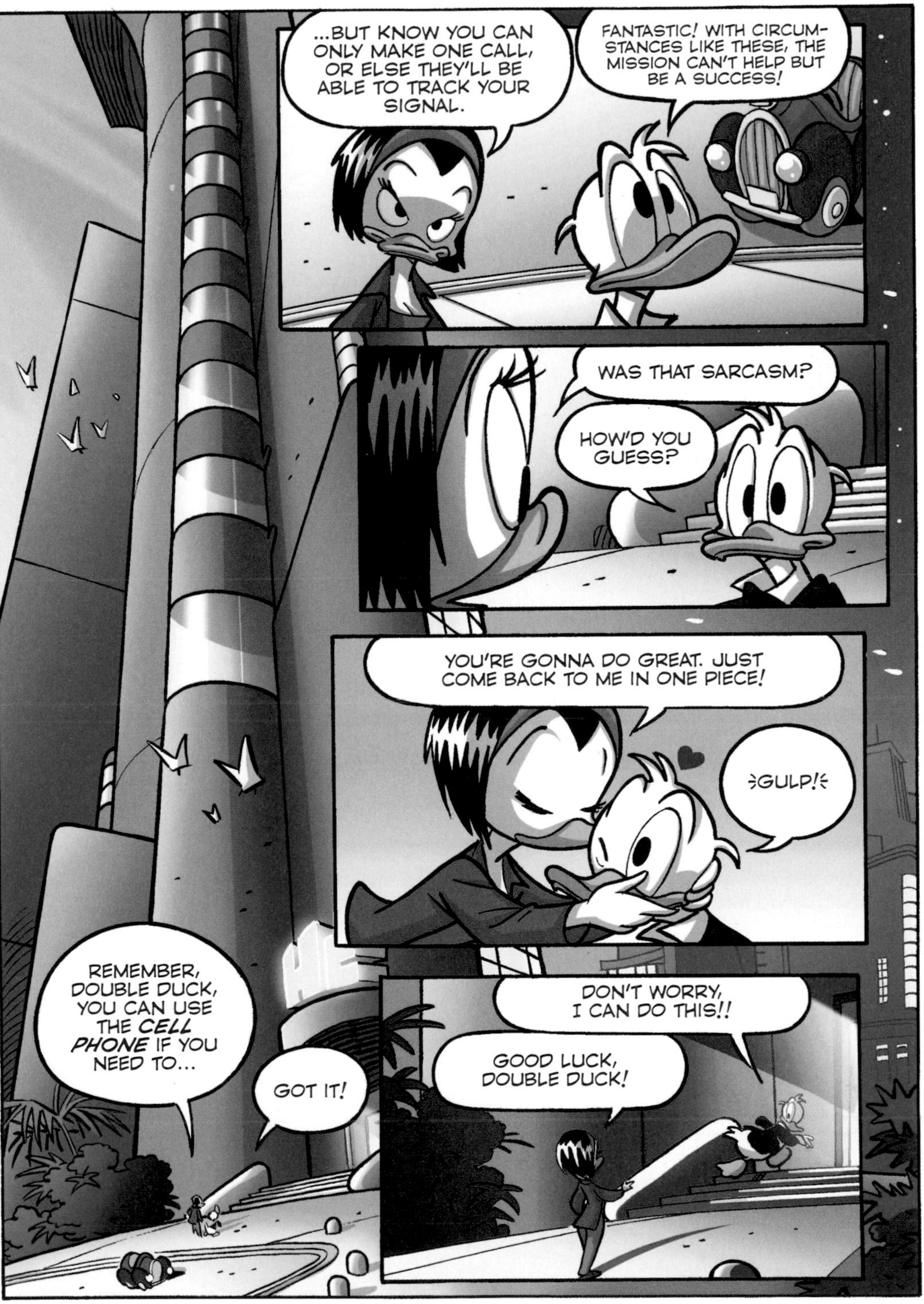
...BUT KNOW YOU CAN ONLY MAKE ONE CALL, OR ELSE THEY'LL BE ABLE TO TRACK YOUR SIGNAL.
FANTASTIC! WITH CIRCUM-STANCES LIKE THESE, THE MISSION CAN'T HELP BUT BE A SUCCESS!
WAS THAT SARCASM?
HOW'D YOU GUESS?
YOU'RE GONNA DO GREAT. JUST COME BACK TO ME IN ONE PIECE!
GULP!
DON'T WORRY, I CAN DO THIS!!
GOOD LUCK, DOUBLE DUCK!
REMEMBER, DOUBLE DUCK, YOU CAN USE THE CELL PHONE IF YOU NEED TO...
GOT IT!

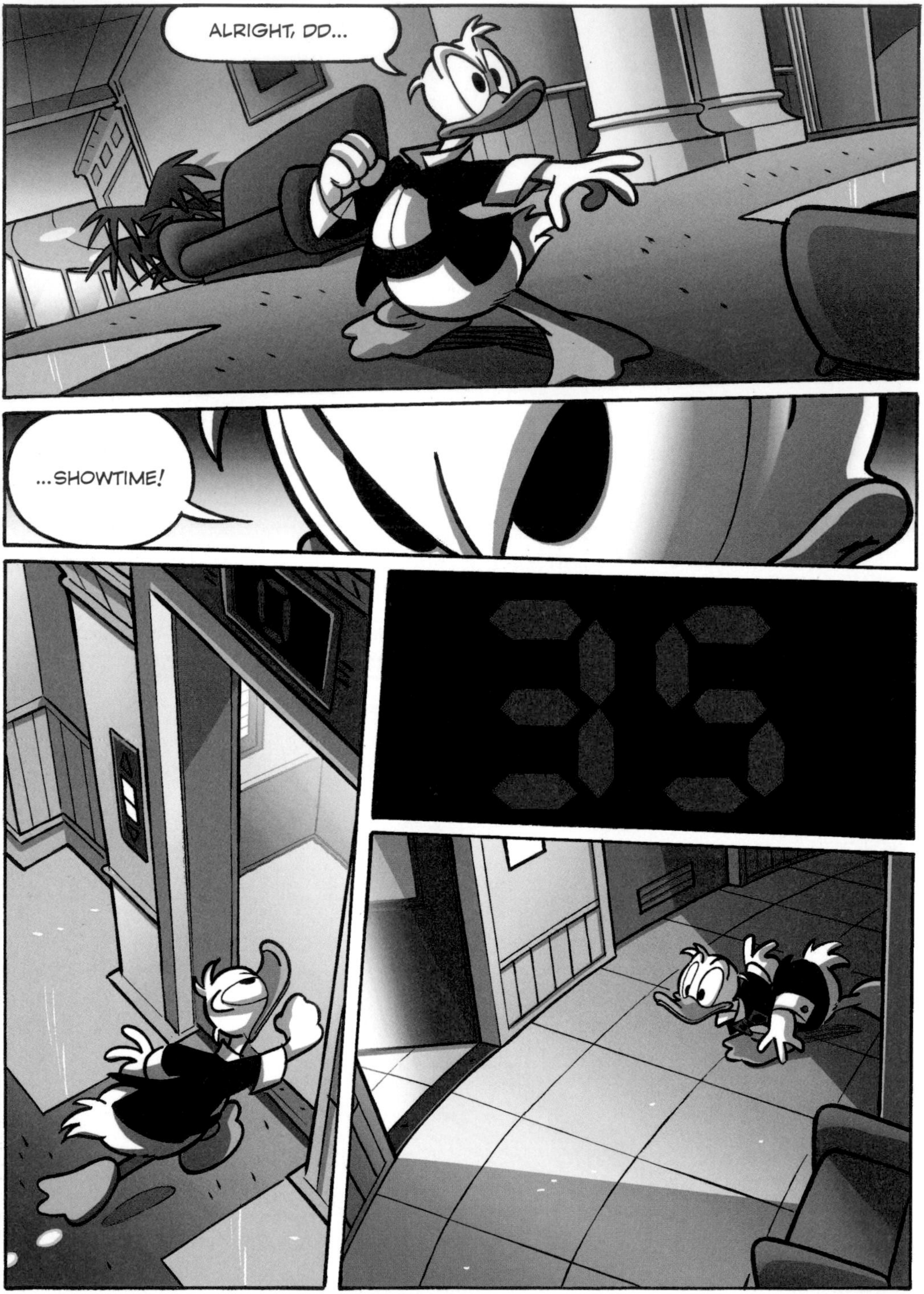
ALRIGHT, DD...
...SHOWTIME!

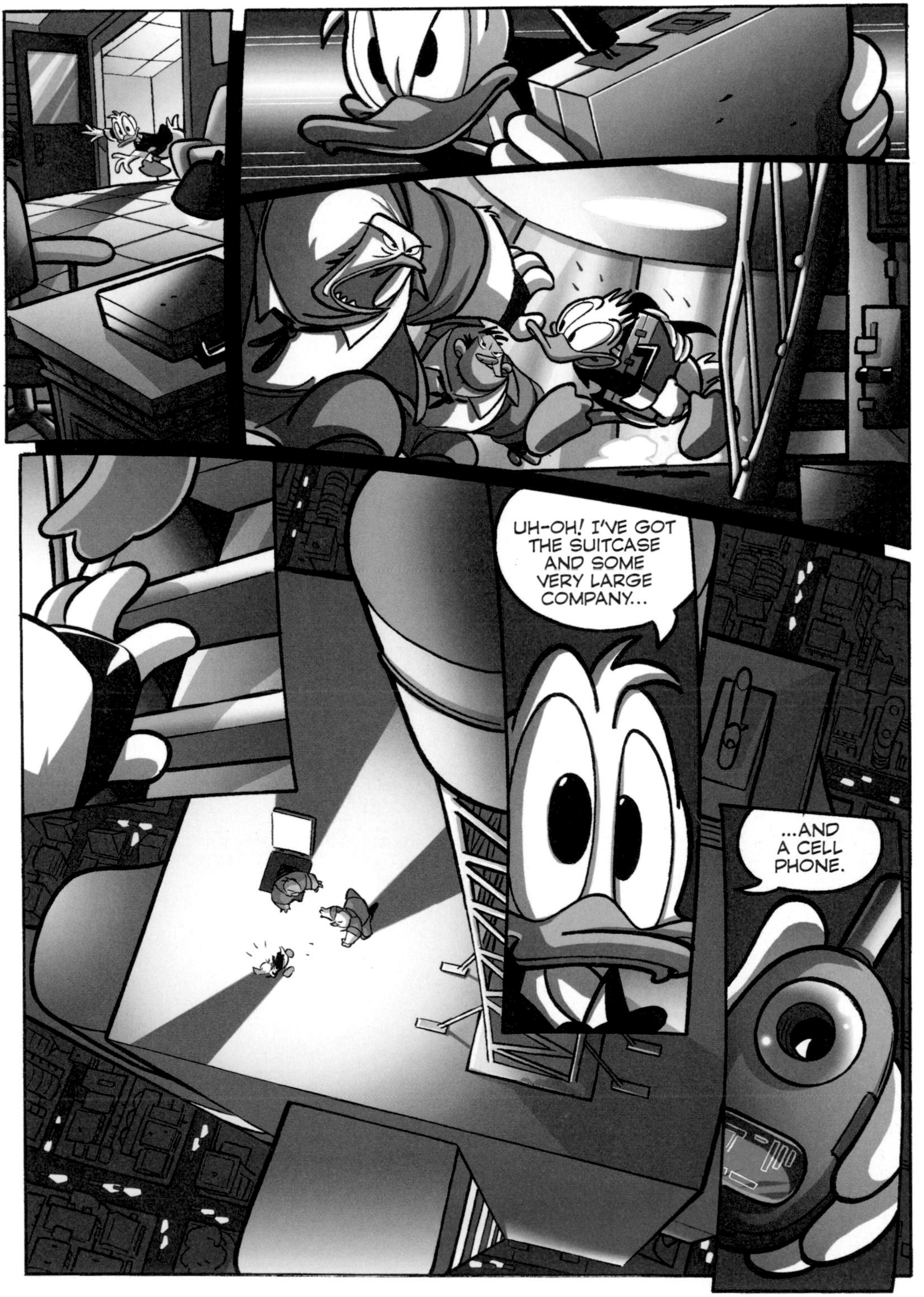
UH-OH! I'VE GOT THE SUITCASE AND SOME VERY LARGE COMPANY...
...AND A CELL PHONE.

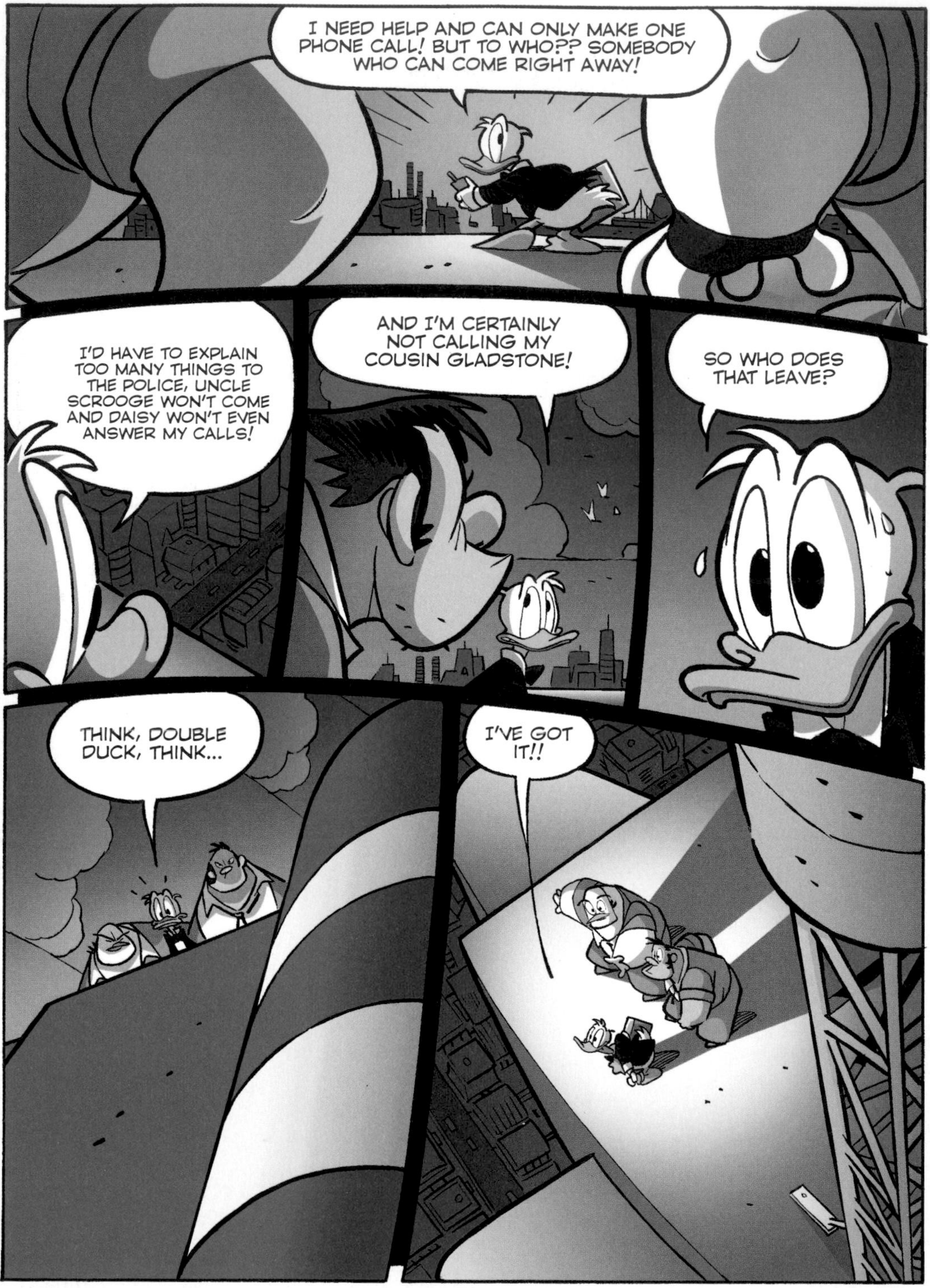
I NEED HELP AND CAN ONLY MAKE ONE PHONE CALL! BUT TO WHO?? SOMEBODY WHO CAN COME RIGHT AWAY!
I'D HAVE TO EXPLAIN TOO MANY THINGS TO THE POLICE, UNCLE SCROOGE WON'T COME AND DAISY WON'T EVEN ANSWER MY CALLS!
AND I'M CERTAINLY NOT CALLING MY COUSIN GLADSTONE!
SO WHO DOES THAT LEAVE?
THINK, DOUBLE DUCK, THINK...
I'VE GOT IT!!

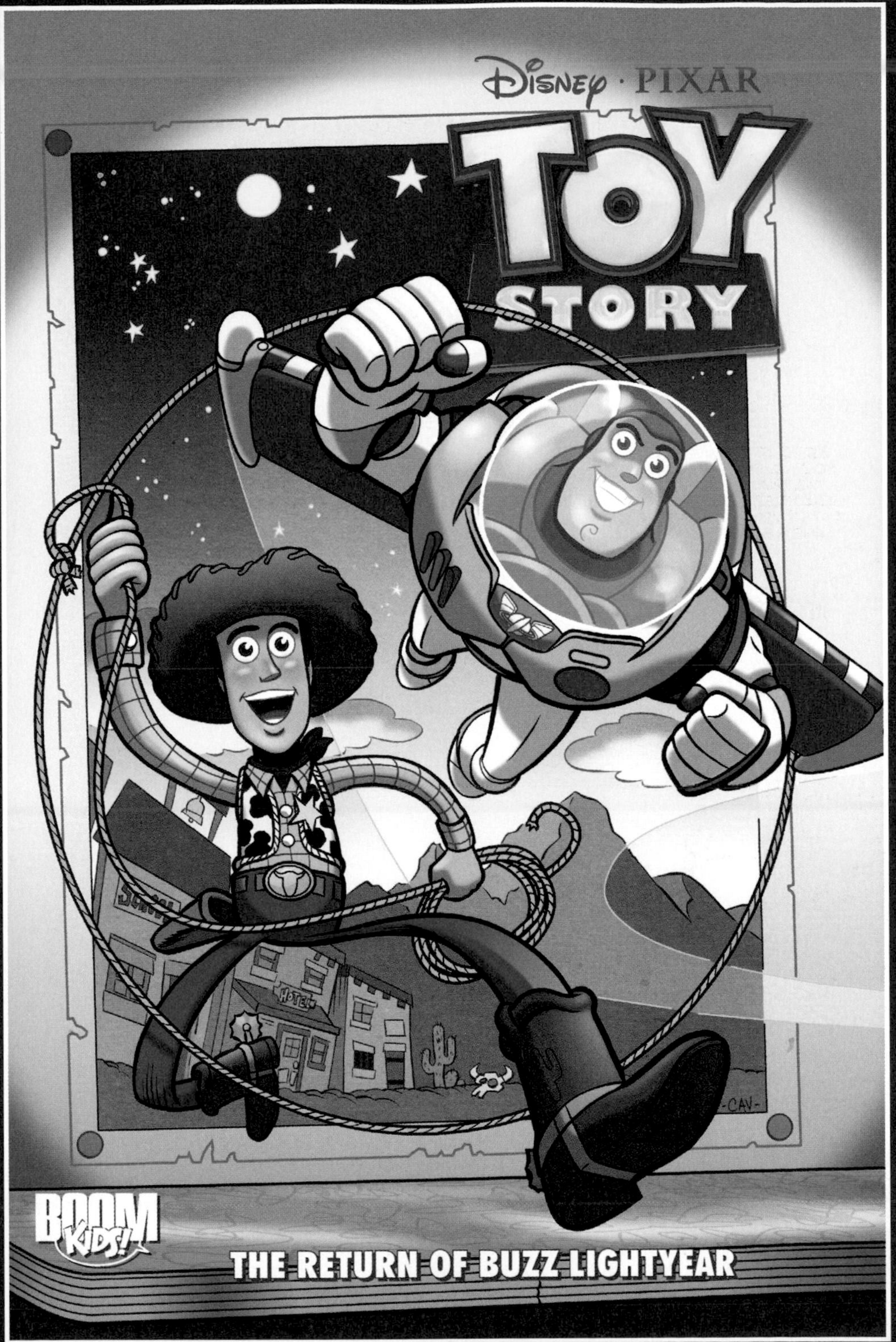

Disney · PIXAR
TOY STORY
BOOM KIDS!
THE RETURN OF BUZZ LIGHTYEAR

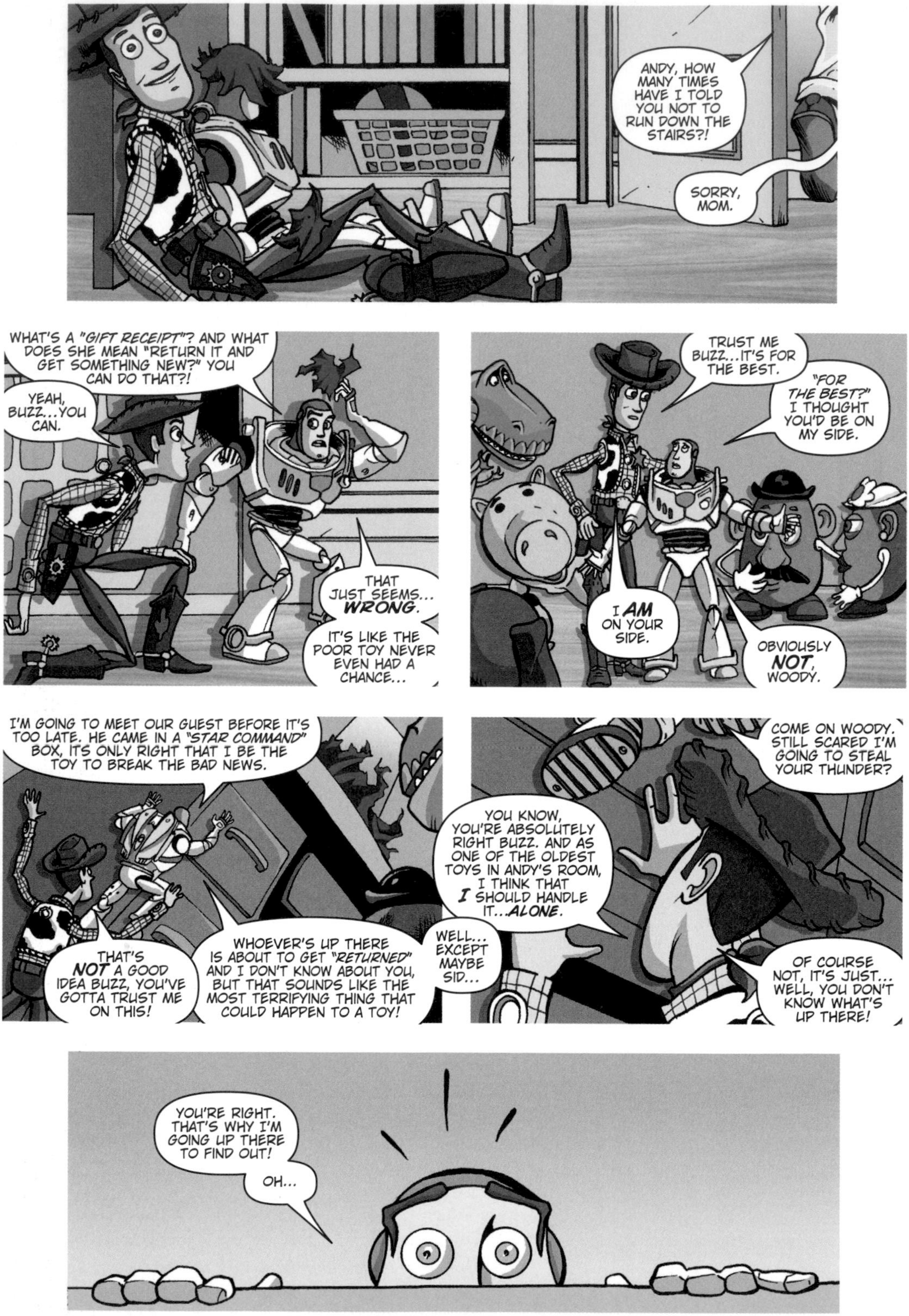
ANDY, HOW MANY TIMES HAVE I TOLD YOU NOT TO RUN DOWN THE STAIRS?!
SORRY, MOM.
WHAT'S A "GIFT RECEIPT"? AND WHAT DOES SHE MEAN "RETURN IT AND GET SOMETHING NEW?" YOU CAN DO THAT?!
YEAH, BUZZ...YOU CAN.
THAT JUST SEEMS... WRONG.
IT'S LIKE THE POOR TOY NEVER EVEN HAD A CHANCE...
TRUST ME BUZZ...IT'S FOR THE BEST.
"FOR THE BEST?" I THOUGHT YOU'D BE ON MY SIDE.
I AM ON YOUR SIDE.
OBVIOUSLY NOT, WOODY.
I'M GOING TO MEET OUR GUEST BEFORE IT'S TOO LATE. HE CAME IN A "STAR COMMAND" BOX, IT'S ONLY RIGHT THAT I BE THE TOY TO BREAK THE BAD NEWS.
THAT'S NOT A GOOD IDEA BUZZ, YOU'VE GOTTA TRUST ME ON THIS!
WHOEVER'S UP THERE IS ABOUT TO GET "RETURNED" AND I DON'T KNOW ABOUT YOU, BUT THAT SOUNDS LIKE THE MOST TERRIFYING THING THAT COULD HAPPEN TO A TOY!
WELL... EXCEPT MAYBE SID...
COME ON WOODY. STILL SCARED I'M GOING TO STEAL YOUR THUNDER?
YOU KNOW, YOU'RE ABSOLUTELY RIGHT BUZZ. AND AS ONE OF THE OLDEST TOYS IN ANDY'S ROOM, I THINK THAT I SHOULD HANDLE IT...ALONE.
OF COURSE NOT, IT'S JUST... WELL, YOU DON'T KNOW WHAT'S UP THERE!
YOU'RE RIGHT. THAT'S WHY I'M GOING UP THERE TO FIND OUT!
OH...

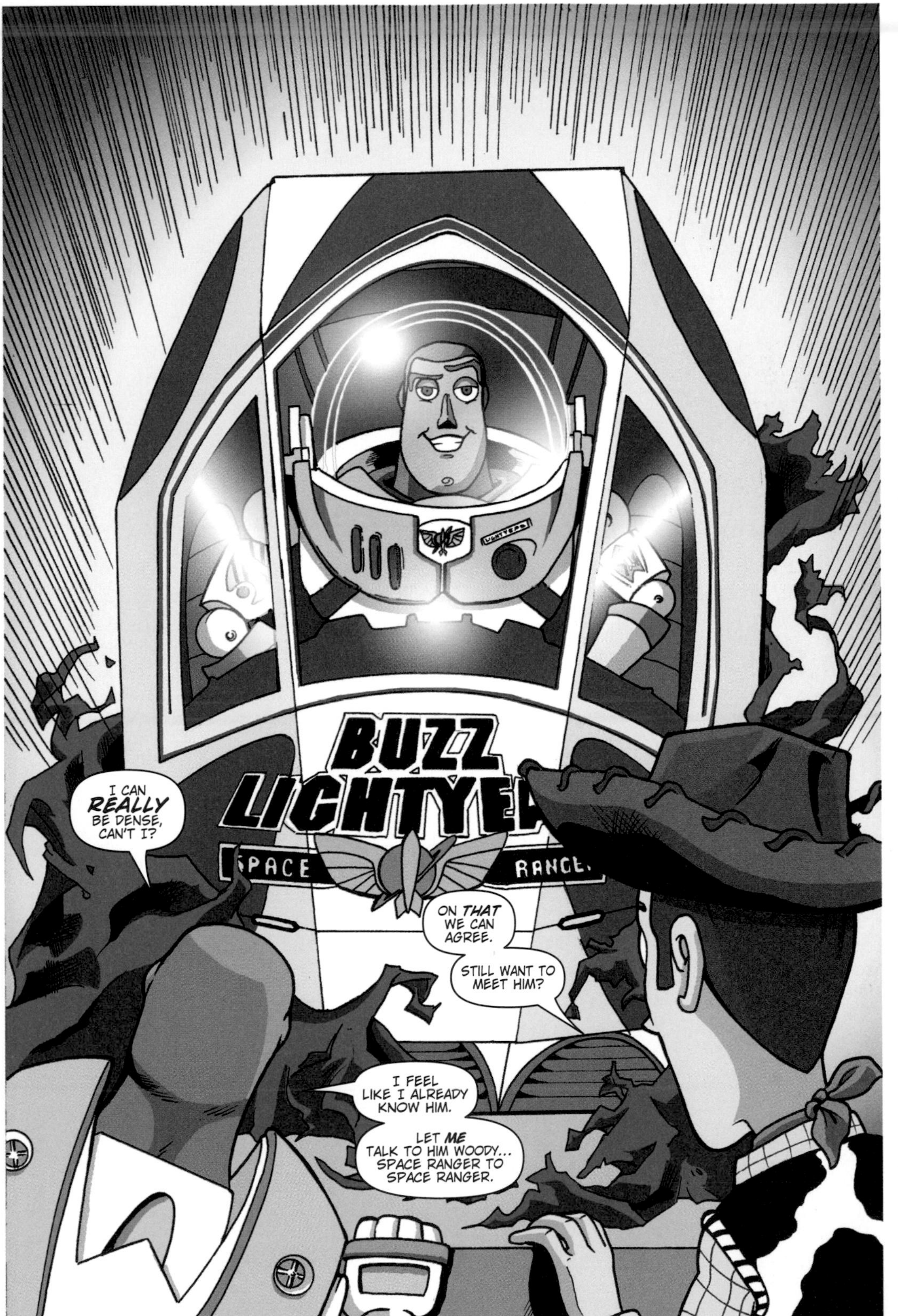
BUZZ LIGHTYEAR
SPACE RANGER
I CAN REALLY BE DENSE, CAN'T I?
ON THAT WE CAN AGREE.
STILL WANT TO MEET HIM?
I FEEL LIKE I ALREADY KNOW HIM.
LET ME TALK TO HIM WOODY... SPACE RANGER TO SPACE RANGER.

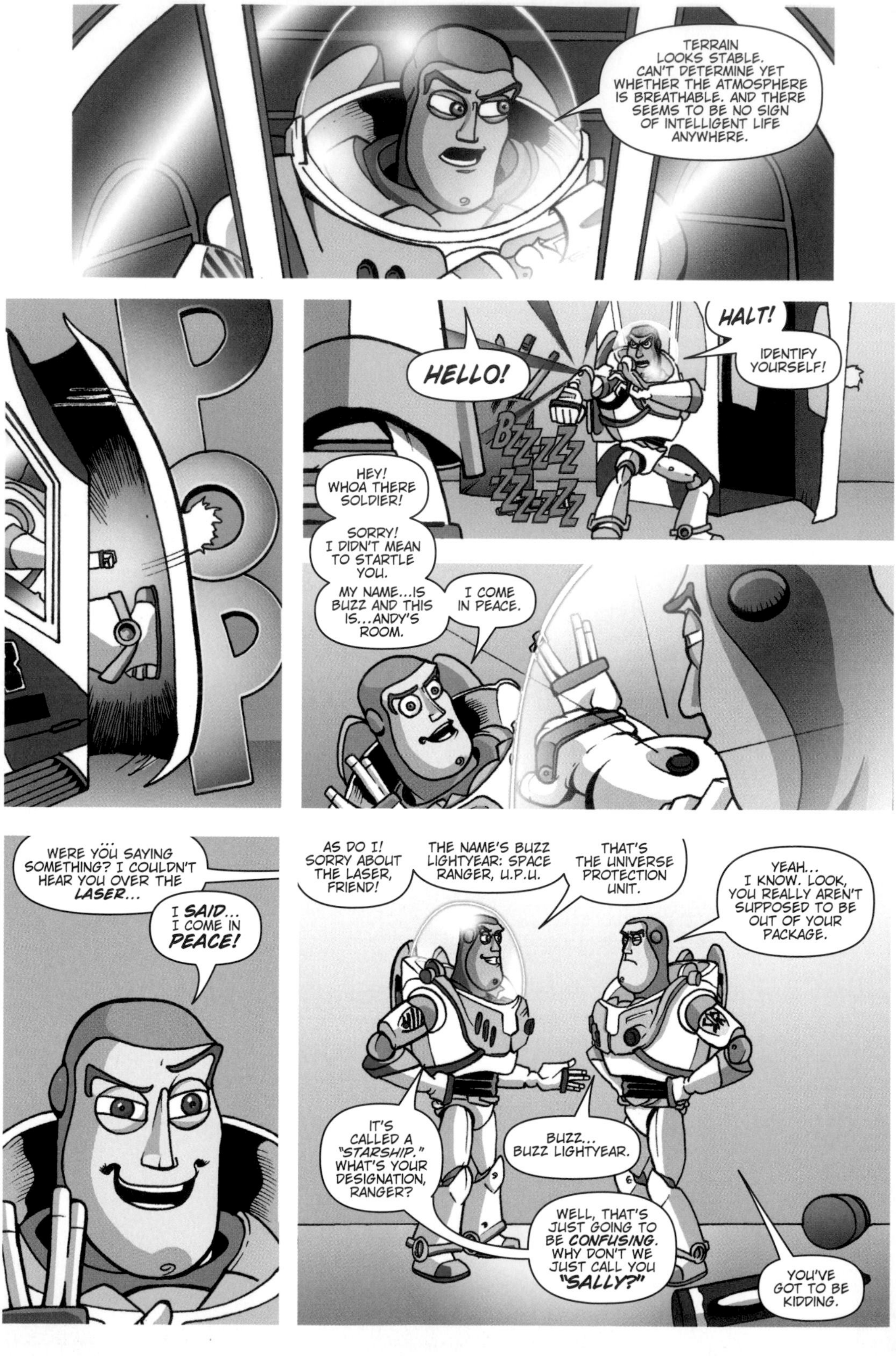
TERRAIN LOOKS STABLE. CAN'T DETERMINE YET WHETHER THE ATMOSPHERE IS BREATHABLE. AND THERE SEEMS TO BE NO SIGN OF INTELLIGENT LIFE ANYWHERE.
HALT!
IDENTIFY YOURSELF!
HELLO!
BZZZZZ-ZZZZZZ
HEY! WHOA THERE SOLDIER!
SORRY! I DIDN'T MEAN TO STARTLE YOU.
MY NAME...IS BUZZ AND THIS IS...ANDY'S ROOM.
I COME IN PEACE.
WERE YOU SAYING SOMETHING? I COULDN'T HEAR YOU OVER THE LASER...
I SAID... I COME IN PEACE!
AS DO I! SORRY ABOUT THE LASER, FRIEND!
THE NAME'S BUZZ LIGHTYEAR: SPACE RANGER, U.P.U.
THAT'S THE UNIVERSE PROTECTION UNIT.
YEAH... I KNOW. LOOK, YOU REALLY AREN'T SUPPOSED TO BE OUT OF YOUR PACKAGE.
IT'S CALLED A "STARSHIP." WHAT'S YOUR DESIGNATION, RANGER?
BUZZ... BUZZ LIGHTYEAR.
WELL, THAT'S JUST GOING TO BE CONFUSING. WHY DON'T WE JUST CALL YOU "SALLY?"
YOU'VE GOT TO BE KIDDING.

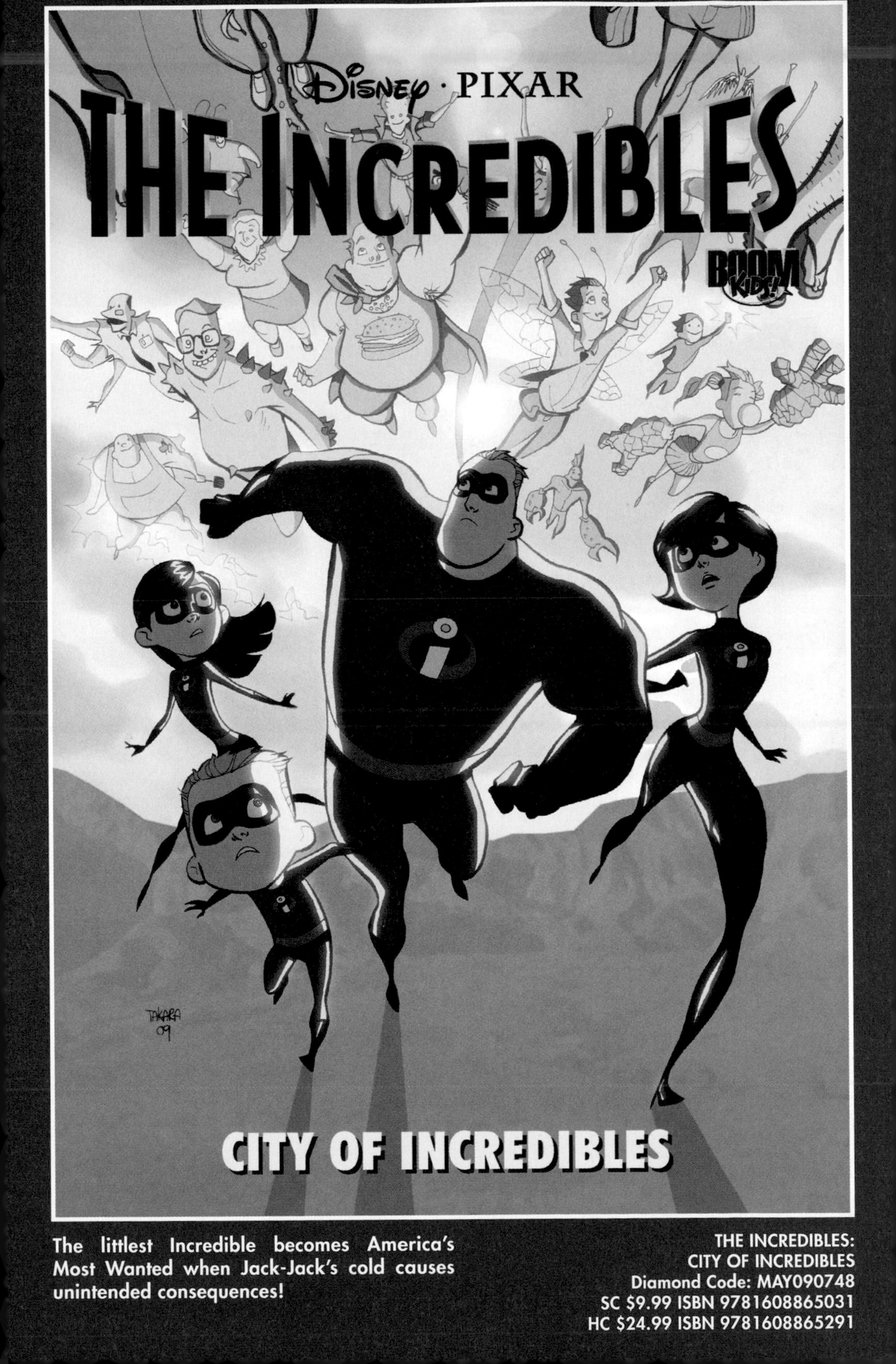
Disney · PIXAR
THE INCREDIBLES
BOOM KIDS!
TAKARA 09
CITY OF INCREDIBLES

The littlest Incredible becomes America's Most Wanted when Jack-Jack's cold causes unintended consequences!

THE INCREDIBLES:
CITY OF INCREDIBLES
Diamond Code: MAY090748
SC $9.99 ISBN 9781608865031
HC $24.99 ISBN 9781608865291

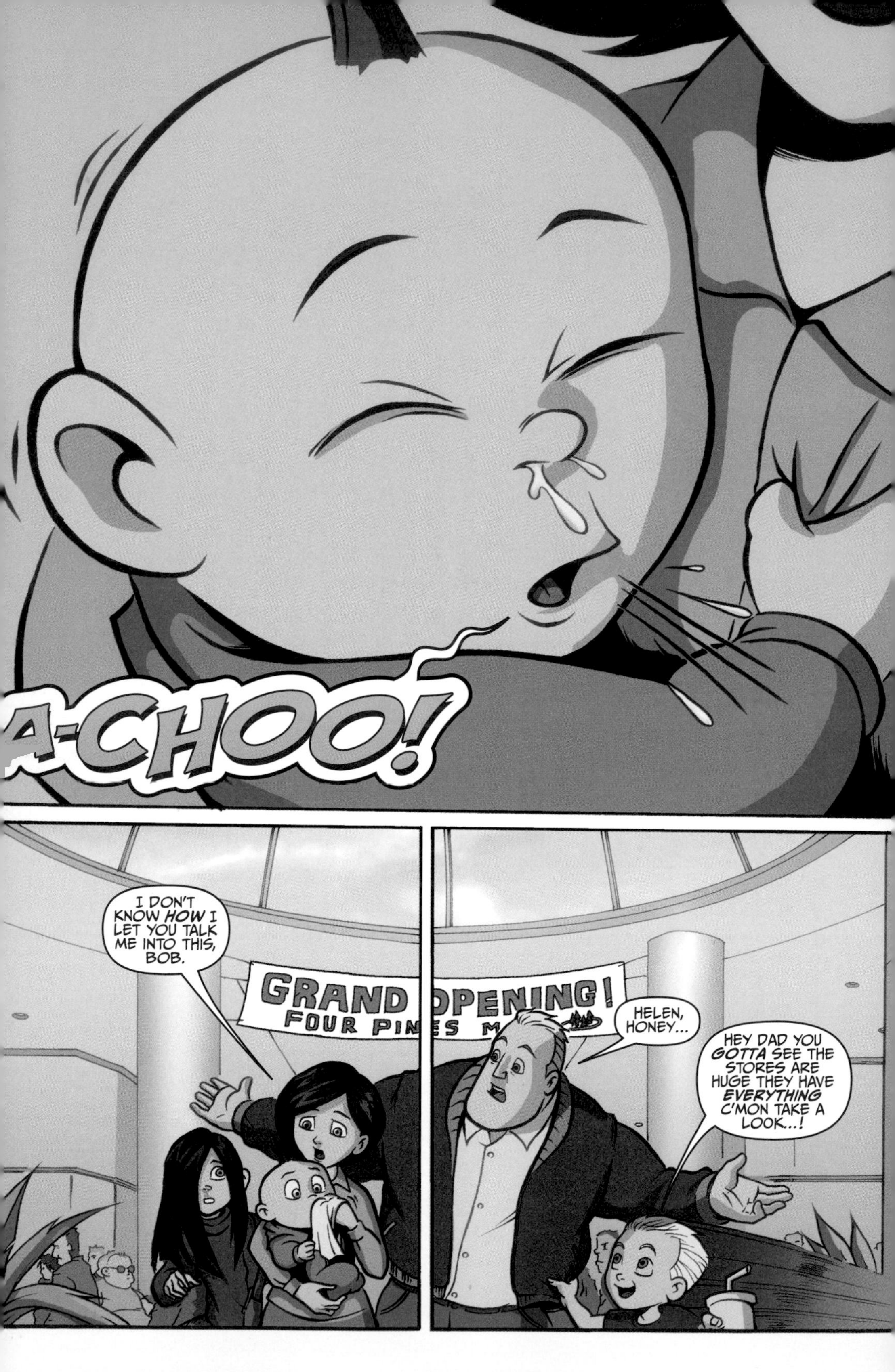
A-CHOO!
I DON'T KNOW HOW I LET YOU TALK ME INTO THIS, BOB.
GRAND OPENING! FOUR PINES M
HELEN, HONEY...
HEY DAD YOU GOTTA SEE THE STORES ARE HUGE THEY HAVE EVERYTHING C'MON TAKE A LOOK...!

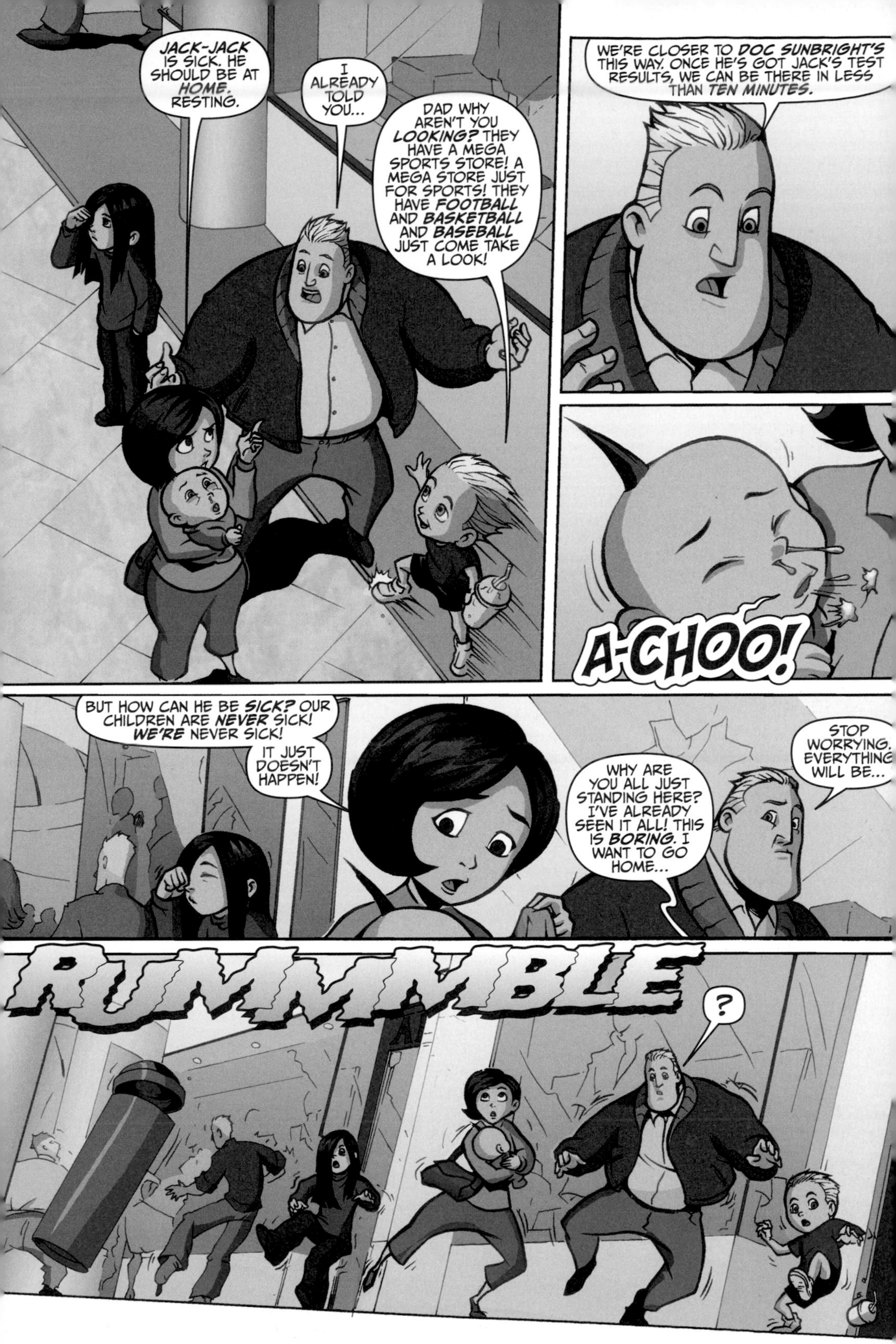
JACK-JACK IS SICK. HE SHOULD BE AT HOME. RESTING.
I ALREADY TOLD YOU...
DAD WHY AREN'T YOU LOOKING? THEY HAVE A MEGA SPORTS STORE! A MEGA STORE JUST FOR SPORTS! THEY HAVE FOOTBALL AND BASKETBALL AND BASEBALL JUST COME TAKE A LOOK!
WE'RE CLOSER TO DOC SUNBRIGHT'S THIS WAY. ONCE HE'S GOT JACK'S TEST RESULTS, WE CAN BE THERE IN LESS THAN TEN MINUTES.
A-CHOO!
BUT HOW CAN HE BE SICK? OUR CHILDREN ARE NEVER SICK! WE'RE NEVER SICK!
IT JUST DOESN'T HAPPEN!
WHY ARE YOU ALL JUST STANDING HERE? I'VE ALREADY SEEN IT ALL! THIS IS BORING. I WANT TO GO HOME...
STOP WORRYING. EVERYTHING WILL BE...
RUMMMBLE
?

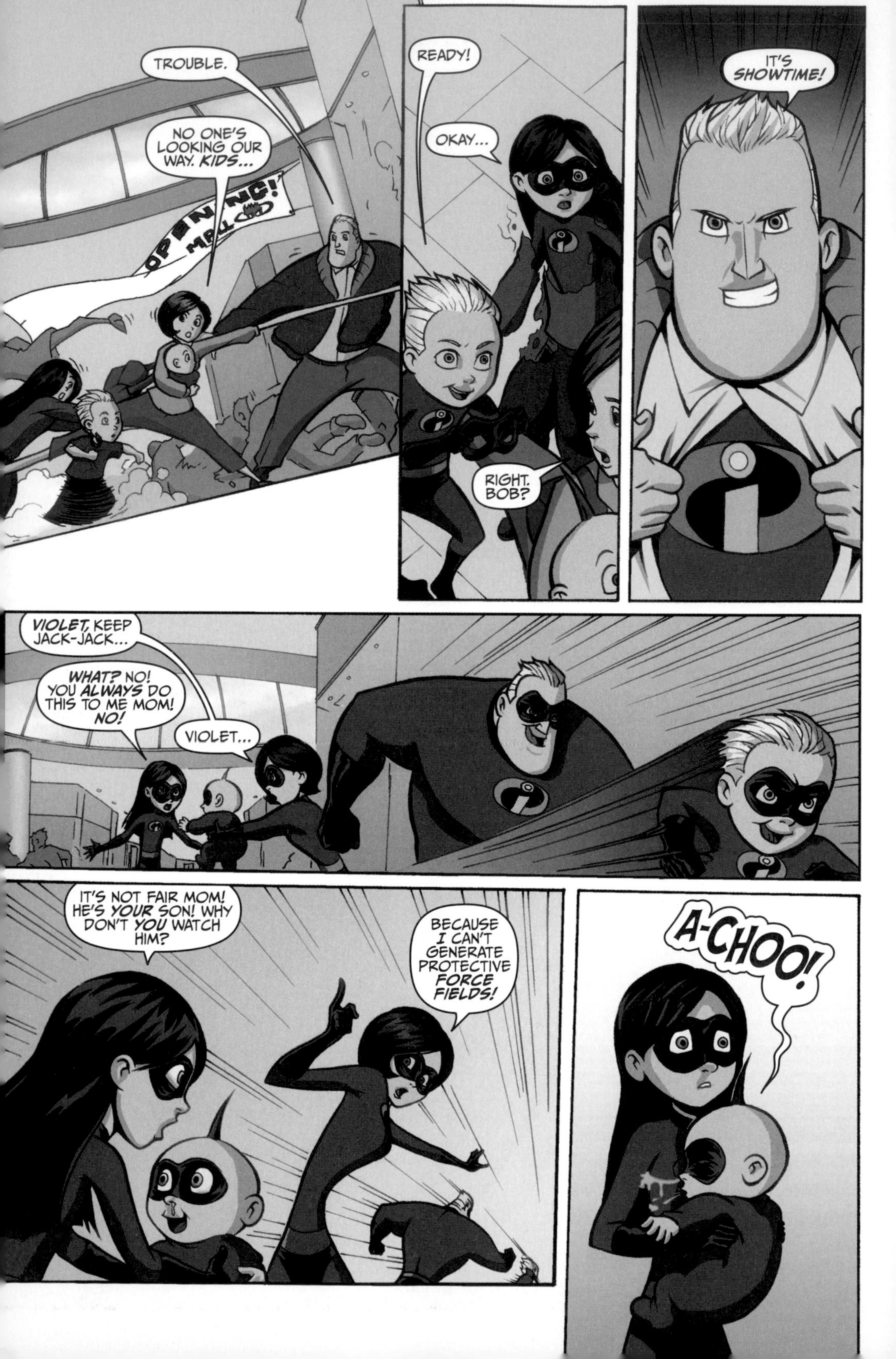
TROUBLE.
NO ONE'S LOOKING OUR WAY. KIDS...
OPENING! MALL
READY!
OKAY...
RIGHT. BOB?
IT'S SHOWTIME!
VIOLET, KEEP JACK-JACK...
WHAT? NO! YOU ALWAYS DO THIS TO ME MOM! NO!
VIOLET...
IT'S NOT FAIR MOM! HE'S YOUR SON! WHY DON'T YOU WATCH HIM?
BECAUSE I CAN'T GENERATE PROTECTIVE FORCE FIELDS!
A-CHOO!

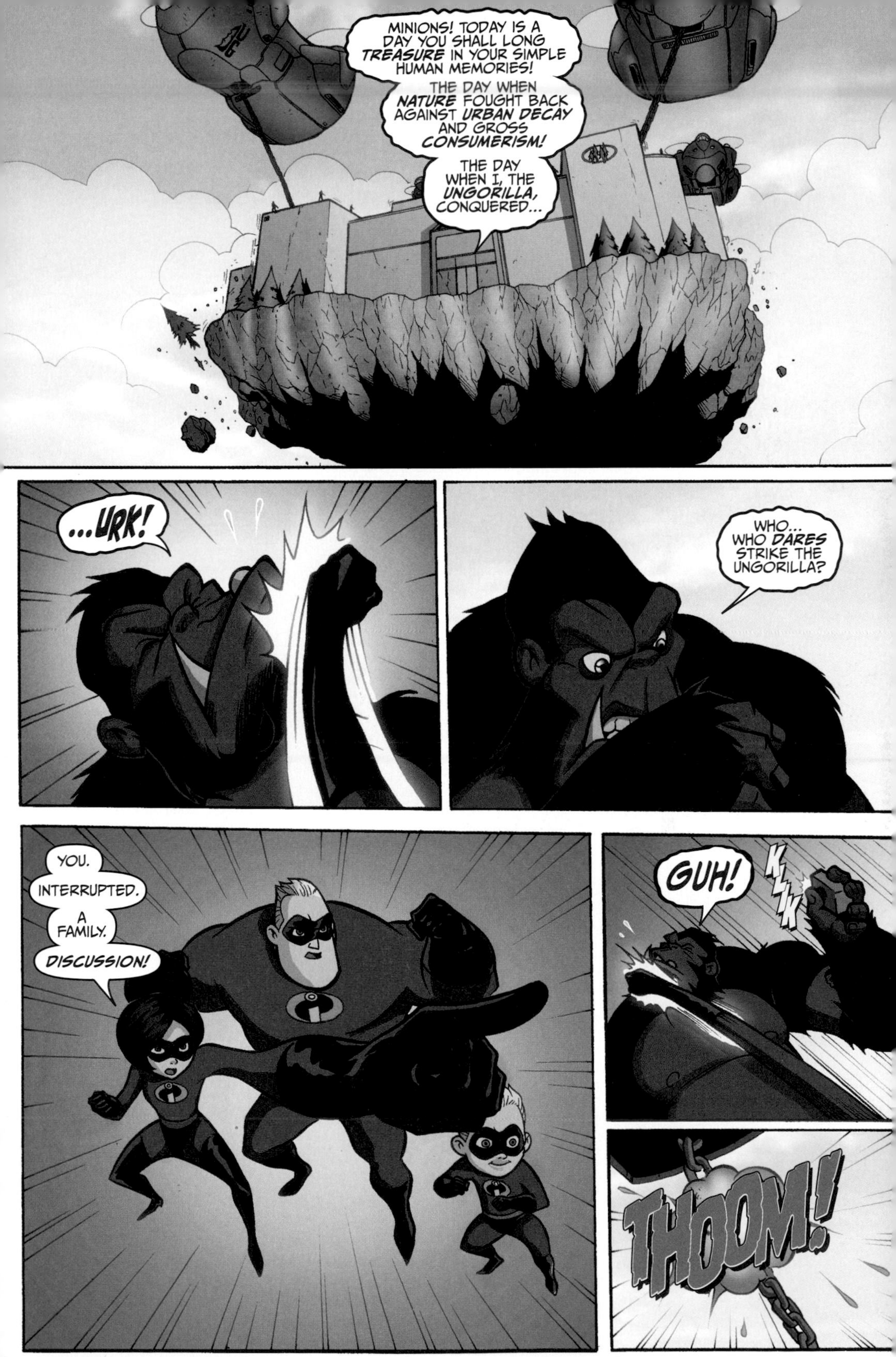
MINIONS! TODAY IS A DAY YOU SHALL LONG TREASURE IN YOUR SIMPLE HUMAN MEMORIES!
THE DAY WHEN NATURE FOUGHT BACK AGAINST URBAN DECAY AND GROSS CONSUMERISM!
THE DAY WHEN I, THE UNGORILLA, CONQUERED...
...URK!
WHO... WHO DARES STRIKE THE UNGORILLA?
YOU.
INTERRUPTED.
A FAMILY.
DISCUSSION!
GUH!
KLIK
THOOM!

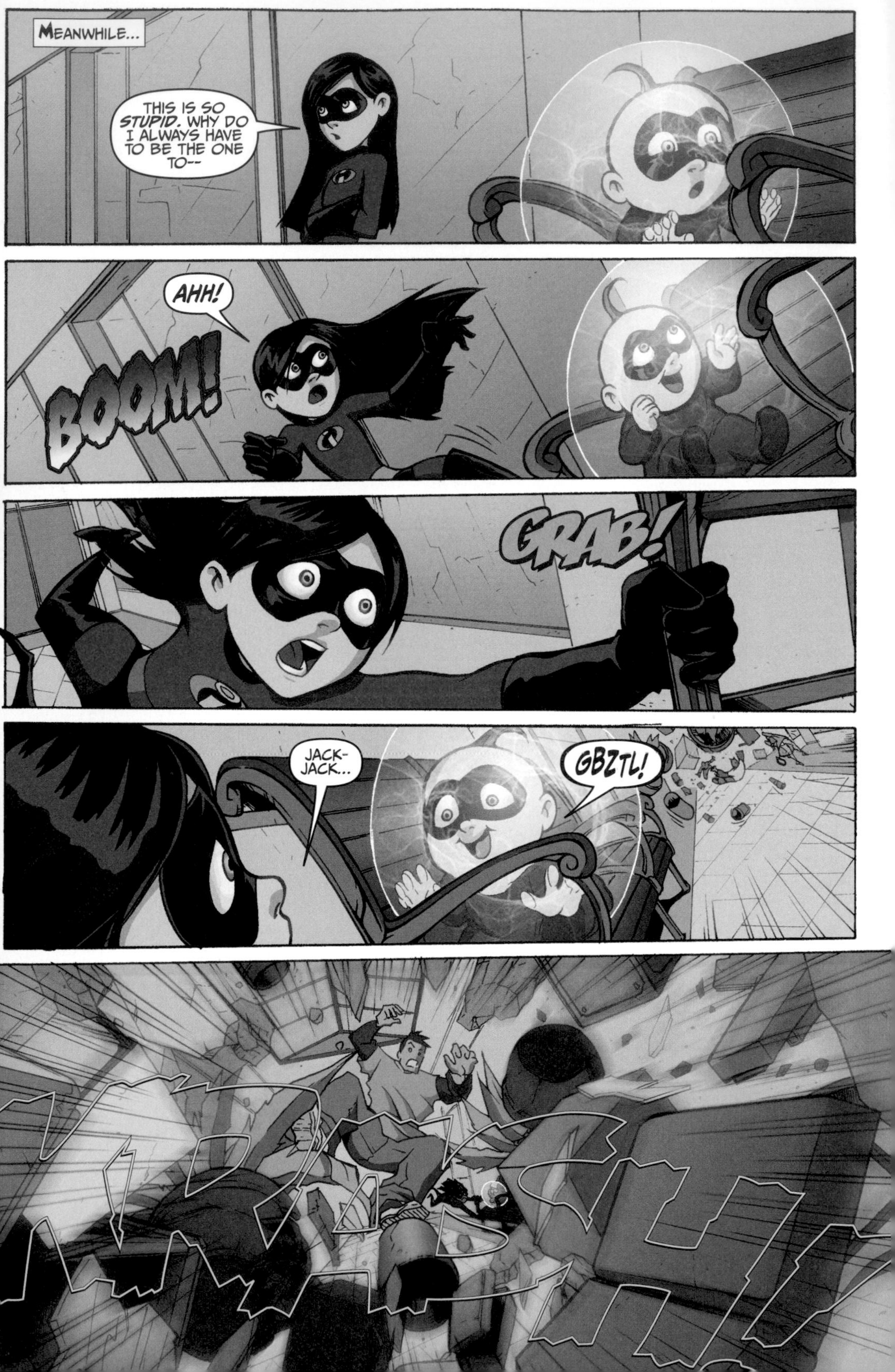
MEANWHILE...
THIS IS SO STUPID. WHY DO I ALWAYS HAVE TO BE THE ONE TO--
AHH!
BOOM!
GRAB!
JACK-JACK...
GBZTL!

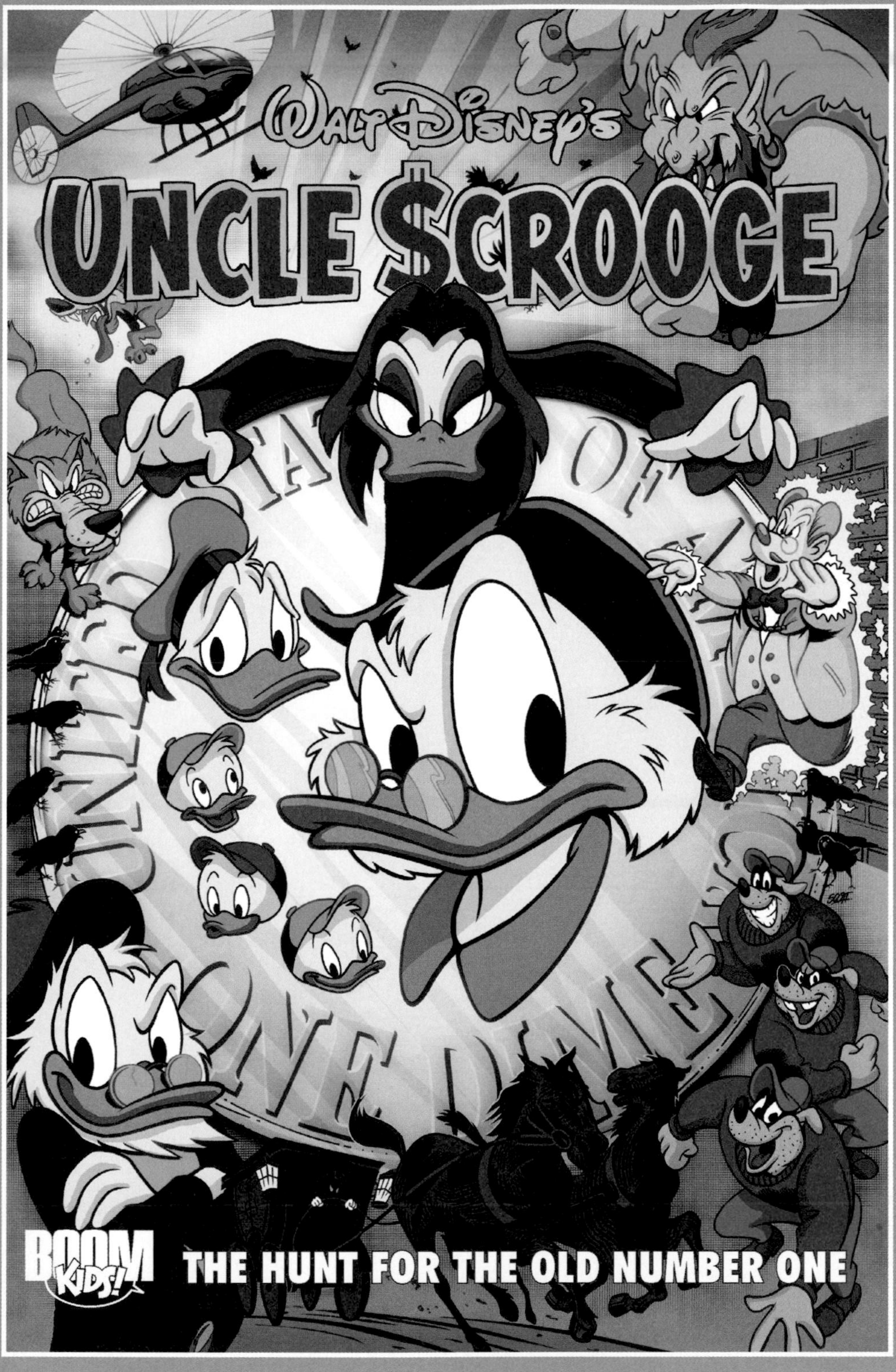
WALT DISNEY'S
UNCLE $CROOGE
BOOM KIDS!
THE HUNT FOR THE OLD NUMBER ONE

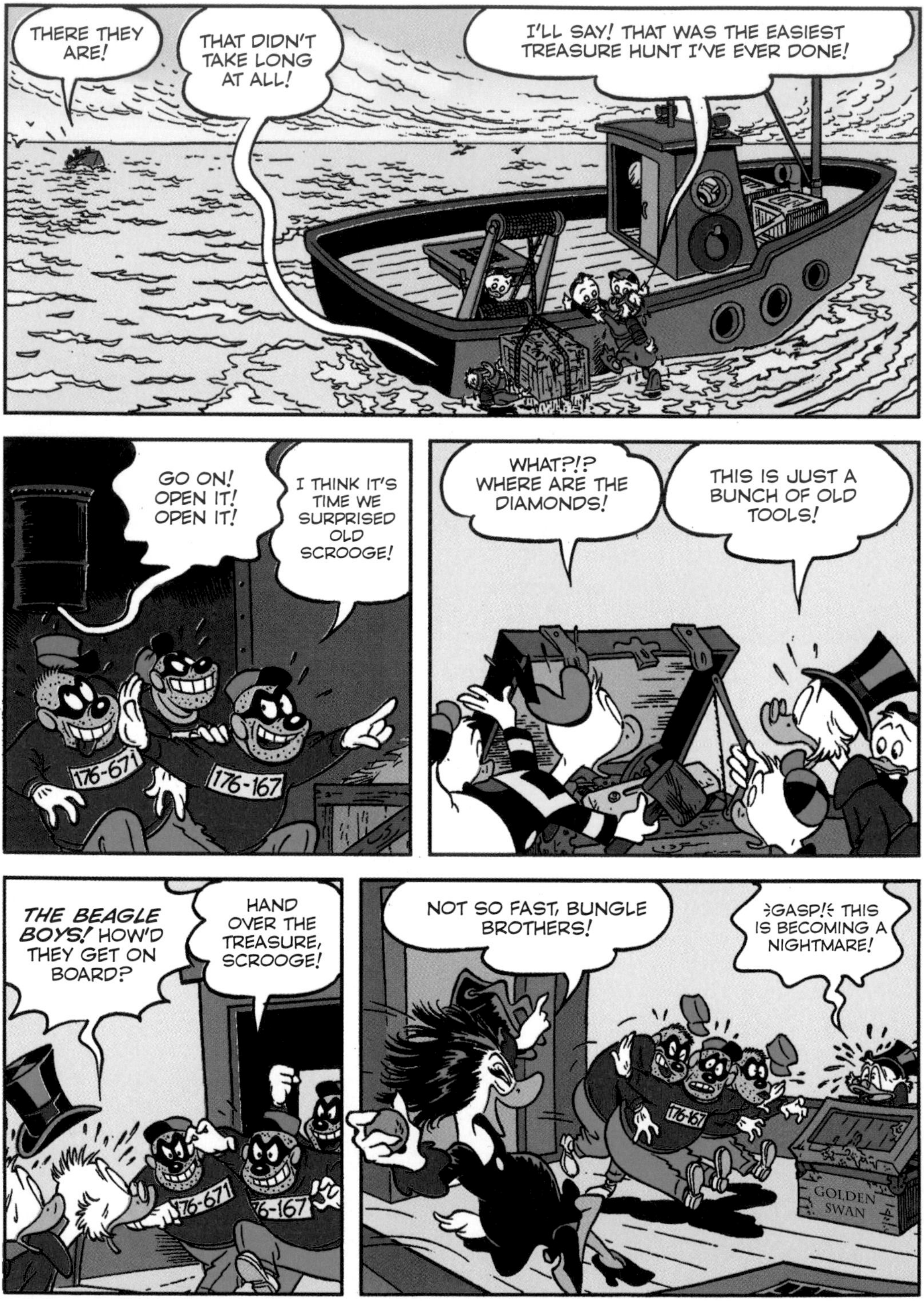
THERE THEY ARE!
THAT DIDN'T TAKE LONG AT ALL!
I'LL SAY! THAT WAS THE EASIEST TREASURE HUNT I'VE EVER DONE!
GO ON! OPEN IT! OPEN IT!
I THINK IT'S TIME WE SURPRISED OLD SCROOGE!
176-671
176-167
WHAT?!? WHERE ARE THE DIAMONDS!
THIS IS JUST A BUNCH OF OLD TOOLS!
THE BEAGLE BOYS! HOW'D THEY GET ON BOARD?
HAND OVER THE TREASURE, SCROOGE!
176-671
176-167
NOT SO FAST, BUNGLE BROTHERS!
GASP! THIS IS BECOMING A NIGHTMARE!
176-167
GOLDEN SWAN

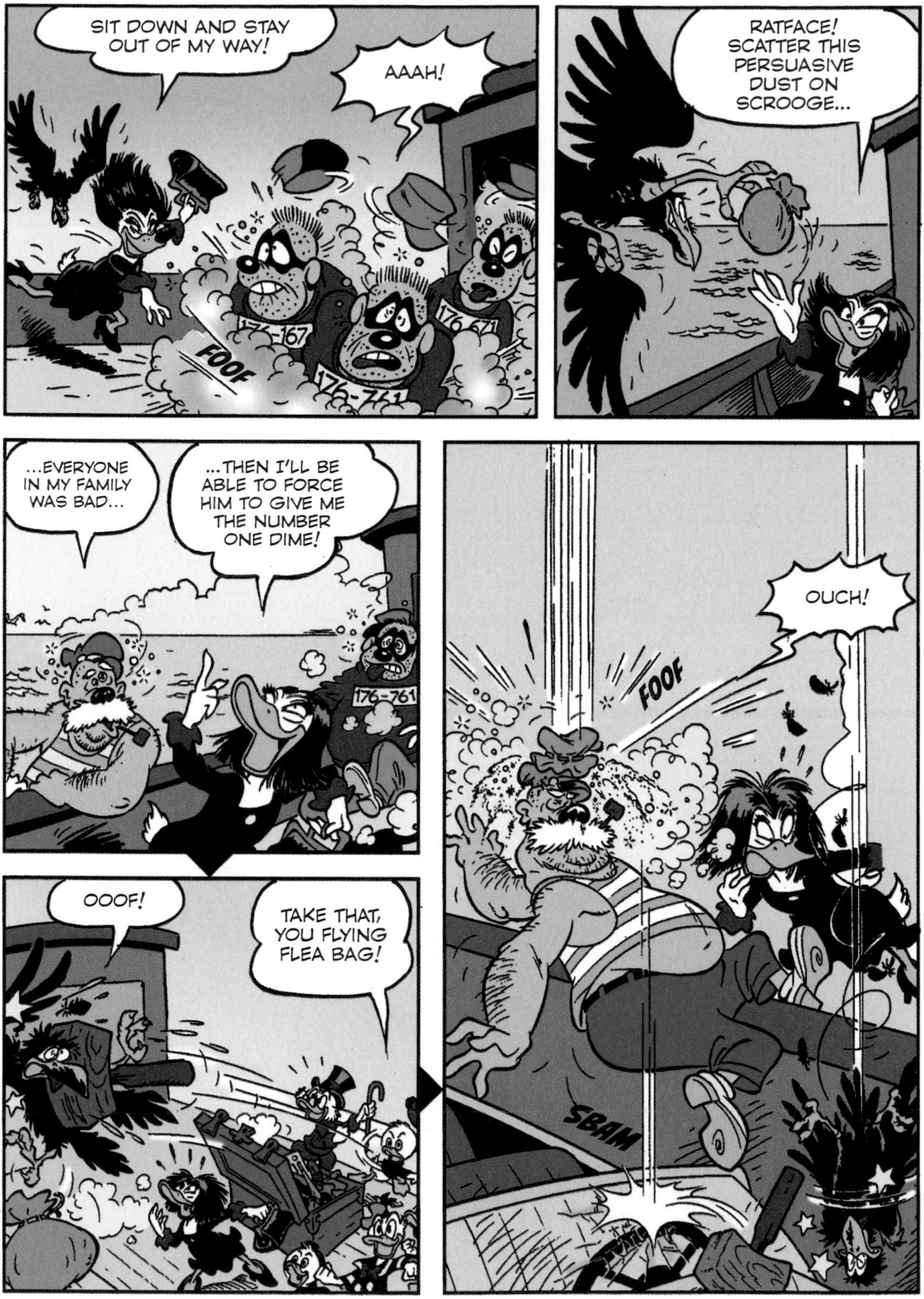

SIT DOWN AND STAY OUT OF MY WAY!
AAAH!
176-167
176-761
176-671
FOOF
RATFACE! SCATTER THIS PERSUASIVE DUST ON SCROOGE...
...EVERYONE IN MY FAMILY WAS BAD...
...THEN I'LL BE ABLE TO FORCE HIM TO GIVE ME THE NUMBER ONE DIME!
176-761
OOOF!
TAKE THAT, YOU FLYING FLEA BAG!
OUCH!
FOOF
SBAM

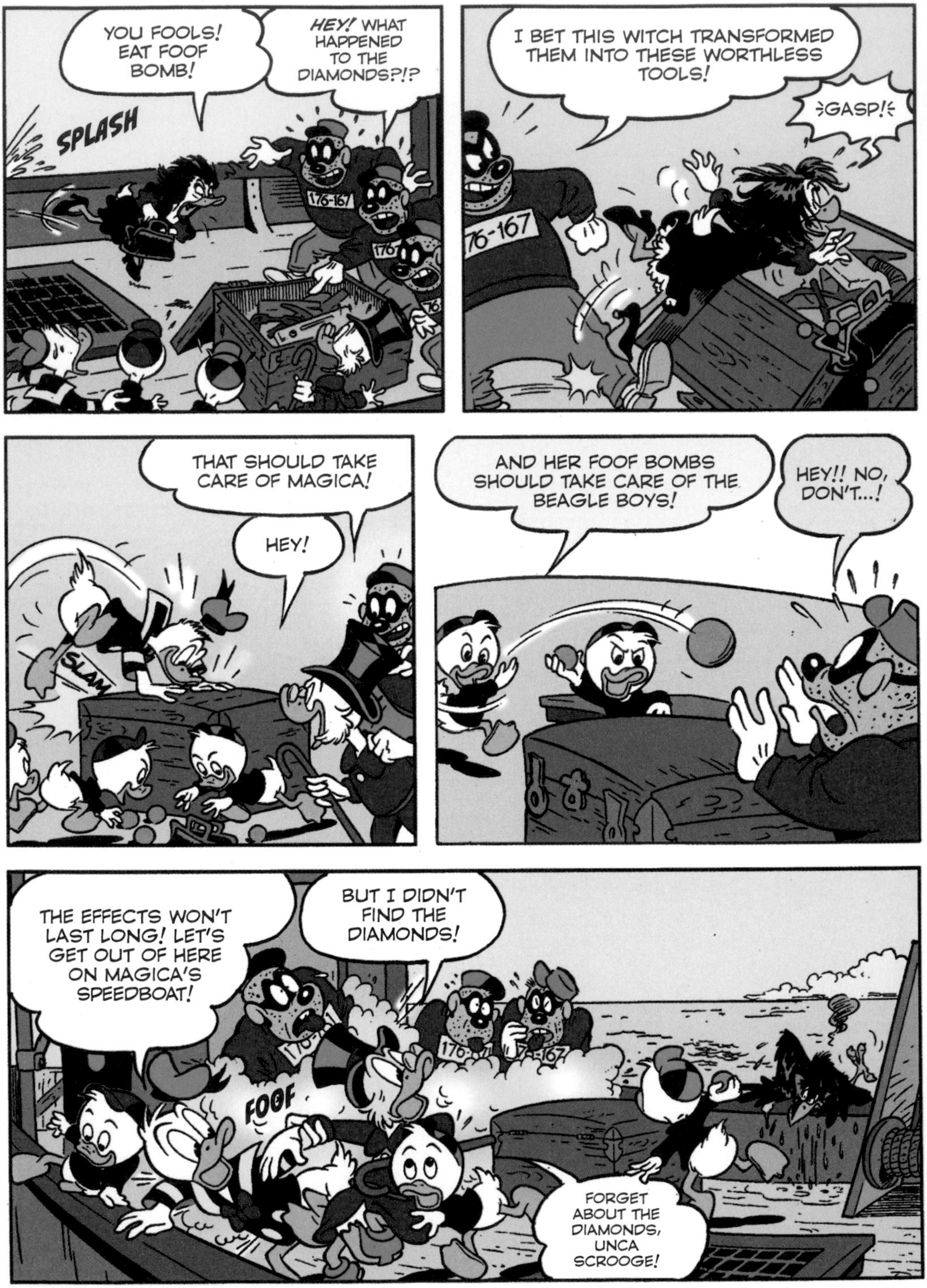
YOU FOOLS! EAT FOOF BOMB!
HEY! WHAT HAPPENED TO THE DIAMONDS?!?
SPLASH
I BET THIS WITCH TRANSFORMED THEM INTO THESE WORTHLESS TOOLS!
GASP!
THAT SHOULD TAKE CARE OF MAGICA!
HEY!
SLAM
AND HER FOOF BOMBS SHOULD TAKE CARE OF THE BEAGLE BOYS!
HEY!! NO, DON'T...!
THE EFFECTS WON'T LAST LONG! LET'S GET OUT OF HERE ON MAGICA'S SPEEDBOAT!
BUT I DIDN'T FIND THE DIAMONDS!
FOOF
FORGET ABOUT THE DIAMONDS, UNCA SCROOGE!

GRAPHIC NOVELS AVAILABLE NOW!

BOOM KIDS!

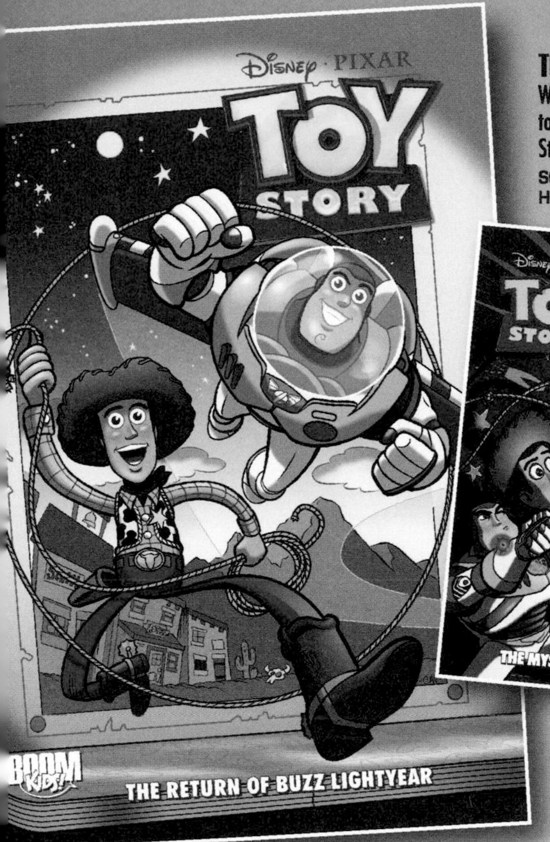
DISNEY · PIXAR
TOY STORY
BOOM KIDS!
THE RETURN OF BUZZ LIGHTYEAR

TOY STORY: THE RETURN OF BUZZ LIGHTYEAR

When Andy is given a surprise gift, no one is more surprised than the toys in his room...it's a second Buzz Lightyear! The stage is set for a Star Command showdown when only one Buzz can stay!

SC $9.99 ISBN 9781608865574
HC $24.99 ISBN 9781608865581

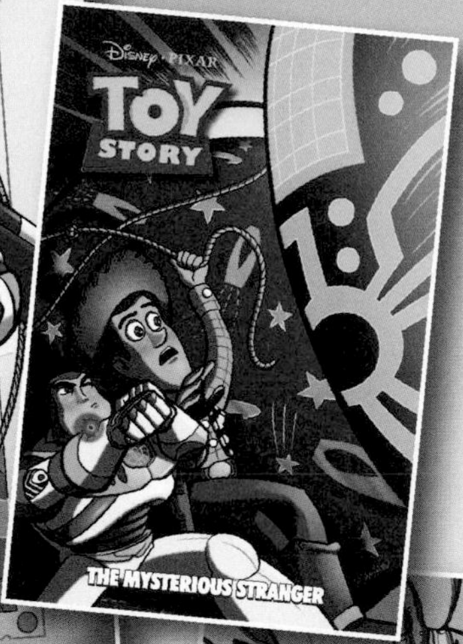
DISNEY · PIXAR
TOY STORY
THE MYSTERIOUS STRANGER

TOY STORY: THE MYSTERIOUS STRANGER

Andy has a new addition to his room—a circuit-laden egg. Is this new gizmo a friend or foe? This adventure kicks off the first of four self-contained stories featuring all your favorite characters from the TOY STORY movies – Woody, Buzz and the gang!

SC $9.99 ISBN 9781934506912
HC $24.99 ISBN 9781608865239

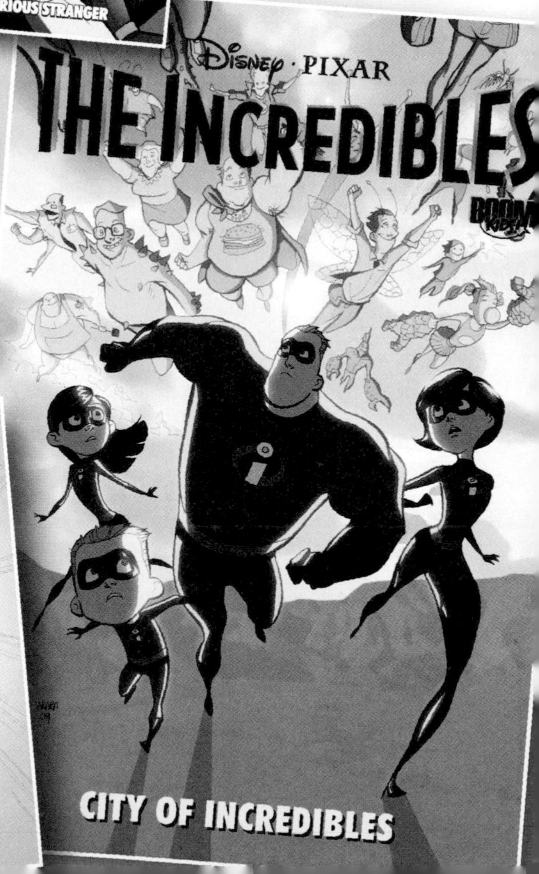
DISNEY · PIXAR
THE INCREDIBLES
BOOM KIDS!
CITY OF INCREDIBLES

THE INCREDIBLES: CITY OF INCREDIBLES

Baby Jack-Jack, everyone's favorite super-powered toddler, battles...a nasty cold! Hopefully the rest of the Parr family can stay healthy, because the henchmen of super villains are rapidly starting to exhibit superpowers!

SC $9.99 ISBN 9781608865031
HC $24.99 ISBN 9781608865291

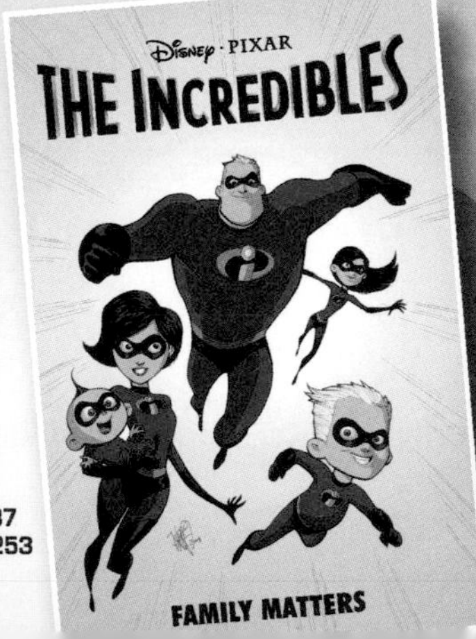
DISNEY · PIXAR
THE INCREDIBLES
FAMILY MATTERS

THE INCREDIBLES: FAMILY MATTERS

Acclaimed scribe Mark Waid has written the perfect INCREDIBLES story! What happens when Mr. Incredible's super-abilities start to wane...and how long can he keep his powerlessness a secret from his wife and kids?

SC $9.99 ISBN 9781934506837
HC $24.99 ISBN 9781608865253

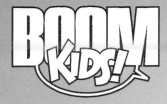

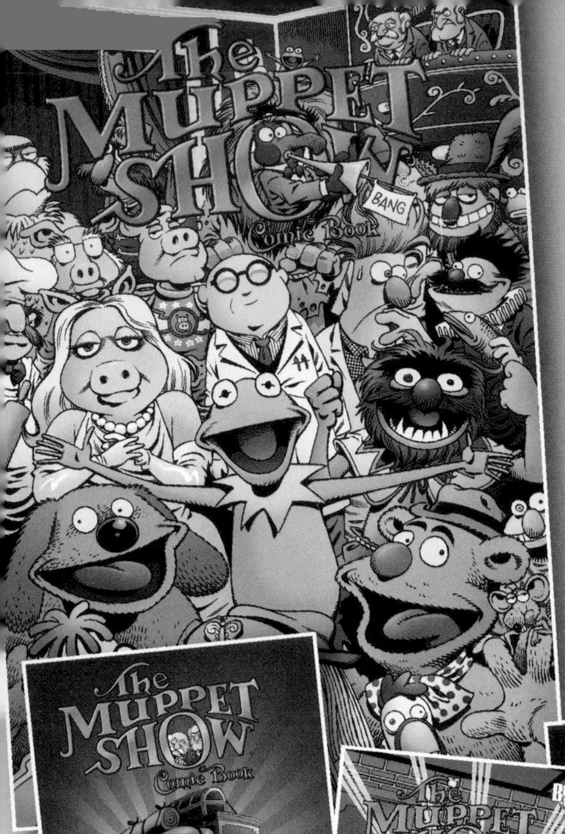
The
MUPPET
SHOW
Comic Book
BANG

THE MUPPET SHOW COMIC BOOK: MEET THE MUPPETS

Collecting the first four issues of the Eisner Award-nominated THE MUPPET SHOW COMIC BOOK, written and drawn by the incomparable Roger Langridge! Packed full of madcap skits and gags, this trade is certain to please old and new fans alike!

SC $9.99 ISBN 9781934506851
HC $24.99 ISBN 9781608865277

THE MUPPET SHOW COMIC BOOK: THE TREASURE OF PEG-LEG WILSON

Scooter discovers old documents which reveal that a cache of treasure is hidden somewhere within the Muppet Theater...and when Rizzo the Rat overhears this, the news spreads like wildfire! Can Kermit keep everyone from tearing the theater apart?

SC $9.99 ISBN 9781608865048
HC $24.99 ISBN 9781608865307

THE MUPPET SHOW COMIC BOOK: ON THE ROAD

With the Muppet Theater destroyed, the Muppets take their act on the road...but with two very familiar hecklers in every town, will the show be a hit, or will our Muppet minstrels be run out of town in tar and feathers? Also: PIGS IN SPACE!

SC $9.99 ISBN 9781608865161

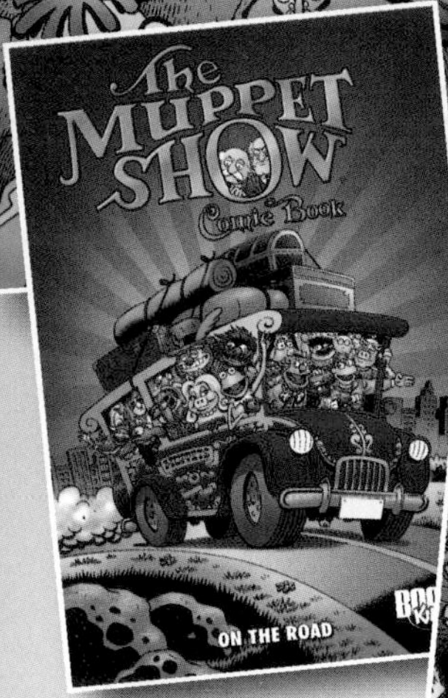
The
MUPPET
SHOW
Comic Book
ON THE ROAD

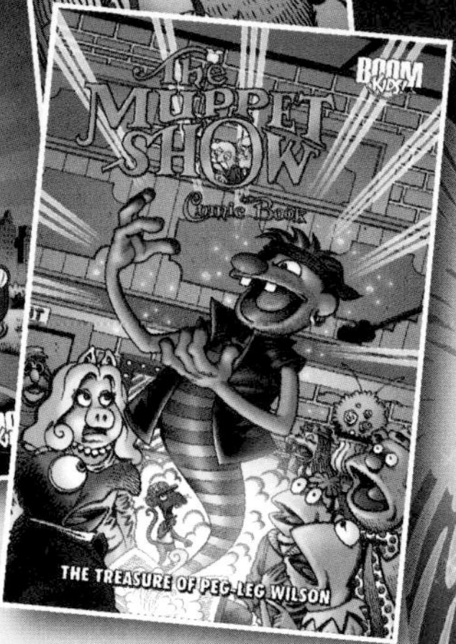
The
MUPPET
SHOW
Comic Book
BOOM KIDS!
THE TREASURE OF PEG-LEG WILSON

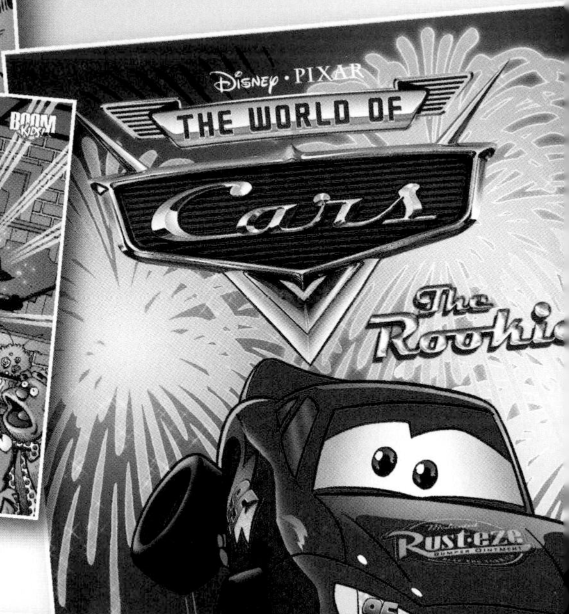
DISNEY · PIXAR
THE WORLD OF
Cars
The
Rust-eze
95

CARS: THE ROOKIE

See how Lightning McQueen became a Piston Cup sensation! CARS: THE ROOKIE reveals McQueen's scrappy origins as a local short track racer who dreams of the big time... and recklessly plows his way through the competition to get there!

SC $9.99 ISBN 9781934506844
HC $24.99 ISBN 9781608865222

CARS: RADIATOR SPRINGS

Lightning McQueen is hanging out with his friends at Flo's V8 Café when he realizes that everyone knows his story...but he doesn't know anyone else's! McQueen wants to know how his friends ended up in Radiator Springs...and more importantly, why they decided to stay!

SC $9.99 ISBN 9781608865024
HC $24.99 ISBN 9781608865284

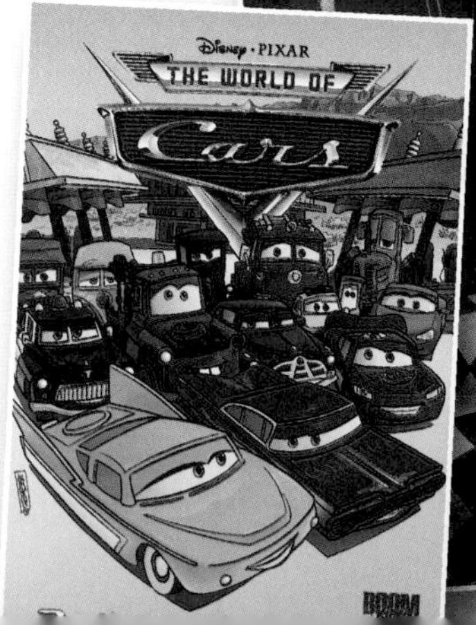
DISNEY · PIXAR
THE WORLD OF
Cars

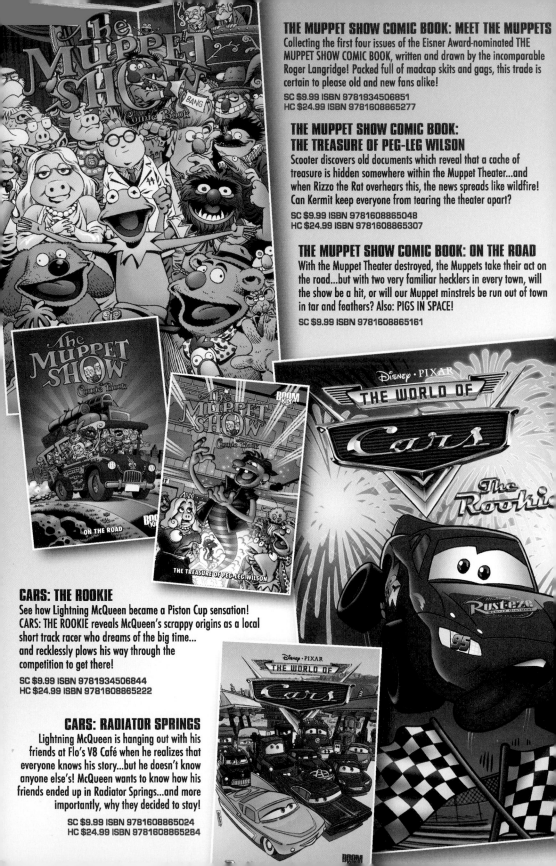

WALL•E: RECHARGE

Before WALL•E becomes the hardworking robot we know and love, he lets the few remaining robots take care of the trash compacting while he collects interesting junk. But when these robots start breaking down, WALL•E must adjust his priorities...or else Earth is doomed!

SC $9.99 ISBN 9781608865123
HC $24.99 ISBN 9781608865543

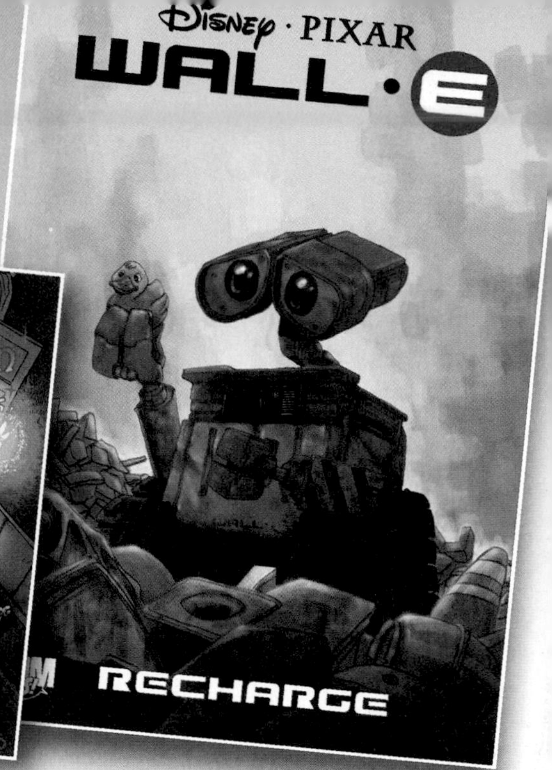
DISNEY · PIXAR
WALL·E
RECHARGE

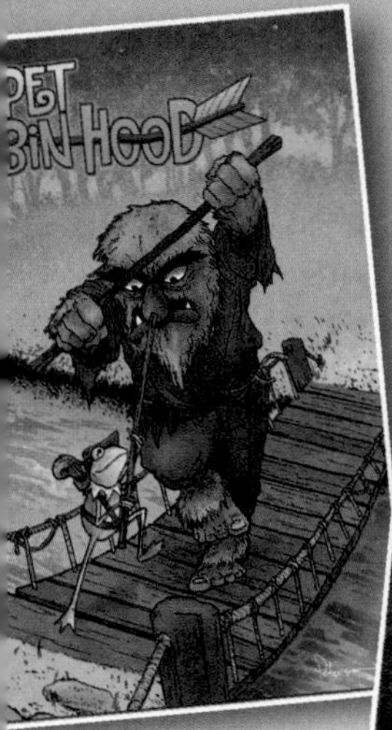

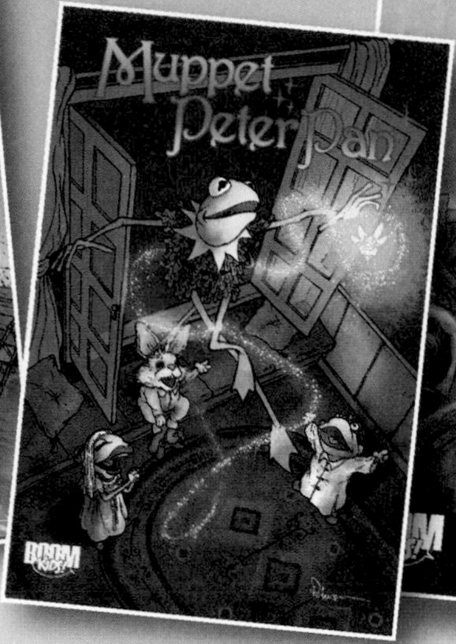
Muppet Peter Pan
BOOM KIDS!

MUPPET ROBIN HOOD

The Muppets tell the Robin Hood legend for laughs, and it's the reader who will be merry! Robin Hood (Kermit the Frog) joins with the Merry Men, Sherwood Forest's infamous gang of misfit outlaws, to take on the Sheriff of Nottingham (Sam the Eagle)!

SC $9.99 ISBN 9781934506790
HC $24.99 ISBN 9781608865260

MUPPET PETER PAN

When Peter Pan (Kermit) whisks Wendy (Janice) and her brothers to Neverswamp, the adventure begins! With Captain Hook (Gonzo) out for revenge for the loss of his hand, can even the magic of Piggytink (Miss Piggy) save Wendy and her brothers?

SC $9.99 ISBN 9781608865079
HC $24.99 ISBN 9781608865314

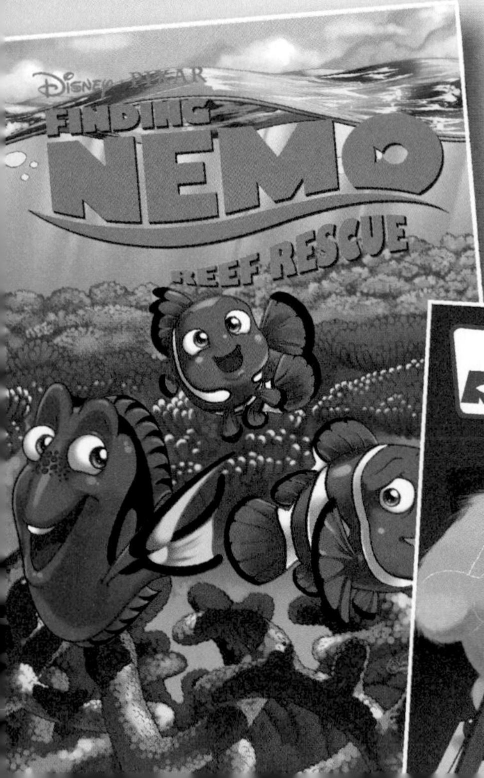
DISNEY PIXAR
FINDING NEMO
REEF RESCUE

FINDING NEMO: REEF RESCUE

Nemo, Dory and Marlin have become local heroes, and are recruited to embark on an all-new adventure in this exciting collection! The reef is mysteriously dying and no one knows why. So Nemo and his friends must travel the great blue sea to save their home!

SC $9.99 ISBN 9781934506882
HC $24.99 ISBN 9781608865246

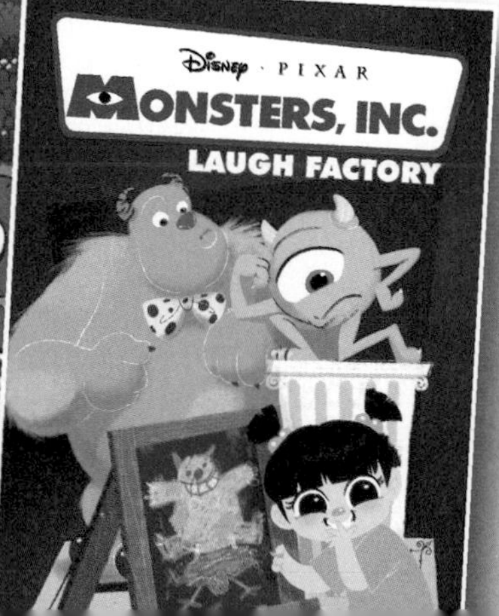
DISNEY · PIXAR
MONSTERS, INC.
LAUGH FACTORY

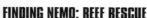

MONSTERS, INC.: LAUGH FACTORY

Someone is stealing comedy props from the other employees, making it difficult for them to harvest the laughter they need to power Monstropolis...and all evidence points to Sulley's best friend Mike Wazowski!

SC $9.99 ISBN 9781608865086
HC $24.99 ISBN 9781608865338

DISNEY'S HERO SQUAD: ULTRAHEROES VOL. 1: SAVE THE WORLD

It's an all-star cast of your favorite Disney characters, as you have never seen them before. Join Donald Duck, Goofy, Daisy, and even Mickey himself as they defend the fate of the planet as the one and only Ultraheroes!

SC $9.99 ISBN 9781608865437
HC $24.99 ISBN 9781608865529

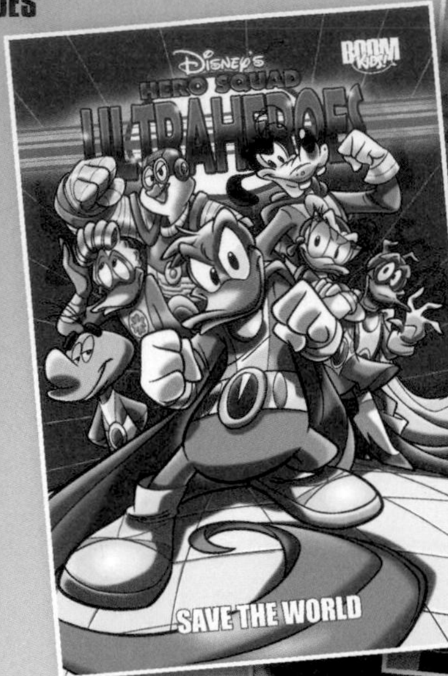
Disney's
HERO SQUAD
ULTRAHEROES
BOOM KIDS!
SAVE THE WORLD

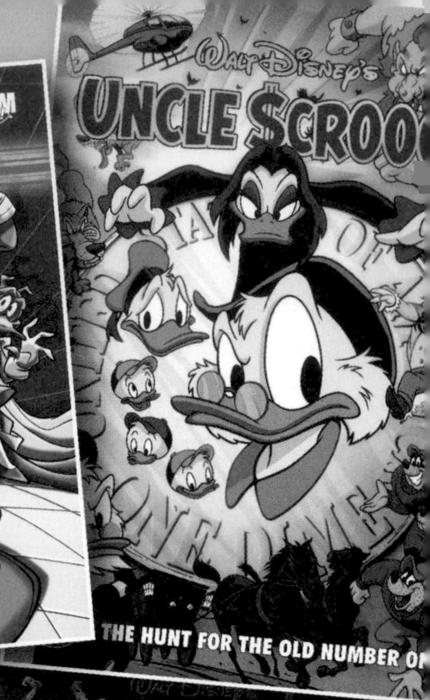
Walt Disney's
UNCLE $CROOGE
THE HUNT FOR THE OLD NUMBER

UNCLE SCROOGE: THE HUNT FOR THE OLD NUMBER ONE

Join Donald Duck's favorite penny-pinching Uncle Scrooge as he, Donald himself and Huey, Dewey, and Louie embark on a globe-spanning trek to recover treasure and save Scrooge's "number one dime" from the treacherous Magica De Spell.

SC $9.99 ISBN 9781608865475
HC $24.99 ISBN 9781608865536

WIZARDS OF MICKEY VOL. 1: MOUSE MAGIC

Your favorite Disney characters star in this magical fantasy epic! Student of the great wizard Nereus, Mickey allies himself with Donald and team mate Goofy, in a quest to find a magical crown that will give him mastery over all spells!

SC $9.99 ISBN 9781608865413
HC $24.99 ISBN 9781608865505

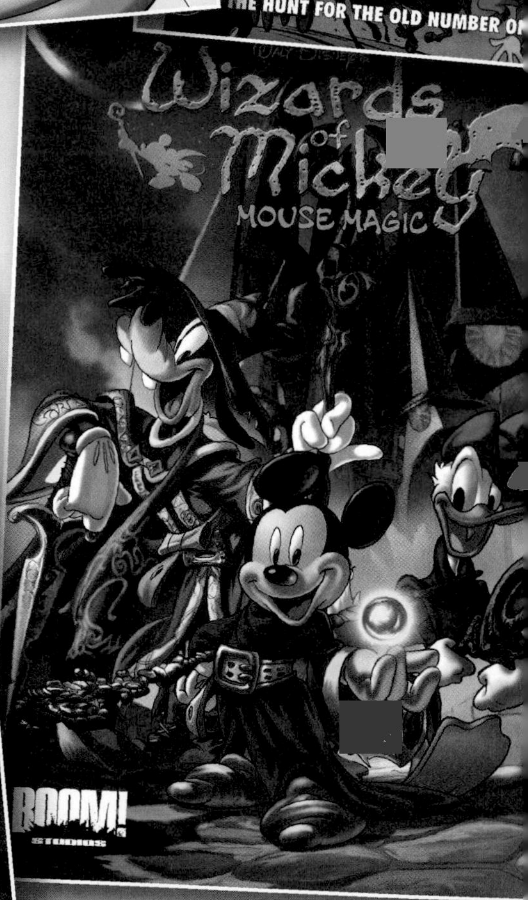
Wizards of Mickey
MOUSE MAGIC
BOOM! STUDIOS

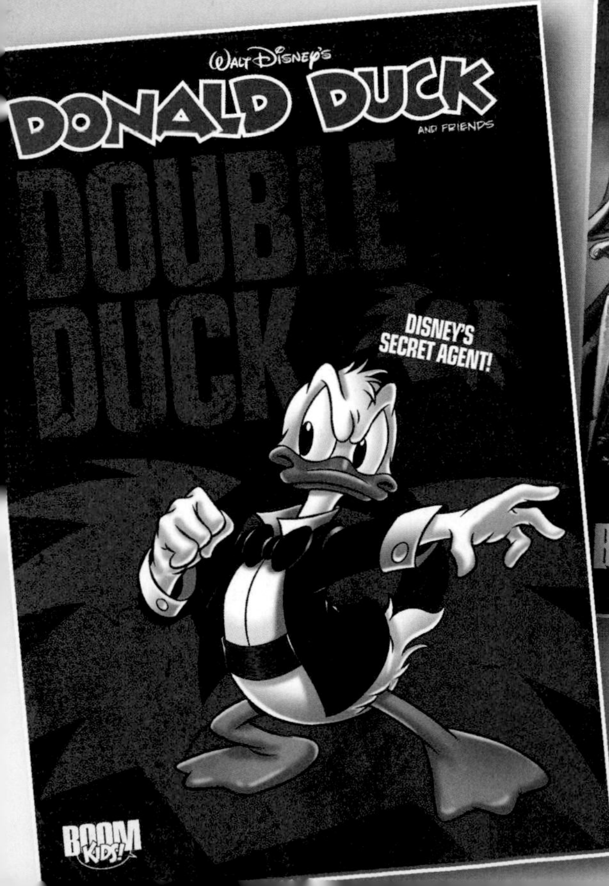
Walt Disney's
DONALD DUCK
AND FRIENDS
DOUBLE DUCK
DISNEY'S SECRET AGENT!
BOOM KIDS!

DONALD DUCK AND FRIENDS: DOUBLE DUCK VOL. 1

Donald Duck as a secret agent? Villainous fiends beware as the world of super sleuthing and espionage will never be the same! This is Donald Duck like you've never seen him!

SC $9.99 ISBN 9781608865451
HC $24.99 ISBN 9781608865512

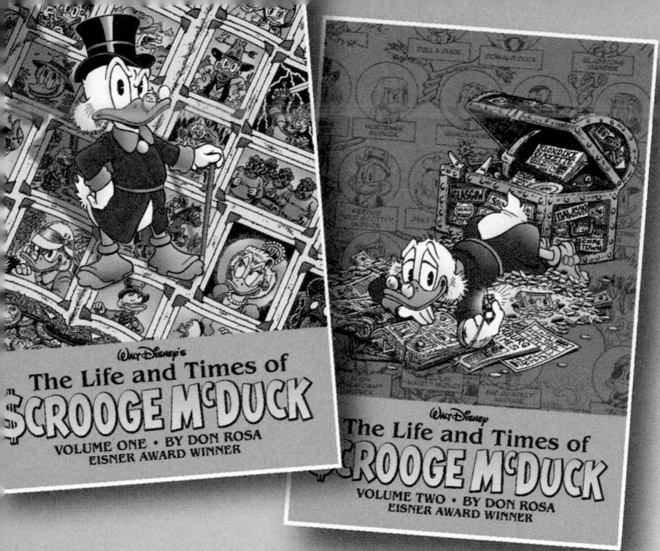
Walt Disney's
The Life and Times of
Scrooge McDuck
Volume One • By Don Rosa
Eisner Award Winner
Walt Disney
The Life and Times of
Scrooge McDuck
Volume Two • By Don Rosa
Eisner Award Winner

THE LIFE AND TIMES OF SCROOGE McDUCK VOL. 1

BOOM Kids! proudly collects the first half of THE LIFE AND TIMES OF SCROOGE MCDUCK in a gorgeous hardcover collection – featuring smyth sewn binding, a gold-on-gold foil-stamped case wrap, and a bookmark ribbon! These stories, written and drawn by legendary cartoonist Don Rosa, chronicle Scrooge McDuck's fascinating life.

HC $24.99 ISBN 9781608865383

THE LIFE AND TIMES OF SCROOGE McDUCK VOL. 2

BOOM Kids! proudly presents volume two of THE LIFE AND TIMES OF SCROOGE MCDUCK in a gorgeous hardcover collection in a beautiful, deluxe package featuring smyth sewn binding and a foil-stamped case wrap! These stories, written and drawn by legendary cartoonist Don Rosa, chronicle Scrooge McDuck's fascinating life.

HC $24.99 ISBN 9781608865420

MICKEY MOUSE CLASSICS: MOUSE TAILS

See Mickey Mouse as he was meant to be seen! Solving mysteries, fighting off pirates, and generally saving the day! These classic stories comprise a "Greatest Hits" series for the mouse, including a story produced by seminal Disney creator Carl Barks!

HC $24.99 ISBN 9781608865390

DONALD DUCK CLASSICS: QUACK UP

Whether it's finding gold, journeying to the Klondike, or fighting ghosts, Donald will always have the help of his much more prepared nephews – Huey, Dewey, and Louie – by his side. Featuring some of the best Donald Duck stories Carl Barks ever produced!

HC $24.99 ISBN 9781608865406

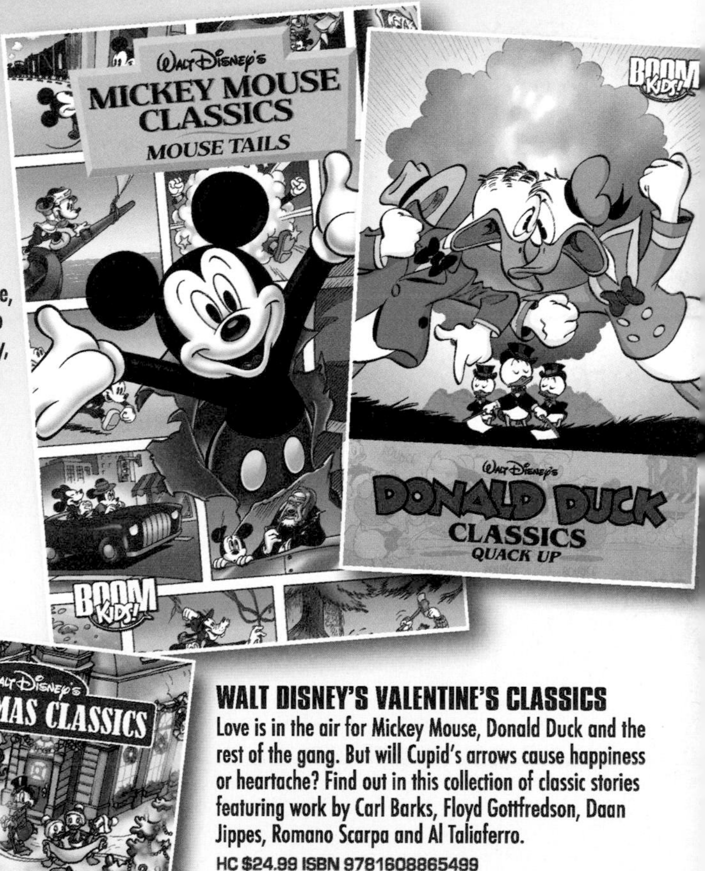
Walt Disney's
Mickey Mouse Classics
Mouse Tails
BOOM Kids!
BOOM Kids!
Walt Disney's
Donald Duck
Classics
Quack Up

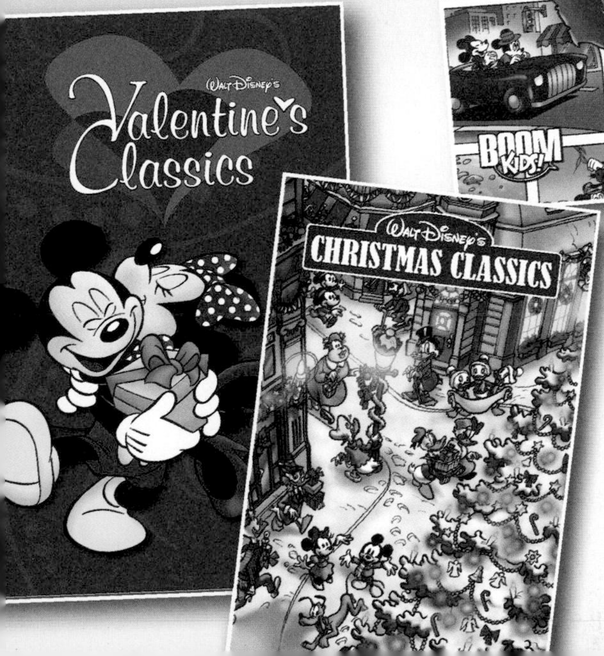
Walt Disney's
Valentine's Classics
Walt Disney's
Christmas Classics

WALT DISNEY'S VALENTINE'S CLASSICS

Love is in the air for Mickey Mouse, Donald Duck and the rest of the gang. But will Cupid's arrows cause happiness or heartache? Find out in this collection of classic stories featuring work by Carl Barks, Floyd Gottfredson, Daan Jippes, Romano Scarpa and Al Taliaferro.

HC $24.99 ISBN 9781608865499

WALT DISNEY'S CHRISTMAS CLASSICS

BOOM Kids! has raided the Disney publishing archives and searched every nook and cranny to find the best and the greatest Christmas stories from Disney's vast comic book publishing history for this "best of" compilation.

HC $24.99 ISBN 9781608865482

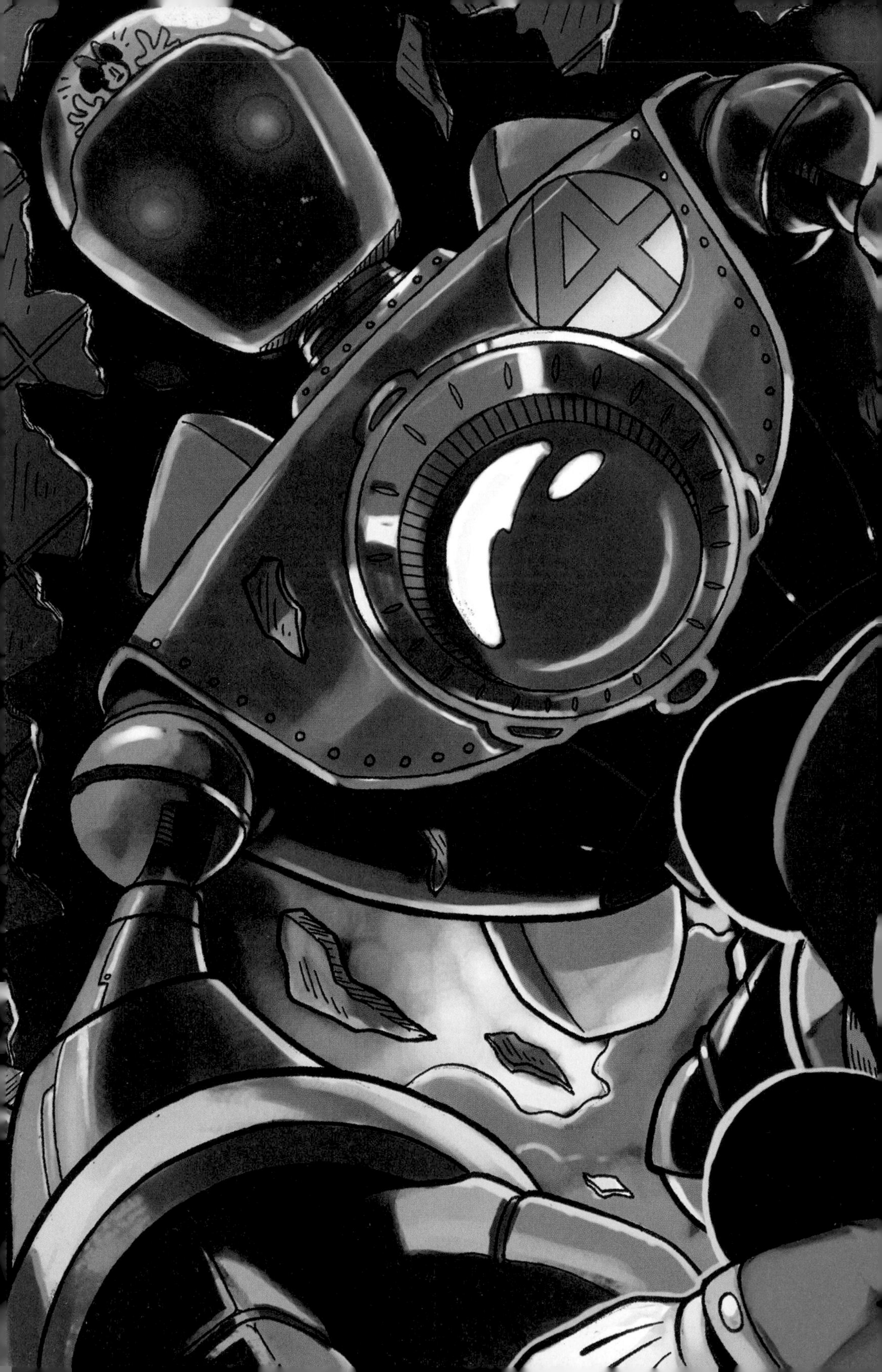